# THE MORTAL BLADE

MW00459477

Christopher Mitchell is the author of the epic fantasy series The Magelands. He studied in Edinburgh before living for several years in the Middle East and Greece, where he taught English. He returned to study classics and Greek tragedy and lives in Fife, Scotland with his wife and their four children.

BY CHRISTOPHER MITCHELL

THE MAGELANDS ORIGINS

*Retreat of the Kell*
*The Trials of Daphne Holdfast*
*From the Ashes*

———

THE MAGELANDS EPIC

*The Queen's Executioner*
*The Severed City*
*Needs of the Empire*
*Sacrifice*
*Fragile Empire*
*Storm Mage*
*Soulwitch Rises*
*Renegade Gods*

———

THE MAGELANDS ETERNAL SIEGE

*The Mortal Blade*
*The Dragon's Blade*
*The Prince's Blade*
*Falls of Iron*
*Paths of Fire*
*Gates of Ruin*
*City of Salve*

*Red City*
*City Ascendant*
*Dragon Eyre Badblood*
*Dragon Eyre Ashfall*
*Dragon Eyre Blackrose*

Copyright © Christopher Mitchell 2020
Cover by Miblart
Map by Irina French
Cover Copyright © Brigdomin Books Ltd 2020

Christopher Mitchell asserts the moral right to be identified as the author of this work.

All the characters in this book are fictitious, and any resemblance to actual persons living or dead is purely coincidental.

All rights reserved. No part of this book may be reproduced in any form or by any electronic or mechanical means, including information storage and retrieval systems (except for the use of brief quotations in a book review), if you would like permission to use material from the book please contact support@brigdominbooks.com

Brigdomin Books Ltd
First Edition, August 2020
ISBN 978-1-912879-40-3

*For the Film Club*

# ACKNOWLEDGEMENTS

I would like to thank the following for all their support during the writing of the Magelands Eternal Siege - my wife, Lisa Mitchell, who read every chapter as soon as it was drafted and kept me going in the right direction; my parents for their unstinting support; Vicky Williams for reading the books in their early stages; James Aitken for his encouragement; and Grant and Gordon of the Film Club for their support.

Thanks also to my Advance Reader team, for all your help during the last few weeks before publication.

# DRAMATIS PERSONAE

**The Royal Family – Gods and God-Children**
    **God-King Malik,** Sovereign of the City; Ooste
    **God-Queen Amalia,** Sovereign of the City; Tara
    **Princess Khora,** Guardian of the City; Pella
    **Prince Montieth,** Recluse; Dalrig

**The Royal Family – Demigods**
    **Aila,** Adjutant of the Circuit
    **Naxor,** Emissary of the Gods
    **Marcus,** Commander of the Bulwark
    **Kano,** Adjutant of the Bulwark
    **Ikara,** Governor of the Circuit
    **Lydia,** Governor of Port Sanders
    **Doria,** Courtier to the God-King
    **Vana,** Advisor to Princess Khora
    **Collo,** Advisor to Princess Khora

**The Mortals of the City**
    **Rosers (Tara)**
    **Daniel Aurelian,** Young Militia Officer
    **Todd,** Young Militia Officer
    **Gaimer,** Young Militia Officer
    **Lord Chamberlain,** Advisor to the God-Queen
    **Clarine,** Suitor
    **Millicent,** Suitor
    **Emily,** Suitor
    **Conrad,** Young Militia Officer
    **Monterey,** Sergeant in Militia
    **Hayden,** Sergeant in Militia

**Hallern,** Captain in Militia
**Nadhew,** Taran Lawyer

**Evaders (The Circuit)**
**Olvin,** Gang Boss
**Bekker,** Gang Member
**Medhi,** Gang Member
**Nareen,** Co-owner of Blind Poet
**Dorvid,** Co-owner of Blind Poet
**Bekha,** Rebel
**Martha,** Servant of Lady Aila
**Tobias,** Servant of Lady Aila
**Joylen,** Gambling Boss
**Letwyn,** Chef

**Blades (The Bulwark)**
**Maddie Jackdaw,** Young Private
**Rosie,** Maddie's Younger Sister
**Tom,** Maddie's Older Brother
**Hilde,** Blade Captain
**Quill,** Wolfpack Corporal

**The Outsiders**
**Corthie Holdfast,** Champion of the Bulwark
**Tanner,** Wolfpack Soldier
**Buckler,** Champion of the Bulwark
**Blackrose,** Prisoner

# CHAPTER 1

# A NIGHT ON THE TOWN

The Circuit, Medio, The City – 2$^{nd}$ Mikalis 3419

Aila crept along the dark alleyway, keeping to the thick shadows. She paused at the entrance to a larger street and saw the tall building ahead of her. Two guards were standing outside the front door, their long iron-clad clubs swinging in the dim lamplight.

Aila concentrated. She knew one member of the gang and conjured an image of his face in her mind.

*You see me as Old Jon.*

She stepped out from the shadows, keeping her head high as she strode across the cobbles.

One of the guards glanced at her. 'Evening, Jon.'

She nodded, and walked past them right to the door, her heart pounding. She turned the handle and pushed it open, then entered and closed it behind her. She glanced around. The hallway was empty, but noise was coming from the rooms on either side.

She pictured one of the guards she had passed.

*You see me as the guard from the door.*

A staircase was at the end of the hallway, and she stole towards it, keeping her tread light on the floorboards.

'Bekker,' said a voice behind her.

She kept walking.

'Hey, Bekker, you deaf? Thought you were watching the door?'

Aila turned and glanced at the man who had emerged from the room. 'Eh, yeah. I was just, uh, going to take a leak.'

The man nodded. 'I'm heading that way, myself; I'll walk with you.'

'Sure.'

She waited until he had drawn level with her, then let him lead the way. They went to the rear of the building, and stopped by a door, from where a foul odour was emanating.

'You better go first,' the man said. 'If Olvin catches you away from your post he'll kick your ass into next month.'

'Thanks,' Aila muttered. 'Wait. What's that?'

She pointed over his shoulder and he turned. Aila whipped her knife out and punched up with her hand, embedding the blade into the side of the man's neck, her other hand going up to muffle his cries as he sank to the floor. She pulled the knife out and wiped it on the man's cloak, then glanced around. She kicked open the door of the toilet and pushed the man inside, wedging him on the floor between the door and the noxious-smelling trough by the wall.

'Damn it,' she muttered. 'I should have asked you what your name was first.'

*You see me as the man I just killed.*

She returned to the main hallway, which was quiet. She should have also asked him where the kitchen was, she thought as she listened to the sounds coming from the side rooms. In the corner of the hall she saw a small flight of steps descending, and she walked over to take a look. She peered over the rail, and heard the sounds of pots and pans, while the scent of roasting meat drifted upwards. She smiled. After a quick glance over her shoulder, she tip-toed down the steps to the bottom, where a passageway led to a kitchen. Servants bustled around, preparing enough food to feed twenty families in large pots that were suspended over a roaring central hearth. Anger filled her at the thought of the many hungry mouths in the Circuit, while the gangs ate like kings.

A red-faced chef glanced over. 'It'll be ready when it's ready. Coming down here isn't going to make the beef cook any faster.'

'The boss wants a bottle of brandy,' she said, noticing a pretty serving girl loading a tray.

'Over there,' said the chef, pointing to a cupboard. 'Take one, and give me peace.'

Aila went over to the cupboard, and selected the most expensive bottle she could see. She picked up a tray and laid the bottle and a few glasses onto it, then carried it back up the stairs.

*You see me as that pretty serving girl, but with a shorter skirt.*

She smiled to herself as she ascended the larger set of stairs. Mortal men could be so predictable at times, and she hoped this would be one such occasion. Her informer had told her that the gang boss Olvin had rooms on the top floor, so she continued upwards, passing guards who were more interested in her illusory legs than who she might really be.

She stopped outside a well-guarded door and looked one of the men in the eye. 'I was told to bring this up for the boss.'

The guards gave the tray a cursory glance and opened the door for her.

'Thanks, boys,' she said, striding in. The room was thick with opium smoke, a scent she readily recognised. Three men and a woman were sitting on a pair of long, low couches. They were passing a pipe around, and from their eyes they seemed to be in a highly relaxed state.

Aila curtseyed before them. 'The boys downstairs asked me to bring this up for you.'

An older man narrowed his eyes and glanced around, as if he hadn't noticed where she had appeared from.

'Is that brandy?' said another.

'Yeah.'

'Well, get it open, girl,' the older man said, leering at her. 'Then you can come over here and sit down on old Daddy Olvin's knee.'

Aila suppressed a grimace. 'Sure.'

She took the tray to a table by the wall, where paint was peeling off in strips. She prised the wax seal from the bottle with her fingernails and opened it, slipping in the contents of the small paper sachet she had brought along. She carried the tray back over to the table and laid it down.

The woman eyed her with suspicion. 'Does your father know you're up here?'

Aila blinked.

'Leave her be,' said the older man. 'If that miserable chef wants to send his daughter up here for me, then that's his business.' He patted his lap.

Aila smothered her revulsion and did as she was told. She picked up the bottle as the man's hand went to her waist, and filled the four glasses on the tray.

The woman raised her hand as one of the men reached for a glass. 'Wait. Get her to drink some first.'

The older man laughed. 'By Malik's crotch, you're paranoid tonight. We just watched her open a sealed bottle.'

'I didn't see her open it,' the woman said. 'Look, I'm just watching out for you, boss; you know how many folk in the Circuit want you dead.'

Olvin puffed on the pipe, and a thick wad of smoke drifted up to the ceiling. 'Relax.'

'I will,' the woman said, 'after she's taken a drink.'

Aila turned to Olvin. 'I'm happy to have some; it's good brandy.'

'Fine,' he said, 'let's humour her.'

Aila picked up a glass and knocked half of it back. She wiped her lips and nodded. 'That's the best thing to come out of Tara since... ever.'

'See?' said Olvin, laughing at the woman on the couch. 'Nothing to worry about.'

He picked up his glass and drank, and the others did the same. Aila watched each of them take a drink as her heart hammered within her chest. She started to feel the poison get to work in her stomach, and she surged her self-healing powers, repairing any damage as soon as it could be inflicted by the lethal concoction.

The woman was the first to notice something was wrong. She

dropped her glass, and it smashed off the edge of the low table. One of the men put a hand to his throat, his eyes wide, then Aila heard Olvin choke. She broke free of his grasp, and turned, watching as the three men and the woman collapsed, convulsed for a moment, then gasped their last breaths.

Aila frowned. She had imagined she was going to have time to deliver a little speech to them before they died, and she had practised it until she knew it off by heart. The stupid mortals had taken only seconds to die, and she felt slightly robbed. They should have known the reasons for their deaths, it hardly seemed right to take their lives without them knowing why.

The poison had left no visible trace on their bodies, so she hauled them back onto the couch and arranged them in positions that might be taken for sleeping if no one checked too closely. While she was moving Olvin's feet, she noticed a small box under the couch and took it out. It was unlocked, and she opened it. Inside was a bag of gold and a large discoloured lump of opium. She pocketed the gold, closed the tin, sat for a moment, then reopened it and took the opium as well. She wouldn't smoke it, she told herself. She would keep it for... a bribe or something. She definitely wouldn't smoke it. She was past that.

She walked to the door.

*You see me as the same young woman, only with her make-up a little smudged.*

She opened the door and stepped outside. The guards turned to look at her, and she gave them a smile as she started to descend the staircase. Though she was still annoyed about the speech, she was starting to feel pleased with her evening's work. She knew that the gang-leaders she had killed would be replaced, but any disruption to their work was welcome.

A high-pitched scream rose up as she was halfway down the final flight of stairs. It was coming from the rear toilet where the body of the man she had stabbed was hidden, and Aila hurried down the last steps. The hallway was filling with people coming out of the side rooms to see what was causing the noise, and Aila put on a concerned face as she squeezed past them.

A woman ran from behind the stairs, her eyes wide in shock.

'Someone's stabbed Medhi,' she cried.

The crowd hurried towards where the woman was standing, and Aila cursed as she was caught up among them.

'Nobody gets in or out!' yelled a man in leather armour, a sword hanging from his waist. He grabbed a younger man. 'Get upstairs and let the bosses know. Run.'

The younger man scrambled through the crowd and sprinted for the stairs. Aila's fear peaked and for a second she froze. There were too many people around for her to change appearance, and the front doors of the building were being locked. Three men dragged the bloody corpse of Medhi through from the toilet chamber, and Aila felt the anger of the crowd surge. She forced her way through the packed mob, heading back towards the stairs. The kitchens, she thought; there's bound to be another way out.

The back of the hallway was a little quieter, and she ran to the top of the small staircase, then skidded to a halt. People were coming up the steps from the kitchen. Leading them was the young, pretty serving girl whose appearance Aila had copied. The girl's eyes glanced up and saw Aila, and she stopped on the stairs, her eyes wide, and her mouth opening to scream. Behind her, the chef frowned at his daughter, then also looked up.

Before the scream could leave the young woman's lips, Aila sprang, colliding with her on the stairs and sending her flying backwards into the arms of her father, whose feet slipped under the weight.

*You see me as the guard known as Bekker.*

They tumbled down the dark stairs together, the chef falling backwards into a row of cooks and servants. They landed in an untidy heap of limbs at the bottom of the steps, and Aila kicked out with her legs, gaining purchase as she scrambled off the chef's daughter and into the small passageway that led to the kitchen.

The chef struggled to his feet, his eyes darting about. He saw his daughter, then looked back up the stairs in confusion.

'Get up those stairs!' yelled Aila, doing her best impersonation of an angry guard.

The chef's daughter rubbed her head. 'But, but...'

'Medhi's been killed, did you not hear?' said Aila. 'No one's leaving until everyone's been questioned.'

*You see me draw a sword.*

The cooks backed away from Aila, and some sped up the stairs. The chef stood frozen for a moment, then took his daughter's hand, and they started to climb the stairs again. As soon as they were out of sight, Aila ran to the kitchen. She stopped by the drinks cupboard to grab another bottle of the fine brandy, then raced past the central hearth and came to a back door. She pulled on the handle. Locked.

The noise from upstairs increased, and she guessed that the bodies of the gang-bosses had been discovered. She ran back to the hearth, and looked around for something to use. Her eyes fell on a wheeled trolley, laden with clean plates and bowls, and she gripped the end. She lined it up with the door, and charged. The wheels rumbled over the tiled floor as she raced towards the exit.

'Hey!' cried a voice from the passageway behind her. 'What in Malik's name are you doing?'

Aila ignored them and rammed the trolley at the entrance. It smashed into the wooden frame, battering the door. It flew open, and Aila leapt up and over the trolley as footsteps rushed towards her. She landed on the slick cobbles of a back alleyway, its walls lined with garbage and kitchen refuse, and a rat scurried away as her boots nearly trod on its back. She sprinted down the alley as shouts echoed behind her, and she could hear the trolley being wrenched aside.

She turned a corner.

*You see me as a young Evader boy.*

She put her head down, and ran.

Ten minutes later, Aila slowed to a walk as she approached her favourite place in the City. She lingered in the shadows of a neighbouring block, its grey concrete eroded and crumbling. The slums of the Circuit had barely changed in the hundreds of years she had known them. Whenever a building collapsed, which was fairly frequently, another shoddily-built block would be erected in its place, where Evader families would be crammed in with ten to each tiny apartment. Despite the extreme poverty and suffering, Aila had come to love the Circuit and the people who lived there. No matter what injustices they faced, or how they were treated by the five other tribes of Auldan and Medio, the Evaders had a resilience that humbled her at times.

She waited for the street to quieten, then pictured in her mind the face of the person she was about to become. For twenty years, she had been using the same appearance whenever she visited the building opposite, being careful to gradually age as time went on, just as the mortals did.

*You see me as Elsie, the swine-trader.*

Aila rolled her shoulders and walked out into the street. Thugs from the gang she had attacked were patrolling the area, and she knew suspicion would fall upon the chef's daughter and the hapless guard Bekker. She felt a twinge of guilt at the thought that others might be unfairly punished for what she had done, but that was one of the risks she ran. Innocent people suffered every day due to the cruelty and fear engendered by the gangs of the Circuit; balanced against that, it was usually easy for her to forget about those hurt because of her actions. Still, the image of the chef's daughter persisted in her mind, along with the nagging guilt.

She crossed the street and glanced at the old building.

The Blind Poet – one of the roughest drinking establishments in the Circuit, and Aila's second home, but only as Elsie, never as herself.

The wardens at the door nodded to her as she entered. The ground floor of the tavern was quiet, with just a handful of regulars and one or two strange faces. The best nights occurred once a month, after the workers had been paid for their soul-crushing labour, and everyone just wanted to get drunk and let go of their inhibitions, but the next such date was more than twenty days away.

'Evening, Elsie,' the woman behind the bar called over; 'your usual?'

'Aye, Nareen, ta.'

Aila sidled up to a barstool and sat. 'Seen all the commotion outside?'

'Yeah,' muttered Nareen as she took a large tankard from a hook on the wall. 'Something's got their knickers in a twist tonight.'

Aila leaned in closer as Nareen opened the tap on a barrel and began to fill the tankard. 'I heard,' she said, keeping her voice low, 'that Olvin's place got attacked.'

Nareen's eyes flickered upwards. 'Yeah? Oh dear,' she smirked; 'that's terrible. Shocking.'

'Disgraceful.'

The two women laughed as Nareen set the ale down for her on the bar. Aila raised the tankard to her lips and took a long drink of the cool ale.

'Not bad,' she said. 'Is this a new batch? Reminds me of the chestnut ale you were serving about, um... twelve years or so ago.'

Nareen shook her head. 'The brewery should employ you; I'm always saying that to them next door. "Give Elsie a job," I tell 'em, "she knows more about ale than any of you clumsy oafs". But nobody listens to little old Nareen.'

'Getting drunk to the ale of the Blind Poet is a passion of mine,' Aila said, 'and I listen to you, Nareen; you're one of the few folk with any sense in this damned City.'

Loud shouting came from outside, and Nareen glanced at the front door as it burst open. Aila took another drink as the sound of boots filled the tavern.

'We're looking for two fugitives,' one of the newcomers yelled. 'A man, and a woman.'

Nareen shrugged. 'As you can see, boys, we're quiet tonight; just a few regulars.'

The gang members fanned out through the tavern. One came up to the bar and stared at Aila.

She raised her tankard. 'Evening. What's going on?'

'None of your damned business. Where were you tonight?'

Nareen let out a long, rattling laugh. 'You think Elsie here was up to no good? That's the funniest thing I've heard in years.'

The gang member frowned. 'I asked her the question, not you.'

'I've had enough of this nonsense,' Nareen said. 'I've got a business to run, and can't have you lowlifes coming in here and harassing my most loyal customers. Elsie's been drinking in here for twenty years, for Malik's sake; she screams if a mouse comes in through the door. Do you really think she's capable of... doing whatever you're accusing her of? I recognise a few of you; run back to Olvin and tell him that if this harassment doesn't stop, then I'll be wanting a refund on the protection money he squeezes out of me every month.'

The gang-members glanced at each other.

'Olvin's dead,' said one.

Nareen's eyes widened. 'Oh.'

'Come on,' said another to his colleagues. 'We're wasting time.' He glanced at Nareen. 'If you hear anything...'

'I'll be sure to let you know,' said Nareen.

The gang-members frowned, took one last look at the tavern, then left by the front doors. Nareen reached under the counter and brought out a bottle. She filled a glass with brandy and slid it across the surface of the bar for Aila.

'Really? For me?'

'By way of an apology,' Nareen said. 'Those cretins were out of order, questioning you like that.'

Aila raised the glass. 'Thanks.'

'Don't thank me; you've brought in a lot of money and business to this place over the years, and I wouldn't want you going somewhere else with your custom.'

'I wasn't intending to get drunk tonight,' Aila said, taking a sip of the rough spirits, 'but I think you might well have persuaded me.'

Four hours later, Aila staggered from the Blind Poet, colliding with one of the wardens Nareen had posted by the door.

'Watch yourself, old girl,' one of them laughed.

'Sorry,' she giggled, swaying as she grabbed his arm to steady herself.

'The state you leave this place, Elsie,' said the other, 'it's a miracle you ever make it home.'

'See you tomorrow, lads,' she slurred as she stumbled down the narrow street. The roads of the Circuit were twisting and chaotic, and seemed to follow no rational plan, but she knew the ways around the Blind Poet well, as if she had been born and raised there. She glanced upwards. The colour of the sky was as good as a clock to her, and she could tell from the shade of purple that it was a couple of hours after midnight.

Damn it, she thought, she was going to be late. She stole into a dark alley, rubbed her face, then used her self-healing to sober herself up. It was a pity; she enjoyed being drunk, but work was work.

*You see me as Stormfire, the assassin and spy.*

Stormfire was one of her favourites. She had once glimpsed a woman with a scar going down her cheek that had given her a sinister, dangerous appearance, and had adopted it decades later as the face she would present when dealing with her informers. An illusory hood shielded most of her face, and a dark cloak made her almost disappear into the shadows. She set off again, moving faster than drunken Elsie had been capable of, crossing the dark alleys until she reached an abandoned warehouse by the side of a murky canal.

She stayed clear of the water's edge, and approached a side door.

'You're late,' said a voice.

'I've had a busy night.'

A figure emerged from the shadows of a woman in her thirties, about halfway through the mortal span of her life. Aila had known her for thirteen years, and she was the latest in her succession of informers.

'The job's done,' she said, handing the woman the bag of gold she had taken from the gang bosses. 'Your information was accurate.'

'I know it was,' the woman said; 'I was nearly killed getting it for you. I don't know how you managed it, but Olvin's gang is in turmoil. You took out four of their leadership in one night.' She shook her head. 'It should be me that's paying you.'

'I have no need for money,' Aila said, 'and I know you'll put that to good causes. Do you have another address?'

The woman nodded and took a slip of folded paper from her pocket. 'Security will be tighter after what you did to Olvin. I'd suggest you wait a while for this one.'

Aila took the paper and slipped it beneath her robes.

'I wish I could tell everyone what you're doing,' the woman went on; 'you're making a real difference to the lives of the poor in the Circuit, whoever you really are.'

'I'm Stormfire.'

'You're a hero.'

'Don't be ridiculous,' said Aila. 'You know that Olvin will be replaced by another thug soon; perhaps he already has. Tomorrow, the gang will be back to work.'

'That doesn't matter; you've disrupted their business, and that means less opium on the streets, less folk forced into prostitution, fewer children snatched from their parents. If only you'd been around when my sister...' The woman tailed off as her voice broke.

'I wish I had been, Bekha.'

The woman glanced around.

'There's no one here,' said Aila.

'Even so, please don't say my name when we're working. The militia are getting closer to finding out what I've been doing, and I'm worried that I might have been followed. If they catch me, then you know it'll be the gallows.'

'They won't catch you,' Aila said. 'I'm watching out for you, remember? Just keep doing what you're doing; every address you get me helps.'

The woman opened the bag of gold and her eyes widened. 'This is a lot more than we agreed. Where did you get it?'

'It came courtesy of Olvin; he doesn't need it any more.'

'And he had this amount lying around?' She took out one of the gold coins. 'This is worth a hundred crowns on its own, and the whole bag is full of them.'

Aila peered into the bag. Bekha was right; the contents came to thousands of crowns. 'Maybe business was good?'

'It's never this good,' said Bekha. 'I know Olvin's accountant; he told me his client was short of funds, which is why he was increasing his activities, in order to bring in more revenue.' She frowned. 'Someone paid Olvin a lot of money for something.'

'I'll look into it.' She put her hand out and Bekha shook it. 'See you soon.'

Aila turned and slipped back into the shadows. She had several miles to go before she could get back to her quarters and relax with her stolen bottle of brandy.

*You see me as an old peasant man.*

She strolled down the narrow streets towards her home. She patted her pocket to make sure she had the slip of paper that Bekha had given her, and felt something lying next to it. A lump. The opium.

There was a locked box under her bed in her quarters; she would put it there for safe-keeping, and use it to trade, or for information. She wouldn't smoke any of it, she promised herself, those days were behind her.

She frowned. Who was she trying to fool? She would have a tiny bit, to ease the long day out of her system.

Just a tiny bit, she told herself, and quickened her pace.

## CHAPTER 2
## ARRIVAL

**P**ort Sanders, Medio, The City – 3<sup>rd</sup> Mikalis 3419

Corthie awoke as the room was flooded with red-infused light.

'They've barred the damned windows,' a voice muttered. 'Hey, lad! Look at this; they must think we'll try to escape, eh? They've taken precautions.'

Corthie rubbed his head and opened his eyes. He glanced around the strange room for a moment, then turned to where Tanner was standing. He had opened the shutters, revealing a sky rippling in reds and pinks, framed by a vertical series of iron bars.

'Is there a fire?'

'What's that, lad? You cold?'

'No,' he said, pulling back the thin sheet and swinging his feet onto the smooth floorboards. 'I meant, is something burning outside?'

The older man shrugged. 'Nah, it's just the sunrise.'

Corthie pulled on a pair of shorts and stood. Fresh clothes had been laid out for him on the back of a chair, while on a table in the centre of the room sat a collection of dishes and plates. From the mess, it looked like Tanner had eaten his way through most of it.

'When did breakfast arrive?'

'Half an hour ago, maybe? I tried to wake you, but with all the drugs Naxor gave you, you were sleeping like the dead.'

Corthie scanned the detritus on the table and picked up an apple. He walked over to the window and stood next to Tanner as he took his first view of his new home. Stretched before them were tidy rows of red-tiled roofs and yellow, sandstone buildings, tinted pink by the glow from the sky. Beyond was a long harbour, and then the sea, reaching into the horizon, where it was swallowed up by a thick bank of luminous fog, shot through with dark, swirling reds. The vast expanse of the sky seemed to burn in every shade of red, from lighter pinks by the horizon, to a deep, blood red overhead.

'Some sunrise,' said Corthie. 'It looks like the end of the world.'

'For all we know it is,' said Tanner. 'Let's face it, neither of us has a clue where we've been sent; we just know there will be trouble, and violence, and danger...'

Corthie laughed.

'Don't know what you find so amusing, lad. In ten years I'll have paid off my debts to Gadena, and will be able to go home.' He turned and glanced up at Corthie. 'You'll be here until you die; they own your ass. I saw Gadena hand over your papers to Naxor.'

Corthie gazed out of the window, his arms leaning on the sill. 'I won't die here. I'm just passing time until...'

'Wait, stop; I know this bit. Until your sister comes and rescues you; that's what you were going to say, yeah?'

'Aye, because it's true.'

Tanner nodded. 'You keep telling yourself that, lad, if it keeps you going.'

At that moment a sliver of sun appeared on the horizon, and the sky lightened as peaches and pinks pushed back the darker shades of red.

'It's like the sky's on fire.'

'It's something to behold, lad, but if this is what it's like here, we'll just have to get used to it. Different place, different rules. I've seen all kinds of strange lands.'

'I thought you said you'd never left Lostwell until now?'

Tanner glared at him. 'Don't be saying that, not even when we're alone; anybody could be listening. Gadena told me to keep quiet about... that place. He threatened to add years onto my time here if I blab about where we're from, so do me a favour, eh?'

'Aye, sure.'

'Good lad. The locals here know nothing of other lands, and Naxor wants it kept that way.'

Corthie turned away from the dawn and got dressed. No armour or weapons had been left for either of them, but the fresh set of clothes were smart, and fitted well.

He heard a faint noise and glanced at the door.

'It's locked,' said Tanner. 'I already tried.'

Corthie sat on the bed and pulled on a pair of leather boots. 'Someone's coming.'

Tanner frowned and cocked his head to listen. 'Are you sure?'

'Aye. Footsteps.'

Corthie stood as a key turned in the lock. The door swung open, and a man stepped into the room, two soldiers behind him.

'Good morning. I trust you slept well?'

'Considering the quantity of drugs you gave us,' Tanner said, 'I think you already know the answer to that question.'

Lord Naxor smiled. 'Quite. Well, the first stage of your journey is complete; welcome to the City. You are part of a long and honourable tradition of selecting the very best to aid us in our struggle against the eternal enemy.'

Tanner raised an eyebrow. 'Last night you said it was a siege.'

'That's right,' Naxor said, amusement flitting over his eyes at the same time his lips were fixed in a diplomatic smile, 'as you will soon see for yourself. If you were wondering what has happened to your old clothes, they have been destroyed. You enter this world naked, bringing nothing with you from your old lives; and saying nothing about them while you are here.'

Tanner glanced at Corthie.

Naxor gestured to the hallway outside the room. 'Follow me.'

The two soldiers stepped aside to allow Corthie and Tanner to leave the room after Naxor, then they followed behind, their crossbows ready.

'You shall be travelling by boat,' Naxor said as they descended a wide, stone staircase.

'Are you not coming with us?' said Tanner.

'My role is to ensure your safe transport here, and then hand you over to the Blades.'

'Is that the name for the army?'

'Almost. The Blades are one of nine tribes that inhabit the City. Their duty is to defend the Great Walls from attack, and to keep the City safe. All tribes have their own militia, but the Blades are the only ones entirely dedicated to the military life.'

He paused as they reached a hallway at the bottom of the stairs. A few servants were standing around, their heads lowering as Naxor arrived. Corthie glanced at them. They were about the same height as Naxor and Tanner; a good foot shorter than he was. He knew his stature was one of the reasons he had been selected by Naxor. His battle-vision powers were another.

The lord turned. 'I'm afraid word has got out that a new batch of champions destined for the Bulwark has arrived, and you may find the streets of Port Sanders a little busy this morning.' He glanced at a servant. 'The engineers?'

'Waiting in the sitting room, my lord,' the old woman said, bowing.

'Fetch them for me, would you? It's time to leave.'

The servant hurried to a side door and opened it.

'Engineers?' said Tanner. 'From the Guild?'

'Of course,' said Naxor. 'Their secrecy and discretion are as renowned as their expertise.'

A dozen dressed in black robes emerged from the side room. Hoods covered most of their faces, and they wore sandals on their feet; and to Corthie they looked more like mystics than engineers.

'Good morning,' Naxor said, greeting them. 'I believe your ship awaits you.'

The head engineer nodded, her hood bobbing up and down, and

Naxor gestured to a servant at the front doors. The man opened them, and a loud roar of voices rose up from the street. Lord Naxor led the way, with Corthie and Tanner behind, while the engineers lined up in pairs to follow them. The noise increased as Corthie stepped outside into the street. There was wealth in the City, he thought, glancing around at the elegant sandstone townhouses. Garlands of flowers hung from windows and balconies, and more were being waved by many in the crowd filling the cobbled road. At least twenty soldiers were lining the entrance to the lord's residence, spilling out onto the street by the neighbouring mansions.

Naxor nodded to an officer, and the soldiers formed up into two columns, flanking Corthie and the others as they walked down the street. Hands emerged from the mass of people, and fingers reached out to touch Corthie and Tanner as they passed.

Naxor glanced at him. 'Smile. Remember you're a champion, fighting to give the people the freedom to live their lives in peace.'

They turned left at a junction and descended a gentle slope towards the sea front as the street narrowed. They passed a market, where the merchants and their customers stopped to stare at the procession. The sky was growing brighter, but the sun remained low, barely brushing the horizon, and a pink light permeated the air. The stalls in the market held a rich assortment of goods, from fresh meat hanging from butcher's hooks, to fruit, vegetables and wine. No one looked hungry, and Corthie smiled to himself, pleased that the place he would be fighting to defend appeared happy and prosperous.

They reached the harbour front, where several dozen vessels were tied up, while others were making their way in or out between the long stone piers that nearly enclosed the basin. Gulls screeched and hovered over several boats as they sailed towards the long wharf.

Naxor directed them to a narrow wooden pier, where a galley was berthed. A dozen men and women were standing alongside the vessel, all in similar uniforms, making it hard for Corthie to tell which were crew, and which soldiers. An officer stood at their head, awaiting the new arrivals. The crowds had thinned as they had walked through the harbour, though a few were still watching. A woman blew a kiss at Corthie, and he smiled.

'Lord Naxor,' said the officer, bowing.

'Major. Good morning.' Naxor put his hand out and one of his servants passed him a roll of documents. He glanced at it for a moment, then passed the bundle to the officer. 'I think you'll find all that you need in there.'

'Thank you, my lord.' The officer glanced at Tanner and Corthie. 'I thought we were only getting one.'

'The older of the two comes courtesy of my contacts,' Naxor said. 'He was due to be executed for failure to repay his debts, but instead has been contracted to serve here for ten years. His details are in the bundle. He has a history as a soldier, so I'm sure you can find a purpose for him.'

'We shall indeed, my lord, thank you.'

Naxor extended his hand. 'Once again, Major, it has been a pleasure. Now, if you'll excuse me, I need to visit my mother in Pella.'

'The pleasure's mine, my lord,' said the officer, shaking hands.

Naxor turned, then paused in front of Corthie and Tanner. The smile faded from his lips. 'You,' he said to Tanner, 'fight well, and if you survive, then I'll see you here in ten years.' He turned to Corthie. 'You are destined for a different life; the life of a champion. If you fight like they say you can, then your fame will be known to every citizen; they will love you, a mortal, as if you were one of the gods that rules the City.'

Corthie glanced down at him, saying nothing.

'Farewell,' said Naxor, then turned and strode down the pier, his guards flanking him.

The officer gestured towards the boat, and the dozen hooded engineers began making their way over the short gangway leading to the deck of the galley.

Corthie frowned. 'Do gods rule the City?'

'You were just speaking to one,' said the major; 'a demigod, to be precise. Lord Naxor is the son of Princess Khora, daughter of the God-

King and God-Queen, and ruler of the City. We mortals come and go, but the royal family lives on. Lord Naxor is over a thousand years old.'

'He doesn't look much older than me.'

The major gestured to the gangway. 'That's immortality for you. This way, please.'

Corthie and Tanner crossed the short plank and boarded the galley. The major and the last of the uniformed crew stepped onto the deck and the vessel began to pull away from the pier, its ropes loosened by harbour workers. A sail was unfurled and the galley slid through the calm waters of the basin. Corthie and Tanner stood by the railings to watch as they drew away from the houses along the sea front.

Someone prodded Corthie's shoulder.

'You first,' said the woman in uniform. She pointed at a wooden stool on the deck. 'Take your tunic off and sit down.'

Corthie frowned for a second, then pulled his top off, feeling the warm wind against his skin. He sat on the small stool as the woman crouched opposite him, the bundle of documents on her lap. A man in uniform took hold of Corthie's left arm.

'You're a big lad,' said the woman. 'What's your name?'

'Corthie Holdfast.'

She flicked through the documents, until she reached a folder made of thick card. 'Here we are; let's take a look.' She opened the folder and skimmed through a sheaf of papers. 'It says here that you're only eighteen. Is that a mistake?'

'No.'

She squinted at him. 'You look older than that.'

He shrugged, then felt a pain in his upper left arm. 'Ow.'

'Keep your arm still,' said the woman, 'or your tattoo will smudge. If the greenhides eat your head, it'll be the only way to identify your body.' Her eyes returned to the papers on her lap. 'What? That can't be right.' She glanced at him again, an eyebrow raised, then turned to the officer. 'Major, sir? Could you come here, please?'

The officer turned from where he had been talking to the Guild engineers. He raised a finger to them, then walked over to the side of the deck. The woman showed him a paper and he read it for a moment.

'It must be an error,' he muttered.

'I've never known Lord Naxor to make a mistake before, sir.'

The officer shrugged. 'No one's perfect, not even a demigod. If I had to guess, I'd say we've been conned.' He glanced at Corthie, his eyes narrow. 'He looks like he could be a tidy fighter, though; disregard the obvious exaggerations and register him as per the normal procedure.'

'Yes, sir.'

The man by Corthie's side let go of his left arm. 'All done, Sergeant.'

Corthie glanced down. Blood was trickling from his upper arm where the needle had stabbed a series of symbols and numbers in black ink, along with a shield with crossed swords.

The woman smiled at him. 'You're a Blade now, lad.'

---

The galley sailed out from the harbour of Port Sanders and along by an enormous wall on their left. To the right, the sea stretched off towards the bright pinks and peaches where the sun sat above the horizon, which was lost in thick mist. After a voyage of less than an hour, they entered a smaller harbour nestled into the massive walls, and the crew tied the boat up next to a long pier.

'Welcome to the Bulwark,' said the major as Corthie and Tanner gazed out at the compact harbour. Beyond the docks rose vast concrete warehouses; shabby, grey and crumbling, while the majority of workers were dressed in the same utilitarian brown tunics, contrasting with the smaller numbers in the darker uniforms of the Blades. They disembarked the galley, and walked to where a row of carriages were waiting. Soldiers led Corthie and Tanner to their carriage, then locked the door once they had clambered aboard and taken their seats.

Each carriage had four ponies harnessed to the front, and they set off at a trot, heading towards a heavily guarded gate in the harbour wall. They emerged onto a long, straight road, high walls on either side. The stone barrier on the right was massive, with battlements, towers, and soldiers on the walkways at the top, while the wall on the left was featureless; cast from tall slabs of the same drab concrete that Corthie had seen in the small harbour. Tanner closed his eyes and reclined onto his bench, as Corthie strained to look out of the tiny window slats.

After twenty minutes the road veered sharply to the left, and Corthie saw the bulk of an enormous fortress on their right, built into the corner where the wall turned. They carried on in a straight line for a further twenty minutes, then slowed as they approached a second huge fortress. The carriages entered under an archway, then drew to a halt in front of a tall building.

The door of their carriage was unlocked and opened.

'Out you get, lads,' said the sergeant.

Corthie climbed down to the large, worn flagstones. 'Where are we?'

'Fortress of the Lifegiver.'

The interior of the fortress was crammed with stone buildings. Six-storey garrison blocks lined the inner walls, while towers reached up over the high curtain wall. Officers were waiting to welcome the engineers as they stepped from the carriages, and within a few minutes they were led away into the shadows of the fortress. A crowd of soldiers had gathered to take a look at the new arrivals, each wearing the dark grey uniforms of the Blades.

The major led Corthie and Tanner between several large buildings. In the corner of the fortress a tall tower loomed, surrounded by its own wall, as if it was a small castle within the fort.

'That's the Duke's Tower,' said the sergeant, 'where the Commander of the Bulwark lives.'

'Is he a god, too?' said Corthie.

'A demigod,' she said, 'like Lord Naxor. Well, not quite like him. He's more your size.'

A tall, well-built man in shining battle armour was standing with a few guards at the entrance to the tower.

'Is that him?' said Corthie.

'No,' said the sergeant, keeping her voice low, 'that's his Adjutant,

Lord Kano. Also a demigod.' She turned to Corthie, and mouthed the words, 'be careful' at him.

'Lord Kano,' said the major, bowing low in front of the armoured man.

Kano glanced at the officer, then turned to the new arrivals. He looked Corthie and Tanner up and down for a moment. 'I thought I'd come down to see our new champions for myself. Are you taking them up to the wall?'

'No, my lord; I was going to book them in with the quartermaster to have them fitted for uniforms.'

Kano gave him a dismissive glance. 'That can wait. I want them to see how summer starts every year in the Bulwark.' He stared at Corthie. 'Is this the one the rumours are about?'

'Rumours, sir?'

'Your soldiers have loose tongues, Major,' Kano frowned. 'I was interrupted a few minutes ago by some ridiculous nonsense being spread by the lower ranks regarding this... mercenary. It seems someone has been telling tall tales; ascribing powers to a mortal that no mortal can possibly possess.'

'Apologies, sir. I have already requested that these exaggerations be struck from the record.'

'A little late for that, you fool. You know how excitable the lower orders get. Next time, stamp on these rumours before your soldiers have a chance to spread them.'

'Yes, sir. Sorry, sir.'

Kano stared at Corthie for a moment, contempt in his eyes. 'Let's see how he copes with his first sight of the eternal enemy.' He nodded to his guards. 'The battlements.'

They trooped off, and Corthie fell into line behind Lord Kano, with Tanner to his side. They crossed a courtyard, and turned left by an enormous building that stood alone, taking up a good portion of the front of the fortress.

'What's that?' Corthie whispered to the sergeant.

'Artillery battery,' she said. 'Up on the flat roof.'

Corthie glanced upwards at the walls of the tall building, but could see nothing from where he was standing. They came to a long set of stairs built into the side of the massive curtain wall, and climbed them. A circular tower rose above the battlements, and they were led inside before they could catch a glimpse of the view. They ascended a spiral staircase and Lord Kano stopped with a few steps to go. He turned to face Corthie and Tanner, a smile on his lips.

'Lord Naxor did well to get you here on this particular day,' he said. 'The storms of Freshmist have passed, and summer began a few days ago; four long, hot, dry months are ahead of us, the greenhides' favourite kind of weather. Their legions have awakened from their slumbers and are amassing by the walls, waiting.' He paused. 'Are you ready?'

Corthie nodded. 'Aye.'

Kano stared at him. 'Half of all new recruits break down at this point. Many weep and cower. One even threw themselves from the battlements rather than stand up like a soldier. Let's see how cocky you are after you've had your first sight of the eternal enemy, shall we?'

Tanner smirked at Corthie as Kano turned and led them up the last few steps. Corthie followed the demigod and they emerged onto the roof of the tower. A four-foot parapet enclosed the small platform, where a lethal-looking bolt-thrower stood, its crew working on it. Kano strode to the parapet, his big hands splayed on the stone edges of the battlements. Corthie and Tanner walked up next to him, and Corthie heard the older man's intake of breath as they gazed out.

The land ahead of them was flat, dark green, and seemed to be moving. Corthie focussed his eyes and stared. The thick green carpet covering the plain before the walls was made up of beasts; tall, muscular beasts with thick green skin, like armour-plating, covering their backs and chests. Their arms were long and powerful, with six-inch claws extending from their gnarled hands. Their faces were insect-like, and devoid of any compassion or feeling. They were rolling in a giant wave across the plain, with the largest concentrations to the right, where portions of the sky were blue, but where the sun remained low.

'By all the gods,' Tanner muttered; 'what are they?'

'Greenhides,' said Kano; 'the eternal enemy of the City. For two and a half thousand years they have attacked us, emerging from their nests in the sunward deserts in their hundreds of thousands to throw themselves at the walls of the Bulwark.' He glanced at Corthie, seeming a little disappointed at his lack of reaction. 'They are like no enemy you have ever faced; relentless, indifferent to pain or injury, and stronger than the mightiest mortal.'

Corthie leaned over the parapet, and glanced down. 'Have they ever breached these walls?'

'No,' Kano said. 'The Great Walls were built over a thousand years ago, and they have protected the City ever since.' He pointed. 'There are three lines of defence; the moat, which is thirty feet deep and the same wide, and shielded by the moat wall; then the outer wall, and finally the inner wall, where we're standing now.'

Corthie frowned. 'Then why do you need us?'

Kano snorted. 'Need you? We don't need you. You're just grist for the mill, bodies sent by Naxor for propaganda purposes so that the mortals of the City have something to distract them.' He shook his head. 'As far as I'm concerned, there's only one champion worthy of the name. But don't worry, we'll find a good use for you two; you're being assigned to the Wolfpack.'

Corthie nodded as he watched the great masses of the greenhides rush across the plain, their thick, sturdy legs speeding over the rough, broken land. They reached the edge of the moat and halted, swarming along the brink of the dark water. On the other side of the moat, an unbroken wall stretched, behind which soldiers were presenting a thick line of pikes that reached halfway over the water. One of the greenhides roared a cry of frustration up at the walls, then hurled itself across the moat. It reached halfway, then crashed into the water, its limbs flailing as it sank into the depths.

'They've never learned to swim?'

'No,' said Kano. 'They're dumb brutes. Thousands drown in the moat each year, and we're safe enough while the water level remains high. The problem is, that the central section of the moat dries up every summer, exposing over a third of the length of the Great Wall to direct assault, and we have four months to contain them before the storms of Sweetmist refill the barrier.' He pointed over to his left. 'This is the Fortress of the Lifegiver, and the next fort along is Arrowhead. Beyond that is Stormshield, and it's at these three forts, and along the walls that lie between them, where the moat dries and the Blades fight every summer. Now,' he said, smiling, 'time for a little demonstration.'

He gestured to one of the crew working by the bolt-thrower, and she raised a large yellow flag into the wind, where it unfurled. More yellow flags were lifted from the other towers of the fortress, and Corthie looked back at the massive artillery platform, its height almost level with the battlements of the inner wall. At a signal, over forty huge throwing machines loosed, their long arms arcing through the air unleashing a barrage of projectiles up and over the defences. The massive rocks ripped into the vast sea of greenhides, each ploughing its way through dozens of the tightly-pressed enemy, gouging bloody furrows across the rocky soil. All along the wall, the ballistae, catapults and mangonels loosed; the pink sky flecked with a hailstorm of yard-long bolts and massive stones. Greenhides fell in their hundreds, but every gap in their lines was immediately swallowed up by more of the creatures. Corthie stared into the distance, but could see no end to them, and the bombardment seemed futile.

A cheer rose from the soldiers on the wall and Corthie glanced up as he saw something move through the sky, above the level of the projectiles.

'Behold our champion,' said Kano, smiling; 'worth more than a thousand mortals.'

The flying beast circled for a moment over the battlements, and Corthie glanced at it. It was a winged lizard, its body stretching twenty yards, and its tail even longer. Its hide was dark red with lighter patches on its underside.

'What do you think?' said Kano.

'I've seen these beasts before,' said Corthie. 'Where I'm from, they're harnessed to carriages, and fly people and supplies around. What do you use it for? Does it drop rocks onto the greenhides?'

Kano stared at him, then shook his head. 'Buckler is no mere beast of burden.'

'You've given it a name?'

'It's what he likes to be called. He says he has another name, but he keeps that to himself.'

Corthie's eyes widened. 'Wait, it can talk?'

'Of course he can, and stop calling him "it".'

Tanner laughed. 'My young friend is thinking of a similar beast.'

'It's a winged gaien,' said Corthie.

'No, it's not,' said Tanner. 'Watch.'

Kano smiled at the older mercenary, then gestured again to a guard, who raised a red flag. The beast banked in the air, then soared down over the plain as every soldier on the wall watched. As the beast descended, it extended its wings, and a great burst of flames came from its jaws, a thick oily gush of fire that incinerated scores of greenhides in one pass. The greenhides tried to run from the flames, but they were packed too closely together, and Buckler soared back for a second pass.

Corthie's mouth opened as he watched the flying beast unleash a further blast of flames, the black smoke rising from the smouldering bodies of the greenhides. Every pass was killing a dozen times what each flung rock had achieved, but even so, the beast's efforts were making little difference to the vast numbers of greenhides. The soldiers on the wall cheered as Buckler returned for a third pass.

Corthie narrowed his eyes. 'What is it?'

'That, my young friend,' said Tanner, 'is a dragon.'

# CHAPTER 3
# THE OLD LADY OF ARROWHEAD

Sector Six, The Bulwark, The City – 4<sup>th</sup> Mikalis 3419

'Maddie!' yelled her mother. 'Get your lazy ass down here now.'

'I'm up!' she cried as she sprang out of bed. Her room was in pitch darkness and she stumbled as she searched the floor for clothes, landing with a thump amid the scattered ceramic bowls and heaps of dirty washing. She scrambled around, pulling on a pair of leggings and her army tunic. She grabbed her boots by the door and bolted to the narrow staircase, leaping several steps at a time.

'Why did no one wake me?' she cried as she burst into her family's small living room, which doubled as their kitchen. She glanced at the window-clock, which showed the sun's reflection at an hour after dawn. 'Malik's sweaty crotch, I'm going to be late.'

'No cursing in this house,' said her mother by the stove, giving her elder daughter a frown.

Maddie sat at the dinner table and began to pull on her boots. 'I wasn't cursing. Referring to the perspiration of the God-King's private bits isn't cursing.'

'You know what I mean, girl.'

'No, I don't. Please explain, mother, how what I said is a curse.'

Her younger sister Rosie looked up from a pile of wood and metal on the table. 'Shut up.'

'You shut up, you little toerag.'

'Don't call your sister that.'

'Why? She is a toerag.'

Her mother put her hands on her hips. 'Stop arguing and get your boots on. Do you realise the favours me and your father had to ask for to get you another chance? Being thrown out of the infantry was bad enough, but when you quit the arbalest course I could have despaired. Do you want to be put in the Rat Company?'

'That's not what it's called,' said Maddie. 'It's the Auxiliary Work Company.'

'Yes,' said her mother, sighing, 'but you do know what job they have to do? If you antagonise everyone you meet, then that's where you'll be sent.'

Rosie smirked. 'She wouldn't survive an hour in the moat.'

'No, she would be ripped to shreds by those beasts on the other side of the wall.'

Maddie shrugged. She laced up one boot, then pulled the other on as her sister shuffled the wooden and metal pieces on the table.

'Is that a crossbow?'

Rosie glanced up. 'It's a siege-bow; longer and heavier. You would know that if you hadn't quit the course.'

'And why have they given one to an idiot like you?'

'It was crushed by a falling boulder over by the mangonel battery, and I'm fixing it.'

'Yeah, right. You?'

'Yeah, me. I'm going to work on it for a couple of hours each day. I repaired Dad's crossbow didn't I?'

'That was pure luck,' said Maddie. 'You were eleven. You didn't have a clue what you were doing.'

'Maybe, but I'm fourteen now, and I'm better with my hands than you'll ever be. You'll see. In a month or so I'm going to shoot my first greenhide with it. I'll cover you while you're shovelling gore from the moat with the rest of the Rats.'

'Girls, enough,' said their mother. 'Maddie, go; there's no time for breakfast, just get yourself along to the fort before registration. You've still got time if you run.'

Maddie glanced around. 'Where's Tom?'

'Your brother left an hour ago. Please, don't make me raise my voice. Go.'

Maddie frowned and got up.

'She won't last a day,' muttered Rosie.

'Right, just for that I will,' Maddie said. She pulled her army coat from a hook and walked to the front door. Her stomach rumbled as she stepped outside into the red glow of morning. She ran down the street, passing the rows of identical cube houses where the other Blades of Sector Six lived. She reached the Sixth Plaza, the centre of her district, and dodged through a crowd of milling recruits, her eyes on the position of the sun on the horizon to her right.

If only one of her useless family had woken her, she thought, then she could have had some breakfast, and would be walking to the fort, instead of running like an idiot. A shadow flitted across the sky and she glanced up at the flying serpent, its red scales shimmering in the morning light. The beast liked to stretch its long wings each dawn and she remembered when Buckler had arrived over ten years before, and how the first thing he had done was to launch himself into the sky and fly away. At the time, most had thought that he would never return, but he had, and every day since had been the same. She shuddered to think what the survival rates of the Rat Company had been like before Buckler had appeared in the Bulwark. He was a gift from the gods, or so they said, a miracle procured by the divine wisdom of the God-King and God-Queen. A few even believed he might be the redeemer, come to save them, but Maddie didn't hold with such wishful thinking.

She sprinted down the wide avenue that linked the Sixth Plaza to the entrance of the mighty fortress of Stormshield. On her right lay the divisional marshalling yards, an open, dusty plain where hundreds of soldiers were holding the repetitive drills that had driven her crazy with boredom during her short-lived time in the infantry.

The huge gatehouse of Stormshield loomed ahead, and she raced past the guards by the open entrance and entered the fort. Hundreds were assembling within the vast forecourt by the towering barracks blocks, and she scanned the raised standards, looking for the unit her parents had talked into giving their wayward daughter another chance. The banner of the Seventh Support Battalion was fluttering in the warm breeze. A small group of officers had gathered next to the young standard-bearer, and were checking a long scroll. Maddie ran to the end of the lines that led from the banner, and put her hands on her knees, wheezing and panting.

She laughed to herself. Just in time.

An officer began to read out a list of names, and the assembled men and women raised their hands in turn.

Maddie straightened, conscious of the looks she was getting, She pulled her hair back and tied it into a long ponytail, and wiped the sweat from her brow. She glanced around as more names were called out, looking for any faces she recognised, and saw a couple of guys she remembered from infantry training. Unlike her, they had been ejected from the front line forces due to sheer incompetence, rather than her annoying habit of pointing out why many of their orders didn't make any sense. If there was one thing officers hated, it was being told they were wrong by the lower orders.

'Maddie Jackdaw,' the voice called out.

She raised her hand, half-expecting to be singled out and told there had been a mistake, but the officer went on to the next name.

Someone nudged her with an elbow. 'You're one of the Jackdaws?'

'Clearly.'

'My sister was good friends with Nahil Jackdaw.'

'There are lots of Jackdaws,' Maddie said. 'I don't know them all.'

'What about Nahil's brother Amon? You must know him, he was...'

'Nope.'

Another recruit butted in. 'She's Tom's little sister. I used to see her play out in the street when I was young. A right little toerag she was.'

'Screw you,' Maddie said. 'You call me that again and I'll break your nose.'

'That's weird,' said the first recruit. 'I met Tom once, and he told me he only had one sister, and her name was Rosie.'

'Probably ashamed,' laughed the second recruit.

Maddie swung her fist and struck the woman in the face. Within seconds, the queuing recruits had transformed into a mass of shoving and shouted recriminations. Hands grabbed Maddie's arms, so she kicked the closest guy in the groin, and he doubled over, shrieking in pain. A fist glanced off her cheek as her left arm was twisted behind her back, and another blow landed in her stomach. She prepared herself for a beating as more fists flew in.

Army wardens piled into the melee, their clubs lashing out. The crowd pulled back as officers shouted out orders. The hands let go of Maddie's arms and she slid to the flagstones, gasping for breath and aching in a dozen places.

'What in the name of Amalia's sacred blood is going here?' cried an officer. 'Who started this?'

None of the recruits spoke, and Maddie opened her eyes from where she lay on the ground.

'I want a name,' said the officer, 'or the entire battalion will be assisting the Auxiliary Work Company today.'

There was a sharp intake of breath from the assembled recruits. Wardens were prowling up and down the lines brandishing their clubs but still, no one spoke.

Maddie raised her arm.

'Speak, Private.'

Two wardens came over and hauled her up by her shoulders.

'Well?' said the officer.

'I was provoked.'

'That doesn't matter; did you strike first?'

'Yeah, but I was...'

'Silence, Private.' She glanced at a junior officer. 'Her name?'

'Private Maddie Jackdaw, ma'am.'

The officer shook her head. 'The one I was warned about?'

'Yes, ma'am; she was discharged from the infantry for insubordination.'

'And she starts a fight within five minutes of joining our battalion?'

Maddie struggled in the grip of the wardens pinning her shoulders. 'This isn't fair; I was provoked!'

The officer looked at her with disdain. 'Yes, you probably were. However, it is your response to that which is the subject of my attention, Private. Your lack of self-control is evident, as is your inability to work as part of a close-knit team.'

'I have self-control. Ma'am.'

'Really? Tell me, Private, if someone were to repeat the same provocation, how would you react?'

'I, uh...'

'As I thought.' She glanced at the wardens. 'Get her out of my sight. I need a little time to decide what's to be done with young Jackdaw.'

'The Rats,' murmured a low voice from somewhere in the crowd.

Maddie's eyes glanced over the other company recruits, searching for the source of the comment; trying to see who had dared to make such a suggestion as her anger bubbled and simmered.

The arms gripping her shoulders started to guide her away from the crowd, leading her towards a stone blockhouse by the iceward walls of the fortress, where the punishment cells lay. She writhed in their grasp, but the hands were strong, and pushed her onwards.

'Guys,' she said, 'this is a mistake; I've done nothing to deserve the cells, come on...'

The two wardens ignored her, and they entered the low block. It was dark inside, and stank of stale urine and worse. A long, double row of barred cells lined the walls of a passageway.

'Who do we have here?' said a man rising from a chair by the door, a huge ring of keys by his belt. He picked up a wax-board and stylus from a small desk.

'Private Maddie Jackdaw,' said one of the wardens. 'Colonel Lichter wants her secured until a decision's been made about her future.'

The jailer nodded, and wrote onto the wax-board. He glanced up. 'Cell seventeen's free.'

The wardens and the man escorted Maddie down the passageway, then shoved her into a damp, filthy cell. The barred gate was closed, and the jailer locked it.

'There's a bucket in the corner,' he said, 'and fresh water in the...'

Maddie glared at them through the bars. 'I know how it works.'

'This is not your first stay, then?'

She shrugged.

'Look at her,' the jailer said; 'she has "Rat" written all over her face.'

'My boot will be all over your face when I get out of here.'

The wardens and the man laughed, then they disappeared down the passageway. Maddie stared at the dark, empty corridor for a few moments, as what had happened began to sink in. Her parents were going to lose it completely when they found out. A grizzled old soldier in the cell opposite glanced up at her from his straw mattress, and Maddie retreated into the darkness of her own cell. There was a narrow opening, but it gave out onto a view of the high curtain wall of the fortress, and was letting in almost no light. She sat on the edge of her mattress, and prepared for a long wait.

---

None of it was her fault. In the infantry, the officers had been pig-headed fools, who had taken a perverse pleasure in issuing the most irrational orders. Move that pile of rocks over there. You've done that? Right, now move it all back again. It had driven Maddie to the edge; how could she obey such foolish commands? It was clear that those in control didn't want the infantry thinking for themselves, but she couldn't bring herself to play along with their silly games. The arbalest course; that wasn't her fault either. No one had told her how much geometry and arithmetic she would need to master, and the equations had frustrated her to breaking point. She was clever; everyone had always said that, but she clearly had no head for numbers. She had walked out during an examination on angles, wind-speed, and the force with which a catapult could hurl a half-tonne boulder over a quarter of a mile. It was pointless. As long as the damn boulder hit the greenhides, who cared about the rate of acceleration?

A cold shiver rippled down her back as she pondered the colonel's decision. She had often watched the Rat Company at work from the safety of the battlements. Even with Buckler and the Wolfpack protecting them, the casualties they sustained were higher than any other unit. Once she had witnessed the annihilation of the entire company in a single outing beyond the walls. The red dragon had tired early for some reason, and the greenhides had surged through the thin cordon of Wolfpack fighters. They had ripped and hacked every member of the Rat Company into bloody pieces, as the onlookers had watched in stunned silence from the walls. The siege-bows and ballistae had been operating at maximum capacity, and hundreds of greenhides had been killed, their bodies heaped up between the dry moat and the outer wall; but it didn't matter how many of the enemy fell, there were always others to take their place.

Maddie remembered a particular greenhide. It had been sitting amid the carnage, eating the remains of one of the Rats, oblivious to both the missiles falling around it, and the six bolts that were already studding its thick, armoured back. Its hideous face was smeared in red blood, its long claws dripping entrails and gore, and Maddie had experienced nightmares about it for years.

She cursed her luck. Why couldn't she have been born a Roser? She would even be happy being an Evader, rather than be forced to join the Rat Company. Then she could have lived her life in blissful ignorance of the daily war that raged along the walls of the Bulwark. What did those stupid civilians know about the struggles of the Blades, or the sacrifices they made so that the rest of the City could enjoy their lives in peace? Cowards, the lot of them.

None of it was fair; was she the only Blade to see that?

A noise came from the end of the passageway, and her eyes flickered up. A young lieutenant appeared outside the bars of her cell, accompanied by two wardens. Maddie got to her feet.

'Private Maddie Jackdaw?' the officer said.

'Yeah.'

'The colonel has reached a decision regarding your future...'

'Then why isn't she here to tell me herself?'

The lieutenant frowned. 'The colonel has more important things to be attending to than one insubordinate soldier. Now, if you'll allow me to continue, Private?'

'Just get it over with. I'm being pushed into the Rats, aren't I?'

He stared at her. 'You have no idea how lucky you are; no idea at all. Jackdaws have served in the Blades for generations; dozens have given their lives to defend the Bulwark over that time.'

'I'm an embarrassment to my family, I know. My dad's always saying that he'd rather...'

'Shut up for one minute, Private. Due to the honour in which your family is held among the lower orders, the colonel has decided that it would be detrimental to morale if you were to be assigned to the Auxiliary Work Company.'

'Wait, I'm not going to the Rats?'

'Let me finish, Private!' the young officer cried. 'By Malik's breath, I can now see why the other officers smirked at me when I was told to deliver this message; you're incapable of closing that big mouth of yours.'

Maddie put her hands on her hips, but said nothing.

'Good. Right, you've been re-assigned, effective immediately, to the Fourteenth Support Battalion based in Arrowhead. They have a vacancy that they've been finding difficult to fill, and the colonel has arranged that you be transferred there. It's a trial position, and the officers of the Fourteenth have been briefed on your record.' He nodded to the jailer, who had been lurking in the shadows to the left of the cell. 'Release her.'

'Is that it?' Maddie said as the gate was unlocked. 'No punishment, just a transfer?'

'This really is your last chance, Private,' the lieutenant said. 'The name of Jackdaw isn't as well known in Arrowhead, and if you mess up there, then the officers of the Fourteenth will have no problem sending you to the Rats. Understand?'

'Yeah, I get it,' she said as she walked from the cell.

'The Fourteenth are expecting you there today,' the lieutenant said, 'so go home and pack a bag, then make your way to Arrowhead and report to the gatehouse.'

'Pack a bag?'

'It's a live-in position; you'll be quartered there. Dismissed.'

Maddie frowned at the officer, then turned and walked past the other cells to the main door. She stepped outside and scanned the sky. The sun was approaching noon, and the sky was almost blue. It was a six-mile walk from her house by the Sixth Plaza to Arrowhead Fort, which meant that if she hurried home, then she would have time for something to eat before she had to leave again. Even better, her mother would be at work, and her sister at school, so she would have the house to herself. She wondered how she would break the news to her parents.

A note, she thought. She'd leave them a note.

---

The sun was setting by the time she reached the gatehouse of Arrowhead Fort. She had been in the fort several times, but as a native of Sector Six, she had always seen Stormshield as her true home. Arrowhead felt like the competition to her, and the rivalry between the forts was intense. She passed under the entrance arch and turned left at a door in the gatehouse. She hefted the bag on her shoulder, took a breath, and opened the door.

She walked into a small chamber, with wooden benches and a long desk. Two soldiers were talking by the slit window, and they turned to glance as she approached.

'Can I help you, Private?' said one.

'My name's Maddie Jackdaw, Sergeant.'

'And?'

She frowned. 'I've been sent over, I mean transferred, from the Seventh to the Fourteenth Support Battalion.'

'Ahhh,' said the man. 'You're the lass from Stormshield?'

'Yeah, that's me.'

The sergeant chuckled.

'What's so funny?' said his colleague.

'She's been assigned to the old lady.'

The soldier's eyes widened.

'The who?' said Maddie.

The sergeant grinned. 'You'll see.' He turned to the other soldier. 'You stay here, and I'll take the lass over to the Fourteenth.'

'Sure, boss.'

The sergeant gestured towards the door, then he and Maddie walked back out into the entrance tunnel of the gatehouse. He led her into a large forecourt, and the noise from the loosing catapults and mangonels rang through her ears. Dozens of machines were up on the wide walls of the fortress, while Buckler was flying high above, circling over the battlements. His lair was somewhere in the fortress, she knew, though she had never seen it. Atop the wall to the right, however, a great wooden platform had been erected, which served as the dragon's perch, where he could sit and look out over the waves of greenhides assailing the walls. The two sides of the fort met at an angle, and the point they created jutted out from the Great Walls; the shape giving the fortress its name. Next to where the walls met was a large, thick tower, the home of the Wolfpack. Seeing it reminded her of something she had heard the day before.

'You got new champions yesterday, yeah?'

The sergeant glanced at her. 'The news reached Stormshield, did it?'

'My brother told me.'

'Oh yeah? Did he tell you the rumours as well?'

'What rumours?'

'It's a load of nonsense, but you're bound to hear it. Apparently, one of the new champions, who to all appearances is a mortal like you and me, though he is a little on the tall side; anyway, apparently, this man has battle-vision.'

'What? That's impossible.'

'I know. Unfortunately, the Bulwark has its fair share of the gullible, the superstitious, and the downright stupid, and you can only imagine what the Redemptionists have to say about it.'

'He's not fought yet, I take it?'

'No, they're giving him a day or two to settle in first, but the sooner the better, in my opinion. Let them all see that he's just a mortal, and hopefully that'll put the rumours and the mystic nonsense to bed.'

'Sounds like you want him to get killed.'

'Better a dead champion than a fort full of religious zealots.'

'Is it that bad? Stormshield only has a handful of Redemptionists, and no one listens to anything they say.'

'It used to be the same here, lass,' he said, glancing up at the sky, 'but Buckler draws them to Arrowhead. Many folk thought he might be the one they've been waiting for; some still do. I'd say we have about a dozen genuine dragon-worshippers in the fort now, and plenty of others who just want to be in the same vicinity as the beast.'

'Weirdoes. He's just a flying snake, basically.'

The sergeant took a sideways glance at her. 'I'd be careful mouthing opinions like that in Arrowhead, especially in front of Buckler, and even more especially...' He tailed off into silence.

'Even more especially what?'

He shrugged. 'Nothing.'

She squinted at him, but thought better of prying. Officers were fair game, but she always felt a little intimidated by sergeants.

They passed a massive barracks block to their left.

'Is that where I'll be staying?'

'No,' he said; 'just a little further.'

To the left and right of the Wolfpack tower were long rows of arches opening into the huge outer walls of the fortress. The sergeant led her through one and they came to a door set in the wall. He knocked on it.

'Delivery,' he shouted through the closed entrance. 'Fresh meat.'

The door opened before Maddie could respond and a middle-aged woman peered out.

'Evening, Hilde,' said the sergeant. 'I've brought the lass from Stormshield.'

The woman eyed Maddie. 'Does she know what she's going to be doing?'

The sergeant chuckled. 'Nah. I thought it would be better coming from you.'

'Is this supposed to be a joke?' said Maddie. 'What will I be doing? Are you the old lady? You don't seem that old to me. My mother looks older than you, and if you called her an old lady, she'd punch you in the face.'

The woman frowned at her. 'Is this why they sent you?'

'Eh?'

The sergeant laughed and raised his hands. 'See you later, Hilde, and good luck.'

The woman watched the sergeant walk back through the archway into the courtyard, then she levelled her gaze on Maddie.

'When you address me, you will call me ma'am; do you understand?'

Maddie stood to attention. 'Yes, ma'am.'

The woman sighed. 'Fine. Well, I suppose you should come in.' She opened the door wider, and Maddie walked through the entrance into a low-ceilinged chamber, lit by an oil lamp burning from the wall. 'Welcome to the Fourteenth Support Battalion, Auxiliary Detachment Number Three.'

Maddie glanced around. 'Where's everyone else? I mean, ma'am, sorry.'

The woman stuck her hand out. 'It's just me and you.'

'Oh.'

The woman glanced down at her hand, and Maddie shook it.

'My name is Captain Hilde, and I've been looking after this detachment for nearly ten years. In that time I've gone through over twenty assistants, and have spent more days working alone than I have with any assistance at all. As my new assistant, forgive me, but I'm not going to bother learning your name until you've lasted at least a few days.'

'It's Maddie Jackdaw, ma'am.'

'Do you ever listen to what you're told?'

'Oh, I listen, ma'am, but I often feel compelled to disagree.'

A hint of a smile appeared on Hilde's lips for a second. 'Come with me,' she said, 'and I'll show you where you'll be sleeping.'

She led Maddie through a door and into a long hallway. Hilde began pointing at side entrances as they passed them. 'Office, stores, kitchen, stores, my quarters; never go in them without my express permission; stores, stores, and here we are.' She stopped at a door and opened it. 'Your room.'

'That was a lot of stores,' Maddie said as she glanced into the chamber. It had a bed, not a straw mattress, for which she felt immediate gratitude. There was also a table with a candlestick, a chair, and a trunk. She slung her bag off her shoulder and threw it onto the bed.

'Don't unpack,' said Hilde; 'not just yet.'

'Am I finally going to be told what I'll be doing?'

Hilde smiled. 'What do you know about dragons?'

'What? Buckler?' she cried, letting out an involuntary yelp. 'I'm going to be working with Buckler?'

'No,' said Hilde; 'not Buckler.'

'Eh? But we only have one... dragon... don't we?'

'Follow me.'

Hilde turned and opened a door at the end of the hallway. They passed into a large cavern, where an earthy animal stench assaulted Maddie's nostrils. Opposite was a huge red door, barred and padlocked, while an equally wide and high tunnel led off to the left.

'Did you know,' said Hilde as she led Maddie towards the tunnel, 'that the fortress of Arrowhead was chosen for Buckler because the walls here are thicker than at any other fort? We could tunnel out a lair for him, so he could live in the fashion he prefers. It took over a year to finish it.' She pointed at a massive red-painted door that spanned the side of the tunnel. 'That gate leads to Buckler's lair. He has a score of Blades attending to his every need and desire; they scurry around like servants in the court of a demigod.' She glanced at Maddie. 'In this lair, there's only me, and now you.'

Maddie swallowed. 'What happened to all of the other assistants?'

Hilde approached a huge, black-painted gate. A smaller door had been cut through it and she put her hand up and unbolted it.

'About half left and refused to come back.'

'And the other half?'

Hilde pushed open the door. 'It's me,' she called out into the darkness. 'I've brought someone new to help out. Do not, I beg you, incinerate her before you have a chance to get to know her. You might like this one.'

A low rumble echoed out from the darkness behind the gate. 'The taste of her flesh in my jaws would be the greatest service she could offer me. Send her in if that's your intention; otherwise I promise nothing.'

Hilde glanced back at Maddie. 'I've had less favourable responses. Come on.'

She stepped through the small door and disappeared into the gloom. Maddie stared at the dark opening. There was another dragon in Arrowhead? How did she not know this? Why would it be a secret? A hundred questions rolled through her mind, fighting against the base fear that was churning her stomach. If she stepped through the door, she might find out the answers, or she might be reduced to ashes; but what was the alternative? The Rats?

Maddie took a breath and entered the darkness, coming into a vast chamber. A dozen high slit-windows were letting in the red light of evening, and in their glow Maddie could see the great bulk of a creature. Scales gleamed a dull red, but that was the light, the dragon looked to be pure black; a beast formed of darkness. Its head was low, almost on the stone ground, but its eyes glistened a deep blood red.

Maddie stepped forward to stand next to Hilde, who was waiting for her.

'Good,' the woman said; 'you've made it this far. Who knows, you may even be the one I've been waiting for.'

'She's not the one I've been waiting for,' growled the dragon, its voice causing Maddie's knees to tremble. 'She's far too scrawny; I would barely get a bite out of her.'

'Yes, very funny,' said Hilde. She turned to Maddie and smiled. 'Say hello to Blackrose. I may be your commanding officer, but she's your new boss.'

# CHAPTER 4

# GRADUATION DAY

**Tara, Auldan, The City – 5th Mikalis 3419**

Daniel sat alone in the small dressing room, the weight of three and a half thousand years on his shoulders. He had been spoiled as a boy, he knew that, but missed his youth; the freedom, the space, the innocence. He had always known that he was the last of the Aurelian line, but as a child that had made him feel special, rather than the sole hope of his family. His cousins had died young, or had grown old without bearing children, and for years he had listened to the plans his parents had made for him. He had been betrothed to the daughter of one of the other nobles lines of Tara since he had turned twelve, and they were due to be married in under two years, as soon as he had reached twenty-one. Clarine, her name was, and he had met her precisely three times since their engagement.

A soft knock at the door roused him from his thoughts.

'Sir? The ceremony's about to commence, and your noble mother is asking for you.'

Daniel put his head in his hands.

'Sir?'

'I heard you,' he snapped.

There was silence for a moment, followed by shuffling footsteps outside the door. 'Apologies, sir, but your noble mother was most insistent.'

'I'm sure she was,' he muttered.

'Sorry, sir?'

'Nothing. Go away. I'll be out in a moment.'

Silence.

Daniel stood, and smoothed the front of his smart new uniform. He glanced into the six-foot mirror on the wall, and noticed the heavy lines around his eyes from lack of sleep. The other sons and daughters of the nobility would already be out on the grand podium in front of the Military Academy, and his mother was no doubt furious that he was taking so long to get ready.

Ready? He would never be ready for what was expected of him. For a fleeting moment, he wished he had been born a peasant. The Rosers were the elite of the City, and the Taran aristocracy were the elite of the Rosers; a tiny proportion of the smallest tribe out of the nine, who controlled much of the economy, and most of the wealth. Would he swap a life of luxury to be free of his responsibilities? He had never been in the vast slums of the Circuit, and had only the vaguest notion of how the poor conducted their miserable lives, but even so, he felt it would be a worthwhile trade.

He opened the door, and found the servant skulking close by.

'I thought I told you to go away?'

'Apologies, sir, but your mother... I was told...'

'Forget it,' Daniel said, sweeping past the old man as he walked along the marble passageway. He reached a large, empty hall, and walked out through the open doors into the sunlight. The sky was a deep shade of blue ahead of him, where the sun sat poised above the horizon. Noon was only a few minutes away, and he hurried down the wide, stone steps. A crowd had gathered by the forecourt of the academy, standing behind a row of Taran militia. Arranged on seats in front of the crowd were the parents and family members of the young graduates, and Daniel glimpsed his mother and father in the front row. His mother was glaring at him, and pointing at the high platform that had been erected by the grand entrance to the academy. He turned away from the crowd and hastened towards the platform. Wooden steps had been constructed at the rear of the structure, and he raced up them. Over two dozen other aristocratic youths were already seated, facing the crowds, and Daniel found the last free chair, hidden in the back row. His mother wouldn't be pleased. She had told him to be early, so that he could be seated near the front, as befit a scion of the most ancient and noble family of Tara. He could already hear her complaints about the second-rate nobility blocking the view of her precious son, but he didn't care. A small part of him was amazed that he had even turned up.

A senior officer glanced over at Daniel, and nodded. She raised her arm, and the crowd began to quieten.

'Good afternoon,' she said, her practised voice reaching to the edge of the large forecourt. 'On this most revered of dates, when we commemorate the life and death of Tara's most illustrious son, Prince Michael, and honour his beloved and divine mother, the God-Queen Amalia, I am pleased to present to you, the people of Tara, this year's new crop of young officers.'

She paused to allow a polite smattering of applause from the common folk.

'The Taran nobility,' she went on, 'has a unique role to play in these troubled times. The peace and security of the City depend on order and obedience, without which the tribes would fall into anarchy and lawlessness. Outside the Great Walls, the eternal enemy waits; seasons change and decades pass, and they will still be there. The weak may tremble at the thought, but it is the task of the best of us to never despair, to fight on and keep the flames of the City alive. We are a beacon of light in this world, the last beacon, and if the day comes when that light is extinguished, then this world shall fall into darkness and oblivion. But, until that day, we pledge to fight on, and to never give up.' She turned to glance at the two dozen youths next to her on the platform. 'Please stand.'

The young aristocrats rose from their wooden chairs.

'Once a year,' the officer said, 'on the birthday of our beloved martyr and prince, we commission our new officers. By swearing the sacred oath to the God-King and God-Queen of the City, they are bound to a lifetime of service to Tara and the Rosers; the first town, and the first tribe. Raise your right hands, and make your oath.'

'In the name of the God-Queen and God-King,' they recited in unison, 'and in the sacred memory of Michael, Prince of Tara, we vow to dedicate our lives to the service of Tara, the tribe of the Rosers, and the City. We swear to obey the orders of our superiors, and shall uphold the dignity and honour of the Rosers, the first and most noble tribe of the City, for as long as we shall live.'

There was another smattering of applause, and the officer gestured to the youths to retake their seats.

'I shall now call out the names of those who have recently graduated from the Taran Military Academy. When you hear your name, please step forward.' An aide passed the officer a thick sheet of cream-coloured paper. 'Lieutenant Daniel Aurelian.'

Daniel blinked. He had finished eleventh out of twelve in his class, and he suspected that he had only passed due to the influence of his parents. He stood, and the crowd applauded as he made his way through the rows of chairs to the front. The aide held out a purple ribbon and a gold badge, and the officer took them as Daniel approached.

'Congratulations, Lieutenant,' the officer said, taking a firm grip of Daniel's hand and shaking it. She passed him the regimental insignia and the officer ribbon. 'Wear these with pride.'

Daniel nodded, unsure if he should reply. His eyes darted over the crowd, and he caught sight of his parents beaming with joy. A few seats to their left sat members of the Chamberlain family. They were applauding politely, but Daniel could see the contempt in their eyes. The officer smiled and withdrew her hand, and Daniel took that as the signal to return to his seat. He squeezed through the chairs as the officer read out another name. Daniel took his seat amid more applause, and gazed at the badge and ribbon lying in the palm of his right hand.

That was it. He was an officer. Not because he wanted to be, or because he had any interest whatsoever in the Taran militia, but because of his name, and what it meant. He kept his head down for the rest of the ceremony, ignoring the polite clapping of the others around him, and meeting no one's glance. When the last graduate to be called had received their ribbon and badge, the officer raised her hand again, and the forecourt fell into silence.

'These twenty-six new officers,' she said, 'have all worked hard to reach this point, and at dawn tomorrow they will take their place in the Taran militia. This evening, however, as is traditional, they and their families are cordially invited to a dance and reception in the banqueting hall of Maeladh Palace.' She smiled. 'Please don't keep our young lieutenants up too late.'

She stepped back and began to applaud the new officers, who stood to receive the acclaim of the crowd. Daniel shuffled to his feet, feeling light-headed and dizzy, as if he were in a dream.

'Hey, Danny,' said a young man to his right, 'you couldn't look more miserable if you tried. What's up? Just think, no more classes, ever. As of tomorrow, we'll be the ones giving the orders, and those stupid sergeants and trainers will have to do what we say, instead of us having to obey them.'

Daniel nodded. His eyes drifted left towards the harbour of Tara, where dozens of small vessels were berthed amid the clear, blue waters of Warm Bay, then at the pretty villas and mansions of the old town, with their red tiled roofs and pastel exteriors, and finally to the right, where the high cliffs of the Sunward Range continued up the coastline to where the gargantuan marble statue of the martyred Prince Michael stood, guarding the entrance to the large bay. The ancient palace of Maeladh was dug into the side of the high, narrow ridge of hills, its huge bulk amended and renovated countless times since its foundation. Along from it nestled Princeps Row, a cluster of streets where the richest Tarans dwelt in great mansions that had been burrowed from the rock. One of the grandest residences belonged to the Aurelians, and Daniel had been born and raised within its solid walls. The palace had once been their family home, he knew; a fact that his parents had pointed out to him while he was still a toddler. One day, his mother had whispered, it would be their home again.

---

Although there were several hours between the ceremony and the reception, Daniel's parents seemed to spend the entire time rushing about getting ready. Tailors, hairdressers, manicurists and make-up artists had all been summoned to the Aurelian mansion. His mother had sent spies out from the family household of servants to discreetly discover what the other parents and family members were going to be wearing to the reception. For the aristocracy, this was one of the biggest events of their lives; the day their noble children took on the mantle of adult responsibilities and became full Taran citizens. As an only child, Daniel's parents would experience the occasion once, and both were determined to take full advantage of the opportunities it would present.

For Daniel, sartorial choices were of no concern; he would be wearing his dress uniform along with the other new officers. A servant had stitched the purple ribbon to the shoulder of his militia jacket, and the golden badge depicting the leopard of Tara had been attached to the breast pocket. At his mother's insistence, the jacket was hanging up in his room to prevent him from creasing it or, Amalia forbid, in case he accidentally stained or ripped it. He retired out onto a veranda to escape the sound of his parents shouting at the servants, and watched as the sun slipped towards the horizon, and the sky resumed its usual shades of red and pink. Their mansion was one of the highest on the ridge, and he could see right across the bay to the outer suburbs of Pella, the home of untold numbers of Reaper peasantry. He envied their simple lives at that moment, and their freedom. Crab-boats and small passenger ferries were plying the waters of the bay, while larger galleys were sailing past the enormous statue of the dead Prince Michael, heading for the straits that led to the Warm Sea to harvest the seaweed, lobsters and shellfish that proliferated in the balmy, saline waters. It was a beautiful view, he had to admit; possibly one of the best views in the City, and he had it all to himself.

There was a tap on the veranda door, and his mother emerged into the early evening light.

'I knew I'd find you out here,' she said, sitting next to him. Her hair was up in rollers, and she had a towel draped over her shoulders, and a glass of wine in her right hand. 'It has come to my attention,' she said, 'that young Gaimer from your class is related to the Hauvern family.'

'Yeah, so?'

She frowned at him. 'The Hauverns are cousins with the Bludwins, and Perpertua Bludwin is married to none other than the uncle of your Miss Clarine. What I am trying to say, my dear child, is that there's a very strong possibility that your betrothed will be present at tonight's reception.'

His eyes widened. 'I thought her parents weren't going to let her leave the house until we were married?'

'Yes,' his mother said, her gaze on the harbour, 'that is indeed what they said. However, graduation day at the academy is a very special occasion, and so I thought I'd prepare you, just in case.'

'Gaimer never mentioned that he knew Clarine.'

'Immaterial, my boy. Now, if Miss Clarine is there, then propriety and tradition forbid you from being alone in her presence. You may dance with her, in fact if you didn't ask it would be seen by her family as a grievous insult, but you must keep a good distance between you; a hand on her waist is fine, but nowhere else. And whatever else you do, do not kiss her. Be courteous, but aloof; interested, but not overly-excited. Keep your conversation to banalities regarding the weather, or how pretty her dress is.'

'You make it sound like I'll be dancing with an old aunt, rather than with the woman I'm going to marry.'

Her mother shook her head. 'Miss Clarine is still only fourteen, Daniel; she is not yet a woman.'

A shiver rippled through him at her mother's words. 'What? But, no, that can't be right. I last saw her when I was fourteen, are you telling me that she was only nine years old at the time?'

'Yes. Her mother went to inordinate lengths to make her appear older than her years, and you saw her for less than thirty seconds. If I recall the occasion correctly, the girl had a veil on for most of that time.'

'You tricked me. I thought she was only a couple of years younger than me. I'm supposed to marry her when I'm twenty-one, and she'll only be sixteen? I feel a bit sick, to be honest.'

'Don't be so melodramatic. When you're fifty, she'll be forty-five, and the difference in age will seem utterly trivial. What's important is that this union will bring our families closer together. She's from very good stock.'

'She's not a pony, mother.'

'You know what I mean. Your father and I had to court her family for months before they would even consider beginning marriage negotiations. A lot of time and money has been invested in this engagement, and I know for a fact that, had you not passed the officer course at the academy, then they had a clause in the nuptial contract that would have allowed them to cancel the whole thing.'

He stared out at the bay. 'Maybe that would have been better. I don't want to be an officer, and I don't want to marry a woman, I mean a girl, that I don't even know.'

His mother slapped him across the face. 'How dare you, you ungrateful child. Do you have any inkling of the sacrifices your father and I have made to get you where you are today? Of course you don't; you're a foolish and immature boy with no understanding of the struggles of life, or the place of the Aurelians. This family has served Tara since the very beginning, and the blood of the last mortal prince runs in your veins.' She took a breath. 'Now, I know it must be hard for you. You are the sole living heir of what was once a flourishing family line, a line that has lasted almost three and a half thousand years. If you fail to marry and produce heirs, then all of that history ends with you. The shame would break my heart and send your father to an early grave.'

'It's too much,' he said, 'and it's all on my shoulders. Why, mother, why didn't you have more children?'

'You wouldn't ask that question if you knew the troubles we had conceiving you, my son. Years of trying; years of disappointment, until you finally appeared. You were like a miracle to us; you still are. This is yet another reason why Miss Clarine is such a perfect match; her family abounds in their fecundity, and I have no doubt that she will bear you a strong and robust litter of children to fill the ranks of the next generation of Aurelians.'

He grimaced as she stood.

'You're a man now,' she said, her hand going to the veranda door. 'Try to remember to act like one.'

---

The banqueting hall of the palace was the most sumptuous chamber Daniel had ever seen. Its domed ceiling rose high above the marble floor, painted in frescoes outlined in gold leaf. Glittering chandeliers hung suspended by chains, each one dazzling from the glow of the dozens of candles that burned within their jewelled holders. The high walls were brightly painted, depicting scenes from the legendary past of the City; the arrival of the Two Gods, the building of the Union Walls, when the City was first united under the rule of the God-King and God-Queen, and the Battle of the Children of the Gods, when Malik and Amalia's six offspring had annihilated the greenhides and pushed them back hundreds of miles, allowing the time and space to construct the invincible Great Walls. The newest scene had been added only a few hundred years before, and showed the infamous slaying of the mighty and beloved Prince Michael, lord of Tara, and eldest son of the God-King and God-Queen. The vile and treacherous Princess Yendra, who had so shamelessly cut down her brother in cold blood, was shown cowering in fear before the king and queen, who had come to mourn their son and deliver justice to their wicked daughter.

Daniel gazed at the picture for a moment, wondering what Queen

Amalia thought of it. The God-Queen had moved into the palace in Tara after her son's death, taking over his old rooms and making them her own, following her separation from the God-King, who had remained in Ooste. In his nineteen years, Daniel had never once seen the God-Queen, whose personal living quarters were far removed from the banqueting hall.

He bowed to the noble lords and ladies as he entered the chamber, his parents a step behind. At least a hundred of Tara's elite were already inside, chatting, and taking food and wine from trays held aloft by uniformed servants. A musical band were tuning up in a corner of the hall, their strings and horns mingling with the hubbub of conversations. Daniel groaned inwardly, but tried to keep a smile on his face. He loathed the aristocracy of Tara, and was already counting the hours and minutes before he could leave. His parents took him on a tour of the room, where he shook hands and nodded along to the many congratulations.

The crowd cleared a space in the middle of the floor when the band began playing, and the first couples stepped up to dance. Daniel retreated to a side wall, and tried to hide himself in the shadows.

'Hey, Danny,' said Todd, one of his academy classmates. 'You having fun?'

'Yeah, right,' he muttered.

Todd shrugged. 'I don't mind it. Free wine, free food, and you get to look at all the girls dressed up.'

'I'm engaged, remember?'

'So? It's only looking.'

'If my mother catches me gawking at other girls she'll string me up.' He sighed. 'Malik's ass, here she comes.'

Todd visibly straightened and tucked his stomach in as Daniel's mother approached. 'Ma'am,' he said, bowing low and kissing her hand, 'might I say what a delight you're looking this evening?'

Daniel's mother raised an eyebrow at Todd, then withdrew her hand from his grasp. 'Quite. Anyway, would you be so good as to fetch me another glass of wine?'

'Of course, ma'am,' said Todd, bowing again, 'it would be my pleasure.'

He scurried off, and Daniel shook his head. Several of his male classmates acted in the same way around his mother, and it had been a source of continual embarrassment.

'What a charming young man,' she said, 'but I felt obliged to interrupt, as a certain young miss has arrived.'

He groaned.

'Hush, now.' She pointed discreetly towards the opposite wall. 'There she is, along with about a dozen of her relations, all here just for Lieutenant Gaimer. Her parents must have known you'd be coming, so we should assume that they expect you to go over and ask her to dance.'

'Mother,' he cringed, 'you can't make me dance with a fourteen-year-old in front of the other officers; I'll be a laughing stock.'

'Don't be ridiculous. Half of the officers present here will also be having arranged marriages, and if any think less of you for dancing with your betrothed, then that's their problem. On the other hand, if you refuse to ask her, then the damage might well be irreparable.'

His eyes scanned the opposite wall. He caught sight of Gaimer and his sister, then behind them, almost unnoticeable, stood a girl in a long green dress. Her face was lowered, but she glanced up as he stared, and their eyes met. She blushed and looked away.

'I can't do this,' he muttered.

His mother frowned at him. 'Remember when I told you to act like a man? Perhaps you should start now. If you don't, then I will go over there and ask her on your behalf and, trust me, that would look considerably worse.'

Todd walked over with a full glass of wine in his hand. 'For you, my lady,' he said, offering it to Daniel's mother.

'Thank you,' she smiled. 'Daniel was just about to go and ask his betrothed to dance.'

'Oh, she's here, is she?' he said, glancing around.

Daniel muttered a curse and stepped away from the wall. He circled the dance floor in the middle of the hall, squeezing past groups of young officers and their families until he reached Gaimer.

'Danny,' his classmate nodded. 'Nice to see you. What do you think of this place, amazing, eh?'

'Yeah. Listen, I actually came over to speak to Miss Clarine.'

Gaimer frowned. 'Eh? My scrawny little cousin?'

'Yeah.'

'Why?'

'Because we've been engaged for nearly eight years, that's why.'

His friend's mouth fell open. 'What? She's the betrothed you've been going on about? The one we were making rude jokes about just a few days ago? She's my cousin; my fourteen-year-old cousin?'

'Look, I didn't know she was only fourteen; I only found that out today. I've seen her three times in my entire life, I had no idea.'

Gaimer gave him a look of disgust. 'Right. Fine. Go on, then.'

Daniel closed his eyes for a second, the embarrassment excruciating. He walked past a glaring Gaimer and approached the girl.

'Hello,' he said. 'I'm Daniel Aurelian.'

'She knows who you are, young man,' said her father, who was lurking behind her.

Daniel tried to smile.

'Well?' said her father. 'Was there something you wanted to say?'

'I was hoping,' he said, 'that she would... I mean, that you would like to dance?'

The girl blushed again.

Her father nodded. 'You took your time in coming over,' he said. 'Another ten minutes and I would have taken the girl home. However, late is better than never, so yes, she will dance with you.'

Daniel held out his hand and Clarine took it, and, while the eyes of her extended family turned towards them, they walked out into the centre of the dance floor. She turned to face him as they stopped, and he placed his left hand lightly on her waist, and took her other hand as they began to glide across the floor.

'I'm sorry that was so embarrassing,' he said.

She opened her mouth to respond, but he was out of practice and trod on her foot as they turned. She closed her mouth again, fighting back tears.

'Damn it, sorry,' he muttered.

She took a breath. 'Why did you wait so long before asking me to dance?'

'To be honest,' he said, 'I only found out how young you were this afternoon. I thought you were about eighteen, not fourteen, and, well, it came as a bit of a shock.'

'You don't think I'm pretty?'

'No, yes, what? I don't know, this is all weird to me. I guess I didn't think I'd be dancing with a child.'

She ripped her hand from his grasp and slapped him across the face, then turned and ran back to her family. Daniel stood frozen in the middle of the dance floor, his cheek stinging as the other dancers glanced at him. He could hear laughter coming from some of his academy classmates, and, not for the first time that day, wished the earth would swallow him up. He turned to face the entrance doors, and walked from the hall with as much dignity as he could muster.

---

He got as far as the long outside terrace that ran down one flank of the palace and sat on a bench under the branches of an orange tree. Blossom was littering the ground by his feet and he put his head in his hands. The sky was a dark and brooding purple and the street lights in the town below looked welcoming. Maybe he should run down there and catch a boat; flee his humiliation. But where could he go? The City was surrounded on three sides by water, and the fourth was besieged night and day by the greenhides. There was another land-mass opposite Ooste, past the Clashing Seas, where the City had once built colonies, but the greenhides had destroyed all of that long before.

The City was a prison. It was large and comfortable, but it was a prison nevertheless, where every inhabitant was serving a life sentence. No wonder some folk despaired, or turned to opium.

'Boy,' said a voice.

'Go away.'

The voice chuckled and Daniel glanced over. He leapt to his feet, and bowed his head.

'Lord Chamberlain, my apologies.'

'Tish tosh, boy, relax,' said the old man; 'I'm not going to bite your head off. I had just come out to assist with the search.'

'What? Are people looking for me?'

'Indeed they are. Your mother looked positively alarmed by your sudden disappearance. She rushed out to look for you, but unfortunately, she went the wrong way.'

Daniel said nothing. The Chamberlains were his family's rivals, enemies even, and the animosity stretched back into the remote past. His mother would be furious to discover that the old man had found him first. He needed to make an excuse and leave.

'Sit,' the old man said. 'I think it's time we had a little chat, young Aurelian.'

Daniel did as he was told. Lord Chamberlain was one of the most powerful men in the City, a mortal who had the ear of the God-Queen. His family had served Prince Michael for over a millennium, and now they served Queen Amalia. He sat down next to Daniel on the bench, both hands resting on his walking stick.

'You're the last of them, aren't you?'

'Sorry, sir?'

'The last Aurelian. If you pass without issue, your line will end, and the Aurelians shall fade into history, where some say they belong.' He paused to glance at Daniel, a smile on the edge of his lips. 'But you are different from many of the other Aurelians I've known. I get the sense that, perhaps, you'd rather not be the sole heir to such a legacy, that the weight of expectation upon your young shoulders sits heavily with you. So much pressure, on one so young. Tsk. A pity.'

Daniel thought of a dozen responses, but kept his mouth shut.

Maybe his mother would come along, or his father, and rescue him from the words of the old man.

'I watched you as a boy,' the lord continued, 'but now you are a man, or so that ribbon on your sleeve would tell me.' He scratched the ground with his stick. 'Make no mistake, I will destroy you, Aurelian. Your family has all but withered up like a dead flower, and my dying dream is to see your extinction before I breathe my last. To know that the line of the accursed Aurelians had been extinguished? Why, then I would die a happy man.' He stood. 'Your family's foolish dream of regaining the throne of Tara is over, boy. With you as their sole hope, the Aurelians are doomed. And, you know, when I look into your mother's eyes, I think that deep down she realises it too.'

He strode off through the orange grove, the walking stick swinging over the gravel.

Daniel closed his eyes. The old man was right. He wasn't fit to be the heir to the Aurelians, but what else could he do? He had sworn an oath to serve Tara, and in the morning he would be expected to take command of a company of Roser militia. The lower orders would see through him in a second, and his famous name would only compound the humiliation.

He got to his feet, and began to walk home.

## CHAPTER 5
## ADJUTANT OF THE CIRCUIT

The Circuit, Medio, The City – 5th Mikalis 3419

Compared to the six other palaces of the City, that of Redmarket in the Circuit was the least pleasing to look at. Damaged at the end of the Civil War in 3096, the palace had never been thoroughly renovated, and much of it had fallen into disrepair. Aila occupied a suite of rooms that had once belonged to one of her cousins, Yearna, the youngest child of Princess Yendra, who had ruled the Circuit for nine hundred years, until her execution for the killing of Prince Michael.

Following two centuries of house arrest in Pella for her role in the Civil War, Aila had been assigned to Redmarket Palace. She had wept upon her return to the place, her memories haunted by the events that had ended the disastrous internal conflict that had destroyed so many lives. Four God-Children, fifteen demigods and over a hundred thousand mortals had perished in the fighting. Aila's own father, and six of her siblings had been among the casualties, and though it may have occurred over three hundred years previously, to a demigod like her it felt like yesterday.

There had still been old traces of bloodstains visible on the worn, stone floor of Lady Yearna's quarters when Aila had first moved in. For a few decades she had left them there, unwilling to give up the reminder of the pointless sacrifices they had made, but eventually she had ordered her servants in to remodel the dilapidated apartment, to make it look more like her comfortable rooms in Pella. Thick, woollen hangings covered the damp patches on the walls, and she had laid warm rugs and carpets over the new floorboards. The light from her lamps was dimmed and diffused through thin sheets of brightly-coloured fabrics, and she had filled the rooms with her favourite style of comfortable couches and chairs, along with the biggest bed that would fit.

She swung open the doors to her wide balcony to let in the morning light, and to let out the stale odour of the opium she had been smoking over the previous couple of days since she had returned from the meeting with her informer. She had been weak, and instead of just having a small puff or two before bed, she had worked her way through over half of the lump she had purloined from Olvin over the course of thirty-six hours, losing an entire day in the process.

Governor Ikara would not be happy.

She turned to Martha, the head of her small band of mortal servants. 'I need you to air the place, please. It reeks.'

'Yes, ma'am.'

Aila frowned. 'Did I say or do anything that I need to apologise for?'

The servant hesitated.

'I'll take that as a yes. Go on.'

'Yesterday, before lunchtime, ma'am, you were rude to one of the governor's officials, who had arrived at your quarters to see why you hadn't turned up for work.'

Aila shrugged. 'Anything else?'

The servant frowned.

'That's not a face that fills me with confidence, Martha.'

'I'd rather not say, ma'am.'

Aila rested her hands on the balcony railings and glanced out over the vast, grey expanse of the Circuit. 'You know me, Martha. Have I ever punished a servant for telling me unpleasant truths?'

'No, ma'am.'

'Let's hear it, then.'

'Well, ma'am, it's just that you're not the most pleasant person to be around whenever you indulge in too much opium and brandy. It was the first time a few of the younger servants had seen you like that and, to be honest, I think some of them were a little shocked and upset.'

Aila sighed.

'Sorry, ma'am.'

'It's not your fault. Dip into my savings and make sure they all get a little extra for their troubles by way of an apology; and if any want to leave my service I'll write them a decent reference. I'm sorry, Martha, my mood swings seem to worsen with every passing century. I have a lot of anger inside me, and occasionally it bubbles up to the surface.'

'I've already spoken to them, and told them that you're the best mistress a servant could hope for in the City. If anything, you're too generous, ma'am, and I worry that you'll be taken advantage of.'

'One last question.'

'Yes, ma'am?'

'Did I say anything... compromising?'

'No, ma'am.'

'Are you sure?'

'I stayed with you the entire time, ma'am, to watch out for that very possibility, but you didn't mention anything that would endanger any of your... friends.'

'Thank Malik for that. Damn it, I need to be more careful.'

'Do you have any opium left, ma'am?'

Aila nodded.

'May I make a suggestion?'

'Yeah.'

'Let me know when you plan to have some, and I'll ensure the younger servants are re-assigned for a while. Tobias and I are well-acquainted with your habits, ma'am; nothing you do has the ability to shock us any more.'

Aila frowned. She could feel the combination of melancholia and her cravings for more opium rise within her, and wanted nothing more than to retreat into her rooms, close the shutters, and sink back into oblivion again. It was all in her head, she knew; her self-healing powers had already expelled the last traces of the narcotic from her system, and repaired the damage it had caused, so her addiction wasn't physical in any sense. And yet, the cravings persisted.

'Are you all right, ma'am? I didn't mean any offence by that last comment.'

'I know you didn't. I'm just wondering what the point of it all is.'

The old servant put a hand on her arm. 'You rescued me from a gang when I was nine years old, ma'am; saved me from a life of degradation and shame, and probably an early death. You're the only one of your illustrious family to lift a finger to help us mere mortals; and I think that's the point, ma'am. You give hope to those who haven't felt any in a long time. There hasn't been a god or demigod who cared about the lives of the Evaders since the days of Princess Yendra.'

'You know you're not supposed to mention her name in this palace.'

'Of course, ma'am. Apologies, but you understand what I mean?'

Aila nodded. 'Yeah, but it feels like I'm fighting the greenhides; no matter how many I kill, there are always more to take their place.' She exhaled. 'Alright, enough wallowing. I'd better go to work.'

'Shall I bring some breakfast up for you, ma'am?

'No, thanks. I'll eat with my dear cousin.'

Martha nodded and Aila strode from the balcony. She left her quarters and went downstairs to the governor's private dining-room. There was a large window in the room that had a sweeping view of the concrete landscape of the Circuit, but the curtains were drawn as she entered.

'Lady Aila?' came a voice dripping with sarcasm. 'Is it really you?'

Aila nodded at her cousin. 'Reporting for duty, ma'am.'

Well,' said Lady Ikara, 'I must say, what a surprise. I thought your opium-induced daze would last at least another few days, yet here you are. Lucky me.'

Aila took a seat at the long table. Aside from her cousin, the only others present were a couple of the governor's mortal assistants.

'What exciting jobs do you have for me today?'

'Well,' said Ikara, 'all of yesterday's work, for a start. Five hundred condemned prisoners have been sitting in our over-crowded cells for nearly a day. They need processed, and shipped off to the Bulwark. No exceptions this time, understand? I'm getting fed up with you making excuses for these mortals, and finding loopholes to prevent them going to the Great Wall. The Blades rely on the prisoners we send them to refill their ranks.'

'But, Ikara, sentenced to life in the Bulwark for stealing an apple? Especially when "life" probably means a few days. The Blades treat the prisoners we send like fodder.'

'That's out of our hands. You know the quota; two thousand Evader criminals every year; like scraping the scum off the top of the Circuit. The summer fighting season has begun, and I've already been receiving messages from your brother, Lord Kano. He's quite insistent that we get those prisoners to him as efficiently as possible. Anyway, that's your first job today, and remember, they've not had any food or water since they were brought to the palace prison.'

'Why not?'

Ikara frowned at her. 'Dealing with prisoners is the job of the governor's adjutant, is it not? Tell me, what is your position here in the Circuit?'

Aila suppressed her anger. Being humiliated by her cousin was part of the role she was playing. If she antagonised the governor, she might lose her job and be forced back into house arrest, which would mean the end of the double life she was leading.

'I'm the Adjutant.'

'That's right! What a clever girl you are! After that, I need you to go to the racecourse to collect my cut from the gambling syndicates. Take guards, and arrest Joylen while you're there.'

'Why?'

'Just do as you're told.'

Aila nodded.

'If there are any protests, speak to the others and calm them down.'

'What makes you think they'll listen to me?'

Ikara shrugged. 'Because they like you.'

'That's only because I treat them fairly.'

'No, they like you because your father was a traitor, and the Evaders remain disloyal at heart. They seem to think that you're one of them, and that, somehow, you are carrying a flame for their beloved, sadly executed, Princess Yendra.' She smiled. 'Imagine that. The fools actually think you're capable of making a difference to their sad, little lives; when I know how much of a coward you are, and how you'd rather sink into the warm embrace of opium than face up to the mess your life has become.'

'You finished?'

'Not quite. Presumably you haven't heard, but there was some trouble a couple of nights ago.'

'Yeah?'

'Paid assassins murdered Olvin and three of his lieutenants.'

'How despicable.'

Ikara narrowed her eyes. 'As you are no doubt aware, Olvin had been paying me a considerable sum to ensure he was immune from such risks. His murder makes me look bad, as if I can't protect my own. Already I've had grumblings from the other bosses, demanding to know what I intend to do about it.'

'What are you going to do?'

Ikara shrugged. 'Sounds like it falls under the role of adjutant, wouldn't you say?'

'Fine. What do you want me to do about it?'

'Catch those responsible and string them up by the Grand Iceward Canal. Be brutal; send a message that won't be misunderstood. Of course, if your investigations hit a dead end, then I still want to see bodies. Half a dozen should suffice; I don't care where you get them from.'

'Alright. Is that it?'

The governor nodded. 'Yes, run along.'

Aila picked up a slice of fruit toast from a dish on the table and strode to the door, as Ikara resumed eating her breakfast. She made her way to the rear of the palace where, amid a wing of crumbling and abandoned rooms, the small jail was located. It had been built to accommodate about a hundred prisoners, but often had more packed behind its walls and barred doors. She descended to the basement, and walked to the guards' quarters. She nodded to the soldier on duty, who seemed half-asleep at his desk, then continued on into the prison wing. Ten large cells ran down each wall, and over two dozen prisoners had been crammed into every one.

The stench was vile, and she covered her nose with a handkerchief. The prisoners began calling out to her as soon as she appeared, stretching their arms between the bars to beg for water. Aila ran her eyes over them. Most were youths, though there were a few older mortals present as well, wrinkled and weathered in the way that afflicted them all if they were lucky enough to reach that age. Once she had despised them, now she pitied them. Their pathetically short life spans flowered and faded in the blink of an eye. A few of the younger ones in the cells before her would be dead within a month of arriving at the Bulwark; what a waste of their limited time alive.

'Help us,' cried a woman. 'Please don't make us go to the Great Wall.'

Aila glanced at her. What could she say? She was sending them to the jaws and talons of the greenhides; the governor had made her decision.

'Are you Lady Aila?' said another.

'It is,' cried a third, 'she's here to rescue us!'

The volume of cries and shouts increased; intense and insistent. Aila could see the faint glimmer of hope in their eyes, but they were wrong.

'You knew Princess Yendra,' said an older woman; 'you fought by her side to the bitter end.'

'Yes,' she said, quietening the cells with a single word. She glanced around. 'But then I was captured. I begged for mercy in front of the God-King and God-Queen, and they spared my life. I am the Adjutant of the Circuit now, and I work for Governor Ikara.'

The cries turned angry, and several of the prisoners spat at her.

'Filthy traitor,' one called out. 'You're worse than the rest of your damned family, because you know what you're doing is wrong.'

Aila lowered her face, then walked back to the guard's desk.

'Wake up.'

The guard stumbled to his feet. 'I'm awake, ma'am.'

'I need to requisition two squads, and enough food and water for five hundred prisoners. Send a message to the canal terminal, we're sending that lot to the Middle Wall by barge. I want them on their way to the Bulwark by lunchtime. No bribes, no exceptions. Understood?'

'Yes, ma'am,' he said, saluting and running off down the hallway.

Aila sat and put her boots up onto the desk. Despite the angle, many of the prisoners could still see her, and they continued with their insults and jibes. Their words hurt, because she knew they were true.

---

After organising the logistics of the prisoner transfer, Aila took a squad of militia and left Redmarket Palace. It was a ten-minute walk through the twisting, narrow streets to the Great Racecourse, the centre of cultural life in the Circuit. She saw the building loom above the roofs of the other buildings as they approached. It was the largest single building in the entire City, vaster even than some of the fortresses on the Great Wall, and bigger than any palace. Constructed from the same grey concrete as the rest of the Circuit, it spanned over a mile in length, and was several storeys high. Every evening the place bustled with thousands of people, come to watch the foot, dog or pony races, or to see a wrestling match, or, every ten days, to witness those sentenced to death by the governor being executed. The complex was riddled with tunnels and arenas large and small, with enough bars to satisfy the thirsts of everyone who attended. It sometimes made Aila despair, but gambling was a central part of the lives of most Evaders, and small fortunes changed hands every day within the enormous building.

A few passers-by nodded to her as she walked, keeping her skirt lifted to avoid the hem trailing in the open sewer running down the middle of the street. Rats, garbage, and open drains; she wasn't sure which aspect of the slums she hated the most. The guards she had brought kept pace with her as she hurried along the unpaved streets. Surrounding the Great Racecourse was a wide, cleared space, that accentuated the height of the monstrous complex, and arched entrances ran along each wall. Aila turned right, and they walked round the narrower end of the building and down its iceward flank, where the shadows were never disturbed. Halfway along, stood a gargantuan statue of Prince Michael, the twin of one that the God-Queen had constructed in Tara. The building of the two statues had famously exhausted an entire marble quarry in the Sunward Range, and both had stood for over three hundred years. Aila imagined that the one in Tara was probably treated with devotion and respect. For the Evaders that lived in the Circuit however, the statue was a symbol of everything that was wrong with the City, and the local inhabitants routinely spat on the tyrant of Tara every time they passed.

Aila turned her gaze from the spittle-flecked base of the statue as they reached it, in case she was tempted to add to the accumulated deposits of saliva. The militia would inform her cousin of anything she did that was unusual or potentially disloyal, and spitting on the memory of Prince Michael was about as unpatriotic as it got.

She knew the truth, though; she had been there.

The syndicates were located in the lower depths of the racecourse, and they entered the building after leaving the statue behind. Aila led the guards down a series of dim passageways, passing a few seedy bars on the way. When she heard the barking from the kennels where the racing dogs were kept she knew she was close. They reached a door, and she pushed it open without knocking.

'Joylen,' she cried, pointing at the man amid a dozen or so of his colleagues; 'hands above the table; you're under arrest. Guards, secure him.'

The gambling bosses stared at each other and began to protest. Joylen's eyes darted towards the window, but the militia were too fast, and two of them grabbed his shoulders and hauled him away from the table where he had been sitting.

'This is outrageous,' said an old woman, the leader of the syndicate. 'On what grounds are you arresting him, Lady Aila?'

'I have no idea. Governor's orders.'

'I know why,' said Joylen, standing calmly as the guards pinned his shoulders; 'it's because I refused to pay the extra bribe that she requested at the Freshmist Festival. Half my takings, she wanted, instead of the usual third.' He stared at his colleagues. 'The rest of you paid it, didn't you?'

No one responded.

'On the subject of bribes,' Aila said; 'sorry, I mean insurance premiums, I'm here to collect this month's. Get your wallets out.'

She watched as the members of the syndicate began to gather the money on the table.

'What would your father think of you?' said the old woman. 'Or Princess Yendra?'

'If either were alive then I wouldn't be doing this.'

'Ikara's a parasite,' muttered Joylen, 'and you willingly do her bidding. She lives in luxury while the rest of us do all the work.'

Aila shook her head. 'You call taking money from gamblers "work"? While we're here, does anyone know anything about what happened to Olvin?'

'And what's in it for us if we do?' said the old woman.

'Depends on the quality of the information, but I'm prepared to negotiate. I'll drop a hundred crowns from your premium if you have a good lead.'

The old woman shrugged. 'There's a chef by the name of Letwyn, and apparently his daughter was up to no good with one of Olvin's guards, a miscreant called Bekker. The chef's gone into hiding with his girl.'

'Where?'

'Folk say near the old ironworks by the Midway Canal.'

'And Bekker?'

'Olvin's mob bashed his brains out and left him floating towards the Union Walls.'

'Did they question him first?'

The old woman shrugged. 'How should I know? Maybe you should go and ask them?'

Aila reached into the pile of money on the table and threw fifty crowns towards her.

'That's only half of what you said.'

'Generous, I thought.'

The old woman scowled at her, but Aila didn't care. She had shown enough interest in the case that the militia could use to put in their report to Ikara. She wondered if she should search for the chef's daughter. A nagging guilt was still eating away at her about the blame for what she had done being placed on the shoulders of an innocent bystander. She tossed an empty bag onto the table and nodded at the militia.

'Gather it all up, then take the cash and Joylen back to Redmarket.'

'Aren't you coming, ma'am?'

'No. There's a boxing match starting soon that I want to see.'

The militia glanced at each other, then took the bag and escorted Joylen from the room.

Aila smiled at the syndicate. 'See you next month.'

---

'I don't care, Naxor,' she said from her seat in the back row of the dark arena, 'I'm not going to work for your mother again; I hate her.'

Her cousin frowned from the next seat along. 'My mother doesn't hate you; you know that? She respects you.'

'She's a hypocrite. If she respected me, then why did she make me Adjutant to her useless daughter? I know she's your sister, but Ikara's a nightmare to work for. She's more corrupt than the worst gang boss. Today she told me to select six innocent civilians and execute them publically because one of the bosses that pays her protection money got killed. What's your mother going to do about that, eh? If Princess Khora can't even control her own children, then how am I supposed to believe she can run the City?'

'She has run the City for over three hundred years, Aila.'

'Yeah? And look at what's happened to it in that time. We've had shortages of just about everything, and prices have doubled in the last few years. People are going hungry again, and the Circuit is starting to boil over. Tell your mother that she should...'

'Stop there,' said Naxor, raising a hand. 'If you have advice regarding the governance of the City, then I shall arrange a meeting where you can speak to my mother face to face. She is willing to do that; are you?'

'No.'

'Then save me the complaints, little cousin. Do you know that I'm the only member of our illustrious family that all of the others will speak to? You refuse to talk to my mother, or your brother, Lord Kano, or Duke Marcus, while the God-Queen won't speak to the God-King, and Marcus won't speak to my mother. I spend all my time passing messages between my relatives.'

'When you're not fetching champions?'

Naxor smiled. 'Did you hear about the new ones I delivered a few days ago?' He puffed out his cheeks. 'One of them was your fairly average skilled warrior; he'll do alright, I think, but the other? By Amalia's breath, what a find he was.'

'Did you bring another one of those flying snakes?'

'No, he's a man. Taller than your brother; taller even than the duke. That's all I'm going to say for the present; I'm sure you'll hear more in due course as word spreads.'

'Give me his name, so I can look smart when they tell me.'

'I can do that. His name is Corthie Holdfast.'

'They have strange names in the mystical lands of the gods,' she smirked.

'One day, Aila,' he said, 'I hope I'll be able to tell you the truth about the work I do. I actually spoke to my mother about bringing you into the secret, as I feel you could help us with those powers of yours... talking of which, I heard a certain gang boss was murdered.'

'Yeah,' she said, 'but what do my powers have to do with that?'

He glanced at her. 'Be careful, that's all my mother and I ask.'

'Wait, Khora knows?'

'What you get up to in your spare time? I'd say she has a fairly good idea. The unsolved assassinations of major criminals in the Circuit oddly began around the time you became Adjutant, and, no matter what else you may think of her, you know my mother isn't stupid. Don't worry though, neither of us would whisper a word to Ikara about it. She may be my sister, but...'

'Olvin had a lot of money.'

Naxor shrugged. 'Isn't that rather the point of being a gang boss?'

'Over and above that. Someone had recently paid him a ton of gold for something.'

'This is the first I've heard of it.'

'Damn. I was hoping you might have an idea or two.'

'I'll make enquiries. Before you go, I want to ask you one more time to consider my mother's offer. It's time to put the past behind us, Aila. You have skills that could make a difference; more of a difference than you're already making.'

'What does she want me to do?'

'Meet with her, and she'll tell you.'

Aila shook her head. 'Sorry, there are some things I can't do, and one of them is forgive Khora.'

Naxor's eyes tightened. 'It's regrettable that you think that way.' He turned to the boxing match and made a face as one of the fighters was sent flying to the ground.

Aila took that as her cue, nodded to her cousin, and slipped away.

## CHAPTER 6
## FIRST DAY ON THE JOB

A rrowhead Fort, The Bulwark, The City – 6th Mikalis 3419

Corthie peered into the night mist. Ahead lay the moat, and beyond that, out of range of the City's artillery, was the vast sea of greenhides. On either side of him, members of the Rat Company were filing out into the space between the outer wall and the moat. A section of moat wall had been breached the previous afternoon, and the infantry had withdrawn behind the outer wall before they could be slaughtered. Corthie followed the other Wolfpack soldiers as they fanned out to flank the Rats. Wheeled and collapsible cranes were rolled out of the gate in the outer wall, and the Rats began assembling them in the darkness.

'Quiet,' growled an officer.

Corthie reached the moat wall. He was tall enough to see over the top without having to stand on the sentry platform, and he gazed out across the plain. The ground was littered with the corpses of green-hides. Many had been pulled away at sunset by their brethren, to be eaten out of range once night had fallen. Corthie had watched them from the walls, learning their simple daily pattern, and now he was barely a few hundred yards of flat ground and a moat away from them.

Ladders were brought up to the wall and lowered into the moat, as the first assembled crane trundled forwards. Corthie stepped up on the sentry platform and looked down into the dark depths. The water level had fallen by over three-quarters in the few days since he had arrived, and at that rate it would be empty in a couple more. So many green-hides had fallen in, that their bodies were visible in places, their rounded backs or thick limbs poking through the surface.

Corthie glanced up at the sky. It wasn't the true darkness he remem-bered from his home, when nights were almost pitch black. Even with hours to go before dawn, there were still streaks of red and purple in the sky, and towards his right; sunward, as he was learning to call it, the patches were brighter still.

When the cranes were in place, two long moat-bridges were brought out through the gate in the outer walls. Rats carried them on their shoulders, with a dozen to each bridge. They laid them down by the moat wall and attached them to ropes dangling from the cranes. Winches lifted the bridges into the air, and the crane arms swung out over the moat in perfect silence. Corthie smiled. The whole operation had taken place in just a few minutes, and not a sound had been made by any of the dozens now behind the moat wall.

The captain in command of the Wolfpack squadron raised his hand and gestured. The soldiers responded, scrambling up the wall and climbing onto the bridges. Corthie pulled himself up and joined the others. He knew his thin leather armour and light shield were designed for stealth, but against the talons of the greenhides he would have preferred something a little more solid. He had practised for years in full plate armour, and had been surprised when he had seen the more basic uniforms of the Wolfpack. Speed and silence saved their lives, he guessed, as he glanced down into the moat.

The other side of the bridge lay flat on the lip of the moat, and the Wolfpack fanned out, creeping over the plains. Corthie knew what was going to happen; it was only a matter of time before the greenhides were alerted to the desperate work of the Rats, as they began pulling the bodies from the moat. The crane arms swept back and forth, lifting the greenhides one at a time and depositing them onto the plain.

Corthie saw Tanner to his right, and gave him a nod. Behind them, up on the battlements of the outer and inner walls, the infantry were getting their nightly entertainment, laying bets on how many Rats were going to get killed. Corthie had seen a chalkboard advertising odds, and had noticed his own death had been estimated at an evens' chance. Everyone believed his powers were a lie, and he had neither confirmed it, nor tried to deny it. He rolled his shoulders and turned back to the greenhides.

The minutes passed. The Wolfpack remained low, watching the plains, while the heap of extracted greenhides was growing. Rats were circling the heap, dowsing it with tar oil in preparation for the inevitable retreat. The cranes were working at full speed, the Rats taking shifts on the winches that raised the corpses from the moat.

A crack ripped through the air as a strained rope snapped. The greenhide it had been lifting fell back to the bottom of the trench hitting one of the Rats and burying him under four hundred pounds of rotting flesh. There was a moment of stunned silence, then the rest of the Rats began pulling the cranes back from the moat wall in a frenzy of movement.

'Here they come!' someone cried.

Corthie drew his sword. It was lighter than what he was used to, but the steel and finish were decent enough.

'Forget about that, big man,' shouted one of the Wolfpack as they began to retreat; 'just get your ass out of here.'

There was a whompf of noise as the heap of dead was lit and the oil ignited. With a flash of flames, Corthie saw the plain light up before him. Charging towards the moat in their hundreds, their thousands, the greenhides were roaring out their rage, their long claws gleaming in the firelight. Corthie stepped back, keeping in formation with the rest of the Wolfpack, his eyes never leaving the approaching tide.

The rule was, the longer you had served in the Wolfpack, the quicker you were allowed back over the bridges, and the veterans clambered up as they reached the lip of the deep barrier. The cranes had been disassembled and were being pushed back along the ground towards the gate in the outer wall, but several Rats were still in the moat, waiting by the ladders for their chance to flee.

'We're not going to make it,' said Tanner, his eyes wide as he stared at the approaching greenhides.

'Of course we are,' said Corthie; 'we're not dying tonight.'

There were screams and the sound of twisting wood behind them, and Corthie watched as one of the bridges buckled and fell into the moat, crashing onto the last of the Rats. Though most of the Wolfpack had crossed, several had still been on it, and they lay groaning in the filthy water at the bottom.

Corthie had no time to react as the first greenhides reached them. A man six yards to his left was ripped in half by a single lash of thick claws. The greenhide stopped to drink his blood as the others piled on.

This was it, Corthie thought, this was what he had trained for. Rather than be on the back foot, he surged his battle-vision and powered forward into the mass of greenhides, swinging his sword into the face of the nearest. Claws ripped through his shield in seconds and tore a six-inch gash down his left arm, but he smothered the pain, and let his battle-vision do the work. With it, he could move faster than his conscious mind could process. His senses and reactions were honed to a razor-sharpness by years of intensive training, and he kept moving, ducking and rolling under the lunges of the greenhides. He struck out, again and again, his balance and speed too fast for the greenhides to keep up with, and he carved his way through them. He killed several, but many more were left unharmed by his attacks; his sword cutting into, but not through the thick hides that covered their backs and chests. A splash of green blood hit him in the face and he was blinded for a moment. A powerful blow sent him flying backwards, his leather cuirass ripped and bloody. He rolled under a swipe and struck upwards. His sword cut through the forelimb of a beast, and it dropped to the ground. As it howled in agony, Corthie swung again, his blade striking the extended talons of another greenhide, and his sword snapped.

Corthie scrambled away as claws raked the ground where he had fallen. He let go of the broken sword, and reached for the hacked-off forelimb. He punched his fist into the soft flesh of the wound, as more greenhides surrounded him, closing in. He grasped the arm bone in his hand, and swung it with all his strength. The talons ripped through the armour of the closest greenhide as if it were made of paper. Corthie pushed his hand further into the bloody limb to get a better grip, then rose to his feet, his eyes flickering in a battle-vision trance. He charged into the beasts, using the limb like an armoured gauntlet, hacking through the tough, green armour back towards the moat.

The moat.

For a moment his head cleared. The other moat-bridge had been pulled back, and the last of the Rats and the Wolfpack were hurrying through the gate in the outer wall. His heightened senses took in what he needed in a second, then he turned back to the greenhides. They were circling him, keeping a short distance away after seeing what he could do with his own set of claws. The trail of those he had slain stretched down across the plain; had he really charged so far? Behind him, the moat was still a good ten yards away. He stepped up onto the thick, rounded back of a dead greenhide.

'You want me?' he cried, brandishing the talons, their edges gleaming in green blood.

There was a low roar behind him. It had been going on for a while, but it hadn't registered in Corthie's mind. It was coming from the battlements. At the same time, there was whoosh overhead, and Corthie blinked as a torrent of bright flame surged down from the sky. It struck the greenhides in a wide swathe a hundred yards from where Corthie was standing, incinerating dozens. The greenhides surrounding him screamed out in rage and fear at the dragon, and charged Corthie. He twisted on his feet, slashing out with the talons, felling them as they came into reach. He had never surged his battle-vision to such a pitch, but, he thought, as the green blood sprayed around him, he had never been surrounded by greenhides before.

A burst of flame crashed alongside him, the heat and blast sending him falling to the side, the hair on his left arm singed. Stupid lizard!

Was it trying to kill him? He leaped up, then rolled as another surge of flame scorched the ground by his feet.

Corthie glanced up at the sky, then at the moat. The damn flying beast was clearing the way home for him. He charged into the few greenhides remaining between him and the moat, cutting them down with his claws. He broke into a sprint. Thirty feet, they said. Looked more like twenty-five to him. His foot struck the edge of the moat and he jumped. For a moment he felt nothing but the air on his face, but the sound coming from the walls was rising to a crescendo. He slammed into the moat wall, and punched the stonework with the talons. They dug in deep, and he dangled for a moment, held in place only by the strength of the greenhide claws. He reached up with his left hand and climbed to the top of the wall.

A roar greeted him. All along the battlements, soldiers and other Blades were watching him. He raised his left hand to them, and the noise increased. He turned to the greenhides. They were screaming hatred at him from across the moat, but their numbers were fast dwindling as most retreated from the dragon's fire.

Corthie brandished the greenhide claws at them. 'Remember me next time,' he cried. 'I'll be coming for the rest of you.'

Buckler swooped overhead, making a low pass across the moat, as if to take a closer look at the man standing on the moat wall. Corthie waited until the last greenhides had fled out of sight, then turned and jumped to the ground. The gate in the outer wall was still open, and some of the Wolfpack ran out.

Tanner sprinted over to him. He stared at Corthie, shaking his head. 'So you weren't joking, then?'

'Malik's ass, check the state of him,' another said. She grabbed his arm, and starting pulling him towards the gate, 'he's got a least a dozen wounds; how is he still standing? We need to get him to a medic. And we need to get that thing off his arm.'

'I'm fine,' Corthie said, though he let her continue to pull him along. 'I heal quick, and the battle-vision masks the pain. And don't touch the claws; I'm keeping them.'

The soldiers shoved him through the gate and into a large forecourt, where hundreds had gathered. They roared out a cheer as Corthie entered. The captain of the Wolfpack saw him and strode forwards.

'Son,' he said, as Corthie stood in front of him, the greenhide talons dripping green blood onto the flagstones. 'Everyone listen,' the officer went on, 'I want you all to hear this. I called this soldier a liar to his face this morning, for we all know that it's impossible for a mortal to possess battle-vision.' He turned back to Corthie. 'I was wrong, and I apologise for my insult.' He gestured to an aide. 'Take him inside and let the doctor attend to his wounds. After that,' he said glancing back at Corthie, 'what would you like, son? Name it, and if it's within my power, I'll grant it.'

Corthie gazed at the crowds. Some were acting as if he had saved the world, rather than kill a few dozen greenhides, and he suspected one or two of them were close to hysteria.

He raised the claws. 'I want someone to take the talons from this and make me a weapon,' he said, 'and then I want a bath, some breakfast, and maybe a couple of drinks.'

---

'Tell us a story!' cried a voice from the crowd.

Corthie smiled, a mug of bitter spirits mixed with red wine in his hand. The Wolfpack common room was packed, with the entire company in attendance, as well as dozens of other Blades who had crammed in. Corthie had been seated at a long table, with his back to the wall, so that as many of the others could see him as possible. His left arm was bandaged, as was his chest, right hip, shin, and there was a dressing on his neck, but the battle-vision was still dulling the pain, and the spirits were helping, too.

'No,' he said. 'I'm the new one here, I want to hear more about the City. Like, for example, what's wrong with your sun?' He lifted his finger to demonstrate. 'In normal places, it rises on one side of the sky, goes up to the top, then goes down the other side. Your one just goes up a little bit, stays there, then goes down again in the same place. I mean, what?'

The crowd looked at him as if he were mad. He laughed and downed the contents of his mug. As soon as he placed it back on the table, hands reached out to refill it. On his right, Tanner was also drunk; a stupid grin glued to his face. On his other side sat the woman who had grabbed his arm by the moat-wall. Her name was Corporal Quill, he had since learned. Since that moment by the wall, she had barely left his side, making sure he had been treated well by the medics, and arranging a massive breakfast that he had finished in ten minutes.

'Fine,' he said. 'How about something less astronomical, and a bit more histroci... historical? I heard that two actual gods rule the City. Why doesn't someone tell me about that?'

'That's easy,' said Quill, 'I can do that.'

'We can fetch a teacher from one of the schools,' said another.

'Let Quill do it,' Corthie said. 'I like the sound of her voice.'

The corporal's eyes widened for a fraction of a second. 'Alright. Um... Right, for a thousand years, there were just the five cities...'

'Five? I thought there was only one?'

'They were more like towns, then, but they called themselves cities. They were Tara, Dalrig, Pella, Ooste, and on the other side of the straits, there was also Jezra. They fought each other for ages, back and forth, blah blah, and not much happened until...'

'Not much happened?' said an incredulous voice from the crowd. 'You missed out the entire Golden Age of Pella, and the Ascendancy of Tara.'

Quill waved her hand at the complainer. 'No one cares about that, I want to get to the good stuff. Right, everything was going fine, yeah, and then, in the year 970, suddenly, out of nowhere, the greenhides arrived. Luckily for us, but not so much for Jezra, they made their first appearance on the other side of the straits. Took them about a day to wipe Jezra from the map, and all the folk here could do was watch and weep. It took them a couple of years to get to this side of the straits...'

'They went via the sunward deserts,' said someone, 'because they like the sun and hate the cold and dark.'

'Stop interrupting!' cried Quill. 'Anyway, by the time the greenhides arrived, the four remaining cities had bound themselves together into an alliance and repaired their defences. Even so, the siege was brutal.' She lifted her fingers and placed them an inch apart. 'We were that close to extinction. If the siege had lasted a few more months, so they say, then the last folk would have been obliterated from this world.'

'Hang on,' said Corthie. 'The "last folk"? You mean there are no other towns or cities in this world?'

Quill shrugged. 'Well, I've never actually seen the rest of the world, but we've got unending deserts two hundred miles sunward of us, and unending darkness and cold a couple of hundred miles iceward. As far as we know, the greenhides rule the rest. Here's the miracle bit. Just as the four cities were starting to starve, and the walls close to being breached, then, like a vision from the sky, the God-King Malik, and God-Queen Amalia descended from the clouds in all their power, and they smote the greenhides...'

Corthie laughed. '"Smote"?'

'I'm quoting from the Book of the Gods,' she said; 'I'll get you a copy and you can read it yourself. After much smiting, the greenhides lay dead in their hundreds of thousands, and the new king and queen moved into Ooste. They built the Union Walls and the Royal Palace, and have ruled us ever since.'

'Praise be to the gods!' cried someone, and others joined in, lifting their hands and bowing their heads.

'I have a question,' said Corthie. 'If Malik and Amalia are so good at smiting, then why are we doing the fighting? Why don't they live in the Bulwark and smite away to their heart's content? Sounds like a load of crap to me.'

Many in the crowd looked aghast at him, shock imprinted onto their features.

Quill glanced at him. 'You might, eh, want to be careful what you say about the God-King and God-Queen.'

'Why? Will they smite me?' He started to laugh, the spirits loosening him. 'I notice that no one has actually answered my question.'

'God-Queen Amalia destroyed the greenhides, unaided, for nearly a thousand years,' said Quill. 'Then she and the God-King had six children, to spread the burden. When Prince Michael came of age, they handed the reins of power to him, and went into a well-deserved retirement in Ooste.'

Corthie chortled. 'Gods need to retire, do they? So this Michael guy's in charge? I thought it was someone else…' He scratched his head. 'Oh aye, I remember. Lord Naxor's mother, whatever her name is.'

'Princess Khora?'

'That's the one.'

'The princess has ruled for three hundred years, ever since Prince Michael was martyred.'

The crowd fell into a hushed and reverential silence.

'Did the greenhides get him?'

'Of course not,' said Quill; 'he was murdered at the end of the Civil War by his sister, Princess Yendra. Only gods can kill other gods.'

Corthie smiled, and took another long swig. 'What I'm about to say, it might come over as bragging.'

Quill smiled back. 'I think you earned the right to brag last night.'

'Mortals can kill gods too.'

Several people gasped, as if his words had offended them.

'And how in Malik's name could you know that?' said one of the Wolfpack.

Corthie shrugged. 'Because I've killed one myself.'

Silence fell over the common room, and, despite the alcohol clouding his mind, Corthie could see how uncomfortable he was making them. He laughed to himself.

'Shall I tell you that story? A god came looking for me and my family; they were trying to wipe us out. One broke into my family home. He killed an entire company of soldiers who were there to protect us. He had these… death powers, where he could lift his hand, and people would die. You heard of a power like that?' He glanced up, and saw the silent nods. 'So in he comes, right, and there are dead soldiers all over the floor. I didn't know I had battle-vision until that moment.' He took another swig.

'What happened?' said Quill.

'I picked up a glass ashtray and bashed his brains in. Hit them faster than they can heal, that's the trick with gods.'

'How old were you?' said Quill.

'Fourteen.'

A small group by the door raised their arms and began to chant, their eyes closed.

'Get those religious freaks out of here,' cried a soldier, and the group was herded out of the common room.

'Who are they?' Corthie said.

'Ignore them,' said Quill. 'How did you avoid the god's death powers?'

Corthie shrugged. 'I'm immune to them; I'm immune to all mage attacks.'

'Mage? What's that? Do you mean god?'

He narrowed his eyes. 'Wait a minute. Am I the only normal person, I mean the only mortal, that you've heard of with powers?'

'Are there more like you where you're from?'

Tanner opened his eyes and put a hand on Corthie's arm. 'Time for some fresh air, lad.'

'I thought you were too drunk to speak.'

The older man stood. 'That's enough stories for today. The big guy needs his rest.'

Corthie frowned. 'I'm fine; I'm just getting into the swing of things.'

Tanner's eyes tightened.

'Fine,' Corthie muttered, downing the rest of his drink. He stood, amid cries of complaints. 'Same time tomorrow?' he said to the crowd.

Corporal Quill also got to her feet, and the three soldiers squeezed through the crowd. Folk reached out to touch Corthie as he passed, and he blew kisses to the prettiest young women. Tanner grabbed his arm, and they emerged into the giant forecourt of Arrowhead Fort. The interior was cast into shade, as it always was, though the sky overhead was almost blue. Tanner began saying something, but Corthie wasn't paying any attention.

'This is what I was talking about,' he said. 'It must be nearly noon, and where's the damn sun?'

He wandered into the forecourt, oblivious to the fresh crowds that were gathering. Many had been forced to stand outside the Wolfpack common room, and they crowded round him. He craned his neck, and saw a high wooden platform, the top of which towered over the battlements.

'What's that?' he said, pointing.

'We need to get indoors,' said Tanner, eyeing the crowds with unease.

'It's Buckler's Eyrie,' said Quill; 'it's where he sits when he's not flying.'

Corthie nodded. 'I need to get up there. Take a look at the damn sun.'

'What?' said Quill. 'You can't. No one's allowed up there except the dragon, and anyway, it's too high to climb…' Her last words tailed away as Corthie wandered off. She and Tanner followed, barging their way through the crowds behind him.

Corthie reached the base of the wooden platform and jumped, grasping hold of a wide crossbeam. He pulled himself up, then clambered onto the next section. Within moments, he was clear above the crowd. He laughed, feeling the gaze of hundreds upon him. His arms were starting to ache a bit as his battle-vision wore off, but he still had enough power to scale a tower. He stretched out and jumped up to a higher level, then climbed a series of crossbeams, each step taking him higher and higher. He reached the height of the top of the battlements, where a group of soldiers were staring at him, and he got a good view of the plains, where the greenhides were roiling in a mass by the moat. The next section was trickier, and he leaped, and almost fell, his left hand slipping on the wood. The crowd below him gasped, and he laughed again, as he hung suspended by one hand from the structure.

He sensed eyes watching him from above, and he glanced up. Buckler was peering down at him over the edge of his wide platform.

'Hey, lizard,' Corthie shouted; 'you'd better not be thinking about helping me.'

'I wasn't,' its voice growled. 'I should warn you, I eat mortals who disturb my sanctuary.'

'Aye? And how many have you eaten so far?'

'None have ever made it.'

Corthie heaved himself up to the next beam, then grabbed the edge of the platform and hauled his legs up and over. He lay for a moment on the platform, the dragon's face less than a yard away.

'None of the others were Corthie Holdfast, lizard.'

'So it seems, ape.'

Corthie rolled over and got to his feet. He whistled. 'What a view! No wonder you love it up here.' He turned to the dragon. 'What's wrong with the sun?'

The dragon gazed at the sunward horizon. 'I'm no astronomer, but I believe it has something to do with the world we are on, not the sun. I'm used to it now; I barely think about it.'

'You've been here ten years, aye? How many greenhides you killed in that time? Did you see me with those talons?' He laughed as he swayed in the breeze, his head starting to feel light. 'And, by the way, lizard, thanks for almost burning my ass to a crisp last night. At first I thought you were trying to kill me, but then I realised you were only trying to help. So, thanks.'

'You amuse me, mortal-with-powers.'

'And you amuse me, ya flying snake. We're going to kill lots of green-hides together, me and you.'

Buckler glanced down at the forecourt. 'It appears that two demigods are waiting for you down there.'

'Aye? Important ones?'

'All of the god-children and demigods of the City feel they are important, and those two feel it more than most. One is Duke Marcus, Commander of the Bulwark, and the other is Lord Kano, his Adjutant.'

'Kano? I've met him. Bit of a bawbag if you ask me.'

'A what?'

'A bawbag. A scrotum. A fleshly vessel containing testicles.'

For the first time, the dragon smiled. Either that, or he wanted to eat Corthie, he couldn't tell.

'Right,' he went on; 'I suppose I'd better go back down.'

'Try not to break your neck, oh fragile one.'

'You think you're talking to an amateur? Watch this, oh scaly one.'

Corthie surged the last reserves of his battle-vision, and launched himself off the platform, to a cry of alarm from the crowd, He twisted in the air and grabbed hold of a crossbeam, then dropped down, level by level, and was back on the ground in under a minute.

He laughed and glanced up. 'Did you see that, lizard-face?'

A loud cough distracted him and he turned. A space had been cleared, and two tall men were standing in full armour, staring at him. Dozens of soldiers were pushing back the other Blades, of which hundreds were packing the forecourt.

'Kano!' Corthie cried. 'I bet you feel stupid now, after you doubted me. I have to say, though, that I very much enjoyed fighting the green-hides last night, sir.'

Lord Kano and Duke Marcus frowned as Corthie staggered forwards. He smiled as he realised he was taller than either of the demigods.

'I've seen this type of thing before, my lord,' Kano said. 'After experiencing a near-death on the battle field, some soldiers exhibit signs of a nervous euphoria that causes them to behave in this manner. It is usually followed by a deep depression and an unshakeable despair.'

Corthie laughed again. 'You're a funny guy.'

'You might not be so amused to learn that, tonight, you are going back out on another Wolfpack mission, where you will have to fight all over again.'

Corthie raised his hands in the air. 'Great! I can't wait to get stuck into those green-assed beasts; I'm going to smash even more of them tonight.' He raised a finger. 'However, I'm going to need a better sword;

the one you gave me snapped; and a decent helmet. And, did you see the way that moat-bridge broke in two? Come on, guys; sort that out, it's basic stuff.'

Kano glared at him. 'You finished, Private?'

'No. I also want the talons I brought back made into a weapon. Like a war-hammer, or a battle-axe, only with the claws at the end. Can you manage that?'

Kano's eyes filled with rage and he opened his mouth; but Duke Marcus raised his hand. The commander stepped forward, and glanced around at the crowd.

'Blades,' he called out. 'Not since the time of the Children of the Gods have we seen a warrior like Corthie Holdfast.'

The crowd roared out in approval. Marcus nodded at them, a huge smile on his face, though Corthie noticed, despite his growing exhaustion and intoxication, that the duke's eyes remained cold.

'I assure you all,' Marcus went on, 'that our new hero will be well-looked after; his requests will all be honoured. As of this moment, I am appointing him the leader of his own squadron, and he will be free to hand-pick those he wants to serve alongside him. We shall send his talons to the best armourers in the Bulwark, and fashion the weapon he has asked for; until then, he and his squadron shall be allowed to choose whatever they need from the arsenal of Arrowhead.' He gazed around, watching the reactions of the crowd. 'I proclaim Corthie our Lone Wolf; may he smite the greenhides from this day forth, and serve the Bulwark as one of the great champions.'

Despite dizziness and exhaustion threatening to overwhelm him, Corthie couldn't help laughing. 'Smite,' he mumbled, staggering and swaying.

The duke glanced at him quizzically.

'Thanks, Commander,' said Corthie. His battle-vision had all but gone, and he could sense the inevitability of sleep as a deep tiredness permeated his bones. 'Where's Tanner?' he cried.

The older soldier raised his hand from the edge of the crowd.

Corthie pointed at him. 'You're in. Select the rest of the squadron for me, I... I...'

'Are you alright?' said the duke.

'I'll be fit and ready for the mission tonight, don't you worry yourself, boss.' He swayed. 'Oh aye, Tanner, find a place for Quill; I like her voice...'

Corthie's eyes closed as he was still standing. He toppled to the ground, and began to snore.

# CHAPTER 7

# SINCERELY

Sector Six, The Bulwark, The City – 6th Mikalis 3419

'And then,' Maddie said, her hands gesticulating above the kitchen table, 'he leaps up and climbs right to the top of the dragon's perch; I couldn't believe it.'

Her mother frowned. 'He sounds like a drunken oaf, dear.'

Rosie smirked. 'It wouldn't be the first of those Maddie was attracted to.'

'Shut it, toerag, I was in the middle of telling the story.'

Her sister batted her eyes and pretended to swoon. 'Oh Corthie, I can't resist you!'

'Is that his name, then?' said her brother Tom, who was standing by the window pretending not to be interested.

'As if you haven't heard,' Maddie said.

'It might be all they're talking about down in Arrowhead,' said her father, 'but us folk at Stormshield like to keep our boots on the ground, literally and metaphorically.'

Rosie whistled. 'That's a big word, dad.'

He smiled at her. 'I know a few.'

'I don't know why I bother,' Maddie said, shaking her head. 'A guy with battle-vision turns up, kills Malik knows how many greenhides, and you don't care?'

'But you didn't actually see him fight?' her mother said.

'I told you, I work nights now, and that's when the Wolfpack's out. And the Rats.' She frowned. Her family were already losing interest. 'He jumped over the moat as well,' she went on; 'no one's ever done that before. Did you hear me?' The others were looking down at their dinner, their attention gone. She glared at them. 'And,' she said, 'he killed a god.'

Her mother sprayed hot soup over the table as she gasped. Her father slapped her on the back as her face turned red.

'Stop making things up,' said Rosie, glaring at her sister.

Their mother stood, her face still flushed, and she started to clear up the mess. 'You've gone too far this time, girl. What possessed you to say such a thing? Your grandmother would have expired before our eyes if you had uttered such blasphemies in front of her.'

Maddie raised her hands in innocence. 'Hey. I'm only repeating what he himself said, in front of an entire room of folk. You can ask any of them, and anyone in Arrowhead; everyone knows about it.'

'And you heard him?' said Tom.

She swivelled in her chair to face her brother. 'Yeah, I did. I'd come off my shift this morning and was getting some fresh air, and I followed these folk into the Wolfpack Tower; and there he was, throwing back the booze and telling these stories. Yeah, I heard him say it. He smashed a god's skull in when he was fourteen.'

Her mother's face went through several expressions. 'But, don't the champions come from the land of the gods? Why would they send us a savage who had killed one, if that can possibly be true?'

'I don't know,' said Maddie, 'maybe as a punishment?'

'It's a load of rubbish,' said Tom. 'He's either a liar, or he's delusional.'

'That's what folk were saying about him having battle-vision, and he proved them all wrong.'

Her brother frowned. 'You're beginning to sound like one of those damned Redemptionists I keep hearing about.'

'Those freaks? Forget it. I'm no believer in that nonsense. He's a good fighter, that's all I'm saying, nothing more.'

'Can we change the subject, please?' said their mother, sitting back down at the dinner table.

'Maddie,' said her husband, 'that note you left us a couple of days ago was a bit vague.'

'That's cause I didn't know what I'd be doing when I wrote it.'

'Yes, but you clearly know now.'

'Obviously.'

'Well?'

She shrugged. 'Can't say. I'm assigned to the Fourteenth Support Battalion, but I'm not allowed to tell anyone what I'm doing.'

'But you're quartered there with them?'

'I have a room, yeah, but it's not in the main barracks, so don't bother asking your old cronies for any juicy gossip about me.'

Rosie rolled her eyes. 'As if.'

'What's that supposed to mean?'

'If by "juicy gossip", you mean a boyfriend, then, as if.'

'I was talking about my job,' Maddie said, 'but what would you know about boyfriends, you little runt?'

Their father raised an eyebrow. 'Enough, girls.'

Her mother frowned. 'Is the work safe?'

Maddie shrugged. 'I've done two nights and I'm still alive.'

'I'd sleep easier if I knew more, but at least it's not the Rats.'

Tom stretched his arms. 'I need to get to the wall; my shift starts in thirty minutes. Maddie, you coming? I'll walk with you as far as Stormshield.'

She glanced at the window clock, and a sense of dread built in her. Another night with Blackrose. When she had returned to her family home that afternoon, for dinner and a chance to pick up more of her things, she had decided that she would present a nonchalant front for the benefit of her parents and siblings, smothering the anxiety and fear that had developed into a twisted knot in the pit of her stomach over the previous two days.

'Sure,' she said; 'no problem.'

Her parents glanced at each other, frowned, but said nothing.

———

'So, when are you going to tell mum and dad?'

Maddie glanced at her brother as they walked along the paved road in the purple light of dusk. 'Eh?'

'Come on, it's pretty obvious what's happened. I heard about the... events at Stormshield, when you started a fight and got banged up in the cells.'

'So? Get to the point.'

He eyed her. 'You're quartered in Arrowhead, after being kicked out of every unit that would have you, and you're working the night shift. You're a Rat, admit it.'

Her fury rose, but she said nothing, turning her gaze away. Her own brother thought she was a Rat? Is that what Rosie and her parents thought too?

'And,' he went on, 'you're spending time with the Wolfpack. You don't have to be genius to figure it out. I know you're getting a kick out of making it all seem a mystery, but it's not fair on mum and dad.' He raised an eyebrow. 'Nothing to say for once?'

'You've already made your mind up. It's beyond your tiny brain to comprehend that I could be worth more than a Rat, so what's the point of even trying?'

'This is serious. You could get killed out there. I know we argue all the time, but I'd actually rather you didn't get ripped to pieces, if it's all right with you.'

Maddie laughed. 'That's the nicest thing you've ever said to me.'

He glared at her and turned away.

'Look, I'm not a Rat, alright? But it is dangerous.'

Tom halted on the road. 'How dangerous?'

She rubbed her chin. 'Ahhh... fairly?'

'As dangerous as being in the Auxiliary Work Company?'

'No... maybe? I don't know. I wish I could tell you, honestly, because I feel like bursting, but I swore I wouldn't. I had to take an oath, it was a condition, otherwise I *would* be headed to the Rats. If I can make it through the next ten days I reckon I'll be alright.'

Her brother stared at her.

'Don't tell mum or dad, I mean it.'

'But...'

She grabbed him by the collar and pulled his face close, her teeth bared. 'I mean it.'

'Fine,' he muttered, pushing her hands away and glancing around; 'have it your way.'

The massive gatehouse of Stormshield Fort reared up before them, and they stopped as the road to Arrowhead branched off to the right.

Tom glanced at her. 'Have a good... shift.'

'You too.'

She turned and headed away from him, keeping her head low as she walked, and hoping that no one from Stormshield would recognise her. She was almost relieved to get away from Tom's questions, but then remembered where she was going. Blackrose. Her heart sank. The beast had a vicious temper, and violence felt like it was only ever a breath away. Or one wrong word. Or if she did something that wasn't exactly to her liking. As she had told her mother, she had survived two nights; could she make it through another?

The guards at Arrowhead Fort nodded to her as she passed the gates just as the sun was setting. Her face wasn't yet well known in the fortress, but the newly sewn badge on her left upper arm displayed the insignia of her battalion. The sergeant who had first taken her to Hilde's offices was standing by the gatehouse doors. He smiled at her, an eyebrow raised.

'When you left this afternoon, young Jackdaw, I thought that was the last we'd see of you.'

'Corthie alone is worth hanging around for.'

The sergeant groaned. 'You've not become another of his crazed followers, have you? I took you to have more sense than that, girl.'

'No, but did you hear what he said to Lord Kano this morning? You can't buy entertainment like that.'

'Oh, I heard all right; the entire damn fortress heard that.' He shook his head. 'The lad will need to watch out for himself. Lord Kano doesn't take kindly to being called stupid, especially by a mortal.'

'Yeah, but what can he do? You must have heard what the duke said as well?'

'I heard, but words like that mean nothing. I saw the glare in the commander's eyes as the lad was climbing down from the dragon perch.'

Maddie frowned. 'I didn't notice that.'

'Of course you didn't. Like everyone else, except me, your eyes were glued to the golden boy. Look, I heard what he did out there, and Malik knows we need someone like that right now. Buckler's saved our asses more times in the last decade than I care to think about, but even so, we're losing ground each year. Every summer, the greenhides get that little bit closer to getting through the outer wall. I want the lad to succeed, get me? But if he makes enemies of the demigods, then he's finished before he even starts.'

Maddie felt like arguing, but she had promised Captain Hilde she wouldn't be late. 'We'll continue this next time. Just note for now that I disagree with nearly all of what you just said.'

He shook his head at her as she raced off through the gateway and into the large forecourt. She glanced up at the dragon perch as she ran, seeing an out-stretched wing silhouetted against the purple sky. Lights were shining from the windows of the Wolfpack Tower at the apex of the fort, and she wondered what Corthie was doing. Sleeping off a monstrous hangover, she imagined, smiling to herself.

She almost barged into someone as she ran past the tower. She skidded, and started to topple. A large hand reached out and caught her.

'Oops, sorry,' said a voice she recognised from that morning.

She flushed and raised her eyes, then kept raising them, all the way up to his face.

'You alright?' he said. He frowned for a moment. 'You were in the common room this morning, aye?'

'Yeah, I was there. My name's Maddie Jackdaw.'

'Corthie,' said a grim-looking man to his right. 'The armoury's waiting for us.'

The champion nodded. 'I'd better go. You live here, aye? I'm sure I'll be seeing you around.'

He turned, and the group of Wolfpack soldiers strode away across the forecourt.

She raised her hand. 'Bye.'

---

Maddie had been cleaning the dark lair for over three hours, and the dragon hadn't uttered a single word to her. It stared instead; its blood-red eyes, with thin, vertical pupils as black as her hide, followed her as she scrubbed the walls to remove the layers of soot and grime. Maddie tried to avoid the cold stare, unsure if it meant the dragon was testing her, or merely wanted to rip her head off and eat her.

The scrubbing brush slipped under her fingers, and her thumb bent back.

'Ow,' she cried, dropping the brush and clasping her thumb.

A low, almost inaudible laugh echoed from the beast.

'You think that's funny, do you?'

'I think you should pay more attention to your work, little insect; you stink of fear.'

'I'm not afraid of you.'

'You're a very bad liar, little insect; I've noticed this about you. Is that why they sent you to me? The deceitful world of the two-legged rejected you for not fitting in? Your kind has raised lying to an art form, and if one isn't proficient in deception, then they are of no use to the others. Is that what happened to you?'

Maddie flexed her thumb. 'So I get nothing from you in hours, and then you come out with that? We're all liars, and I must be a bad one?'

'You are a bad one.'

'I don't know about that; I did a pretty good job of lying to my family earlier this evening.'

The dragon chuckled. 'This rather proves my point about your kind. Tell me, little insect, what untruths did you feel it necessary to use against your own blood?'

Maddie picked up the brush. 'I'm not allowed to talk about you.'

'Of course, I should have guessed. I am the dirty little secret that shames the hearts of those who know the truth. A mighty queen such as I, imprisoned within a filthy dungeon, her wings cramped and aching from lack of space, her mind tormented by unceasing tedium and fetid air.' Her eyes were glowing with rage. 'Is it any wonder that I have lashed out at the insects they send to mop my floors? I should have courtiers; instead, I have you.'

Maddie shook her head as she resumed scrubbing. She was terrified of the beast, but her curiosity was, as it had been throughout her life, stronger than her fear.

'You used to be a queen?'

A blast of fire roared out, and Maddie threw herself to the filthy flag-stones as the flames swept a yard over her head, the heat roasting her back. She panted, her body shaking in terror as she turned to face the dragon. Blackrose had raised her head as high as the lair would allow, and she was gazing down at Maddie with hatred welling in her red eyes.

'I am still a queen, you disgusting insect,' she said, her voice filling the large chamber.

Maddie scrambled up, her back to the blackened wall. 'Would it help if I called you, "your Highness"?'

The dragon stared at her, then began to laugh, a cruel sound that made Maddie clasp her hands to her ears. She settled her head back down again, the rage in her eyes dimming a little.

'And would you bow to me, little insect, and sing my praises like a good courtier should?'

Maddie scanned the ground for the scrubbing brush. She saw it and sighed. The flames had reduced the thick bristles to ash, and the handle was nothing more than a charred lump of wood.

'No,' she said, standing and wiping ash from her clothes. 'A good courtier should be brave enough to tell their sovereign the truth, regardless of the consequences.'

The dragon glared at her. 'As I have already said, your kind knows little about the truth, except how to pervert it.'

'But I haven't lied to you.'

Blackrose laughed, then fixed the young woman with her eyes. Maddie felt a fleeting pain pass through her mind.

'What did you do to me?'

'A little test, for a little insect.'

'It hurt.'

'The truth does, sometimes.'

'The truth?'

'Yes. I have gone into your weak little mind, and made it impossible for you to lie.'

'What? But.. I need to... What about my oath?'

'It'll wear off soon, you foolish creature, but note how panicked you became at the very notion that you would not be able to lie. Right, let's begin. What frightens you most, little insect?'

Maddie opened her mouth to say 'the greenhides', but something else came out.

'Being trapped in the Bulwark. Being a Blade, which means I can't leave the defence of the walls, ever.'

'Now we're getting somewhere,' said the dragon. 'What are your true feelings towards this noble City of yours?'

'I hate it. The Rosers, the Sanders, and all the rest of them. They sit behind the Middle Walls, and forget that we're even here. They live their lives in peace, and never have to think about what happens every day in the Bulwark. They're cowards, and our sacrifices are wasted on them.'

She blushed as she said the words, but couldn't help herself, and she heard Blackrose laugh again.

'Good,' the dragon said. 'Tell me more; what do you think should be done to these cowards?'

'I would have them swap places with the Blades; and the poor Scythes and Hammers, and make them defend the Great Walls for a change; see how they like it. Then the three tribes of the Bulwark could live in the palaces and mansions of Auldan, and rest; and maybe we'd be able to forget about the greenhides for a while, just like they do now.'

'I see you are fired by injustice,' the dragon said, 'but sentiment alone will never achieve your dreams. You rail against unfairness, but are a willing accomplice in the iniquities you so despise. In other words, you are a hypocrite. Do you admit it?'

She hung her head. 'Yes.'

'I sense you hate me, little insect, but I am only allowing that which lies within your heart to rise to the surface. Does it not feel good to tell the truth for once?'

'No, it feels terrible.'

'This is no surprise to me; in fact it confirms everything I've been saying about your kind. You fear and loathe the truth, and depend upon your lies to survive. Like insects with two legs instead of six, your species is worthless. You swarm over every world you inhabit, destroying and polluting everything with your towns and cities. This is the first world I've seen where that is not the case. Here, you are confined, walled in; assailed by forces you cannot defeat. Tell me one more thing; in your darkest moments, do you not sometimes wish the greenhides would break through the Great Walls? At least then, the endless struggle and suffering would end, and those cowards you were talking about would finally realise how much you had done for them over centuries of strife. Do you not long for that, sometimes?'

Maddie tried to clench her mouth shut, but her lips refused to obey. 'Yes.'

She burst into tears as the dragon laughed. She didn't really believe that, did she? Was it a truth buried so deep within her that she had never acknowledged it, or was the dragon trying to trick her? The thought of the greenhides breaching the walls was a common nightmare of her youth, no doubt one shared by many in the Bulwark; surely she didn't long for it. That would make her a monster.

'Your tears prove your weakness, little insect,' Blackrose said; 'don't try to hide who you truly are; embrace the dark corners of your mind, where your twisted fantasies lie. You are sick, little insect, vile and sick, but I can help.'

Maddie wiped her face. 'How?'

The dragon stretched her neck, until her head was a yard away from Maddie, and she could feel the beast's breath on her face. 'I can end your pain, if you want me to. I know you want me to, I can feel it. You hate yourself; you loathe your miserable, unfulfilling life; you desire the slaughter of everyone you know.'

Maddie stared at the dragon; the beast's eyes holding her in their deep gaze.

'Speak the truth, little insect; you want it to end, don't you?'

'I... I...'

'You want to embrace the darkness, where there will be no more pain, no more suffering, no more greenhides.' Her head moved closer, her jaws starting to open, the rows of teeth gleaming in the lamplight. 'Say it. Say but one word, and I will ease you from this life of misery.'

Maddie felt her will crumble. The dragon was right. What did she have to live for? She would be as well to end it all now, and find some peace. Peace.

'I...'

'Stop!' cried a voice. 'Blackrose, get back from the girl. Now.'

Maddie blinked as if a spell had been broken. Blackrose turned to Hilde, who was standing by the gate of the lair, and let out a long peal of harsh laughter.

Hilde ran over, and shoved Maddie behind her. 'I've told you about this before,' she yelled, pointing into the dragon's face.

'What's all the fuss?' said Blackrose. 'I was only trying to help the little insect.'

'Yeah? The way you "helped" my other assistants?'

'Not all of them. Some I incinerated due to a variety of objectionable personality traits. This latest one is so consumed by her own fears and doubts, that I felt it would be a mercy to eat her.'

Maddie said nothing as tears spilled down her cheeks. Shame was burning inside at what the dragon had made her admit. She had thought that it would be her deepest fears that would have left her exposed, not her deepest desires.

Hilde took her hand, glared at the dragon, then led Maddie from the vast chamber. They squeezed through the small door in the gate, and Hilde closed and locked it behind them. Maddie let Hilde escort her to the office, where the officer placed her into a chair. She rummaged in the drawer of a desk and withdrew a bottle. She rubbed a few marks from a couple of glasses, and filled them.

'Here,' she said, handing Maddie a glass; 'drink this.'

Maddie's fingers trembled as she raised the glass to her lips and took a sip.

Hilde sat opposite her. 'I knew she'd do that to you sooner or later; it's an old trick of hers.'

'Why didn't you warn me?'

'What difference would it have made? The truth is the truth; there's no dressing it up. What did she make you admit to? Wait, actually, I don't want to know. We are weak creatures; she's right about that, and our minds are full of contradictions. It's possible to love and hate the same person at the same time, for example. Do you see what I mean?'

Maddie shook her head.

'Look,' said Hilde, leaning closer; 'the truth about, say, an event is clear cut, right? Either it happened or it didn't, yeah? What about feelings and emotions? They're also true, but not in the same way. A brother punches you as a child and you want to kill him at that moment; does that mean you're a murderer, or capable of becoming one? Of course not. Anger and fear drive our emotions to dark places sometimes, and that's what Blackrose is playing on. She knows us better than we know ourselves. What I'm trying to say is that whatever she made you admit to, it doesn't define you.'

'She's done this to you as well, hasn't she?'

Hilde smiled. 'Many times. I once told her that my deepest desire was to kill Duke Marcus, after he had been particularly unpleasant one day. Another time I admitted that I'd rather Blackrose hadn't been born at all; I was lucky to get out of her lair alive that day. It's been a few years though, since she's tried it on me. I probably bore her now; she's heard everything I have to say.'

Maddie wiped her face again, embarrassed that she had broken down. 'Apart from the ones who refused to come back, did she kill the rest of your assistants?'

'Yes. Half of them begged her to, after she'd forced them to divulge their darkest desires. The other half, as she said, just annoyed her. So, what's it to be? I won't hold it against you if you refuse to go back in there.'

'But then I'll be sent to the Rats.'

'So? The Auxiliary Work Company is filled with damn heroes, in my opinion. The infantry may take bets on how many of the Rats will survive each night, but deep down they know it's a job that requires as much courage as that of the Wolfpack. To calmly operate those cranes in silence every night, knowing that the slightest noise could mean their deaths? I won't have a word spoken against the Rats in my presence, understand?'

Maddie narrowed her eyes. The captain was the first person she had met to show any respect to the most hated company of soldiers on the wall.

'Well?' said Hilde. 'Are you staying or going?'

'I don't know.'

The captain nodded. 'Alright, you've made it through your third night, because no matter what you decide, I'm not sending you back in there for the rest of your shift. Despite her belligerence, Blackrose hates being left alone, and I want to punish her for what she did to you.'

'Me not being there would punish her?'

'Of course. The fact that you're still here, and still alive is a good sign. Let's allow her to assume that you've run away in terror. When she sees you tomorrow, she might be a bit prickly, but deep down, I know she'll be glad you're back.' She smiled. 'That's if you decide to come back; it's up to you.'

'What is the aim?'

Hilde frowned. 'What do you mean?'

'Long-term, what's the plan? Do we just look after Blackrose in her lair forever, or are we trying to achieve something else?'

'You're a bright girl, Maddie. No other assistant has ever asked me that question. I'll tell you the answer because I want you to stay; I see something in you that makes me hope you do. This falls under the same oath you swore not to tell anyone about what you're doing; no one else must hear these words; do you understand?'

Maddie nodded.

'Duke Marcus wants Blackrose to fight, just as Buckler does. She refuses, that's why she's locked up down here in the depths of Arrowhead. My job, ultimately, is to try to persuade her to drop her objections, and to get her back in the air.'

'Why does she refuse?'

'You must have heard her talk about us. "Two-legged insects", and all that nonsense. She hates us. I still don't really understand why.'

'She used to be a queen.'

Hilde's eyes widened. 'She's told you that already? Yes, she was a queen once, or so she says; I have no way of verifying it.'

'I want to know,' said Maddie; 'I can't help it; I want to know everything about her. She scares me, and I don't want to play the truth game with her ever again, but I can't bear the thought of not knowing more. If I walk away, I'll never find out if she really was a queen, or what her realm was like.'

'So curiosity is winning out over terror?'

Maddie smiled. 'For now. Alright, I'll stay.'

## CHAPTER 8
# CONRAD'S BIRTHDAY

Tara, Auldan, The City – 11th Montalis 3419

Daniel sighed as he watched the sunset from the veranda of the regiment's Junior Officers' Club. He had his feet up on a low railing, and a glass of gin flavoured with citrus resting in his hand. The blossom on the trees had gone, and the leaves were a rich, luscious green. Between the neat rows of trunks, he had a glorious view of Warm Bay, the wind-clipped surface of the water reflecting the peaches and pinks from the darkening sky.

'This is what we joined up for, eh boys?' said Todd as he reclined on the wooden chair next to him.

'Yeah,' said Daniel, 'maybe the military life isn't so bad after all.'

'I'm bored,' said Gaimer, from Daniel's right. 'I thought we'd be seeing some action.'

Daniel disagreed. Strongly. His relationship with his friend was only beginning to recover from the incident at the dance reception, so instead of voicing his objections, he nodded along.

'What action?' said Todd, raising an eyebrow. 'The City's been at peace for three hundred years.'

'Not a war,' said Gaimer; 'nothing quite so extreme. A moderate uprising, perhaps, that would pitch us against one of the more backward tribes.'

'Which one?' Todd said. 'There are a lot to choose from.'

Gaimer laughed. 'Never a truer word spoken. Those bandy-legged thugs that inhabit the Circuit; I'd like a go at them. Or those filthy peasants in Outer Pella; force them all to take a bath in the Inner Bay while we sit on the beach.'

Daniel shook his head, but continued to keep his mouth shut. Negotiations with Clarine's family were at a very delicate stage, and his mother would go wild if he endangered them by getting into a row with one of her relatives.

'I don't know why you care,' said Todd. 'So long as they stay in their slums and leave the good folk of Tara unmolested, then why should I give a moment's thought to what the lower orders get up to?'

'Their tribal territories are nests of crime and corruption.'

'And?' said Todd. He glanced at Daniel. 'Come on, Danny, back me up here.'

'I'm not getting involved.'

Gaimer turned his glare onto him. 'It's a simple enough proposition. Tara has the best trained and equipped militia in the City. The choice is – should they sit in their barracks and watch the pretty sunset each evening, or should they actually be used? With the resources at Tara's disposal, our regiments could root out the gangs and crooks that infest the slums, and restore order to the more... feckless tribes.'

Daniel frowned. 'Have the other tribes asked us to intervene?'

'What does that matter? Do you wait for a diseased limb to ask for help before you cut it off?'

Todd and Daniel exchanged a glance.

'I get the feeling,' said Todd, 'that our friend just wants an excuse to bash people's heads in.'

Gaimer laughed. 'Maybe you're right. It's just that I'm bored out of my mind hanging around the barracks all day while the troopers drill in the yard. The commanders have nothing for us to do, so we each try to look busy, when in reality we're doing sod all. At least some action would break the monotony.'

Todd raised an eyebrow. 'You could always apply to go to the Bulwark.'

The three young officers roared with laughter.

---

'Thank Malik he's gone,' Daniel muttered as he walked along the edge of the gardens with Todd.

'Who, Gaimer? Have you fallen out with him?'

'No, it's just that I can't speak in front of him. I'm too nervous I'll say something that'll get back to Clarine's family.'

'Ahh,' said Todd. 'That explains the way you were behaving. Still pining after Clarine? I thought you blew that at graduation?'

'I thought I had too, but after a dozen letters of apology, her family finally replied a few days ago. My mother will have me flayed if I mess it up again. Look, I wasn't lying to you before; I don't want to marry her, but my mother's threatening all kinds of savage reprisals if I try to back out of it.'

Todd shook his head. 'You wrote her a dozen letters?'

'I may have written them, but my mother dictated the words, then stood over my shoulder to make sure I got them right.'

'Lady Aurelian is a fierce woman.'

'She'll be fierce if I'm late for dinner tonight.'

'Wait, are you using your ten-day pass for that? You'll miss Conrad's birthday this evening; we're all hitting the bars by the waterfront.'

'I know. What can I do? Mother insisted; said I couldn't miss it.'

'Oh Danny, sorry to be the one to say it, but the chaps in the mess are already referring to you as a mummy's boy, and this is hardly going to improve your reputation.'

Daniel shrugged. 'I don't give a donkey's ass what the "chaps" think.'

'You're not making many friends in the militia, Danny. Aside from me and Gaimer, that is, but we already knew you. You should maybe try to fit in a bit more, otherwise people will just assume...'

'Assume what?'

'That you're being a stuck-up Aurelian who does whatever his mother tells him to.' He smiled. 'Sorry. I say it as a friend.' He gestured towards the entrance to the barracks' mess-hall. 'This is where I leave you. Have a wonderful evening.'

Daniel stared at Todd for a moment, his rage simmering below the surface. Is that what they all thought of him? He had only partly been telling the truth before; the jibes of the other officers had hurt, though he hadn't let it show.

'I've changed my mind,' he said. 'The waterfront, did you say?'

Todd grinned.

---

'A drink for Prince Michael!' a drunken lieutenant called out from atop a bar table.

The crowd of young officers roared and raised their glasses. Most of the locals had cleared out of the bar not long after their arrival, leaving the ensigns, lieutenants and the odd captain alone to occupy the tavern. A couple of off-duty sergeants had wandered in, but had left as soon as they had seen the officer insignia emblazoned on every sleeve.

Daniel swayed as he downed the exorbitant but cheap-tasting brandy. The tavern-keeper was probably rubbing her hands with joy at the gold the officers had been handing over for her low-quality fare. A couple of officers slapped him on the back as he slammed the empty glass onto the counter.

'If you break it, you pay for it,' said the serving boy from behind the bar.

Daniel reached into his pocket and threw some gold onto the counter. 'That should cover any breakages in advance. Now, fill up the glass; no, in fact, just give me the bottle.'

The serving boy swept the coins into his hand, then glanced at the tavern-keeper, who was standing with her arms folded, eyeing her rowdy customers. She glanced at the gold, nodded, then resumed her stance.

Daniel took the bottle and turned. Rival regimental songs were competing, as groups of officers cried out the words; out of tune, and out of time. Daniel laughed at the cacophony, and raised the bottle to his lips. His stomach rumbled, and he frowned. He was hungry; he should get something to eat; maybe think about dinner.

Dinner.

He lowered the bottle, a sick feeling replacing the hunger in the pit of his stomach. The raucous shouting, singing and laughter seemed to fade away as he pictured his mother's anger. He needed to get away, but without making a scene.

'Hey, Danny,' said Todd, approaching him from along the bar; 'you've got a bit pale; you alright?'

'Just a bit drunk. I think I might be sick.'

'Not surprised, if you're swigging it from the bottle.'

'Have some,' he said, passing the bottle to Todd. 'I'm just going to pop outside and throw up somewhere not too obvious.'

Todd frowned at him. 'You will be back though, yes?'

'Five minutes, that's all I'll need,' he said, 'unless I'm lying unconscious in a gutter covered in vomit; in that case you'll have to come look for me.'

He heard Todd's laughter as he staggered to the door. He dodged a swaying group of singers, their arms round each other's shoulders in an unsteady circle as they made up new, and increasingly vulgar, verses of their regimental song. He slipped through the door and into the dark street.

He kept his pace to a stagger until he reached the corner of the building, then broke into a run. He passed the harbour front on his left, and turned up one of the well-lit streets towards the centre of Tara. The houses were all detached, two-storey villas, with wide balconies, where many families were sitting, enjoying the warm evening air. The quickest way home was right through the middle of Prince's Square, past the enormous marble fountain with a gigantic sculpture of Prince Michael as a child swimming with dolphins, then towards the ridges of the Sunward Range.

He slowed to a walk as he crossed the great plaza, the fountain spraying water high into the dark sky; the droplets glistening in the light of the many lamps that ringed the square. He avoided the strolling couples and the peasants selling roses, and kept his head down as he attempted to walk in a straight line, with only the occasional sway giving any notice of his inebriation. His guts churned as he walked, from the combination of no food and lots of nasty spirits, and it was with a sense of relief that he started to climb the steps that led up the ridge to Princeps Row and the palace. There were many ways up to the aristocratic and royal quarter of the town, and he had selected one he hoped would be quiet, and one where no carriages would be able to knock him over if he stumbled.

He glanced at the sky as he ascended the switch-backed steps. He had lost track of time in the tavern; hours could have passed. He smiled. Despite the coming storm, he didn't regret going out with the other officers. He didn't like them, but at least they had seen him join in, if only for a while. He prayed to Malik that his early departure wouldn't have been noticed by too many. The state they were in, they would be lucky to remember anything.

The top of the stairs joined a road that snaked up the side of the hill, and Daniel trudged on, each step an effort. The refrain from his regimental song came into his mind for some reason, and he mumbled the lines as he made his way along the road. Maeladh Palace loomed up to his left, the front portion spread out over a terrace that jutted from the hillside. The gates to the palace were at the end of the paved road, and Daniel was about to take the side-branch that led to Princeps Row when he saw the palace gates swing open. A carriage raced out, pulled by six white horses, their hooves pounding off the cobbles. Daniel jumped to the side of the road, and stared as it passed.

He squinted. Lord Kano? What was he doing so far from the Bulwark? He stepped back out onto the road and watched the carriage as it disappeared down the hill. Why would Duke Marcus's Adjutant be visiting the God-Queen? The demigod had been on the losing side of the Civil War, as were the rest of the traitor Prince Isra's children. Kano had then been taken under the wing of Duke Marcus, but his bloodline showed, and he had a reputation for cruelty and brutal ruthlessness.

It was what the Bulwark needed, he supposed; iron discipline.

He turned back to the side-branch of the road and continued on. Trees thick with leaves lined the way, and beyond glistened the domes and towers of the enormous mansions that housed the City's best families. The Aurelian mansion was the biggest of them all. The Chamberlains claimed that theirs was bigger, as the entire extended family lived within a wing of the palace, but that ridiculous claim didn't count. Stupid Chamberlains, he muttered to himself as his guts groaned again.

The front of the Aurelian mansion was obscured by a thick fence of hedges and trees, and as he staggered up the driveway, he saw a carriage parked outside the front door. He heard the crunch of boots on gravel, then noticed a small group of people by the carriage door.

'My humblest apologies for wasting your time this evening,' he heard his mother say. 'One can only presume something unexpected has occurred; I pray the boy hasn't fallen into the bay.'

A lower voice replied, but Daniel couldn't make out the words. He stumbled round a row of shrubs, and staggered out by the carriage. Three people turned to him; his mother, Clarine's father, and Clarine herself, wearing a long dress with a veil covering her face.

'Daniel!' cried his mother. 'Are you alright, darling?'

'I'm fine,' he muttered. He swayed, groaned, fell to his knees, and vomited all over Clarine's dress and her father's high, leather boots.

---

The pale, pink light seeping through the shutters hurt his eyes, and he closed them again.

His bed was warm and comfortable, and as long as he didn't try to move his head, pain-free. Why did he have a headache? Had he been out...? Oh yes, he remembered, he had been drinking with the other officers. Memories came back to him in bits and pieces. The drunken regimental songs, swigging brandy from the bottle, throwing up over Clarine...

He shot up in bed, then immediately regretted it as the pain behind his eyes pounded out afresh. He groaned, rubbing his temples. Clarine. Malik's ass, what a mess he had made of everything. If only he hadn't listened to Todd, and gone straight home. It would even have been better if he had stayed out all night with his colleagues; coming home drunk halfway through the evening had been the worst of all possible choices. He swung his legs onto the floor. And now he had to get back to the barracks before work began, otherwise he would forfeit his next ten-day pass. At least the other officers would be as hungover as he was.

He stood, and dressed in silence, pulling on his spare uniform as his other was reeking of booze and had vomit splashes down the front of the tunic. His hair was a wild nest of tangles, and he needed a bath, but his desire to get out of the house unseen was more important. He crept out of his room, and descended to the ground floor of the mansion. The front door was too obvious, so he sneaked through the quiet and cold hallways until he came to a side entrance. Just a few more yards to go.

'Sit,' said his mother's voice.

He jumped, then turned. His mother was sitting by the glass doors of the veranda in her dressing gown, a mug of something in her hands.

'I'm not going to ask you again.'

He glanced around. 'How did you...?'

'Honestly, Daniel, you're so predictable. Except for last night. That, sadly, I did not predict.'

He stood in an awkward silence for a moment, then sat on a comfortable couch by the wide windows.

'I need to be at the barracks on time.'

'If you left now, you'd be an hour early, dear.'

He frowned. He should have glanced at the window-clock in his room, but had been in too much of a panic. His mother signalled to a servant. 'Get my son a glass of water, and have it flavoured with fresh mint; his breath stinks like a sewer.'

The servant bowed, and walked away.

Daniel attempted a smile. 'Is it time to write another letter?'

'I'm afraid we're a little beyond the letter-writing stage. Your antics last night have destroyed any last hope I had of continuing with the engagement. I've already sent a short note this morning to break it off formally.'

Daniel felt an intense surge of relief but tried to hide it. 'Why?'

'To prevent her family from doing it first; that would have been the final humiliation. It will be bad enough when the Chamberlains find out, at least this way we emerge with a shred of dignity. Not that it matters; the Aurelians are a laughing stock, or they will be as soon as word gets around.'

His mother seemed calm, which made Daniel's nerves screech with anxiety. She had made no demands for an apology, or an explanation, as if she had moved beyond the point of simple rage.

'I'm sorry.'

Her serene countenance almost cracked, and he edged back in his seat. 'Too late for "sorry". The only useful course open to us is to plan our way out of this catastrophe.'

'Do you have a plan?'

'I have several. Unfortunately for you, many of them end up with your head on a stake by the side of the hedgerow, dear. Do you have the slightest notion of how much money last night's little escapade has cost us? Your father and I invested thousands in your engagement, merely to match the bribes the Chamberlains paid out to every noble family with an eligible daughter to refuse to speak to us. Clarine's family have done very well out of this. They took the Chamberlains' money, and then they took ours as well. We now have to start right at the beginning again, only with our funds in rather a depleted state.'

'I've let you down.'

She frowned at him. 'If all you can do is utter banalities, dear, I'd prefer you kept quiet.' She sipped from the mug and Daniel noticed that her gaze continued to avoid him. The servant re-appeared with a glass on a tray, and Daniel took it. He sipped, savouring the fresh, clean taste, then downed it in one, his parched mouth wanting more.

'The problem,' his mother went on, once the servant had departed, 'is that I have already approached, and been rebuffed, by every major family line in Tara. Thanks to the bribes of the Chamberlains, none of them wish to discuss any possibility of marrying into the Aurelians. Therefore, to find you a wife, I must be prepared to lower my sights. The middle-classes are absolutely out of the question, so I am left with one alternative; I must turn to Ooste, Port Sanders or Dalrig, and begin my search anew.'

'You'd let me marry a Gloamer, or a Reaper?'

'Of course not! Don't even think of such foolishness. The Aurelians have always intermarried with Rosers, and always will. Fortunately for us, there are a few Roser families living outwith our territory, many of whom are clustered around the Royal Academy in Ooste, or live in the large estates by Port Sanders. It's true that some of them have "gone native", so to speak, but as long as their blood is Roser, I'm prepared to overlook any rustic elements that may have entered their speech or manners. Once your bride is firmly ensconced within the four walls of our home, I can get to work on eliminating any bad habits.'

'Won't Lord Chamberlain have bribed them as well?'

'Possibly. If it comes to it, we can sell the family villa. It would be a pity, but we have the mansion here, and that may have to suffice.'

Daniel groaned. The best memories of his youth were centred around the vacations they had taken every winter to their estate in the countryside. The sprawling villa was surrounded by acres of vineyards, and was miles away from the eyes of prying neighbours.

'I shall start with the territory of the Sanders,' she went on. 'The Rosers there will be most grateful to learn that someone is interested in elevating one of their number to a higher station. From bordering the Circuit, to the heights of Princeps Row; quite a leap it would be for one lucky girl. My first question will be to ask if they still have all of their own teeth, and then I shall check their hands for calluses; you can't marry someone who has toiled in the fields.' She eyed him. 'These are the depths to which we have sunk, Daniel; I hope you are proud of yourself.'

He didn't want to say it, but a farm-girl from the citrus groves of Sanders sounded far preferable to being joined to Clarine's family. Anyone other than an aristocrat from Tara, sounded fine to him.

He stood. 'I'm off to the barracks, mother.'

There was a moment of startled silence as he walked into the regimental mess-hall, followed a second later by a roar of laughter. Daniel's cheeks flushed as he stood frozen to the floor. Lieutenants were miming throwing up at him, their glee at his humiliation evident. He scanned the room for Todd, but his eyes noticed someone who wasn't laughing.

'You!' cried Gaimer, his face red with fury.

Daniel felt an urge to flee, but his feet wouldn't obey.

'You utterly embarrassed my cousin, you cad,' Gaimer said, walking right up to Daniel and pointing a finger in his face. 'You made a fool out of my whole family.'

Daniel's shame started to edge towards anger. 'They only cared about the money. I'm sure with all we gave them, they can afford to clean some sick off a dress.'

He pushed past Gaimer as the atmosphere in the room quietened. The officers who had been laughing were now watching, their eyes wide.

'You besmirch my cousin's honour?' he heard Gaimer bellow behind him. 'Get back here, Aurelian; face me like a man.'

Daniel halted. Aurelian? Gaimer had never addressed him by his family name before. Daniel, Danno or Danny, but never Aurelian.

Officers moved out of the way to clear a space round where the two men were standing. There was no one in the room with a rank higher than lieutenant, so it was unlikely that anyone would intervene if a fight broke out.

'Well?' Gaimer cried. 'Are you a man?'

Daniel turned, his head still pounding from the hangover. This was the last thing he wanted, but he had already decided; he wasn't going to back down.

Gaimer was standing with his feet apart and his fists raised. 'If you apologise for your comment, and beg for forgiveness, I'll go easy on you.'

Daniel kept his hands loose at his sides. 'I'm not apologising to you. Your relatives have been milking my family's fortune like a prize cow for years. Last night, that ended.'

A few of the lieutenants laughed. Gaimer was known as a solid fighter, and Daniel had no doubt who they expected to win. What none of them realised, not even Todd or Gaimer, was that Daniel's mother had paid for more than just his commission, and the engagement gifts given to Clarine; she had also paid for intensive, physical combat training for her son.

'You're going to regret those words, Aurelian,' cried Gaimer. 'It's time someone brought your family down a peg or two.'

He charged forward and swung his fist. Daniel ducked back and to the side, and Gaimer's arm flew through empty air. A few of the lieutenants glanced at each other.

Gaimer roared in fury and lashed out again. He was big, and strong, but Daniel was faster. He skipped back, dodged, then unleashed his fists. One cracked Gaimer square on the nose, and then the other sank into his waist. Gaimer staggered, a hand going to his bloody face, and Daniel punched him again, striking his old friend on the chin and sending him to the floor.

The room descended into a silence for a moment as the lieutenants stared at the body of Gaimer sprawled across the floorboards.

'I don't suppose anyone else would like to question the honour of my family name?' Daniel said, keeping his tone light; his hands down by his sides again. 'I find that a good scrap does wonders for my hangover.'

The lieutenants glanced away, and the group surrounding the two men dispersed. Todd hurried forward and Daniel narrowed his eyes at the sudden appearance of his, by now, only friend. Todd stared at Daniel, then knelt by Gaimer, a hand feeling for a pulse in the man's neck.

'He's out cold, and I think you've broken his nose.'

'Sorry. Obviously, I should have let him win.'

'I've never seen you fight once, and then you do this?' Todd shook his head. 'Do I even know you?'

'He lunged at me with fists swinging; I didn't want to fight him.'

'Then you should have apologised.'

'For what? I'm sick of this; all of it. I can't win, no matter what I do.' He shook his head and headed for the door. He stopped, telling himself not to antagonise the only person who still liked him. 'I'm going to my company; they've got drills I'm supposed to be supervising. Will I see you at lunch?'

Todd said nothing. Daniel waited for a moment, then nodded and left the mess-hall.

# CHAPTER 9
# ILLICIT CARGO

The Circuit, Medio, The City – 4<sup>th</sup> Izran 3419

Thick, grey mist drifted in sheets over the cold waters of the canal as the barge glided between high, abandoned, concrete warehouses. Ahead, the battlements of the Union Walls loomed like a dark shadow against the swirling purples of the sky beyond. Dawn was fast approaching, and all over the Circuit workers would be rising from their beds and leaving their tiny, squalid apartments for another day of toil.

The summer sun would soon burn off the dawn mist, as it did every day during the hot month of Izran. Named in honour of her father long before he had been executed, it was Aila's favourite month. At the end of the Civil War, the old month of Yendran had been renamed to Balian at the command of the City's new ruler, Princess Khora; such was the loathing felt towards Princess Yendra at the time. Aila had been worried that Izran would also be renamed, but nothing had happened, and she imagined that it was the killing of Prince Michael that had made the difference.

She dug the bargepole against the bottom of the canal to slow down their movement as her arms began to ache. She may appear to any onlooker to be a burly bargeman, but her muscles were her own, and although they were stronger and more toned under her clothes than Lady Ikara might imagine, no amount of training and practice would turn her into a six-foot-plus muscle-bound oaf like the new champion of the walls was rumoured to be. Lord Naxor had been correct, as, annoyingly, he usually was – Corthie Holdfast had proved himself over the first two months of summer as a renowned slayer of greenhides, thrilling the peasants of the Circuit with his daring and with the tales of the crazy risks he took, seemingly because he enjoyed it. The propaganda machine of the City was in full operation, and Aila doubted half of the stories were true, especially the one about him having battle-vision. She almost wished she were allowed to go into the Bulwark to see for herself, but the law was clear, and the authority of Princess Khora's rule came to an end at the dividing line of the Middle Walls; beyond, the Bulwark was under the control of Duke Marcus, and to enter she would need his permission. That would mean talking to a man she despised almost as much as she had hated Prince Michael, the duke's father, and, as she had spent three hundred years avoiding talking to him, she wasn't about to start.

The barge slid to a slow halt and bumped off the side of the canal. A wooden gate tipped with iron was blocking the waterway as it went under the ancient Union Walls on its way to Outer Pella, and a handful of soldiers emerged from a small guardhouse built by the base of the wall.

*You see me as Stormfire, assassin and spy.*

She laid the bargepole down and threw a rope to the approaching soldiers. Their pale green uniforms marked them out as Reapers, members of the Pellan militia, and Aila waited until the ropes were secured before stepping off the barge to join them.

She handed their sergeant a bag of gold, and the soldier slipped it into the folds of her long overcoat.

'I have two for you this morning,' Aila said.

The sergeant nodded. 'Anything we need to know?'

'The gangs are after them. They're going to have to lie low for a while until the hunt has calmed down.'

The sergeant nodded. 'They do something bad?'

'Mistaken identity,' Aila said; 'they're innocent, but the thugs searching for them won't listen to reason.'

'Alright, bring them out.'

Aila went back onto the barge and unlocked a below-deck compartment. Lying side by side in the cramped space were two figures, a man, and a younger woman. They both looked terrified, and stared about at the mist and the faces of the nearby soldiers.

'Get up,' Aila said, and the young woman glanced in fright at the scarred features of Stormfire.

'Where are we?' said the man, as he clambered out of the hold, his eyes darting around.

Aila nodded upwards at the dark bulk of the battlements. 'Union Walls. These soldiers will take you as far as a safe house on the edge of Outer Pella. Do not try to return to the Circuit, understand me? If you do, I won't be coming to rescue you again. Do exactly what the soldiers say, you can trust them.'

The young woman started to cry. 'Why can't we go home? We haven't done anything wrong.'

'For some reason,' said Aila, 'the gangs believe you killed Olvin. Several witnesses say you delivered the poison.'

'But it wasn't me! Someone was dressed like me, and.. and...'

'I believe you,' said Aila. 'I know it wasn't you.' She passed them a bag of gold. 'Take this; it'll help you start a new life in Pella.'

The man took the gold, then helped his daughter get up out of the compartment. They walked to the edge of the barge, and the soldiers stood back as they crossed to the wharf. The sergeant eyed them both up and down, then nodded to Aila; and the demigod watched as the two civilians were led away by a pair of soldiers towards the tunnel that led under the walls.

'Before you go,' the sergeant said to her, 'can I ask your advice on something?'

Aila nodded. Her relationship with the Reapers guarding the canals on the Union Walls stretched back decades, with generous bribes going to each new batch to secure their silence and cooperation. The sergeant led her towards the low arch where the canal went under the walls. A small dockyard had been built there, with a wharf large enough to hold several barges. In the darkness under the heavy bulk of the walls, Aila could see a vessel tied up.

'Don't be offended, Stormfire,' the sergeant said, 'but you're not the only person who bribes us to be allowed safe passage under the wall.'

'I'd be surprised if I were.'

The sergeant pointed at the barge. 'Contracts are usually on a no-questions-asked basis, but something about the demeanour of the two bargemen didn't sit right, and I had their vessel searched.'

Aila's heart sank as they walked towards the barge. She had seen the depths to which some people could sink, and a mixture of nausea and dread began to rise within her. She stopped. 'Look, if it's children in there I don't think I can handle...'

'It's not,' said the sergeant as she stepped onto the deck of the barge. She crouched down, and removed the thick chain and padlock from a long compartment. She slid the three bolts free, and opened it. Aila flinched, then peered inside.

'Weapons?' she said.

'Yeah,' said the sergeant, raising a nail-studded club, 'but none of them are regulation, or look like they've been stolen from the stores of any militia. They appear handmade, but look at this.' She dropped the cudgel and picked up a flail. It had a short handle, and a chain that linked it to a spiked metal ball the size of an orange. The sergeant held up the base of the handle. 'This has been converted from use as a mace, and the armoury stamp has been scratched off.'

Aila leaned over to take a closer look.

'Altogether,' the sergeant said, 'if we include the other compart-ments, I estimate maybe six hundred weapons.'

'And they were coming from Auldan, into the Circuit?'

'Yeah, and many of the ones I've looked at have the same scratched-off stamps; like someone's gone to a lot of effort to pretend that they haven't been stolen from an armoury.'

Aila picked up a machete, its blade gleaming in the dim light. Were the bosses stock-piling for a gang-war?

'Anyway,' the sergeant said, glancing at her, 'I knew you were coming here this morning, and thought you should know.'

'What do you plan on doing with it all?'

The sergeant shrugged. 'We've already been paid, so I guess we'll have to let it through.'

'Don't you think you should alert the governor, or her adjutant?'

'What, and have them find out about the money we've been taking? The entire platoon would be clapped in irons. No, agreeing to take the gold was the same as agreeing to keep our mouths shut.'

Aila nodded. 'Where are the two bargemen?'

'They're currently... resting in the guardhouse.'

'May I see them, alone?'

'Do you promise not to harm them?'

'Alright.'

The sergeant nodded, and locked the compartment, sliding the bolts back into place. They went back onto the wharf, and walked to the rear of the blocky guardhouse. The sergeant opened a door and they entered a lamplit passageway. She took a key from a belt and unlocked an inner door, then swung it open. Inside a small room were two men. One was sitting in his corner with his knees drawn up onto the bench, and looked terrified, while the other, who was a little older, glanced up at Aila, his features calm.

The sergeant nodded to her. 'Five minutes.'

Aila stepped inside, and the door was closed behind her.

She let her black cloak open slightly, so they could see the array of illusory weapons that Stormfire had strapped to her belt, then smiled at the two men.

'Who is the delivery for?'

'There's been a mistake,' said the older man. 'We were promised no questions, and no hassle. If you touch a hair on my head, there will be consequences.'

'You're narrowing my choices with every word. If you refuse to tell me the truth, then I will kill you both. I don't care how much you paid the soldiers, I guarantee that my pockets are deeper than your boss's. The only question is whether I kill you here, then hole your barge and let it sink to the bottom, or whether I accompany you to your destination, then kill you after I find out who is waiting to take the delivery. Then kill them too.'

The younger man shuddered, and cowered behind his knees. The older man glanced at him with contempt, then turned back to Aila.

'I was warned about you,' he said; 'a ruthless, scar-faced assassin that haunts the streets and canals of the Circuit. You're a worthy opponent, but don't underestimate the power of those I work for. You'll find killing us a lot easier than trying to escape the punishment that will come after you. So, go on, do your worst, cause I'm saying nothing.'

'He doesn't speak for me!' cried the younger man. 'I had to come, they have my family and said they'd kill them if I didn't help. Please, I'll tell you everything, I...'

The older man lashed out, his hand concealing something that glinted in the light. With a controlled swipe, he slashed the younger man's throat then, before Aila could react, he plunged the short blade into his own thigh. He grimaced in pain as next to him the younger man toppled dead onto the rough, stone floor. Foam appeared on the lips of the older man, and Aila saw a faint green tinge to the edge of the knife blade that was protruding from his leg. With a groan, he slipped onto the floor, and sprawled lifeless over the body of his companion.

The door behind her burst open and the sergeant ran in. She stared at the ground, her mouth opening.

'I didn't touch them,' Aila said. 'The older man killed the younger, and then poisoned himself.'

The sergeant eyed her. 'And you had nothing to do with it?'

'I threatened them, but I was bluffing. Apparently my reputation precedes me.'

'Malik's ass,' the sergeant muttered. 'You're going to have to help me clean up this damn mess, and I don't just mean the bodies. If those weapons aren't delivered, there's going to be trouble.'

'No,' said Aila; 'your responsibility ends as soon as the barge clears the walls and enters the Circuit. After that, if it happens to be attacked and ransacked by a band of Evader criminals, then that would be no fault of yours. Let's get these two weighted and slung into the canal, and I'll take care of the rest.'

Aila knelt down and turned the older man over onto his back. 'I wonder...' she said, then took out a knife and sliced through the man's thick tunic, uncovering the upper left arm. A wide, red patch of scar tissue appeared through the ripped fabric, and Aila glanced up at the sergeant. 'Exactly where a Bulwark tattoo would be.'

'How did you know?'

'There was something funny about his accent.'

'He sounded Reaper to me.'

'Yeah, but he sounded like someone trying to sound like a Reaper, if you know what I mean.'

'A Blade?'

'That would be my guess, unless he's deliberately trying to mislead us, and make us think so. He certainly acted like a soldier; he obeyed his orders to the end.'

'But what in Malik's name is a Blade doing out of the Bulwark? That flouts the most basic laws of the City.'

'Well, either he deserted and somehow got through the Middle Walls undetected...'

'Or?'

Aila frowned. 'Or someone sent him.'

---

Aila punted the purloined barge for over a mile of deserted side-canals, until her arms were exhausted. For most of the journey, she had made herself appear like the older bargeman, in the hope that at least one witness would be able to back up the soldiers' story that they had allowed the vessel to pass in peace. The sergeant and her squad by the wall blamed her for the trouble that they imagined was coming, and Aila had found it necessary to dip back into her purse to placate them.

She switched back to appearing like Stormfire as she saw the building she had been looking for, and steered the barge into a tight canal that finished in a dead-end. She pushed the pole against the far side of the narrow waterway and the barge bumped against the crumbling brickwork of a wharf. She stepped up onto the solid surface and tied a rope to an iron hoop attached to the side of the canal.

'Raise your hands, slowly,' said a quiet voice from the shadows, and Aila caught a glimpse of a crossbow.

'It's me, Stormfire.'

'Stormfire?'

Aila stood, and turned, her empty palms facing outwards. The young man's eyes widened.

'Is Bekha here?'

'Yeah. I'll.. I'll eh, get her.'

He ran off into the building and Aila followed him inside. It was an old warehouse, but had been converted into a series of makeshift rooms, and they walked to a large open space in the centre, where a dozen people were sitting or standing. They stopped talking and glanced over.

Aila nodded to Bekha. 'I need your help.'

'Stormfire? I thought you were lying low for a while?'

'I was, but there was something I needed to do and, well, one thing led to another.'

Bekha nodded. 'We'll help if we can. What do you need?'

Aila led her and a few others out to the wharf as the sun was rising over the tops of the buildings behind them. It was going to be another warm day in the Circuit. She clambered down to the barge, and opened the compartment so the others could see.

'Weapons?' said Bekha. 'How can we help you with those?'

'Take them off my hands?'

'How much do you want for them?'

Aila frowned. 'Nothing.'

Bekha smiled in confusion. 'You're giving us all these weapons?'

'Look, you'd be doing me a massive favour if you were to take them; but not the barge. The barge has to go to the bottom of the canal.'

'And why would taking them be a favour?'

'Because the people who paid for the weapons are going to be a little annoyed that they didn't arrive where they were supposed to.'

'Ahhh. I see. And who are the rightful owners?'

She shrugged. 'No idea, but the guy bringing them in killed himself rather than tell me.'

Bekha jumped down onto the deck of the vessel then leant over and picked up a short mace from the compartment. She hefted it in her hand, then examined it closely.

'This has been stolen from a City armoury,' she said, her eyes scanning the base of the handle.

'Yeah, that's what I...' Aila's voice tailed off as she heard a low rumble in the distance, followed by what sounded like drum beats. Her heart sank.

Bekha's ears pricked up, and she climbed back onto the wharf, the mace still gripped in her hand. 'Everyone, get inside and bar the doors.' She glanced down at Aila. 'Grab something useful, then lock that compartment and come in with us; it'll be safer than out here.'

Aila closed the compartment and fitted the padlock. 'Thanks, but no.' She tossed the key to Bekha.

'But you know what those drums mean?'

'Of course I do.'

'They're coming this way.'

'Yes, they are.'

'You don't seem concerned. You should be.'

Aila smiled. 'This won't be my first riot, and I doubt it'll be my last.' She climbed up onto the wharf and shook Bekha's hand. 'Remember, sink the barge when you've taken what you need; either that or dump it somewhere far away; it's the only connection leading the weapons to you.'

'Sure,' said Bekha, her attention distracted by the approaching sound of drums, screams and breaking glass. 'Good luck.'

Aila waited until they had gone back into the building, then she began walking along the side of the canal towards the torrent of noise. She wondered what appearance would best suit the situation; should she present a strong or a weak face to a mob of rioters? Both had their uses. She turned a corner but remained in the shadows. Away from the canal, the streets of the circuit deteriorated into unpaved tracks and twisting alleyways that made their way between the grey, concrete houses that towered four or five storeys into the sky. The first wave of rioters were moving from street to street fifty yards from her, smashing every window, setting fires, and destroying whatever they could lay their hands on.

It was a sight Aila had seen before, and it broke her heart every time. The poorest tribe, living in the worst conditions; she knew the many reasons for their anger, but despaired whenever they took it out on their own communities.

*You see me as an enormous man, wide-shouldered, scarred and brutal-looking, wielding a three-foot length of steel pipe.*

That should do it, she thought, as she stepped out into the narrow street.

'Any closer and I'll smash your brains in,' Aila roared to the approaching crowd as she swung her illusory weapon.

The lead rioters took one look at her and scattered into the maze of nearby alleys, drawing the riot away from the canal, and from where Bekha and the others were sheltering.

Cowards, she smiled to herself, slipping back into the shadows.

*You see me as a fellow rioter.*

She re-emerged, and joined the fringes of the mob as it tore through the streets. Whistles and horns were blaring out over the steady beat of drums. The locals shuttered their windows and barred their doors, and prayed to the gods that the mob would pass in peace. Some houses were lucky, others not. The part of the mob Aila was with reached a ceramics plant, and burst in through the wide doors, dispersing into the building, and smashing everything in sight. A few workers protested and were given a vicious beating, but most stood aside or fled as their stocks and equipment were destroyed.

Aila glanced at the faces of the rioters. Most were young, and all were caught up in the chaos and thrill of violence; their pent-up anger seemingly satisfied by the destruction they wrought with their own hands. The mob reached the far end of the plant, and crashed through another set of doors, spilling back onto the streets. Ahead, the road had been blocked by Circuit militia, a double line of stout shields and extended pikes that was sealing the route towards the Great Racecourse and the centre of the district. The mob wheeled away, spreading to the left and right to avoid the soldiers.

Aila dodged into the alcove of a boarded-up shop, and waited for the mob to pass.

*You see me as... myself.*

She strode back onto the street and headed toward the forest of pikes facing her. She halted a few inches from the razor-sharp points.

'Good morning, troopers. I'd be awfully obliged if you could part so that I can get to Redmarket Palace.'

An officer opened his mouth to shout at her, then paused as he realised who was standing in front of the shieldwall. 'Clear a path for the Adjutant!'

Aila waited until the startled militia shuffled out of her way, then she squeezed through the gap.

'Sorry, ma'am,' the officer said, bowing before her. 'I wasn't informed that you were out in the districts today.'

'No need to apologise, Captain. Now, if you'll excuse me, I need to report to my cousin, the Governor.'

'Of course, ma'am,' he said, saluting as she turned away.

She hurried the rest of the route to the palace, hearing the sound of the riot rumble on behind her. She passed the cordon of militia by the entrance, and went in, walking straight to Ikara's office. The chamber was in confusion, as militia officers and tribal officials shouted at each other, while Ikara sat stony-faced in her large chair.

'Good morning, Governor,' she said.

Ikara cocked an eyebrow at her as the room began to quieten. 'Where were you earlier? You weren't in your quarters.'

'I left the palace before dawn; I had a couple of matters to attend to. While on my way back, I ran into the riot.'

Her cousin frowned. 'Which one?'

'There's more than one?'

Ikara shook her head at her. 'Over a dozen riots are currently raging throughout the Circuit, dear cousin; a fact you would have known had you been here. From Iceward to Sunward, and from the Union Walls to the Middle Walls; the Circuit is ablaze.'

Aila pursed her lips. 'Co-ordinated?'

'That,' Ikara said, waving her hand at the people in the room, 'is precisely what they've been arguing about.'

'The violence has clearly been orchestrated,' said one of the militia officers. 'If one area was leaking chaos into another it would be explicable, but for a dozen separate locations to erupt at the same time? A hidden hand is at work.'

'It's the gangs,' said another; 'they've been waiting for this opportunity for months. They're showing us how powerful they've become, and daring us to respond.'

'Madam Governor,' said one of the officials, 'with our militia already stretched to capacity, and our entire economic infrastructure under threat, is it not time to request assistance from the other tribes?'

Ikara gave the man a withering look of contempt. 'What, after a few hours of rioting? Are you unable to hold your nerve for a single morning? Do not fear, mortals, for I will have the Circuit under control long before any assistance could possibly arrive.' She turned to Aila. 'My Adjutant shall see to that.'

'I will?'

'You most certainly will,' said Ikara, glaring at her cousin. 'I want you to crush the riots with all the force at your disposal, which means everything; I'm putting you in charge of the militia, and your sole remit is the restoration of order, by whatever means necessary. Do you understand?'

'Of course, cousin,' said Aila, repressing the warning sounding in her head, 'as you will it.'

## CHAPTER 10

# THE GRAND TOUR

Arrowhead Fort, The Bulwark, The City – 6th Izran 3419

'And this,' said the clerk, opening a thick set of shutters, 'is your new view, sir.'

Corthie smiled as he gazed out from the large window. The panes were set into a wide curve that occupied a third of the entire wall, and he could see the Bulwark laid out before him, and, in the distance, the dark line that marked the Middle Walls.

'Funny,' he said, 'I expected the window to be on the other side of the tower.'

'As the leader of the Wolfpack has to see the greenhides every day, sir, the architects felt this way would be better. You see what you are defending, not those you are fighting against.'

Corthie nodded. 'The quarters are beautiful, but...'

'And don't forget, sir, that they include not only this, the upper floor of the tower, but also the rooms on the level below us, where there is a living space, a dining-room, and small apartments for two officers or assistants of your choosing.'

'Only two? I don't know. I'd miss being around the rest of the company.'

The clerk paused for a moment, as if he had never considered that Corthie might refuse.

'There is also access to the roof, sir. Private access. Would you like to see?'

Corthie noticed Buckler's Eyrie through the window. The platform was at the same level as the top of the Wolfpack Tower, and he would have a good view of the flying lizard whenever he was using it.

'What about the officer who lives here now?'

'Commander Bilston has been re-assigned to the Sunward Fort, sir. He departed Arrowhead yesterday.'

'So he's already gone?'

'Yes, sir. The quarters would lie vacant if you decide you do not wish to move in.'

Corthie glanced around the spacious chamber. There was a large, comfortable bed, wardrobes for his clothes, and a private bathroom with hot, running water. It was palatial, and reminded him of his childhood home for a moment. On the other hand, it was five flights of stairs from the barracks rooms where the rest of his company would sleep, and he would miss being in their close proximity. He knew the real reason the commanders wanted to move him somewhere else; his daily presence in the Wolfpack common room had attracted an ever-growing number of spectators, some of whom barely hid their religious-like devotion to him. It was flattering, but annoying, and they followed him around the fort wherever he went.

'I have also, sir,' the clerk went on, 'been asked to inform you of some other perquisites that befit your position. Food of your choosing, brandy, opium, and any other luxury you require will be available upon request, and Duke Marcus has authorised a harem of no more than three concubines.'

Corthie laughed. 'What?'

'A harem, sir. We can begin the selection process immediately. I have a dozen potential concubines ready downstairs for you to take a look at.'

His heart began to race at the clerk's words, and his imagination turned cartwheels. A dozen beautiful women were waiting downstairs for him, and he could pick three? Something didn't sit right, though, and a nagging feeling formed in the back of his mind.

'How did they come to be concubines?'

The clerk frowned. 'Sir?'

'Did they choose this... path?'

'They have all been selected from the duke's central harem at the Fortress of the Lifegiver, sir. They're all clean, and have been thoroughly vetted for disease.'

'And how did they end up in the duke's harem?'

'Many were born there, sir. Others were sold to the harem by their Hammer or Scythe parents.'

All desire left him. 'No, thanks.'

'Sir?'

'I'd rather do without than take something not freely given.'

'But, sir, it would be a great honour for whichever concubines you chose, and,' he hesitated for a moment, 'it might be perceived as an insult if you refuse.'

'An insult to who?'

'Duke Marcus, sir. Being assigned a harem is generally a privilege reserved only for demigods and God-Children. I believe the God-King himself has one numbering several hundred occupants. As a mortal, you have been shown a special honour, sir.'

'Tough, I don't want it. I'll take the quarters though.'

The clerk's face fell.

'Tell him it's cultural or something; I don't want you getting into trouble on my behalf. Or, I could just tell him myself.'

'And is it... cultural?'

'Aye. My culture despises slavery, and that's what this set-up sounds like to me.'

'I'm not sure, sir, that telling the noble duke that you despise his traditions would help.'

Corthie shrugged as he walked to the bed. 'What else can I say? I'll kill greenhides all night long for you; does that mean I have to like every aspect of your lifestyle?'

He sat on the bed. Firm and comfortable. His thoughts flashed to an image of him sharing it with three gorgeous women, and he shook his head to clear it. He hated powerful men who took advantage of the weak, and if that meant sleeping alone, then at least he would have a beautiful room to do it in.

---

Corthie walked into the common room, brushing someone's hand from his sleeve as he scanned the hall for his sergeants.

'Hey, you two!'

Tanner and Quill looked up from the table they were sitting at.

'You got a minute?'

Corthie avoided a woman praying on her knees in front of him, and nodded to the guards to escort her out of the building. More and more of his devoted followers were managing to get into the Wolfpack Tower, and the guards on the doors had been doubled in recent days. The commander of Arrowhead was on the verge of expelling all religious zealots from the fort, despite the long tradition of allowing the Blades free access to the facilities, as they were starting to interfere in the day to day military operations that engaged the defences all summer. Corthie still smiled at most of them; they were deluded, but harmless.

'Boss?' said Quill as she approached, with Tanner a few feet to her side.

'I'm moving.'

'What? Where? Have you been assigned to a different fortress?'

'No,' he laughed, seeing the look of worry on her face. 'Just upstairs. They've offered me the old commander's quarters.'

'Wow. I heard it's like a palace up there.'

'Aye, it's pretty nice, but there are a lot of stairs between there and here. Just getting to bed will be a ballache, specially if I've had a few to drink.'

'You're an officer now, lad,' said Tanner. 'The commanders probably don't think you should be drinking with the lower orders any more. I assume there's a fully-stocked bar somewhere in your new rooms?'

'Aye. Food, booze, whatever I want.'

'You got servants?' said Quill.

Corthie shrugged. 'A few, but I'd rather do without to be honest; they just get in the way.'

'So, are you needing a hand moving your things, or will your new servants do that for you?'

'I never thought to ask. The main reason I'm telling you is that the quarters come with two small apartments on the lower floor...'

'You've got more than one floor?' said Tanner.

'I've got three, if you include the roof. Anyway, guess who I'd like to move into those two wee apartments?'

Quill's eyes widened.

'Grab your stuff and head up; I've already told the guards on the stairs to expect you.'

A young man dressed as a courier approached through the busy room.

'Pack Leader Holdfast,' he said, bowing low before Corthie.

'Aye?'

'I have an invitation, sir,' the man said, straightening, 'from the noble Lord Naxor. He awaits your presence at the Fifth Gate on the Middle Walls, and has sent a carriage to take you there.'

'Lord Naxor? Will it take long? I still haven't slept after last night's shift, and I need a good seven hours before I go back out tonight.'

'Lord Naxor has successfully requested that you be excused duty this coming night.'

Corthie frowned. Who would protect the Rats if he wasn't there? He was about to say no, when Tanner glanced at him.

'Come on, lad. You've been here over two months. Surely you're not going to turn down a night off?'

'It's not fair, though. Why should I get a holiday while the rest of you are still having to go out there?'

'Because we're Blades,' said Quill, 'it's what we do. For Malik's sake go, boss. The moat's been clear for days, thanks to what you've done out there. We'll cope.'

'We'll do better than cope, lass,' said Tanner. 'Let's show the big guy here we can manage for a single night without him.'

Corthie narrowed his eyes. 'And you won't go beyond the moat?'

Quill laughed. 'We promise.'

He turned to the courier. 'Alright; let's go and see what Lord Naxor has planned for me.'

---

The carriage was large and comfortable, and Corthie watched the view as the Bulwark passed on either side of the wide road. On his right were the neat streets and plazas where the Blades lived, but on the left, set twenty yards back from the road, was nothing but the long wall that separated the Blades from the Hammers and the Scythes. The two other tribes of the Bulwark were names only to him, and he still had no real idea how the City worked.

The straight, dark line of the Middle Walls grew with every minute that passed. So many walls, he thought; thick lines that split the City, dividing its people.

He had to disembark the carriage when it reached a large gatehouse at the end of the road. The entrance tunnel was walled up, but a small postern door led into the gatehouse. Blade wardens patrolled the area, ensuring no one was able to pass through. Corthie was led into the building, where Lord Naxor rose to greet him.

'The famed champion,' he said, a smile on his lips.

'Morning, Naxor,' Corthie said, shaking his hand.

'I've completed the requisite paperwork,' he said, 'and am free to take you out of the Bulwark for the day.'

'Aye? You laying on a tour?'

'The City's too big to see all of it in one day, but I have picked out a few highlights. There will be food to eat, fine wines to taste, and, yes, several hands for you to shake. I was able to pare down the number of requests I received from people clamouring to meet the new hero of the Bulwark, but there were a few I couldn't refuse.'

'I pretty much guessed that'd be the case. It's fine; I'll shake all the hands you want.'

'And, if it's not too much to ask, can I request a certain level of civility from you today?'

'You can.'

'But?'

'I'll be civil to folk who are civil to me.'

Naxor chewed his lip for a moment then nodded. 'Let's begin.'

They passed through a guarded gateway, then emerged out into the pink light of morning. Corthie glanced around. The City was densely populated on the far side from the Bulwark, with streets of tall, grey tenements leading off from the gatehouse.

'This is Medio,' said Naxor as they walked towards another carriage. He pointed over to the right. 'See the hilltops over there? Beyond lies the town of Icehaven, capital of the Icewarder tribe. These suburbs we're in are part of the Circuit.'

'I've heard of that.'

'Yes? And what have the Blades told you about the Circuit?'

'Nothing good. It's inhabited by a tribe they don't like, the Invaders?'

'The Evaders.'

'Aye, that's them. Most Blades say they're dirty, thieving scum, basically. The cesspit of the City, I heard someone call them.'

Naxor sighed. 'Yes. Unfortunately, the Blades are not alone in their opinion of the Evaders.' He gestured to the open door of the carriage and Corthie climbed inside and took a seat. Lord Naxor joined him, sitting on the bench opposite. 'As I was saying, the Evaders have earned themselves a certain reputation among the other eight tribes of the City.'

'Why?'

'It stems, I think, from the fact that they were the last to join the City. They migrated thousands of miles, fleeing from waves of greenhides, and started to arrive in the middle of the City's second millennium. They spoke a different language, and had their own customs, and found it hard to integrate. As soon as the Royal Walls were built...'

'The Royal Walls? I've not heard of them.'

'They've been called the Middle Walls ever since the Great Walls were completed. For seven hundred years, the Royal Walls were the City's only defence against the Greenhides, and the Evaders were moved, en masse, to the area where the Circuit now lies.'

'Do they still speak their own language?'

'No. The education policy was strict, and all Evader children were taught the language of the City right from the start. It took many generations, but eventually their old tongue died out.'

'Seems a little harsh.'

'The government of the time felt differently.'

'So it wasn't your mother?'

'My mother inherited control of the City when the illustrious and mighty Prince Michael was slain.'

'I've heard of him. Duke Marcus's father, aye?'

'Yes, and my mother's eldest brother. Prince Michael ruled for over a thousand years, in the time known as the City's Golden Age.'

Corthie laughed. 'Aye? What age are we in now?'

'The Age of Iron. The official recorders of history in Ooste say that it began with the onset of the Third Great Siege, in other words, just after the end of the Civil War.'

Corthie eyed the young-looking demigod sitting opposite him. 'How old are you?'

'Let me see,' said Naxor, a glint in his eye. 'You are eighteen years old, yes?'

'Aye.'

'Then I am exactly one thousand years your elder.'

'Why do you look not much older than me? Is it a choice, or do you not age at all? The reason I ask is that I've seen a few gods, and they all looked older than you.'

Naxor said nothing, as if he hadn't heard. 'We'll need to make one quick stop on the way.'

'On the way to where?'

'Ooste; I'm taking you to the Royal Palace.'

Corthie gazed out of the window at the narrow streets of the Circuit and the monotonous grey concrete that surrounded them. 'Where are we going first?'

'I need to speak to someone briefly.'

'Another demigod?'

'Yes, as a matter of fact; one of Lord Kano's sisters.'

As Corthie peered through the glass, he noticed several plumes of smoke rising over the grey, concrete buildings to the left, or sunward, of the carriage. 'Trouble?'

'The Circuit occasionally boils over; this is one of those times.'

'Why?'

'I'm sorry?'

'Why does it boil over?'

'Let's see, poverty, over-crowding, a lack of basic amenities, short-ages of decent jobs; the list is long.'

'Why doesn't your mother fix it?'

Naxor smiled, though his eyes remained cold. 'Do you remember when I brought you here, how quiet you were? You hardly uttered a word to me. When I started to receive reports of your outspoken behaviour, I put it down to sheer exaggeration, but now I see I was mistaken. Lord Kano, he... well, let's just say that he's not your greatest admirer.'

Corthie pointed out of the window. 'Half of your City's on fire; I'd say you have more to worry about than my big mouth.'

Naxor glared at him.

'I'm not going to stop asking questions,' Corthie said, 'and you can send me back to the Great Wall if you don't like it; it makes no differ-ence to me whether I see your fancy palaces or not. And, I'm warning you now, if you give me alcohol, I'm apt to say or do whatever pops into my head, regardless of company.'

Naxor said nothing. The carriage continued onwards down a dusty street, then slowed outside a grand stone-built building situated alongside a canal, where several barges were tied up. A group was standing by the wharf, watching the carriage as it halted. A woman stood forward, short and slight for a demigod, Corthie thought. She had dark hair that fell down past her shoulders, and her piercing grey eyes had a gleam to them that caught his attention.

'Lady Aila,' said Naxor as he climbed down from the carriage; 'so good to see you again, cousin. How are you doing?'

The woman raised an eyebrow. 'How in Malik's name do you think I'm doing, Naxor? A dozen riots have been raging through the streets for over two days.' Her eyes flickered up to where Corthie was sitting in the carriage, but the woman made no acknowledgement that she had seen him. She turned away, and walked with Naxor towards the stone building.

Corthie sat back in the carriage. Damned demigods. He closed his eyes for a quick nap.

---

A cough awoke him, and he realised the carriage was moving again. He glanced out of the window and saw an ancient structure looming into view.

'The Union Walls,' said Naxor, 'built after the Two Gods first arrived. Beyond lies Auldan, the oldest part of the City, and home to its four original settlements.'

Unlike at the Middle Walls, the gates of the Union Walls were open, though soldiers were stopping and checking carts and wagons as they passed through. Naxor's carriage over-took the queue and went straight to the front, where militia in pale green uniforms waved them through the gates ahead of the rest.

'This is now the territory of the Reapers,' he went on, 'once the home of Prince Isra, and now administered by the Governor of Pella.'

'Let me guess; another demigod?'

'Yes, my brother Lord Salvor as it happens.'

'What happened to Prince Isra?'

'He fought on the losing side in the Civil War, and paid for it with his life.'

Corthie looked out of the window. A vast settlement of red-brick and red sandstone buildings and houses spread for miles. The roofs were mostly flat, and many of the streets seemed to be dug out below the natural surface level.

'That is Outer Pella, the suburb that grew up long ago outside the old walls of the town. The plain here experiences high winds for much of the year, and the Reapers have learned to keep their heads down.'

Corthie nodded, then noticed Naxor catch his eyes and hold him for a second in his stare. A faint tingle appeared around his temples, and he realised that the demigod was trying to read his mind. They have vision powers, he thought, smothering a smile. His sister had long before protected him against such attacks, and he watched as Naxor's mouth opened in surprise.

'You alright?'

'Em, yes,' Naxor muttered.

'You look a little flustered.'

'Do you... ah, understand what just happened?'

'Aye. You tried to sneak your way into my thoughts and I didn't let you.'

Naxor's eyes widened. 'But that's impossible.'

'Clearly it's not. What is it with you guys and mortals with powers? You act as though you've never met any before.'

'That's because we haven't,' Naxor snapped. 'No mortals have powers; they're the sole preserve of gods and demigods. This truth is fundamental to everything we understand. Gods have powers, mortals do not.'

Corthie smiled. 'I'm starting to see why so many folk follow me around Arrowhead like sheep.'

'Yes, I heard about that too.'

'And I thought it was just my winning smile.'

'You're an aberration of nature.'

Corthie laughed.

'Part of me regrets bringing you here.'

'We can still go back to the Middle Walls. We could stop off for a drink on the way. Any good alehouses in the Circuit? I fancy a cold beer in the middle of a riot.'

'I wasn't referring to this journey today; I meant I'm starting to regret bringing you to the City at all.'

'A few thousand greenhides would agree with you.'

'A few... thousand?'

'Aye. Did you know that some of the infantry keep meticulous records of each night's Rat and Wolf expedition beyond the walls? They have an unbelievably complicated betting system going on. Soldiers have made small fortunes on the odd night I've managed to put away more than a hundred of the green-assed runts. So, aye; a few thousand.'

'You average over fifty kills a night?'

'Aye, although that's fallen a lot in recent days, ever since the green bawbags learned to fear me. Some of them run away when I come out of the gate in the walls; it's pitiful. I have to actually chase them.' Something outside caught his attention. 'Wait. Can we stop?'

Naxor seemed distracted for a moment, then he blinked. 'You wish to stop?'

'Aye, just for a minute.'

The demigod gestured to the driver, and the carriage pulled over to the side of the road. Corthie opened the side door and jumped down, breathing in the fresh air. The road had gone through the suburbs of Outer Pella for a few miles, but then it had reached the side of a bay, and Corthie stared at the still waters, turned pink by the mid-morning sun.

'That's a beautiful view.'

'It is,' said Naxor, joining him by the side of the road. Beyond the paved surface was a long beach that extended round half of the bay. Some people were on the golden sands by the edge of the water, children ran with dogs, and they splashed in the shallows.

'From left to right,' Naxor said, 'that town with the harbour is Pella, then, on the far side of the other bay in the distance, that's Tara. Do you see it?'

'Aye. I can see the cliffs, and a town at the bottom. And a big statue.'

'Prince Michael. Then, over to the right a bit, that's Ooste, the town we're travelling to. The white building you can see is the Royal Palace, the grandest edifice in the entire City.'

'Are we going to see the king and queen?'

'No.'

'Probably for the best.'

'The God-King and God-Queen are separated. Queen Amalia no longer lives in the Royal Palace; instead, she has made Maeladh Palace in Tara her home.'

'Did they fall out? Let me guess, was it over the Civil War?'

'Yes, it was, actually. Did someone already tell you?'

'No, it just seems that a lot of your troubles stem from the war you gods had amongst yourselves. Two princes were killed as far as I can tell.'

'And two princesses, along with many demigods.'

'There were six children of the gods, aye? Your mother is obviously one, and four died in the war. What about the other one?'

'The other is Prince Montieth of Dalrig. He doesn't involve himself in the affairs of the City. He seldom leaves his palace there, as far as I know.'

'When's the last time you saw him?'

Naxor smiled. 'I've never seen him.'

'Not once in a thousand years?'

Naxor shook his head.

'How do you know that he's even there? Maybe he left centuries ago.'

'Lady Vana, the other surviving daughter of Prince Isra, has a certain ability. She can sense the location of the gods and demigods; she can feel their life-force. She would know if Prince Montieth had left. Now, perhaps we should move on; my mother is expecting us.'

The Royal Palace was a spectacular building, towering and majestic, but it was well past its prime. It sat half-buried into the cliff-face of a range of hills, the same range that continued in Tara, after being broken by the narrows that allowed access to the bay. Lord Naxor accompanied Corthie up the white, marble stairs that led to the great entrance doors of the palace. Soldiers in polished steel armour lined the front of the building, standing to attention in the warm rays of the summer sun. They passed through the doors and walked into a grand hallway, with a frescoed ceiling that hung high above them, and statues of the gods and their children lining the walls.

Courtiers bowed low, then escorted them into a grand state room, where enormous paintings in gilt frames covered the four walls. Guards stood by the doors, and a small group were in the centre of the room, surrounded by a larger body of officials and courtiers. A path opened up through them as Lord Naxor and Corthie approached. Once again, he was the tallest in the room, by over a foot. He smiled as he saw a woman gaze at him. She looked to be in her mid-twenties, a few years older than Lord Naxor, who bowed before her. He gestured for Corthie to approach.

'Is this the champion we have heard so much about?' said the woman.

Corthie glanced at her. Something in her eyes made it seem as if she would rather be elsewhere, but she had a professional smile balanced on her lips. He guessed she had better things to do than meet a thug from the walls.

'This is Corthie Holdfast, your Grace,' Naxor said; 'and this,' he said to Corthie, 'is the High Guardian of the City, Princess Khora of Port Sanders and Pella.'

Corthie stuck his hand out and smiled. 'Nice to meet you, ma'am.'

Princess Khora gazed at his hand for a moment, but kept her own clasped to her waist. 'I'm told you're doing a wonderful job on the Great

Walls, and your feats of bravery and daring have fired the hearts of many in the City with hope and joy.'

'I'm happy to do my bit, ma'am. I'll kill greenhides every night for you and the folk that live here. Well, at least until my sister comes for me.'

A hint of a genuine smile found its way onto Khora's lips. 'Your sister?'

'Aye, but that could take a while, so until then, I'm all yours.'

'Excellent. I have, however, heard certain rumours concerning you. I'd be obliged if you could assist me in squashing them.'

'Sorry, ma'am; you'll have to be more specific.'

The woman glanced to her left. 'This is Lady Vana, whom I have asked to attend this reception today.'

Corthie glanced at her. She looked a little similar to the woman Lord Naxor had met in the Circuit, though a little taller, and her eyes were lacking the spark that Corthie had seen in Aila's. She was staring at him, her mouth slightly open.

'Lady Vana,' Khora went on, 'has an unusual gift.'

'Your son's already told me about it. She can sense gods or something.'

'Not quite; she senses powers. All gods and demigods burn residual self-healing powers continuously; that is why she can sense them, but she should, in theory, be able to sense any being with powers. To dispel these silly rumours, I now ask...' She paused as she saw Vana stare at Corthie. 'Lady Vana?'

The demigod tore her gaze away from Corthie and turned to Khora. 'It's not just a rumour.'

Fear passed over the face of the princess for a brief moment.

'He has battle-vision,' Vana went on, 'a powerful strain of it, but there's something else; a shield, a web of protection that surrounds him. I can feel his battle-vision leaking through it, but there's no way in from the outside.'

'I can vouch for that part,' said Naxor. 'He blocked my vision powers on the way here.'

Khora frowned, then stared at Corthie, her eyes narrowing, and he felt the pull at his temples again, a strange fuzzy feeling as the princess's powers were rebuffed.

She lowered her gaze and shook her head. 'This is something I need to ponder on. This audience is at an end. Son, ensure the champion is back in the Bulwark promptly. Corthie Holdfast, it was a pleasure to meet you.'

Without another word, Khora turned, and strode from the hall, Lady Vana and the others of the group hurrying after her.

'I think that went quite well,' said Corthie.

Naxor sighed.

'What do you think she meant by "promptly"? It's still only the early afternoon. If I've got the night off, I want to find some dodgy tavern and get drunk with the locals.'

'I could do with a drink myself.'

'Can demigods actually get drunk?'

'Of course, if we choose to,' Naxor said as they turned back towards the exit, 'but we don't get hangovers.'

'I bet you know a good few places to drink, and the best ale in the City. Let's get some lunch then hit a few taverns. Or are you scared I'd drink you under the table?'

'Now, that sounded like a challenge.'

Corthie laughed. 'You're on. Let's start with Pella, and then when we're feeling dangerous, we'll head into the Circuit.'

'I'm starting to like you, mortal, but, I warn you, playing drinking games with demigods could lead to all kinds of trouble.'

Corthie slapped Naxor on the back, nearly bowling him over. 'Sounds like my kind of fun.'

## CHAPTER 11
## DRAGON CLAWS

A rrowhead Fort, The Bulwark, The City – 8th Izran 3419

The warm summer air felt wonderful on the bare skin of Maddie's arms and legs as she moved through Arrowhead fort. Captain Hilde was strict about many things, but sometimes she would surprise Maddie, and when she had seen how hot the day was likely to be, she had told her she could dispense with her usual thick and heavy uniform. Maddie had grabbed one of the few summer dresses in her possession and pulled it on before the captain could change her mind.

It felt strange to wander the fort dressed as a civilian. Folk looked at her differently, and she was sure that one or two people hadn't recognised her. The sergeant at the gatehouse had given her an approving wink from his office by the entrance archway, but the glances of a couple of other soldiers she had talked to more than once had passed over her without recognition.

The dress was sleeveless, which was her only worry, as it showed, in tattoo form, her chequered past. Each new division or unit she had joined had been inked into her skin in small letters and numbers, and she had a series of them usually only matched by old hands and experienced veterans. Some Blades went through their entire lives serving the same battalion or company, whereas Maddie was already on her fourth.

She eased her shopping basket into her other hand as she browsed the market stalls lining the inner walls of the fortress. Unlike Stormshield, with its strict rules on decorum and behaviour, the atmosphere in Arrowhead was more like a busy village at festival time. Large groups of merchants congregated to finalise deals, or to sell their wares to the crowds that came from the nearby Blade housing. The variety of goods on offer was far wider than at Stormshield, a consequence of Arrowhead's policy of not looking too closely at the trading licences the merchants were all supposed to have, and the captain had asked Maddie if she could obtain a few items for her. With gold in her pocket, and the sun on her skin, she had set out, her spirits lightening away from the dark shadows of Blackrose's lair.

For two months she had been with the dragon, easily surpassing the previous record for one of Hilde's assistants. She had suffered bruises, scrapes, cuts, and one time Hilde had been forced to trim her hair after the last couple of inches had been singed by a blast of fire. It would grow back, the captain had told her as Maddie had wept in front of the mirror. Blackrose, needless to say, had found it all highly amusing.

There were fresh apples in from the Scythes, along with honey and butter, and Maddie loaded her basket. She filled the wine flagon she had brought with her from a barrel, and purchased a ceramic flask of seaweed-infused gin distilled by the Hammers, complete with a little stamp on the base displaying their tribal arms.

A loud commotion arose behind her and she glanced up to see if Buckler was in the air. The pink sky was empty, however, so she brought her glance downwards towards the base of the imposing Wolfpack Tower. She smiled. Corthie Holdfast was walking out from the building, flanked by his personal retinue, and the crowds were surging around him, stretching out their hands to try to touch the champion as he smiled and shook his head at them. There had been near-hysteria on the battlements a couple of nights previously, when the young Pack Leader had not emerged from the Outer Walls with the rest of the Wolves and Rats. Rumours had spread that Corthie was ill, injured or even dead, and an officer had to be dispatched to the soldiers watching from the walls to assure them that he was well, and merely enjoying his first night off since arriving. The doubts and rumours had persisted right up to the previous evening, when there had been an explosion of cheers and chants as Corthie had been seen leading the Wolf Pack again. The multitudes of his religious followers had taken this re-appearance as nothing less than a miracle, and their hymns of worship and thanksgiving had kept half the fort up all night.

He knows my name, she thought to herself as the tall warrior passed through the crowds on his way to the armouries. She chided her weakness. Who cares? He's just another muscle-bound oaf. Good-natured maybe, and handsome. Very handsome. And strong. She had a crush on him, she couldn't help it, but was determined not to become just another one of his legion of female admirers, who were almost as numerous as the religious fanatics. Wearing ever-shorter skirts, and showing ever more cleavage, they followed Corthie about, trying to catch his eye, or touch his arm as he passed.

Maddie liked how Corthie would be polite to them, but never seemed to show any real interest. As far as she knew, the young warrior had never taken any of them to his bed, and some were beginning to wonder if he wasn't interested in girls, but as he hadn't shown any interest in boys either, maybe he was just fussy. Keeping it in his pants had only increased the level of desire felt by his followers, and had made their efforts to sleep with him more desperate and embarrassing as far as Maddie was concerned.

Buckler swooped low overhead, as if to remind the crowds in the fort that Corthie wasn't the only champion toiling day after day to keep the walls safe. The beast and the warrior clearly had respect for each other, as was seen every night in the way they co-ordinated their tactics, but there was also a fierce competition between the two, and both had a tendency to show off for the crowds watching from the battlements.

The volume of noise quietened a little as Corthie disappeared through the entrance to the fort's main armoury. Buckler circled over-head a few more times, then landed onto his high perch, where he folded his long wings and gazed out over the enemy-held plains.

Maddie squeezed through the busy crowds and headed towards the tall curtain wall. She still had a few minutes before she had to return to Captain Hilde, and wanted to get as much sun on her skin as she could. The battlements were bathed in the pink glow of morning, and she smiled as she climbed the steps to the top. She laid her basket down and leaned her arm on the battlements. In the distance, the waves and masses of greenhides rolled across the plain as they always did, but the scene directly below her was unprecedented. For the first time in any summer that she could remember, the moat was clear, and no green-hides were between it and the outer walls. A long row of stakes stretched along the front of the moat, and each one had the head of a greenhide impaled upon it; the work of Corthie and the Wolfpack. The lifeless, rotting heads were staring back at their fellow greenhides, and the effect upon them was noticeable. Their loathing and clamouring hatred were undimmed, but they also knew fear, and avoided the stakes as if unable to look at the evidence of their failure.

Good, Maddie thought. It was about time the greenhides felt fear, and she hoped it would long continue. She crunched her way through a shiny red apple, then tossed the core over the side of the walls.

---

Maddie sat on one of the captain's rickety wooden chairs as the older woman went through the shopping basket.

'And how was the forecourt today?'

'Mobbed. Could hardly move through the market.'

The captain shook her head. 'It's too busy for my liking. I abhor crowds at the best of times, but it's gotten out of hand these last couple of months.'

'I guess having Corthie and Buckler based here brings the folk in.'

The captain smiled. 'I didn't realise you were on first name terms with the young Pack Leader. Know him well, do you?'

Maddie's cheeks flushed. 'What? No, I...'

The captain laughed. 'Just teasing. He's nice to look at, I agree, but I hope you're not getting too wrapped up in the cult of Corthie Holdfast. He may be a good warrior, but he's a mortal like us, and it would only take one mistake, one split-second bad judgement, and he'll be as dead as all those greenhides he's dispatched.'

'Don't say that. I mean, I know it's true, but I don't want to have to think about it.'

'Always best to be prepared for the worst, Maddie; that way if it happens, you'll be ready.' She withdrew the flask of gin from the basket. 'Ah, here's what I was looking for. Fetch a couple of glasses.'

'Is it not a bit early for that?'

Hilde frowned at her, so she got up and went over to the cabinet against the wall of the captain's office, and collected two glasses. She brought them back to the table just as Hilde was breaking the seal on the flask. She poured out two generous measures and handed one of the glasses back to Maddie.

'Is it a special occasion?'

The captain took a sip. 'You could say that. I received a message informing me that we're going to be having a visitor today.'

'And we're getting drunk for that?'

'One gin shouldn't make you too drunk; well, I hope not, but a little lubrication will certainly help.'

'Who's coming? Is it Duke Marcus?'

'If it were, I wouldn't be drinking, I'd be hiding and pretending we're not in.'

Maddie's eyes flashed. 'Is it Corthie? I mean, Pack Leader Holdfast?'

'Gods preserve us, no,' Hilde smiled. 'The lad I could deal with; his crazed followers on the other hand? Come on, drink up.'

Maddie glanced at the glass. 'I feel a bit weird, drinking this early.'

'I'm sure you've done it before.'

'But not in front of my boss.'

Hilde shook her head. 'Stop arguing and get it down you, girl.'

'If you insist.' She lifted the glass to her lips and sipped. 'So, we're getting a little bit... fortified for someone's visit. Who could it be?'

'Shall I just tell you?'

'No! I want to guess. Is it someone I know?'

'I'm sure you've heard of them, and seen them often.'

'One clue; a boy or a girl?'

'Male.'

'I hope it's not Lord Kano. That would be a bit of a let-down, to be honest.'

'I agree, but thankfully it's not him either.'

'The God-King?'

The captain gave her a funny look.

'Alright, not him. Handsome?'

'Not my type.'

'A mortal?'

'He is mortal.'

'Ahh, but not "a mortal"?'

Hilde shrugged, smiling as she sipped more of her gin. 'Think bigger.'

Maddie frowned.

'Think big and scaly.'

'What? You mean... Buckler?'

Hilde laughed. 'Yes. Remember the big red gate in the tunnel outside Blackrose's lair? Today it opens, and the dragons will have one of their rare meetings.' Her laugh fell away. 'They don't always go to plan.'

'When was it arranged? Blackrose said nothing to me about it.'

'She doesn't know. I only got word while you were out shopping. I think it should be you that tells her.'

'Why?'

'I thought you'd want to.'

'It depends. How is she likely to react?'

'I think that after two months you probably know her well enough to answer that yourself.'

Maddie took a larger drink of gin, swallowed it, then downed the rest. The captain had already finished hers, and they stood.

'When is he coming?' Maddie said.

'Now. The note said as soon as possible, so I told them that I'd unlock our side of the red gate when we were ready.'

'Sounds important.'

'Buckler's a young dragon. He's quite impulsive, so he may have decided to do it just because he was bored.'

Maddie paused as they approached the door leading to the lair. 'Should I get changed out of this dress first?'

'Leave it on. It makes you look pretty, and I'm curious to see what Blackrose thinks. She might treat you differently out of a soldier's uniform.'

Maddie said nothing for a moment. Had Hilde just said that she was pretty? Weird, she thought; the captain rarely gave her compliments, but she had just finished a large gin, so was probably a bit drunk. Hilde took the keys from her belt, and unlocked the door. They stepped through into the vast cavern that led to Blackrose's lair, and Maddie saw the massive red gate ahead of them.

'Go and tell her ladyship,' Hilde said, 'and I'll get the gate ready.'

'Don't open it until...

'I won't. I'll wait for your signal.'

'What signal should I make?'

'Whatever you damn well feel like, girl,' Hilde said waving her hand at Maddie.

The captain walked away towards the gate and Maddie turned for the corresponding black doorway that led to the lair of Blackrose. She slid the bolts free in the small door inset into the gate, and walked through.

The dragon opened an eye, its head low to the ground in the near darkness.

'Good morning. Blackrose.'

'I would say that the world has made another revolution, but I don't think that's the case here.'

'What?'

'Never mind. Your insect brain wouldn't comprehend it, anyway.'

'How are you today?'

'Hungry.'

'That's good.'

The dragon fixed her with a stare. 'Get on with delivering whatever bad news you've come to say.'

'How did you know?'

'The terrified look on your face gave it away. I know how my day's going to go as soon as you walk in here and I sense your mood. The best days are when you're sad; I enjoy those. The worst days are when you walk in here with an inquisitive air about you, then I know I'm in store for a hundred stupid questions.'

Maddie smothered the first reply that came into her head. The dragon loved to talk about herself, yet seemed to hate answering any of Maddie's questions. 'It might not be bad news. The truth is, I don't know how you'll take it.'

'If it's not that I am to be released and escorted back to my home, then it's bad news.'

'What? Released? That doesn't make any sense. If you agreed to fly, then you could just... fly. Fly away and go back to your home.'

The dragon laughed, a noise that filled the lair. 'Your stupidity does amuse me at times, little insect. Either that, or it makes me want to eat you; it's hard to tell.'

Maddie's cheeks flushed, and she felt her anger rise. 'Maybe if you explained things to me properly then I wouldn't say stupid stuff.'

'You're claiming your stupidity is somehow my fault? If we play the truth game, I'm sure we'll get to the bottom of your insecurities regarding your lack of intelligence, and I'll wager a shiny gold coin that I'm not the real cause. How about it?'

'I know I'm clever, despite you trying to trip me up all the time.' She took a breath, trying to remember the reason she entered the lair in the first place. 'You have a visitor.'

The dragon hesitated for a fraction of a second, and Maddie smiled.

'Who?'

Maddie met the beast's gaze. 'Buckler.'

The dragon closed her eyes and reached out with one of her great fore-limbs, with the claws extended. She brought it down and began drawing it back, scraping the heavy claws against the blackened stone floor. The flagstones split and buckled as the claws dug deep into the ground, and Maddie jumped back, her hands covering her ears to block out the harsh noise. She stared at the gouges in the floor, then at Blackrose.

'You finished?'

Blackrose opened her eyes. 'Yes.'

'That's it? No arguments?'

'I never argue with insects. Open the gates and send the boy in.'

'Boy? Someone told me Buckler was about eighty years old.'

'Exactly. A youth among dragons. It's my misfortune that the only other of my kind on this world is an impressionable, foolish child.'

Maddie smiled. Blackrose's reaction had been milder than she had been expecting. 'When did you last see him?'

'Two years ago, I believe.'

'Oh. That's a while.'

'It didn't end well.'

'What happened?'

'I ripped his wing with those claws you just saw, and he was unable to fly for three months.'

'Wait! I remember that. Well, not the reason, but I remember when Buckler was grounded for a while. We all thought the greenhides had injured him.'

Blackrose laughed again. 'I think of that day whenever the tedium of this prison taxes me; it always makes me smile.'

Maddie shook her head, then turned to the gate. She poked her head through to the cavern outside, and waved at Captain Hilde, who was standing by the red gate.

'Her Majesty's ready!'

Hilde nodded, and began opening the bolts that kept the gate secured. Maddie pulled her head back from the door to find Blackrose's face a foot from hers.

'Never call me that again.'

'But...' Maddie said as she cowered backwards, 'I thought you said you were a queen; you told me that when I first arrived.'

'I am a queen, and you used that title to mock me. I heard the sneer in your voice, insect.'

Maddie raised her hands. 'I'm sorry.'

'Do it again, and I'll rip your body in two. The next time you refer to me by that title, you will be kneeling before my throne, do you understand?'

'Yes!'

Blackrose pulled her head back. 'Open the gate. Oh, and by the way, wear more clothes the next time you come into my lair. All that bare flesh just makes me want to eat you more than I usually do.'

Maddie turned, shaking. Her fingers went to the bolts, but they were trembling so much that she couldn't grip them. A low rumble of laughter echoed from behind her, and anger rose up to fight her paralysing fear. Damned lizard. She was nothing more than a bully. Maddie cleared the last bolt and began to heave on the door. She had only opened it herself once or twice, and had been surprised at the ease with which she had been able to shift the huge gate. Its hinges and rollers were thick with grease and the gate made no sound as it slid open. On the other side, Hilde had done the same with the red gate, and was standing in the cavern talking to a couple of people whom Maddie assumed were the Blades who looked after Buckler.

She walked out from Blackrose's lair, and when she was halfway to Hilde she noticed Buckler appear down the high tunnel that led to the red gate. Further caverns and tunnels stretched out behind his bulk, as if his lair was considerably larger than where Blackrose stayed. Maddie halted as she watched Buckler. He had always seemed like such a huge dragon, but after being at close quarters for so long with Blackrose, she estimated that he was about half her size. Even so, the stone floor was shaking at his approach. He leaned his long neck into the cavern, and glanced towards the open black gate.

'Hello, Buckler,' she shouted up. 'I'm Maddie Jackdaw.'

His eyes flickered down for a moment. 'I hope Blackrose is treating you fairly, girl, but I know her well, so I doubt it.' He laughed at his own joke, but the sound felt weak compared to the noise Blackrose made. He glanced back up again, a hint of wariness in his eyes as he peered past the black gate. 'Blackrose, are you there?'

A dark shadow loomed behind Maddie. 'Of course I'm here. What do you want, child?'

'It's been a while. I've been thinking about you, stuck down here. I wanted to see you with my own eyes, to make sure you were alright.'

Blackrose lifted the thick, heavy chain that bound one of her rear legs to the wall of her lair. 'Do these shackles not tell you everything you need to know?'

Buckler's large, snake-like eyes narrowed at the sight of the chains. 'It doesn't have to be this way.'

'If this is the point where you're going to attempt to convince me to fight for the insects of this world, then save your breath. If you couldn't persuade me on the dozen occasions you've tried before, what, apart from your stupidity, makes you think I'll change my mind now?'

For a moment, Maddie thought Buckler was going to attack. He tensed his forelimbs, his claws scratching the flagstones, scoring them deeply. The temperature in the cavern rose as smoke emerged from his open jaws. Blackrose laughed, and this time the cavern echoed with the thundering sound. Buckler lowered his head, calming himself, as Maddie crept away from the area between the two dragons.

'For a start,' he said, 'you would be free to fly again, every day. I kill greenhides for the people of the City, it's true, but for most of the time I can fly where I will, for as long as I wish, and feel the air over my wings. Don't you miss the clouds, and the stars? The rain? Seeing the frost on the ground shimmer a hundred feet below you? And the killing is good. The greenhides have no nets or spear-throwing ballistae; they don't even possess the capacity to make simple bows. And the people, they're grateful for what I do. I have all the food I require, and company, and an airy, warm lair. They even built me an eyrie, from where I can see almost the entire City. They treat me like a king.'

'You are a slave!' Blackrose roared, making Buckler flinch back a yard. 'A pampered pet, a tail-wagging poodle begging treats from your master for performing tricks for him. You are no dragon; you are a disgrace to the name. If the high dragons of our home were to see the way you have abased yourself for these worthless humans, they would rip you limb from limb.'

'*Your* home,' Buckler said. 'It was never mine. I have never seen the home you talk of. You are blaming me for not living in a manner that I have never known. I was born in chains, and raised as a slave-mercenary, but I am still a dragon. You, though, are a coward.'

Blackrose pushed her head through the gate, her teeth bared as her jaws opened. Buckler faced her, and adopted the same pose, and the two dragons stared at each other, separated by a few feet. Hilde grabbed Maddie's arm and pulled her back.

There was a roar of fire as Blackrose sent flames out to engulf Buckler. His neck darted forward, and his jaws closed on the older dragon's left shoulder. Blackrose let out a roar of pain, and brought her right forelimb down, its claws ripping deep scratches across Buckler's left flank.

'Stop!' yelled Maddie, running out towards them, her hands waving in the air.

Blackrose's forelimb was still raised, and it swung towards Maddie before the dragon had even glanced at her. At the last second, the claws were retracted, but the force of the blow sent Maddie flying across the length of the cavern. She crashed into the floor and skidded and bumped another few yards before coming to a halt. She opened her eyes but could see nothing, and her chest and limbs were screaming in agony. She tried to move her legs, but nothing happened. Someone was calling her name, but her mind fell into oblivion before she could tell who it was.

She awoke in her own bed, her head throbbing with a dull pain. She felt groggy and nauseous, and half of her body seemed to be wrapped in bandages or strapped to splints. She took a breath, and her chest heaved in agony.

'Malik's ass,' she groaned.

Captain Hilde lifted her head from the chair where she had been reclining. Her eyes widened and she rushed over. 'Don't try to move.'

'Water.'

'Sure; of course,' Hilde said as she glanced around. She reached out and picked up a mug from the small bedside table. 'Here.' She held it out so Maddie could take a few sips. 'The good news is; you're alive! Hurrah. I really thought Blackrose had done it again, though yours would have been the first accidental death so that's something, I suppose.'

'Being alive is good,' said Maddie; 'what's the bad news?'

'You can still talk. Only joking, that's good news as well, of course. I look forward to hearing all of your many irritating questions while you convalesce. The real bad news is that your recovery may take some time. Your left leg's broken in two places, as is a bone in your left forearm. That was from hitting the floor. You've also broken several ribs, and your collar bone; that was from Blackrose hitting you.'

'What happened to Buckler? Is he alright?'

'Not really. They separated after you were almost killed, and he went back to his lair, dripping blood along the way from that wound she gave him down his flank. I doubt he'll be in the air for a few days after that.'

'Was he not burnt as well? I remember fire.'

Hilde shrugged. 'Dragons are very resistant to fire. It would have hurt, but it didn't do any lasting damage. To seriously wound, they use their jaws and claws against each other. Blackrose took a nasty bite to her shoulder, and you saw what her claws did to him. You were lucky; if she hadn't retracted her claws when she swung at you...'

'Why did she?'

Hilde sat on the edge of the bed. She glanced down at Maddie, and moved a strand of hair that had fallen over her face. 'Apart from me, in the last ten years you're the only person she's known for more than a few days.' She smiled. 'I guess the old lady has a heart after all.'

# CHAPTER 12

# THE LEOPARD AND THE
# HONEYBEE

Roser Territory, Auldan, The City – 10<sup>th</sup> Izran 3419

Dust was rising along the entire length of the road that ran from the suburbs of Tara to the ancient castle of Torwood on the Union Walls. It was a six-mile march from the first town of the City to the fort; the first three miles of which traversed a built-up area of streets and buildings, while the second half was through the peaceful fields and farms of Outer Tara.

Daniel and his company moved to the side of the road as another pony-carriage trotted by, carrying high-ranking officers to the castle. As a junior officer, Daniel was marching with the regular soldiers of his regiment, and his sole duty was to ensure none of them absconded along the way. He wasn't worried about the prospect of that; judging from their faces, the Taran militia were keen to get involved in what was developing into a crisis in Medio. Daniel didn't know much about what was going on. He had heard the rumours of riots in the Circuit, and knew that the governing authorities of the Sander tribe had officially requested assistance, but no explicit orders had been given, except to report with his company to Torwood along with the other regiments that had been called up.

Wheat fields stretched out on either side of the road, their stalks still green in the warm sunshine. Any spare water was directed to the irrigation channels, and the road was a dry, dusty mess, trampled by the boots of hundreds of militia over that day and the previous one. On their left, the wheat fields were coming to an end, replaced by enormous paddocks holding the herds of Roser ponies, while on their right the fields extended to the base of the Sunward Range of hills. The lower slopes were crowded with terraced olive groves and orchards, while the higher land was reserved for the great vineyards and estates that produced the finest wine in the City. Only a tenth of Roser territory was built-up, the lowest proportion of any tribe except the Icewarders, but as most of their land consisted of the barren mountains of the Iceward Range, it was hardly a fair comparison. Nowhere else in the City had such an abundance of green spaces and quiet meadows; woods, glades and gentle hillsides where one could walk and not see anyone else for an hour; the contrast with the concrete slums of the Circuit could not be starker. With half of the City's food supply coming from the Cold and Warm Seas, the other half had to be grown somewhere, and Daniel knew he was lucky to live in a place that seemed almost rural within the heart of the vast metropolis.

He halted and turned to gaze back down the road, making sure his company was keeping together in marching formation. The soldiers' eyes avoided him as they passed. To them, he was just another useless aristocratic officer, untried and junior; a liability to their cohesion rather than of any benefit. He didn't care; he felt much the same way about his own commanding officers. All he could do was his job, and make sure the same number of troopers returned to the base in Tara when the mission was over as set out in the first place.

In the distance, he saw another junior officer leading the next company along the road, but he had no desire to wait to speak to them. Since his confrontation with Gaimer, his peers had avoided him as his reputation had altered in a few well-aimed punches from mummy's boy to reckless thug. No one had taunted him since then, Gaimer's broken jaw had made sure of that, but none had said a friendly word to him either. Even Todd had been distant, though whether it was due to peer pressure or the fact he was genuinely disgusted by Daniel's behaviour was unclear.

He turned back to the road ahead and continued the march. Each trooper was weighed down by the huge amount of equipment they had been issued with; not only weapons and clothes, but tools, tents, cooking utensils and enough food and water for several days. Their shields and mailed armour were strapped to their packs along with their helmets, and many were sweating under the hot sun of Izran. Daniel was fortunate; his equipment had been put onto the back of a wagon and would be awaiting him in his new quarters, wherever they were.

The line of the Union Walls grew steadily closer as they marched. It was the most dilapidated section of the ancient defences, and had seen no major repairs in centuries. As the land it straddled had Rosers on one side and Sanders on the other, many had even campaigned for a two or three mile stretch to be demolished, to allow the two neighbouring tribes more freedom to move between the two territories.

Conversely, Torwood Castle had been renovated several times, and was kept in a high state of repair; and Daniel noticed its tall towers as they approached. Roser and Sander standards were flying high from the battlements; the black leopard and the honeybee. In many ways, the Sanders were seen as a junior branch of the Rosers, and their family and trading connections went back to the younger tribe's foundation. Formations of Taran troopers were standing in the open areas by the Roser side of the massive fortress, waiting for officers to assign them to their positions. A captain on the road signalled to Daniel as his company arrived in front of the gatehouse.

'Report, Lieutenant.'

'Third Company of the Queen's Own, ma'am.'

'And you are?' the captain said as her eyes scanned a scroll.

'Lieutenant Daniel Aurelian, ma'am.'

She glanced up at him, and he could see that she was debating whether or not to make a comment about his name. 'Park your company somewhere close by where I'll be able to see them, Lieutenant, then make your way inside. The Major-General is expecting you.'

'Yes, ma'am.' Daniel saluted, then walked back to his troopers. He found the company's sergeants and gestured to them.

'Sir?' one said as they gathered by him.

Daniel glanced at them, seeing the contempt they held for him in their eyes. 'I've been told to go inside, presumably for our orders, so sit tight out here for now.' He glanced around and saw a clear space fifty yards away. He pointed. 'Over there will do. Don't let the troopers wander off; I might need to find you again in a hurry.'

'Yes, sir.'

He turned away and strode towards the gatehouse. The entrance was heaving with troops and wagons, and he squeezed past. Another captain was directing traffic beyond the gates, and he pointed over to the tall keep when Daniel asked where he should go. He approached the keep and entered through the guarded gates. The ground floor was bustling with staff officers and porters carrying luggage and crates, and Daniel ascended a series of stairs until he reached the top storey, where an orderly directed him to the commander's briefing room. He knocked and entered, coming into a crowded hall packed with officers. Maps were spread out over tabletops, and were hanging from the high walls.

'Can I help you?' said a colonel.

'Yes, sir. I was asked to report to the Major-General.'

'Every arriving officer is directed up here.' He gestured to a clerk, who handed him a thick folder. 'Name?'

'Lieutenant Daniel Aurelian, sir.'

The colonel chuckled. 'Ah, so we have been blessed by the presence of a great and noble Aurelian, have we?'

'It seems so, sir.'

He skipped through the pages of the folder until he found what he was looking for. 'Come with me.' He walked over to a large table, where a map of the sunward half of Medio was displayed. Daniel gazed down, noting the thick black lines marking the Union and Middle Walls, and a red line that showed the frontier between Evader and Sander territory.

'Let's see now,' said the colonel, as he glanced between the folder and the map. 'You have been assigned to patrol and guard this section of the border here,' he said, pointing at a stretch of the thick red line.

'Which officer am I under?'

'Captain Hallern is in overall command of the sector, but you shall be personally leading a detachment of forty troopers from your company. Is that a problem, Lieutenant?'

'No, sir.'

'Very good. Well, what are you waiting for? Take your detachment and go.'

'May I ask, sir, what are our objectives?'

The colonel gave him a scathing glance. 'Haven't you been briefed on the situation?'

'No, sir.'

'Damnation, I haven't time for this nonsense,' the colonel muttered. 'Very quickly, then; our position is that we, the Taran militia, have been asked to reinforce the frontier between the Evaders and the Sanders. Your objective, Lieutenant, is to prevent the recent troubles from spilling over into Sander territory. No one is allowed to cross the frontier from the Circuit without the express permission of Captain Hallern. You and your troopers will be quartered in local Sander housing on the frontier, and the length of border you are responsible for stretches for, let me see...' He paused as he scanned the map. 'About a quarter of a mile, I'd say. Now, get your Aurelian butt out of here and make your way to Captain Hallern's command post. Check in with him before moving onto your quarters, understand?'

'Yes, sir. What about my equipment and baggage, sir?'

'I'll have it transported to your location by wagon before the end of the day.'

'Thank you, sir.'

The colonel turned away and began speaking to someone else, so Daniel took that as his signal to go. He retraced his steps down and out of the keep, then shoved his way through the press of people and carts in the fortress's marshalling yard. He had to wait as a huge wagon made its way into the fort, then he hurried through the gates and emerged back onto the road outside Torwood Castle. He glanced over to where he had told the company to wait, and saw a far fewer number of troopers sitting or standing on the dusty ground. He frowned and walked over.

'Where's the rest of the company?' he said to the nearest sergeant.

'The other officers from the regiment have already been and taken most of the squads, sir.'

Daniel frowned as he glanced at the troops he had been left with. It was a mixture of the youngest recruits, with a smattering of very old hands. Two sergeants were present, along with thirty-four troopers.

'Get them on their feet, Sergeant; we have another couple of miles to walk.'

---

Daniel led his detachment back through the packed castle. At the gatehouse at the far end, the guards let them pass, and they emerged into Medio. Torwood was located at the junction of three tribes. On the Auldan side, all of the territory belonged to the Rosers, but on the Medio side, the frontier between the Evader and Sander tribes ran practically from the fort's entrance. A wide road led off in a straight line, with a deep ditch on the iceward side of it. The road was busy with troops and wagons, and Daniel led his detachment to a quiet spot by the ditch. He had the sergeants line them up in a double column as he waited.

'Troopers,' he said to them once they were in position, 'in case any of you were wondering; yes, that's the Circuit behind me.' He gestured to the vast sprawl of grey concrete rooftops and narrow alleys, the sky above hazy with smoke. 'The ditch marks the frontier, and we are going to be patrolling a section of it. Take a good look. Despite whatever you may feel, the Evaders are not our enemy, and I want no action taken that will inflame the situation. Treat the civilians with respect, and carry out your duty, and we will be back in Tara as soon as the current troubles die down. Any questions?'

The troopers and sergeants had barely acknowledged that he was speaking, and none seemed motivated to ask a question.

'Very well,' he said. He glanced at the sergeants. 'Captain Hallern is based in an old dance hall about two miles from here; lead on.'

The sergeants nodded, and the two columns began moving again, marching along the wide road, with every step taking them further from Tara. Both sides of the road were built-up, but the houses on the Sander side were large and spacious, with red-tiled roofs and gardens, while the concrete sprawl on the Evader side was filthy, cramped and chaotic. The ditch was over-grown in places, and half-filled with building debris and garbage, and everywhere, watching them, were pairs of eyes. Children in dirty, torn clothes stared at them from alleyways, or from the flat roofs of houses. A stone flew at them, arcing over the ditch and bouncing off the paved surface of the road.

'Taran scum!' a voice cried, though Daniel couldn't make out the source. One of the sergeants glanced at him, but he shook his head. They were only a few hundred yards from Torwood Castle, and he didn't want his detachment getting mixed up in anything until they had reached their position.

They arrived at a crossing point, where a thick bridge spanned the ditch. It was guarded by a unit of Sander militia, their black uniforms trimmed in yellow. A barrier had been erected on the bridge, refusing passage to a large number of Evader citizens gathered on the other side. Families with dust-smeared children stood or sat next to over-loaded carts; their flight from the riots halted at the frontier.

Daniel's detachment marched past without stopping at the bridge, and continued along the road. Sander and Taran militia were present in large numbers, lining the ditch and constructing tall, wooden watch-towers. The amount of smoke in the air increased as it drifted sunward from the fires raging in the Circuit. After a further twenty minutes, Daniel reported to Captain Hallern, a gruff man who had set up his headquarters in an old dance hall. Daniel received a hastily-drawn sketch of the area his detachment had been assigned, a list of addresses, and was sent on his way. He and his troopers set off again, the soldiers grumbling and cursing about the weight of their packs in the summer heat. They reached a stretch of frontier with a crossing point, and an officer from the Sander militia approached.

'Are you Lieutenant Aurelian?' he said, his accent sounding rustic to Daniel's ears.

'I am, sir.'

'Excellent. This bridge, and the frontier for two hundred yards on either side of it, are now under your authority. Good luck.' He turned and gestured to his black-garbed militia. 'The Tarans are here, finally. Let's go.'

The Sander soldiers pulled back from the makeshift barricade blocking the bridge, and from their positions along the ditch. They eyed the Tarans, some with wariness, others with relief, and they pulled back to the road and began marching away.

'Your orders, sir?' said one of Daniel's sergeants.

Daniel gazed along the ditch, taking in the arrangement of buildings on either side. The alleys and streets of the Circuit opposite presented a vast, grey mass of potential trouble, and he frowned.

'Sir?'

'Split the detachment into two columns; just as they marched here. One sergeant takes each half. Your column will be on duty first; have your troopers dump their packs on the road, and get them kitted up for sentry work. I want you and another six on the bridge, and the rest spaced out along the ditch.'

'Yes, sir.'

Daniel turned to the other sergeant and handed him the list he had received from the captain. 'Have your column take their own packs to these addresses, then I want them back here to collect the rest of the detachment's things. I expect you to allocate the quarters fairly, Sergeant; we may be here for a while.'

'Yes, sir. Which address will you be wanting, sir?'

He glanced at the buildings on the Sander side of the road. 'I'll take a room in the one closest to the frontier, and I want a sergeant in the same building.'

'Yes, sir. Will you be coming with us?'

'No, I want to take a closer look at the crossing.'

The sergeants saluted and got to work. Daniel strode towards the bridge. It was made of the same concrete as the entire Circuit seemed to be, and jumped the ditch in a single span. Halfway across was a heap of debris that had been piled into a barricade. On the other side, at least a hundred Evaders were gathered. Some had carts or luggage, but many seemed younger and were staring at the Taran militia with rocks in their hands. Daniel stepped onto the bridge and approached the barrier. Beyond, the Circuit seemed to stretch away forever. He had seen it once before, on a trip to Port Sanders, but it had been in the far distance, just a grey smudge on the horizon. He shook his head at the sight. Two hundred and fifty thousand Evaders lived within an area of just a few square miles, sealed off in every direction by walls, ditches and canals.

He heard someone by his right shoulder. 'What's your name, Sergeant?'

'Monterey, sir.'

'And the other one?'

'Hayden.'

'Do you see the way they're staring at us?'

'Yes, sir.'

'I've a feeling they're planning something to welcome our arrival, but what in Malik's name do I know? They didn't cover this in the Taran Military Academy.'

The sergeant said nothing.

'If rocks start to fly,' Daniel went on, 'I want no retaliation. No loosing crossbows, and no throwing the rocks back. Many of them look to be no more than children.'

'And if they attempt to cross the ditch, sir?'

Daniel frowned, and tried to remember anything from his years of training. 'If there's only a handful, we'll arrest them; a dozen or so, we'll loose a couple of crossbows and try to disperse them; and if there's hundreds of them, then we run for it.'

'Are those tactics from the academy, sir?'

'Nope, I just made them up on the spot. You have any objections?'

The sergeant saluted. 'Of course not, sir.'

'It was an honest question, Sergeant, not a reprimand. This is new to me, and if you have any suggestions that will help, I want to hear them. This detachment's been saddled with the most inexperienced lieutenant in the company, and most of the troopers look fresh out of school. As well as fulfilling our orders, I would very much like to get all of us out of here alive, and I'd also prefer we didn't massacre a bunch of civilians at the same time.'

The sergeant frowned. 'You might not be able to do all of those things, sir.'

'I know, that's why I'm asking for your opinion.'

'You're the officer, sir.'

'Fine,' Daniel said, turning away. 'I'll do my best, and then after-wards you and the other sergeants can complain about all the mistakes I made. I just hope that some of the detachment is still alive by that point.' He glanced down at the barricade. 'I do want this barrier replaced though, with something a bit more sturdy. A brick wall with a few crossbow loops would be ideal.'

'You get me the bricks and mortar, sir, and we'll get that built for you.'

Daniel frowned, and walked away from the barrier. Back on the main road he scanned the wide ditch, noticing how far apart each of his sentries were as they stood on the roadside facing the Circuit. They needed three or four times their number to adequately secure the ditch; if a mob rushed them, they would have no chance. He found a low wall in a patch of shade and settled down onto it, stretching his legs out as he kept watch over his new domain.

The first stones arrived at sunset, hurled by a growing gang of youths on the other side of the ditch. They skittered off the road, or thwacked against the troopers' shields. Daniel stirred from the stone wall where he had been sitting for hours in the shadows.

'Stay in line!' he cried. 'Do not retaliate.'

The sergeant and a few of the troopers looked round in surprise at him, as if they hadn't realised he had remained close by all afternoon. A stone ricocheted off the paved slabs by his feet as he strode across the road. He had no shield, and wasn't wearing his heavy, mailed armour, but he wasn't going to show fear in front of his troopers. He approached the bridge, where the Taran militia were holding their shields out.

'I advise you get your head down, sir,' said Sergeant Monterey. 'It seems you were right about them putting on a welcome for us.'

Daniel ducked behind the barrier, his eyes trained on the crowd. 'Send a runner back to Hayden; tell him to send half a dozen of his column's troopers up here as soon as he's able.'

'Yes, sir,' the sergeant said. He turned to one of the soldiers next to him and passed on the orders.

More youths were gathering among the deep shadows of the Circuit. There was an inexhaustible supply of rubble and debris for them to throw, but none of them had yet tried to enter the ditch. From the left, a cry rose into the air, and Daniel twisted his neck to see. A trooper was down, her hand clutching her leg. He ran out before the sergeant could say anything, and sprinted up the side of the ditch. The crowd whooped and began aiming at him, an easy target, as he raced by the roadside. A rock bounced by his foot, and another glanced off his right arm as he dodged and weaved. He reached the trooper and hoisted her shield into a position that covered them both as he crouched by her.

'Can you walk?'

'I don't think so, sir; I took a sore one on the ankle.'

He pushed his back against the shield and pulled the strap over his head as the rocks rained down on them. He put his left arm under the trooper's shoulder and hauled her up as he stood, the shield rising to protect them. With the trooper in his grip, he rushed across the road, and pulled her behind a brick wall on the other side.

'Soldiers are coming from our quarters,' he said to her as she sat up against the wall. 'One of them will take you back there. Get your ankle checked out, and rest. I'm going to need to borrow your shield for a while.'

He stood up before she could say anything, slung the shield round to his front, and ran back across the road to take up the injured trooper's space by the ditch. From the barricade to his right he saw the sergeant shake his head at him. He probably thought Daniel was an idiot, but he didn't care.

Stones bounced off the shield until Daniel's left arm was aching, then their frequency lessened as the youths started to disperse. Daniel lowered the shield and glanced around. The road was littered with rocks and half-bricks. Behind him, he saw Sergeant Hayden arrive with half of his column; the troopers running across the road.

'Lieutenant?' the sergeant said as he glanced at Daniel with a puzzled expression on his face.

'One of your column can take my place, Hayden,' he said, turning back from the ditch. 'I think your arrival might have persuaded the Evaders that they've thrown enough stones for the evening. Oh, by the way, there's an injured trooper behind that wall beyond the road.'

'I saw her, sir.'

'Make sure she gets her ankle seen to.'

'Yes, sir.'

Sergeant Monterey walked out from the bridge and gave Hayden a side-glance.

'I'm going to walk to my quarters now,' Daniel said, 'so I can get cleaned up and a bite to eat. Make sure the troopers are rotated in shifts; twelve on, twelve off; and ensure everyone gets their evening meal. Do you have the address of the building I'm in?'

'Yes, sir,' Hayden said, passing him a slip of paper.

'I'll be back before midnight.'

'Why, sir?'

'I want to spend the night out here, to get a feel for it. If the troopers have to do it, then I should too.' He glanced at them. 'I know you're thinking, "just another clueless officer", but I couldn't give a rat's ass.'

'Actually, sir,' said Monterey, 'I was thinking that you didn't do too bad, for your first day.'

Daniel narrowed his eyes for a moment, then smiled. He nodded to them, turned, and began walking across the road.

All of his troopers were alive, and they hadn't killed any civilians. His first day had been a good day.

He only hoped the days to come would be the same.

## CHAPTER 13

## UNMASKED

The Circuit, Medio, The City – 11<sup>th</sup> Izran 3419

'This is your fault, Aila,' cried Ikara as she raged from behind her desk. 'I expressly ordered you to quell the riots, and instead they've turned into the worst outbreak of trouble in a hundred years.'

'There are lots of reasons, cousin, why it's been impossible to stop the violence. Firstly...'

'I'm not interested in your excuses!' she yelled, throwing a full glass of water at her cousin's head.

Aila ducked, and watched the glass smash off the opposite wall. The gathered officers and officials in the chamber remained silent, their heads bowed.

'I need more troops,' Ikara groaned; 'the casualty list grows every day...' She stared at Aila again, her eyes tinged with fear. 'What do the rioters want? Surely you must know that?'

'They have a list of demands, cousin.'

'Why is this the first time I've heard of a list?'

Aila frowned. 'I, eh, put the list on your desk some days ago. You told me you would read it and get back to me.'

'You're lying,' said Ikara, her lips turning into a snarl. 'I've never seen this list; I don't know what you're talking about.'

'They want Princess Khora to resign her leadership of the City,' said a voice from the crowd of officials; 'along with all of her children.'

Ikara half-rose from her chair. 'Those ungrateful... After all we've done for this place... They deserve to hang, the lot of them.' She sat again, putting her head in her hands. 'I'm going to have to request more assistance; more reinforcements, from the other tribes.'

Some of the officers glanced at each other. 'Is that wise, ma'am? If foreign tribal troops enter the Circuit, it might inflame the situation more.'

'Foreign?' Ikara snapped. 'Are we not all part of the same, happy City? Soldiers from Tara or Dalrig aren't foreign; they're your fellow citizens.'

Aila coughed. 'I'm not altogether sure, cousin, that every Evader sees it that way.'

'Anyone who doesn't is a traitor; simple as that. Does any mortal in this room believe that the, say, Rosers, are a foreign people?'

No one spoke.

'Excellent,' Ikara went on, daring anyone present to meet her eyes. 'Then there will be no objections if I were to ask the beloved God-Queen of Tara if she could spare some soldiers? Or my most noble mother of Pella? A few Dalrigian legions would help, no?'

The group of mortals kept their eyes on the rug. Aila sighed. Her cousin was making a terrible mistake, but would only dig her heels in if Aila tried to reason with her.

'I'll do it tomorrow, unless...' Ikara swung her eyes to Aila. 'Dear cousin, you have until tonight to end the riots, or I'm going to ask Tara, Dalrig and Pella for troops, do you understand?'

'Yes, ma'am.'

'Dismissed, all of you; you make me sick.'

The officials crowded round Aila as soon as they had left the chamber, clamouring to know what she was going to do to end the riots that night.

'Don't worry,' she said to them; 'I'm heading out now. I've got a plan.'

'Praise Malik!' said one of the officials, raising his eyes skyward.

'Why?' she said. 'Is he coming to lend a hand?'

The officials stared at her for a moment as she brushed her way past them. She turned for the stairs to the entrance hall, and hurried along, leaving the group behind her. She had a plan all right; one that involved the Blind Poet and a barrelful of brandy.

———

It took her twenty minutes to get from the palace to the shabby streets where the Blind Poet lay. A riot had passed through the neighbourhood a few nights previously, but the area had been quiet since. She sighed in relief as she saw light trickle from under a set of shutters; she had a dread that, one of these days, she was going to turn up in front of a burnt-out shell.

*You see me as Elsie, the swine-trader.*

She knocked on the door and waited. Things had changed since the riots had torn the Circuit apart and left half of it in smoking ruins, and people were wary and scared. A slot in the door opened and a pair of eyes peered through. Aila heard the sound of a few bolts sliding free, and the door swung open.

'Evening, Elsie,' said Dorvid, the husband of Nareen, the tavern-keeper. He beckoned her inside, his left hand clutching a two-foot iron bar.

'Evening,' she said as she walked in. The bar was almost deserted, as few liked to be out when a riot could come their way. Nareen was standing behind the bar, drying a row of glasses.

'Elsie, it's been a while,' she cried; 'I feared the worst. I even said a prayer to Yendra and the Three Sisters.'

'I've been sitting in my little apartment,' Aila said, taking a seat at the bar, 'dying for a drink but, well, riots, eh?'

'Your usual?'

'Aye, ta.'

A broad smile spread over Nareen's face as she filled the tankard with ale. 'I have some pretty amazing news.'

'Can it wait, Nareen?'

The tavern-keeper gave her a hurt look.

'Sorry, but I've got a raging headache, and I'm really only after a quiet drink.'

'Suit yourself,' Nareen said, passing her the full tankard. 'Maybe you'll be more talkative after a few ales.'

'Aye, maybe,' she said, picking up the tankard and getting off the stool. She spotted a dark alcove in the corner of the tavern and took a seat in the shadows by a table. She sipped the ale and tried to relax, but felt guilty about the way she had brushed off Nareen. She just wasn't in the mood for the trivial nonsense most mortals found so important. So-and-so was having a baby, or was getting married to her second cousin, twice removed. You'll never guess what happened to old George, he fell down the stairs! All of it; pointless. The mortals lived, aged and died so quickly it was becoming a blur to Aila. No, it had always been a blur, but in the past she hadn't cared about the mortals. Did she care for them now?

Some of them. Over the long years, she had developed a few bonds with mortals; friends, occasional lovers, but it always ended the same, with her unchanged, and the mortal growing old and dying, leaving Aila bereft and grieving. The other gods and demigods had hardened their hearts to this sad reality a long time before, if indeed some of them had possessed a heart to begin with.

Dorvid brought over a fresh chestnut ale for her every time she finished the one she had, but the alcohol made no difference to her foul mood. A few customers came and went, and Aila hardly noticed when a loud knock came from the front door. Dorvid grabbed his iron bar and went to the little shutter at the entrance. He grinned and opened it, sliding the bolts free.

A very tall man walked in, with two shorter, more normal-sized people at his side.

'Hey, Nareen!' he called over. 'You're looking good this evening. Line up the drinks, hen; you up for another all-nighter?'

Aila glanced at the tavern-keeper, and much to her surprise she saw the older woman blush and giggle. Nareen giggle? What in Malik's name could possibly make Nareen giggle?

The tall man approached the bar and lowered himself onto one of the stools, which looked tiny under him. He stood again, smiling and shaking his head. 'My ass feels like it's too close to the floor; you got any bigger seats?'

Aila kept to the shadows of the alcove, watching the man and trying to place him. His face seemed familiar...

'Here you go, son,' Nareen said, placing the first three ales before the new arrivals. 'The brandy'll just be a second.' She flashed her eyes at Aila. 'See, Elsie? This is what I was trying to tell you earlier; look who I've got as a customer!'

The tall man turned to peer into the shadows of the alcove.

Malik's beard, she thought, it was Corthie Holdfast.

'Elsie?' he said, a strange look on his face. 'Is that not...?'

Aila stared at him, a panic starting to rise inside her. 'Aye, my name's Elsie. You got a problem with that?'

'Eh, no, I suppose...' he said, winking at her. 'Elsie.' He turned back to the bar, laughed, then downed his ale in one. 'That was beautiful, Nareen; I think I love you.'

A few of the regulars wandered over to the bar to see what the fuss was, and Aila watched as Corthie shook their hands, and engaged them in conversation. What was he doing in the Blind Poet? Wasn't it meant to be her secret place? She started to feel a little jealous. This was her territory, not his. Did he think he could just walk in and take over? She simmered with anger as she watched him smile and laugh with the locals.

She finished her beer and decided to leave, her night ruined. Something was niggling at her though; the way Corthie had looked at her, as if he had seen through her illusions and realised who she really was. No, that was impossible. Her powers worked on everyone, even the God-King and God-Queen.

There was a thump on her table and she looked up to see Corthie plant himself onto a seat in the alcove opposite her, a full bottle of brandy and two glasses laid out before him.

'What do you want?' she said, her eyes narrow as she edged back in her seat.

'I'm curious,' he said as he filled the two glasses. 'Something's bugging me. I already knew that you drank here, your cousin told me, but how come you use a different name? Why does nobody recognise you?'

Aila's mouth dried up and she stared at his green eyes like an idiot.

'If you're too drunk to speak, that's fine,' he said. 'I hope to be joining you soon.'

'Corthie,' said the man he had come in with; 'me and Quill are getting a table. You coming?'

'In a bit. I want a minute with Elsie first.'

'Oh, I wouldn't be bothering her tonight,' said Nareen; 'she's had a foul temper since she walked in.'

Corthie narrowed his eyes and glanced from Nareen to Aila. 'Oops, have I made a colossal ass of myself?' he whispered. 'Are you really Elsie? I could have sworn you were someone else; your face... and I'm usually good with faces. But I suppose it would be a bit strange for the Adjutant of the Circuit to be drinking in here, even if Lord Naxor said that it was her favourite place, or used to be.'

Aila felt the blood drain from her features. 'Lord Naxor?'

'Aye, he brought me here a few days back, when we were on our night out. He said it was the only place in the Circuit he knew, because you... I mean, the person I, em, thought you were, had brought him here once.'

'Asshole.'

'What was that?' he laughed. 'Is Elsie calling a demigod an asshole?' He winked at her again. 'Come on, drop the act, I know who you are. You've not even bothered to change your clothes. What's getting me is that nobody else seems to realise; are you playing some sort of trick on them?'

She stared at him. 'Who do you see me as? I need you to say my name.'

He leaned in close to her ear and whispered, 'Lady Aila.'

She shuddered, partly due to his proximity, partly due to the realisation that Corthie could see through her powers. In fact, it seemed as though he was unaware she was using any powers. How could that be possible? It wasn't, she told herself. It couldn't be happening. Naxor or someone else must have told him about her powers, and this was an elaborate set-up.

'What brooch is pinned to my jacket?' she said.

He raised an eyebrow. 'You're not wearing a brooch. You have a necklace, with... a little silver dog pendant, and your hair's tied up with a black ribbon. You have a ring on the fourth finger of your right hand, silver again, with a blue stone. You have....'

Aila leaped to her feet. 'Stop!' she cried, making everyone in the tavern turn to stare.

Nareen frowned. 'Champion or no champion,' she said, 'Elsie's been a loyal customer for years, and I don't want you upsetting her.'

Corthie raised his hands. 'Sorry, Nareen, just a misunderstanding.' He turned to Aila. 'Do you want me to leave?'

She did, but her mouth seemed frozen. She sat back down again. How was this possible; she needed to know. 'No, it's fine.'

'You should know something about me,' he said, lowering his voice again. 'Powers don't have any effect. Naxor tried to read my thoughts, but he couldn't. No one can, except my sister.'

'You're resistant to the power of the gods and demigods?'

He smiled. 'Aye. So, your trick; how does it work?'

'I can make others see me as a different person, but, as you've already noticed, I don't actually change. It's an illusion. I convince their eyes that I'm someone else, and their minds accept it.'

'Nice,' he said; 'I can see how that could be useful. One question. When you brought Naxor here, did you come as Elsie?'

'No, I came as myself. It was over a hundred years before I'd even thought of Elsie. And Naxor remembered.' She shook her head. 'That boy's getting a slap in the face the next time I see him.'

'Why?'

'Because this is my place; he had no right to invite you along. What are you doing here anyway? You are aware the Circuit's burning to the ground as we speak?'

'Unexpected night off,' he said, refilling the brandy glasses, 'and out of the many taverns I went to with Naxor that night, this one's the closest, and has the best ale.'

'Yes, but the riots?'

He shrugged. 'They don't bother me. The people in the Circuit are the friendliest of any I've met in the City; they remind me the most of the folk I knew back home.'

Aila's annoyance switched to curiosity as if a lever had been pulled. 'Your home?'

'Aye, before I was taken and sold to slave-dealers.'

'And... where is your home?'

'In relation to here? I have absolutely no idea. The sun's all wrong, and the stars... there are so many. My sister would probably know. She's coming to rescue me, by the way, so I won't be here forever.'

'Your sister? Does she have powers too?'

'Not battle-vision; she's hopeless at fighting, but aye, she has powers enough to rival any of your gods.'

'And she's a mortal?'

'Aye, just like me. Why do none of the mortals here have any powers? Everyone acts like I'm the freak, but where I'm from, there are many who have powers; vision, death, flow, fire... It runs in families. My mother and father were both powerful, and my idiot brother too. My sister though, she's the greatest of them all.' He paused for a moment, his eyes drifting. 'I miss her.'

'And are there other gods in your world?'

'Aye, unfortunately. We've killed quite a few, but some were still there when I was taken. Hopefully, my sister will have got the rest of them by now.'

Aila said nothing. Could any of this be true? Was Corthie delusional, or mad? Or was he just a good liar, for he seemed honest? Other
worlds, with other gods.

'You're a demigod, right?' he said. 'How come you don't already
know this stuff?'

'I knew there were secrets; mysteries. Where the champions come
from, for a start. Naxor swore an oath to the God-King, and he's never
uttered a word to me about how he brings the champions here, or how
he... obtains them.'

'He bought me with a big bag of gold. Well, I presume it was gold; I
didn't actually look inside.'

It wasn't gold, she realised with a start. So much was beginning to
make sense.

'Can I ask something else about Naxor?' he said.

'Sure.'

'Why does he look so young? You look older than me, say in your
mid to late-twenties, and Duke Marcus is the same, but Naxor looks the
same age as me; it's weird. Kano too, looks about eighteen or nineteen. I
knew gods that looked old, or middle-aged at least, but here you all
seem so young. How come?'

She narrowed her eyes. Corthie clearly didn't know anything about
the salve, but he had already guessed that the gods and demigods were
using something to maintain their youthful appearance.

'I don't know you well enough to tell you a secret like that.'

Corthie laughed. 'Fair enough, though at least I now know there is a
secret.'

'Do you see much of my brother?'

'Kano? More than I'd like.'

Aila felt her eyes well. Damn it. She hated her stupid brother, why
would the thought of him make her cry?

Corthie glanced at her. 'Sorry.'

She wiped her face. 'He wasn't always like that. He wasn't always
an... asshole. He used to be kind, and generous, and would help
anyone.'

'What happened to him?'

'Duke Marcus.'

They sat in silence for a moment as Aila suppressed her tears. She thought back to the cheerful and happy brother she had grown up with. She had lost that version of Kano forever.

'I'll leave you alone if you want,' Corthie said; 'I didn't mean to bring you down.'

She glanced over at the table where the champion's two colleagues were sitting. 'Are your friends missing you?'

'I see them night and day in Arrowhead; they're probably glad to get some peace.'

Aila observed the way the two mortals were looking at Corthie and doubted that was true. The man was watching him as if he were a proud father, while the woman either wanted to mother him, sleep with him, or both.

She downed her brandy. 'I'd like you to stay.'

He refilled the glasses. 'Good, because I'm enjoying chatting to you. You don't seem much like the other demigods.'

'Do you not like Naxor?'

'He's alright; slippery though, as if you're never sure if he's telling you the whole truth.'

'Yeah, I know what you mean. Out of all of them, he's probably my favourite, but that's not really saying much. So, I thought the fighting on the walls never ended; how come you have a night off?'

Corthie smiled. 'Buckler's got an injury; he can't fly. The greenhides are getting harder to kill anyway, so it makes sense to leave them be for a night.'

'Why are they getting harder to kill?'

'Because they keep running away from me.'

Aila's mouth opened, and she let out a loud laugh. 'What? That's impossible.'

He shrugged. 'I have a thousand witnesses every night who would tell you the opposite. They flee as soon as I step out of the outer walls. When Buckler's fit again, I'm going to ask him to fly me out a bit further, then drop me right into the middle of them.' He chuckled. 'That'd be a laugh.'

She stared at him. Was he mad? Was it possible that he didn't fear the eternal enemy? 'How did Buckler get injured? Did he fly too low over the greenhides?'

'Nah, I don't think it was them that got him. I went down to his lair, but he didn't want to show me the wound. Seemed a bit embarrassed about it to be honest, but I caught a glimpse of it when he wasn't looking. Three deep scores down his flank, as if he'd clawed himself, though I don't think even Buckler's that stupid.'

Aila smiled. She couldn't tell Corthie about the salve, but she knew another secret. 'Come in close,' she said. 'I want to tell you something.'

He leaned over.

'There's another dragon,' she whispered.

His eyes widened and she cackled with glee. 'What?' he said. 'Where, in Arrowhead?'

'I'm not exactly sure where the beast is kept. It's another one of those deep, dark secrets of which there are so many in the City. She arrived at the same time as Buckler, but I think she refused to fly or help in any way.'

'How do you know this?'

She smiled. 'Naxor isn't always as discreet as he'd like to be. He was gushing with excitement when he brought the two dragons here, and I guess he had to tell someone. He's denied it since, right to my face if you'll believe that, but I remember.'

'What else do you know about her?'

'Nothing, sorry. Just that she's a "she", and that she won't fly.'

'I'll need to look into this,' he said. 'Thanks.'

'No problem. Why were you out with Naxor anyway?'

'He took me to Ooste, to meet his mother.'

Aila sneered and narrowed her eyes.

'Let me guess, you don't get along with Aunty Khora?'

'Not exactly. How did you find her?'

'She was busy when we arrived. Polite, but aloof, as if she had more important things to be doing than meeting a greenhide-killer. She was interested in my immunity to her powers, though; that got her thinking.'

'Listen to me, Corthie; do not trust Khora. She might seem like a reasonable sort of person, but I know what she's really like, and it's not pretty.'

'Let me guess, has this something to do with your Civil War?'

'How did you know that?'

'Naxor told me a bit about it.'

'Oh yeah? I can imagine what he would have told you; and what he missed out.'

'You were involved in it, were you?'

'You could say that.'

'Your father was a rebel leader, aye? I'm guessing you fought on the losing side.'

Aila nodded. Should she tell Corthie the truth? She had kept her mouth shut about what had happened, especially at the end of the war, but there was something about the champion that made her want to divulge every dirty little secret the City held. She downed her brandy and Corthie refilled her glass.

'Are you trying to get me drunk? I'm not going to sleep with you.'

Corthie laughed. 'A little bit presumptive of you.'

'Come on, I'm sure the girls of the Bulwark are throwing themselves at you. I bet you never sleep alone.'

'I've slept alone every night since I got here.'

'Oh, sorry.'

'Why?'

'Well, I'm guessing that the slavers must have...' She made a snipping motion with her fingers.

'Any slaver that had tried would've lost his head.'

'Are you religious, then? A virgin? Did they keep you all pure and unblemished?'

'No. There were girls in the training grounds where I was kept for four years. I had a couple of girlfriends. One, in particular, I saw for several months.'

'Yeah, what happened?'

'We drifted apart, I guess. Believe it or not, I could be quite arrogant when I was sixteen.'

'What, and you're not arrogant now?'

He shrugged. 'No, just confident.'

She glanced at him. Damn it, now she quite fancied sleeping with him, just to see what he was like. It had been a while, but her emotions couldn't bear the thought of falling in love with a mortal, and then seeing him wither away before her eyes. She shook her head and looked away.

'So, why shouldn't I trust Khora?'

Aila said nothing for a moment, as an idea formed in her head. 'Do you want to go for a walk?'

'In the middle of a riot? Alright, as long as we can take a bottle with us.'

'Won't your friends mind?'

He frowned. 'I imagine they'll insist on tagging along. They're supposed to be looking out for me; making sure I don't get into too much mischief.' He drained his glass and stood. 'Come on, let's tell them.'

He stretched his long arms then staggered. 'Oops.'

Aila got to her feet and eased her way past him. 'Remember,' she whispered, 'they still think I'm Elsie.'

'Oh aye,' he laughed, 'I'd forgotten that. Hey, Tanner, Quill. I'm going for a walk with Elsie.'

The two mortals frowned at him, while Nareen raised an eyebrow.

'You're going with Elsie? The hog-trader?' said the tavern-keeper, a jealous edge in her voice.

'Aye,' she said, 'I've some pigs I want to show him.'

Corthie started to laugh, and he stumbled into a table, sending it flying.

'Maybe we should be heading back to the Bulwark,' said the man

Corthie had called Tanner. He glanced at Elsie. 'This is not the first tavern we've been in tonight, and I think the lad's had quite enough to drink.'

'Ah, shut yer face,' Corthie said, straightening himself. 'I'm fine.' He threw some gold onto the counter. 'Any chance of another bottle, my sweet Nareen, for the road?'

Nareen fetched a fresh bottle from under the bar, and passed it to Aila, who was standing closer. 'Next time you're in,' she whispered, 'I want to hear all the details.'

Aila winked at her, and then joined Corthie as they left the tavern. Tanner and Quill got up too, and followed them out into the dark streets of the Circuit. Flames were lighting up patches of the sky in the direction of the Union Walls, and there was a low rumble that echoed off the concrete buildings. Aila started up the street and Corthie strolled by her side, swigging from the bottle.

'A beautiful night,' he said, gazing upwards. 'I still can't get over how the sky can be that colour though.'

'Yeah? And what colour's the sky where you're from?'

'It gets dark at night there; there's no colour at all. Just darkness.'

'Weird.'

'So, where are we going, Miss Elsie?'

'I want to show you something.'

'Your pigs?'

'No, not pigs. A couple of them were unpleasant at times, but even I would never have called them pigs.'

'Oh, intriguing.'

'It might explain a bit more about the Civil War.'

'I think I'd prefer pigs.'

'Tough. You asked about Khora, and I'm going to give you an answer.'

The streets were deserted, and they passed through them in peace. Aila led them round Redmarket, avoiding any sight of the palace, and through a confusing maze of alleys. They went down a narrow, almost hidden side-alley, and she stopped outside a nondescript door. She glanced at Corthie's friends.

'You two will have to stay outside.'

They looked up to the champion.

'Do as Elsie says,' he said. 'Wait for us out here.'

'But, boss...' said the woman.

'I'll be fine; you worry too much.'

Aila pushed the door open and stepped inside. Corthie followed her and she closed the door behind them. He gazed around at the small, walled garden. The trees were heavy with thick, green leaves, and the beds of flowers looked well-tended.

'I wasn't expecting this.'

'It's the Shrine of the Three Sisters. I like to come here sometimes, and remember.'

She walked forwards and sat on one of the benches, then watched as Corthie explored the garden. He got down on one knee to look at a rosebush, his fingers touching the petals and thorns; then his eyes were distracted by something against the far wall.

'Are those graves?' he said.

'Yes, three of them. The daughters of Princess Yendra; a rebel leader like my father.'

He stood, and walked over, peering down at the words engraved into the thick granite headstones.

'Kahlia, Yearna and Neara,' he read. 'Did you know them?'

Aila felt her throat catch. 'Yes.'

'They died in the Civil War, did they?'

'Yes. Princess Khora was responsible for them all.'

He nodded. 'Tell me.'

'Halfway during the war, Khora sailed to Icehaven, and murdered Princess Niomi, her own twin. Neara happened to be in the palace at the time, and died in the fire that Khora started. But that wasn't the worst of her crimes. At the end of the war, she betrayed Princess Yendra; tricked her into believing she was helping, when all she was doing was leading her into a trap. I live in Redmarket, and every night I go to sleep in Yearna's room; the woman I watched being hacked to pieces by Prince Michael on the steps of the palace. That monster may have wielded the sword, but it was Khora who tricked Yendra and made it possible.'

'I heard that Yendra was the villain; that she'd murdered Prince Michael.'

'She killed him all right; I was there. Kahlia died, struck down by Michael's death powers, but Yendra got him in the end. And all the time, Khora was watching from the shadows, and as her reward, she was given the entire City to rule.'

Corthie lay down on one of the benches, and for a moment Aila thought he was falling asleep.

'Not the entire City,' he said; 'not the Bulwark.'

'You're right; her rule ends at the Middle Walls, and she has no authority over the Bulwark. That was the God-King and God-Queen's doing. They assigned Marcus to the Bulwark and Khora to Medio and Auldan.' She shook her head. 'The two most vile people imaginable, ruling half the City each. I couldn't even begin to think up a worse scheme for the City's governance. Look, I know I was warning you about Khora, but don't even get me started on that obnoxious sack of donkey dung the duke. He's a real nasty piece of work, I...' She paused, and squinted at Corthie. The champion's eyes were closed, and his chest was rising and falling. 'You awake?'

'Aye, just listening.'

'Pass me the bottle.'

Corthie got up and sat next to Aila on the bench. He took a swig then handed her the brandy.

'You never really answered my question before,' she said.

'What question?'

'About why you haven't taken anyone to your bed.'

Corthie was silent for a moment as she slugged the brandy down. She was drunker than she had been in a long time. She knew she could surge her self-healing powers to sober herself up, but at that moment, with Corthie sitting next to her on the bench, she didn't want to be sober.

'I guess I grew up watching my brother,' he said. 'He was such an asshole to girls that I always swore I'd try not to act the same way. I suppose I want to get to know someone first, but it's been hard, because every girl I meet either throws herself at me or starts praying.' He laughed. 'I'm not sure which is more annoying.'

She eyed him. 'Not every girl.'

Corthie turned his face and his gaze met hers. 'Some are harder to impress than others.'

He moved closer to her and Aila's heart jumped. This was a mistake; she shouldn't do this; he was mortal and she couldn't allow her heart to be broken...

His lips touched hers, and she forgot everything else.

## CHAPTER 14

## THE BEST DAY OF THE SUMMER

Arrowhead Fort, The Bulwark, The City – 15<sup>th</sup> Izran 3419

'Circle round again, lizard,' Corthie cried as the wind swept through his hair.

'I am not your beast of burden, wolf-man,' said Buckler, 'and my limbs are tiring. If you insist on continuing to annoy me, I shall drop you without warning.'

Corthie glanced down as the dragon turned in the air. Buckler's fore-limbs were clutching the champion by the shoulders as he flew, and Corthie marvelled at the view of the City on one side, and the never-ending sea of greenhides on the other.

'Hey, see that big one over there on the little hilltop?'

'I do.'

'Take us in low; I want to kick the bawbag in the face.'

Buckler made a rasping noise that Corthie interpreted as a sigh, then surged downwards at speed. Corthie gave an exhilarated howl of laughter as the air rushed past. They came in low, and he aimed his steel-capped boot just as they soared over an enormous greenhide. The studded heel connected with the greenhide's face and it roared in agony as Buckler rose again.

Corthie whooped. 'That was fantastic.'

'You're a child at times, Corthie Holdfast. What am I saying? You're a child all of the time. A murderous child. You enjoy killing, don't you?'

'Don't you?'

'It is a necessary evil. Humans lust after death; I was taught this in my youth, and you are the living exemplar; the idea made flesh.'

'It's us or them with the greenhides, lizard, whether you like it or not.'

'As I said; a necessary evil. You don't have to enjoy it so much.'

'Shut up and drop me off down there, on that big boulder. All this time talking could be better spent.'

Buckler swooped down in a graceful motion, and deposited Corthie on top of the high boulder as the greenhides swarmed around. Corthie slipped the visor down on his helmet, and nodded to the dragon. Buckler soared away, leaving Corthie on the rock, his full set of fitted steel armour shining in the dawn's rays. He drew Clawhammer from over his back and hefted the weapon that the best armourers in Arrowhead had fashioned for him.

'You weren't expecting me to turn up here, were you, ya green runts!'

The swarm of greenhides turned towards him, and screams of rage rose up around the boulder. Some broke in panic, the sight of Corthie enough for them, but others scrambled up the side of the enormous boulder, their jaws snapping.

Corthie leapt into their midst, laughing as he swung Clawhammer in both hands.

---

Corthie staggered as he strode across the moat-bridge, leaking blood from a dozen places. His whole body felt drained, and the weight of the armour was bearing down on him in the summer sun. The crowds on the walls were cheering, and the rest of the Wolfpack had lined up by the gate in the outer wall to applaud him in. A shadow flitted across his path, and he waved up to Buckler, his arm aching from the effort.

'That was the craziest thing I've ever seen,' said Quill as she walked with him to gates. 'You've outdone yourself this time.'

Tanner joined him on his other side, sighing and shaking his head. 'One tiny mistake, lad...'

'I might have misjudged how far away I was when I got Buckler to drop me.'

'No kidding?' Tanner narrowed his eyes. 'You had to wade through a mile of greenhides.'

'Stop nagging me, Tanner; I'm aching, and bleeding, and I just need to sit down for a bit.'

They went through the gates to a roar of cheering voices from those assembled in the courtyard. An old man shook a large bag of gold at him.

'I'm rich, sonny, because of you!'

Corthie smiled. 'I get over a hundred, did I?'

'You smashed your own record, sonny; the best day of the summer!'

A hymn rose up from the gathered ranks of his religious followers as they greeted his passage through the courtyard. Corthie couldn't make out the words, but smiled at them anyway.

'Which way's Arrowhead?' he muttered to Quill.

She gave him a worried glance. 'Left.'

'Don't look at me like that; I got distracted out there, and lost track of where I was. And, I was half-blinded by all the smoke and flames that Buckler was spewing all over the place. I could hardly see a...'

A man ran out from the crowd, something glistening in his hand. He rushed towards Corthie and plunged a blade into his right side, between the plates of steel. The courtyard erupted into pandemonium. As Corthie sank to the cobbles, a hand clutching his side, he saw dozens of his religious followers surround the man who had stabbed him. In a flurry of frenzied blows and kicks, the man fell, his cries lost amid the cacophony of violence. Corthie felt arms pull him along the ground, and saw Quill draw her sword, fending off the jostling and surging crowds. The rest of the Wolfpack piled in, shoving the civilians out of their way and clearing a space round the champion. The courtyard felt like it was shaking from the noise of the crowds. Some were screaming out lamentations, while dozens were on their knees, tears streaming down their cheeks as they prayed for Corthie the Redeemer.

'We need to get him out of here!' yelled Quill.

'He's bleeding too much,' said Tanner, his voice low. 'We can't move him.'

Corthie tried to turn, but his vision was swimming, and his head fell back, the rim of the helmet hitting the cobbles with a crack. For some reason, his thoughts went to Aila. He pictured sitting with her in the Blind Poet, getting drunk together, and he focussed on the image, as the pain threatened to swamp him. He had liked spending time with the demigod, and had assumed he would see her again at some point, but he had been in no rush; after all, neither of them were going anywhere. But maybe not; maybe his life was ending and he would never see her again. That would be a pity, he thought, as his mind drifted into oblivion.

---

Corthie rolled over and stretched, then grimaced from the pain in his side. He opened his eyes. He was in his room in the Wolfpack Tower, and from the purple light coming in through an open shutter, it was the middle of the night. He pulled back the sheets and placed his feet onto the rug that lay by the bedside. He was naked, except for a clean pair of shorts, and there were bandages on his legs, shoulders, and a wide swathe of them over his torso. He glanced down at his right side, where the blade had entered, then staggered to his feet.

'Hey!' cried the familiar voice of Quill. She threw off the blanket from the chair where she had been sitting and rushed over. 'Get back into bed, now. Where in Malik's name do you think you're going at this time of night?'

'Up onto the roof,' he said as she escorted him back to bed. 'I fancied some fresh air.'

'I can open a window for you. Sit down. That's it. Legs under the sheets.'

'Stop fussing.'

She sat on the edge of the bed, staring at him. 'You were stabbed yesterday morning, boss; you shouldn't be attempting to get out of bed for days.' She reached under the mattress and showed him a chamber pot. 'I brought this for you. Use it. Don't get up to go to the bathroom, not until the fortress medics have cleared you.'

He frowned at the ceramic pot. 'There's no chance I'm going in that thing. I don't know what you're worried about; I'll be up in no time. Is there anything to eat? And can you get me a cold ale? And that window you were talking about...?'

Quill got up, her gaze lingering upon him for a moment. He thought she was going to say something, but she turned and walked to a window. She unlatched it, letting in the cool night air. She then went to a cabinet, lit another lamp, and began to fill a tray with food and drink.

'So who was he?'

She turned. 'The guy who stabbed you? I'm not sure. The Redemptionists didn't leave much of him behind after tearing his body limb from limb. I think soldiers are searching for his left arm; if they get it, they might be able to identify him from his tattoos.' She brought over the tray and set it down for him on the bed. 'There are all kinds of rumours. The demigods are jealous of your success, or it was ordered by a rival religious group who claims you're the anti-redeemer, whatever that is. Everybody's speculating, but no one knows.'

Corthie nodded, his mind on the food. He was always ravenous after being injured, and the more he ate, the quicker he would heal. He slurped down half a tankard of ale and wiped his lips.

'The Wolfpack are out tonight without you.'

'I guessed as much,' he said, picking up a roasted hunk of meat; 'I'll be back out tomorrow night, though.'

Quill's face flashed in anger. She clenched her fists as she rose to her feet. 'You are staying in bed, for at least three days, and then you'll be staying up here in your quarters for another three days, before me and the rest of the Wolfpack will even consider you going back out there, boss. Don't you understand? You're wearing yourself out; they're wearing you out, the idiots in command of the Bulwark. I saw the state of you this morning, and that was before you were stabbed. Out of the sixty-nine days since you first went beyond the walls, you've had two nights off. Your body can't take it; I can see it starting to break down before my eyes...' She paused as tears rolled down her cheeks.

Corthie put the hunk of meat back on the tray. 'Alright. I hadn't realised you felt that way. Look, I'm fine, I'm half Kellach Brigdomin.'

She sat down again, her eyes red. 'Half what?'

'The people I'm descended from, on my father's side. I never get sick, Quill; never catch a disease, and I can eat things everyone else finds poisonous. And we heal; not as quickly as those with self-healing powers like your demigods, but much faster than other folk. My old tutor once told me that he had a theory that the Kellach Brigdomin were bred by a god to be warriors. It's that, mixed with my mother's battle-vision that makes me who I am.' He caught her glance. 'A compromise. Three days off in total, but I'm warning you, by the third day I'll be so bored that I'll be a right pain in the ass.'

'You can still die, Corthie. You might walk around like a god, but you're not.'

'I know that, Quill.'

'Do you? Do you understand the consequences of failure?'

'Of course I do, but I'm not going to dwell on them. When I'm out there, I let my battle-vision consume me; if I stopped to think about getting killed I'd hesitate, and then... well, I'd end up being dinner for the greenhides. Let me worry about being Corthie Holdfast. So, three days, aye?'

She lowered her head. 'I'll speak to Tanner and the others.'

'When?'

'When they get back in at dawn.'

'Alright, thanks.'

She watched him as he tore through the hunk of meat. 'There's something else.'

'Aye?'

'Yeah, Tanner.'

'What about him?'

'He was... concerned about that woman you went off with from the Circuit. Elsie, was it?'

Corthie said nothing, but groaned inside. Neither Quill nor Tanner had said anything to him about how the evening in the Circuit had turned out. They hadn't seen him kiss Aila, though, he was sure about that.

'He's been doing some investigation,' Quill went on.

'It's none of his business.'

'It is if it affects us.'

'And how would me hanging out with Elsie possibly affect you?'

Quill edged away a little, as if seeing the anger rise in Corthie's eyes. 'I'm sure Tanner didn't mean any offence, boss, but that place she took you to?'

'Aye?'

'It's a rebel shrine, boss.'

'A what?'

'It's a memorial to three rebels killed in the Civil War. Apparently, the only folk who go there, or even know exactly where it is, are rebels; outlaws opposing the government of the City.'

'So?'

'Boss, you went there in the middle of the worst riots in a century. The main demand of the rioters is the resignation of the entire government of Auldan and Medio. Do you not think that might look a little suspicious?'

'I'm not planning on overthrowing the government, so, no.'

'And this Elsie woman, did she try to talk you into joining a rebellion?'

'Of course she didn't.'

'Then what were you talking about in there, boss? I mean, if Elsie was a couple of decades younger, then I wouldn't be asking these questions, but she's in her fifties at least and she's not what I would have thought was your type.'

He frowned. 'What is my type?'

'Oh, I'd imagine someone tall and buxom, with thighs that could wrestle a greenhide into submission, but don't change the subject. What were you discussing with Elsie?'

'None of your business.'

'I don't think Tanner will like that answer.'

'Tanner's not here.'

'Well, I don't like that answer, either, boss. If word gets out...'

'And how would that happen, unless you or Tanner spread it around?'

'Our lips are sealed, boss; you know that, but can we trust Elsie to keep her mouth shut?'

'I trust her.'

'Why, boss? You only just met her; you don't know what her plans are, or what her connections to the rebel movement might be. You were as drunk as I've ever seen you, and I already worry about you being led astray.'

'I'm not a child, Quill.'

'I know, but all the same, Tanner and I think you should avoid that tavern in the Circuit from now on.'

Corthie decided to keep his mouth closed. He wasn't going to tell Quill the truth about Aila, and in a way he was relieved that his two closest colleagues had misunderstood the situation. He had no idea what 'Elsie' was supposed to look like, or even what age she appeared to be, but from Quill's words he guessed that she would rather suspect him of naive treachery than believe that anything romantic had taken place between them.

'Do you agree?'

'I'll think about it.'

'No, in other words?'

'I said I'll think about; I'm committing to no more than that. Besides, with this injury, I don't imagine I'll be going out on the town any time in the next few days.'

She nodded, then lifted her eyes towards him. 'I'll let you rest, then.' She paused for a second, her gaze meeting his. 'Do you need anything else from me tonight?'

He glanced at her. Was she…? He hoped not. He liked Quill; she was a good sergeant and a loyal friend, but the last thing he wanted was to get involved with someone from the Wolfpack.

'No, thanks. I think I'll get some sleep.'

She glanced away. 'Alright.' She stood. 'I'll be downstairs in my room if you need me.'

He watched her walk from the large bedchamber, and wondered if he had made a mistake. He could do a lot worse than Quill, but sleeping with her would change everything. Aila popped into his mind, and he smiled. His sergeant had been right; he barely knew anything about the woman he had kissed at the shrine, and she wasn't any of the things that Quill had considered to be his 'type'. He was intrigued enough to want to see her again, though, even if he was going to have to wait. He pushed the tray, now filled with empty dishes, to the side, and lay down to get some more sleep.

---

'Wake up, lad.' A hand shook his shoulder and Corthie opened his eyes to the pink light of morning.

'Hey, Tanner. How was last night?'

'Fine,' said the older man. 'How are you?'

'Hungry again,' he said, sitting up on the bed. 'Did you speak to Quill?'

'Yeah. Three days, eh? You're a fool.'

'Thanks, I like you too.'

'Six days.'

'Three.

'Five?'

'No, three. I don't even need three; it's a compromise to shut you all up.'

'You're a stubborn pain in the ass at times, lad. Anyway, you've got visitors.'

'Aye, who?'

Tanner smirked. 'Pretty much the only folk we couldn't refuse entry to, lad. Arrowhead's swarming with people; they've come from all over the Bulwark after hearing about you getting injured. Soldiers are keeping them from entering the tower, but we couldn't say no to this pair.'

Corthie groaned. 'I'd rather have some peace.'

'Tough. Come on, it's not every day you get a visit from two demigods.'

'Fine. I suppose you'd better let them in.'

Tanner went to the door of the bedchamber, opened it and called down the stairs. After a few moments, Corthie heard the heavy tread of boots on the steps, then Duke Marcus entered, followed by Lord Kano.

'Good morning, champion,' said Marcus as he breezed in, a broad smile on his face. 'I'm so glad to see you sitting up. The reports were that you'd sustained a nasty wound.'

'It's not too bad, sir.'

The duke's eyes scanned the large room.

'Have a seat, sir.'

'Thank you, I will.' He gestured to Kano, who carried a chair over from the table by the window. He placed it down by the bed and the duke sat. 'I wish to express my gratitude, Pack Leader,' Marcus went on, 'in fact, not only the Bulwark, but the entire City owes you its thanks. The feats you have performed have not only cleared the moat of green-hides, but they've also inspired the citizens of the City, and put fire into their hearts.'

'Thank you, sir.'

Behind the duke, Kano's eyes shone with contempt, and a sneer was on his lips as he regarded Corthie.

'Furthermore,' said the duke, oblivious to his Adjutant's expression,

'I want to let you know that your personal security is taken very seriously. Arrowhead has always had a rather... lax attitude to civilians coming and going, but that ends now. I have ordered the commander of the fort to implement a stricter regime of control with immediate effect; it's time to crack down on some of the more fanatical elements that have been allowed to roam free.'

'That's a pity,' said Corthie; 'I like the crowds being able to see what I do.'

The duke frowned for a moment, then his composure returned. 'I understand, truly I do. One must weigh up the risks; we cannot afford to take the chance that some disturbed individual will get that close to you again, and if that means a few innocent civilians are also barred from certain areas, then that is indeed a pity, as you say.'

Corthie nodded, but said nothing.

'The attempt on your life has profoundly shocked us all,' the duke continued, 'but rest assured that no effort will be spared in tracking down those responsible.'

'Have they managed to find his arm yet, sir?'

Duke Marcus looked puzzled for a moment, then glanced up at Lord Kano.

'The would-be assassin was ripped to pieces by the mob, sir,' the Adjutant said, 'making identification nigh impossible, unless we can locate his upper left arm.'

'Ahh, for his tattoos? Now I understand.' He fell silent for a few moments. 'Leave us, Adjutant, if you would.'

Kano glared at Corthie, then saluted and walked from the bedchamber.

Duke Marcus rose. 'Do you mind if I get myself a drink?'

'Help yourself, sir.'

He walked over to a cabinet, and poured himself a brandy. 'Can I get one for you, Pack Leader? I know it's early, but you deserve it for all your efforts.'

'Aye, thanks.'

Corthie watched the duke prepare the drinks, sure that this arrangement didn't happened often. What did he want?

Marcus came back to the bed and sat in the chair. He handed one of the glasses to Corthie.

'To your health, Pack Leader,' he said raising the brandy high.

Corthie lifted his glass, then took a sip.

'I understand you've been out of the Bulwark a couple of times?'

'Aye, sir.'

'How did you find Lord Naxor's tour?'

'I liked the view over the bay at Pella.'

'Ah yes, it's a fine vista, though you should try it from Tara; it's quite spectacular.' He took another sip. 'Did you happen to see much of the Circuit?'

'A bit.'

'And what were your thoughts?'

Corthie glanced at the duke, measuring how honest he should be. 'The folk there are nice; friendly, but they live in awful conditions.'

'And would you say it is well run?'

'I don't know enough about the workings of the City to make more than a guess, sir.'

'Of course; of course. That would be natural.'

'Then why are you asking me, sir?'

'Because, my young Pack Leader, your rise through the ranks from lowly warrior to commander of the Wolfpack has earned you the right to be brought into some of the inner counsels of the Bulwark. I rely on a handful of picked Blades to assist me in the running of the land between the Middle and Great Walls, and I would like to bring you in a little closer. Do you have any objections?'

'I'm not a politician, sir; I kill greenhides.'

'And you do it with aplomb. Unfortunately, however, your responsibilities outweigh your personal feelings. Hundreds, maybe thousands of Blades look to you for inspiration and leadership. I assume you are utterly loyal to the cause?'

'I'm a soldier, sir; I do as I'm told.'

Duke Marcus smiled. 'Quite the answer; are you sure you're not a politician? However, I digress. The situation in Medio and Auldan has had me troubled for some time now. While the Blades on the Great Wall fight every day to defend this City, sometimes it seems as though the others carry on as if the threat from the eternal enemy means nothing to them. Squabbling and petty recriminations plague the six tribes that lie protected and insulated beyond the Middle Walls. Poverty and riots are the result. For nearly half a month now, the territory of the Evaders has been engulfed by disorder, and I received news a few days ago that the governor there, one Lady Ikara, has requested military assistance from the other tribes.'

Corthie frowned. 'Including the Blades, sir?'

'No, no, no. The Blades are forbidden from interfering in the politics of Auldan or Medio, our sole duty is to defend the City from the green-hides. One simply has to hope, in such circumstances, that the internal militia of the other tribes will suffice to quell the disturbances and restore calm to the Circuit. For if not...' He tailed off, frowning as if he were considering the dreadful choices that he would have to face. 'If not, then the City will once again descend into civil war, and the government of Auldan and Medio will have done the work of the green-hides for them.'

He stared at Corthie. 'If that were to occur, then I, as Commander of the Bulwark, would have some difficult decisions to make. I'll need loyal and trusted allies around me, Pack Leader. Can I rely on you?'

'Aye, sir.'

The duke gave a broad smile. 'Excellent. Well, I'll leave you to your rest. Think on what I have said. The time for hard decisions may be coming sooner than we'd all like.'

He stood, and placed his half-full glass on the bedside table.

'Thank you for visiting, sir.'

The duke smiled again. 'I wish you a speedy recovery, Pack Leader.'

Corthie watched as the commander left the room. He waited a few minutes, then got out of bed. He straightened his legs, keeping the weight off his right side, and hobbled over to the door.

'Quill!' he shouted down the stairs.

'Boss?'

'Get your ass up here.'

He heard the sound of her boots approach, and he limped back over to the bed and sat. Quill came through the door.

'Yes, boss?'

'Have they left?'

She nodded.

'Duke Marcus said some things to me, and I need them interpreted into language I can understand.'

Quill frowned as she walked over. She sat in the seat that the duke had been using. 'I'll try.'

Corthie glanced at her. 'You'll keep this quiet, right? Not a word, not even to Tanner.'

'Of course.'

He picked up the half-full glass of brandy. 'He was talking about the riots in the Circuit, and how, if they get really bad, it'll lead to a civil war in Auldan and Medio.'

'Right,' she said. 'Seems a little far-fetched, but go on.'

'He then said, if that were to happen, he would have a difficult decision to take. What did he mean?'

She chewed her lip for a moment. 'You've heard about the Civil War that happened a few hundred years ago?'

'Aye?'

'And you've heard how it ended?'

'With Princess Yendra killing Prince Michael?'

'Yeah, that's right, but Duke Marcus was involved in the last days of fighting as well.'

'Was he in charge of the Bulwark then?'

'His father, Prince Michael, had just appointed him as commander. For his first action, he ignored a thousand years of precedence, and led two divisions of Blades into the Circuit.'

'What? I thought that was banned? He told me that himself.'

'It goes against everything the City stands for. To our lasting shame, the Blades went on a day-long rampage. They put down the last remnants of the rebellion, and in the process slaughtered over twenty thousand Evader civilians.'

'Twenty thousand in a day?'

'Every Blade is a professional killing machine; the civilians had no chance. They were called off at nightfall, by order of the God-King and God-Queen, the gates in the Middle Walls were resealed, and the Blades have never left the Bulwark again.'

Corthie frowned. 'Do you think that's what he was hinting at? That if the riots don't stop, he might send the Blades through the Middle Walls?'

'I don't know Duke Marcus,' she said. 'Until you joined the Wolf-pack I'd only ever seen him from a distance, and had never heard him speak. You already know him better than I do. Trust your feelings; what do you think?'

'I think... if a civil war comes, then I need to stay out of it. I'm here to fight greenhides, that's it, not to get involved in the political bickering of a few entitled demigods.'

'I hope you're right,' she said, 'but something tells me it might not be that easy.'

# CHAPTER 15
# HEALING

Arrowhead Fort, The Bulwark, The City – 7th Koralis 3419

'I can't do it!' Maddie cried, sweat mixing with the tears in her eyes.

'You can,' said Hilde; 'just put your weight on the crutch and ease yourself up.'

After four weeks of bed-ridden recovery, Maddie's limbs felt like rubber. A splint was still securely attached to her left leg, while her left arm was in a sling; yet somehow Hilde was expecting her to hobble about on a crutch. She leaned on her right leg and pushed herself into a standing position, the crutch wedged under her left shoulder. She swayed, grunting with the effort.

'That's good,' said Hilde. 'Now, all you've got to do is walk over to the little table. Move the crutch forward, that's it.'

Maddie struggled for a few inches, easing the crutch forward, then hopping on her right foot. Pain was shooting up her left side and spine, and her ribs felt like a dragon was grasping her in its claws. She got halfway to the table and stopped, the sweat almost blinding her.

'I can't go any further, Captain; it's too sore.'

'I'm sorry, girl, but you must try. Recovery is a painful process, and it would be too easy for me to let you go back to bed. Besides, Blackrose misses you.'

'Yeah, right.'

Hilde moved over to the table and pulled out a chair, setting it down closer to Maddie.

'There,' she said, 'I've made it a little easier for you. Just get to the chair, and you'll be done for now.'

Maddie gritted her teeth, and hobbled forwards, each inch a blur of pain and exhaustion. She would never take walking for granted again, she thought; or having the use of both arms. The long days trapped in bed had felt never-ending, and she pushed herself onwards. She reached the chair, collapsed onto it, and burst into tears.

'Well done, Maddie,' Hilde cried, clapping her on the back. She passed her a hankie. 'Here, wipe that snot off your face.'

Maddie took the hankie and blew into it, then dabbed her eyes.

'Good girl. I'll let you rest for a while, before you attempt the return journey.'

'Does she really miss me?'

'Blackrose has gone through a wide range of reactions to your injury. At first she denied it was anything to do with her; that it was your fault for getting in the way. Then, a while ago, she asked where you were. I told her you were still in bed, recovering, and she seemed a little surprised. She hadn't forgotten, she'd just assumed the injuries weren't that bad. She feels guilty about that; I can see it in her eyes, though she hasn't admitted it to me. Her mood has been down ever since, that's why I want you up and about, so I can report some progress to her.'

'She feels guilty about what she did? But it wasn't her fault; I did get in the way.'

'She had her claws raised, and she knows what those things can do to us mere insects.'

'Tell her I don't blame her.'

Hilde smiled. 'I've already taken the liberty to do that, I hope you don't mind. It didn't make any difference; she feels responsible, whether you blame her or not.'

'Tell her she owes me a big favour, then. Once she carries it out, then things'll be square between us.'

'That's not a bad idea. Do you have a favour in mind?'

'No, not yet, but I'll think of one.'

'Alright. Now, onto your parents.'

Maddie groaned.

'Look, I don't begrudge looking after you, but they're your family. You should be grateful to have people who love you.'

'I don't want to go home.'

'I know, Maddie, you've told me often enough, and they know that too, but they still want to visit. You can't keep saying no.'

'Fine,' she snapped. 'I'll write to them, and tell them they can come and see me.'

'There's no need to write to them.'

'Why not?'

'Because they're waiting in a room along the hallway.'

'What? But, I said...'

'I know what you said, but I could hardly turn them away at the door. They threatened to speak to the fortress wardens if I didn't let them in, and I don't want all that attention, thank you very much.'

Maddie narrowed her eyes as she watched Hilde. The captain rarely got animated, but she seemed a little put out. 'I'm sorry. It sounds just like my family to come barging in where they're not invited.'

'Can you blame them? They got a letter telling them their elder daughter had been seriously injured. What did you expect them to do?'

'So, are you going to let them come into my room?'

'Eh, yes. You can't exactly go to them, can you?'

She glanced round at the general untidiness of the room. 'My mum's going to flip when she sees the mess. Where should I be? Bed or chair; and do I have time to sort my hair and put some make-up on? You've been hiding that mirror from me, don't think I didn't noticed it suddenly disappear; so I'm guessing I must look a right state. How many came? Was it just my parents, or...?

'Quiet, please,' Hilde cried, 'you're giving me a headache. Listen, before I go and get them, there are a few rules.'

'I thought there'd be. Don't mention the dragon is at the top of the list, right?'

'Yes.' Hilde sighed. 'Go on, then. Guess the rules; I know you want to.'

'Right, sure, em.. no dragon, no lair, remember to call you "ma'am", no crying, no complaining about the conditions, no mention of what I do here in any way...' She paused. 'What are we going to tell them that we do? And how do I explain the injuries?'

'I'm an engineer; you're my assistant. We were surveying the damaged wall by the gatehouse, and part of it fell on you.'

Maddie raised an eyebrow. 'You've thought this through.'

'Of course I did; I didn't want to spend an hour debating the details with you. Just stick to the story.'

'Will you be here?'

'I'd rather not, to be honest.'

'Well, I'd rather you were.'

Hilde glanced away, looking uncomfortable. 'Wouldn't you prefer a little privacy?'

'Come on, ma'am, don't desert me now. You know my family are going to ask me loads of questions; for example, why is repairing walls so secret that I had to swear an oath not to tell them? What am I going to say? I'm bound to start making stuff up; I'll have to. You should be here to stop me saying anything too crazy.'

'Damn it,' Hilde muttered.

'You hate it when I'm right, eh?'

'And just how am I going to stop you?'

'Let's see.. if you mention, um... the weather, then I'll know I'm about to go too far.'

'This'll never work.'

'It will. Go get them, I'm ready.'

Hilde waited.

'Sorry,' said Maddie. 'Go and get them, please, ma'am.'

The captain strode to the door. 'I'll be back in a minute.'

Maddie sat, her eyes on the door. She pulled the dressing gown closer round her with her right arm. Her left leg was splayed out straight, the skin mottled and bruised. What a disaster. If only she had been given a few hours' notice, she might have been able to smarten herself up. As long as her brother wasn't there, or her sister; or her dad. She hated people knowing she was ill or sick, and had hidden countless illnesses from her parents when she had been growing up. It was the sympathy she objected to, and that fact that they would remember seeing you at your most vulnerable.

The door opened, and her mother walked in, closely followed by her father and Rosie. Hilde came in last, and closed the door behind them.

'By the sweet breath of Amalia,' her mother said, raising her hands to her face as she saw Maddie.

'Hi, mum.'

Her mother rushed over, then paused, as if unsure which bit of her daughter it was safe to approach. She leant over and kissed her on the forehead.

'Must have been some wall,' her father said, shaking his head. 'My poor little petal...' His eyes welled a little, and Maddie watched him suppress his tears. Please don't cry; please don't cry, she muttered to herself.

Her mother turned to Hilde. 'How could you let this happen to my daughter?'

The captain frowned. 'She ignored my instructions and failed to secure the site before she began work on the wall. It was a lesson I don't think she'll forget in a hurry.'

'I knew it'd be your fault,' said Rosie. 'How many bones did you break?'

Maddie glowered at Hilde for a second, then turned to her sister. 'I see you're still an annoying little toerag.'

Rosie leaned in close, flicked Maddie's ear, then skipped back out of range.

'Quit that!'

Rosie smirked at her. 'Or what?'

'Girls, enough,' said their father. He glanced at Maddie. 'So, how many bones was it?'

'Eh, seven, I think. Maybe eight. Ribs, leg, arm.'

'And this is the room,' her mother said, 'where you've been living these last few months?'

'Yes.'

'Then tell me what's so wonderful about it that you didn't want to come home? I'm not sure which was worse; hearing you had been hurt, or hearing that you had decided to stay in your battalion quarters. Maddie, do you have any idea what you've put us through? It should have been me looking after you this past month.'

Her father put a hand on his wife's shoulder. 'It's not too late, Maddie. You still have at least another twenty days before you'll be fit again; come back with us now, we have a carriage waiting in the forecourt.'

'I can't.'

Her mother glared at her. 'Why not? Why can't you come home? Is it her? Is this officer making you stay?'

'Of course not.'

Her mother glanced at the captain with suspicion in her eyes.

Hilde shrugged. 'I've offered her the choice; she can go home if she wants, or she can stay here.'

'You should have made her go home.'

'Maddie's eighteen. I figured she was old enough to make up her own mind.'

'She's still a child.'

'She's my assistant and I'm her commanding officer; that gives me a duty of care over her as well.'

'It sounds like you've been negligent to me.' Her mother's eyes scanned Hilde's uniform. 'Captain, please order Maddie to return with us immediately.'

Hilde's eyes hardened a little. 'No.'

'It's not her fault, mum.'

Her mother turned to glare at Maddie. 'Stay out of this, girl.'

'No, I won't. Captain Hilde has told me a thousand times that I should go home, but I told her I'd rather sleep rough in the castle fore-court, and so she had to let me stay...' Maddie's mouth froze as she realised what she had just said. 'I didn't mean it like that. I...'

'I don't want to hear your excuses,' her mother said, raising her chin. 'At least we now know what you really think of us.' She turned to her husband. 'We're leaving.'

Her father shook his head at Maddie. 'Take a good, long think about what you just said, and about everything this family's done for you.'

He nodded to the captain and opened the door, letting his wife walk out before following her. Rosie was the last to leave. She shook her head. 'I'm taking your room when we get back. Mum wouldn't let me before, but I bet she does now. See ya.'

Maddie stared at the door as her sister slammed it behind her.

'Oh my,' said Hilde. She took a fresh hanky from her pocket and handed it to Maddie.

'I'm not going to cry; I'm too stunned to cry. Did that really happen? What did I say?'

'You told them you'd rather sleep rough in the forecourt than go home with them.'

'Oh. Yes. Whoops.'

'I don't get it,' Hilde said, walking over to the bedside cabinet and extracting a bottle of gin. 'Your family seems normal. Your mother was upset, but who'd blame her? Why in Malik's name wouldn't you want to go home?'

'I don't know if I can explain it.'

Hilde poured a large measure for herself, and a smaller one for Maddie. 'I'm sure you'll give it your best.'

'It's like, I feel I belong here. I know that sounds weird, because I've never felt like I've belonged anywhere before. And I know this last month's been tough, but I still felt better being here, close to... well, her, I guess. I don't want to be too far from her. Does that make sense? No, it's stupid, I can see that. It's not like I can see her or anything, so why would it matter where I was? It's just that it does matter, to me. It matters to me.'

Hilde sipped her gin.

'And now my stupid need to be near a dragon that I can't see, and who despises me anyway, has made my family think that I hate them. I told you I'd sleep in the forecourt because it would still be close to Blackrose...' She lifted the hanky to her eyes as tears rolled down her cheeks. 'Damn it. Do you know that I never used to cry before I met that stupid dragon? It was like nothing could penetrate my armour, and now everything does.'

'I feel partly responsible.'

Maddie glanced at her. 'Why?'

'What you described,' she said; 'it's what happened to me. Before Blackrose arrived ten years ago I was out-going, lively; I even had a man I was going to marry. But then I got this job, and the beast got her claws into me. Me and my fiancé drifted apart, because I started to prefer coming here, rather than being with him, and he knew it. Over time, the same thing happened with my friends, and before I knew what was going on I was alone; alone with her. I should have warned you, but I was too eager to see you settle in after so many assistants had come and, eh, gone.'

'Do you think she does it...?'

Hilde held up her hand. 'Wait. Something's wrong. The air, it's warmer.'

'Is it?' She turned as Hilde strode towards the door. 'What would make the air warmer?'

A roar rumbled through the thick walls, and Hilde broke into a run. She flung the door open and sprinted in the direction of the lair.

'What about me?' Maddie cried after her. She heard the gate to the lair swing open, and the sound of Hilde's boots fading into the distance.

She was going to have to go. Hilde might need her help. She caught herself and almost laughed at the thought. Her body was in no fit state to help anyone. Nevertheless, for some reason she found herself lodging her crutch into place. She gripped the side of the table with her good hand and pulled herself up. It wasn't too far to the lair. On a normal day she could be standing next to Blackrose in less than a minute after leaving her room. She had timed it.

She leaned to her right, moved the crutch then shifted her body forward a pace. That wasn't too hard. Just another hundred to go. Another roar came through the open door, and Maddie could hear the pain in its cry. She hurried her pace; lean, crutch, swing. Sweat began to appear under her nightshirt as she reached the door to her room. She peered out, and saw that the gate to the lair was lying open. Just a few steps to the gate, she thought. Lean, crutch, swing. Onwards, as the pain ran down her left side and the sweat started to blind her. She wiped her eyes with her sleeve as the cries from the lair rippled through her. She ignored her own pain. Blackrose was suffering, and that was all that mattered. She passed the gate without pausing, entered the lair, and kept going, her body refusing to give up.

She reached the small door cut from the massive black gate, leaned through and was nearly overcome by the rancid stench of burnt flesh. Hilde was by Blackrose, who was lying on the floor of the lair, foam at her mouth; her eyes closed. At the rear of the deep alcove where she usually slept, the chain that linked her limb to the wall was glowing red-hot, and her flank was covered with blistered scorch marks. Her jaws opened and she let out another cry of agony.

'Blackrose!' Maddie cried.

Hilde turned, her mouth falling open. 'By Malik's ass, what are you doing here?' The captain ran over to the door and took Maddie's arm as she started to sway. 'You should be in bed, girl.'

A deep groan came from the dragon. 'Bring her here.'

Hilde turned to the dragon. 'She needs to go back to bed, Blackrose; look at her. Listen, I'll be back in a minute after I take her...'

'Bring her here.'

'Fine.' Hilde turned back to Maddie, a frown creasing her lips. 'I'm not impressed, young lady. You could have seriously put back your recovery, and I need you fit. Now, take my arm.'

Maddie reached out with her right arm, and Hilde helped her over the lip of the door. The captain placed her left arm under Maddie's shoulder and supported her as they walked over to Blackrose. The dragon opened one eye a sliver and stared at her.

'Well, I brought her,' said Hilde.

The dragon didn't respond.

'Look, my arm's getting sore; I'm going to rest her against your forelimb, alright?'

Hilde edged Maddie towards the dragon's enormous limb, and Maddie stared at the claws as the captain lowered her to the floor, her back against the jet black scales. Hilde stepped away.

Maddie glanced at the red-hot chains. 'What happened?'

'She tried to burn her way through the chains again. Dragon fire's hot, but it's not that hot. I need to get back to our quarters and raid the stores for ointment and balm for her burns. Are you going to be alright on your own for a bit?'

Maddie glanced at Blackrose. 'I'm not alone.'

Hilde nodded, then turned for the gate. Maddie listened as the sound of her footsteps dwindled into nothing.

'Why did you do it?'

The dragon's eye turned to her. 'I know you're here to mock me. I wounded you, and now you have come here to be satisfied by the sight of me in agony. I hope it was worth it; I hope you are sufficiently pleased by my suffering.'

'You don't really believe that, do you?'

'I do. I am not a liar and if you think I am then you should hobble or crawl out of here now.'

'Alright then, you're mistaken.'

'Oh, how mighty you must feel right now, attempting to chastise your better. The woe of this life embitters me, but I still see and speak the truth. Perhaps I should make you do so also.'

'No! Please, let me lie. Let me keep that.'

'So you've come to the realisation that I was correct at last? You have finally accepted that your kind is beholden to lies as fish are beholden to the sea?'

Maddie shrugged. 'You have your fire and claws; we have our lies. We need them, but we don't have to use them all the time. I'm telling you the truth when I say that I'm not here to mock your wounds.'

'Then perhaps you would deign to enlighten me as to the true reason?'

'I came here because I heard your cries, and I wanted to help.'

The dragon laughed, but it wasn't a joyful sound, and Maddie shuddered.

'You could hardly help me when you were healthy; how do you expect to help me when the frailty of your body is so evident? I snapped your bones like you would snap a twig. You are broken, girl.'

'I will heal, and I can help you heal. We can heal together.'

The dragon tilted its head. 'Those burns I inflicted upon myself will heal, but there are wounds you cannot see that time is useless to repair.'

'Were you trying to escape?'

'I could escape any time I wished; you said so yourself. All I would have to do is demean myself for a few moments, pledge my allegiance to some self-important maggot, and I could lift my wings and simply... fly away. Or maybe I would turn, and send a wave of fire over the fortresses and walls of this cursed City; blast their gates open and allow the greenhides to enter. Yes, burn the tower of Duke Marcus, and raze this pit of sickness and death to the ground. Let it all burn! How the humans would flee in terror as the greenhides overwhelmed the walls; this was your desire too, wasn't it, girl? Close your eyes and picture it in your mind; the annihilation, the destruction, the glory.'

'That's not what I want,' Maddie said, her voice sounding weak and thin next to the dragon's.

'Lie to me then, go on. Tell me a human lie.'

'No, I won't. I want to help you, that's the truth.'

'There is only one way you could help me, but you are too weak.'

'How?'

'By helping me end my life.'

Maddie's eyes widened.

'As much as I feel the shame of the words as I say them,' the dragon said, 'I cannot achieve it on my own. I cannot burn myself, or claw myself, as my skin is too thick, and it heals too quickly. However, if you weren't lying, and you truly wish to help me, then help me end it.'

'I'll never help you do that.'

'So, you were lying.'

'No, I wasn't. Ending your life isn't helping you.'

'And who are you to judge what I consider to be helpful?'

'I'm Maddie Jackdaw, and I judge things the way I see fit.'

The dragon paused for a moment. 'Maddie Jackdaw?'

'It's my name, you ninny, and that's the first time you've said it since I met you.'

'It's a foolish name.'

'So's Blackrose.'

'That is not my real name, you silly girl.'

'Oh yeah, what is it then?'

'And what makes you think I would tell you?'

'Is it a secret? Are there no humans you tell it to?'

'The only two-legged mortal a dragon gives her name to is the one she chooses to ride upon her, Such, anyway, were the traditions of my world.'

'That's a coincidence.'

Blackrose glared at her for a moment. 'Fine. What is?'

'That's the favour I was going to ask.'

'What favour? You're mistaken, girl; I don't owe you anything.'

'You broke eight bones in my body; I say you do.'

The dragon paused, and swung her head away. Maddie glanced up at her, seeing the black scales shimmer in the lamplight of the lair. Beautiful and brutal, elegant and savage, all at the same time.

'Perhaps you are right.'

Maddie's heart leapt. 'I am?'

Blackrose lowered her head, her long neck turning in a sinuous curve to bring her eyes level with Maddie's face.

'Perhaps I do owe you a favour.'

'Then I want to ride upon your back.'

Blackrose opened her jaws and laughed, her breath blowing through Maddie's hair. This time, she noticed that the dragon's laughter lacked the spite and venom that had filled it before.

'What's so funny? A favour's a favour; you can't get out of it.'

The dragon's laughter stopped, and she made a noise that sounded to Maddie like weeping. That can't be right. Dragons don't cry.

The dragon lowered her head and laid it on the ground. 'Maddie Jackdaw. You ask for something that I cannot give. I know what you're doing; you're trying to distract with favours and names and your endless questions. There's nothing for me here but this prison cell, and these chains. Give me one good reason why I should choose to live rather than die.'

Maddie tried to smile, but her heart was breaking. She leaned back into the dragon's limb. 'I don't have an answer, Blackrose, unless "because I love you" counts as one.'

# CHAPTER 16

# ACCEPTANCE

The Circuit, Medio, The City – 8th Koralis 3419

Daniel walked down the line of troopers, checking they had everything they needed for the patrol. For almost twenty days, the Queen's Own Regiment had been based inside an abandoned soap factory deep within the territory of the Circuit, after being moved up from the frontier. In that time, Daniel had watched the appearance of the troopers under his command degrade; their professional uniforms now filthy and perpetually coated in the grey dust that permeated the Circuit.

'You look like a bunch of peasants,' he said to them. 'I know this will be your eleventh dawn patrol in a row, but there's no excuse for letting your standards slip. I can see four men here who seem to have forgotten what a razorblade looks like, and several with holes or rips in their uniforms that could easily have been repaired.' He paced down the line again, knowing full well that the troopers were barely listening to him. 'You're wondering, who cares about keeping your uniform neat and clean when every day we have to go out onto the streets and face... rocks, stones, fire, dog turds, crossbow bolts, and whatever else the rebels and rioters throw at us. The answer is that I care. When the Evaders look at us, I don't want them seeing savages, I want them to see a professional force that is in the Circuit to protect them from the rebels, not to bully or harass them. I'm perfectly aware that many of the Evaders loathe us, but that's no excuse for discarding what makes us civilised. Instead, it means that we have to work even harder to gain their trust, to prove to them that we are fellow citizens who are here to help.'

He shook his head. No one was listening. The eyes of the troopers were already distracted, as each pictured themselves being out on the streets. He glanced at Sergeant Monterey. 'Let's go, Sergeant; lead us out.'

'Yes, sir,' the man saluted. 'You heard the lieutenant; form up and move out.'

The two dozen troopers turned, and began marching through the old warehouse, passing stacks of crates and barrels of fresh water. Groups of Taran soldiers were sitting around, some displaying signs of exhaustion from the previous night's patrols, others getting kitted up for the day ahead. The large sliding door at the entrance was closed and heavily guarded, and the captain on shift nodded to Daniel as his platoon arrived. Their details were scribbled down in the regimental logbook, and two burly soldiers pulled the massive door open, letting in the pink light of dawn, and the stink of smoke.

Sergeant Monterey led the way out, followed by Daniel and the troopers, with Sergeant Hayden at the rear. The forecourt of the factory resembled a fortress, with concrete barriers and guard posts, and a high wooden tower that overlooked the neighbouring streets. No Evader civilian was allowed to approach the front entrance, and a new bolt-throwing ballista had recently arrived to help enforce the rule. Three soldiers were standing behind it, and its long stock was pointing at the street. It had yet to be used in anger, but Daniel had seen the machines being operated and knew that a single bolt had the power to pass through two or three bodies, and that the crews had been trained to loose six bolts a minute.

Daniel frowned as they passed the killing machine, but said nothing. What was the point in making a fuss about it? No one listened to his opinions, not the troopers under his command, nor his superiors. None of them seemed to care how the ballista appeared to the civilians they were supposed to be protecting, as yet another example of the disparity in power that existed between the tribes; another reminder of who was in charge, and who was powerless.

The barricade at the entrance to the forecourt was lifted, and the platoon filed out into the narrow streets. Their patrol route was varied daily according to a formula that was supposed to be random, but which anyone with a head for numbers could have worked out in two minutes. They turned left, and headed down an alleyway that was enclosed on both sides by high concrete housing blocks. Several of the apartments were burnt-out shells, their narrow window slits blackened holes. A group of filthy children in rags were playing on the street, jumping over a gutter that ran with raw sewage down the middle of the lane. When Taran forces had first been sent into the Circuit, the children had fled from them, but their courage had grown since, and now they jeered at the soldiers as they passed, or made slitting motions across their throats. A stone ricocheted off the track by Daniel's feet. 'The first of the day,' he thought as he stepped over it.

In response to the stone, two troopers raised their shields and rushed a few steps towards where it had been launched from, and the children broke and ran, disappearing into the labyrinth of twisting lanes and derelict buildings. The soldiers laughed, then resumed their places in the column.

Daniel frowned, but said nothing. A pall of smoke drifted over from the right, but from the smell of it, Daniel judged the fire to be some distance away, and decided not to investigate. Getting every one of his troopers back to the soap factory alive at the end of each patrol had become his sole purpose; everything else was blurring at the edges.

They reached a major junction, where five different roads intersected around a plaza. In the centre was a ruined fountain; crumbling and vandalised, and it looked like it hadn't worked in decades. A permanent guard post watched over the traffic passing through the plaza, and Taran soldiers stood at each of the roads leading away from the centre. Daniel's patrol reached the first check point and he approached the officer on duty.

'Good morning, Captain. Any news?'

The officer nodded as his eyes scanned the crowds of Evaders milling through the plaza. 'Plenty, and none of it good. I received a report that a convoy of supply wagons was hit last night over by Candlemaker Row, and I've got no one spare who can go and check it out. Your route this morning will take you close to the location, so I want you to secure the site and await reinforcements.'

'Yes, sir. What was the convoy carrying?'

'Malik alone knows. It was destined for the Third Supply Depot by the quarters of the Seventh Taran Regiment of Foot, so it could be anything. There were four civilian wagon drivers and six troopers protecting it. If those Evader scum have killed our people I want to know first. Understood?'

'Yes, sir.'

'Get to it, then.'

Daniel saluted and returned to his platoon.

'Trouble, sir?' said Monterey.

'Could be. We're being diverted to Candlemaker Row; a convoy might have been hit.'

The sergeant nodded, and gestured to the troopers, who started moving again. Evaders cleared a path for them as they marched through the busy plaza, and Daniel ignored the looks of hatred and the muttered curses as they passed. Didn't they understand that the Tarans were there to help? Without tribal intervention, the riots had rumbled on with no sign of them ever ending; with the Tarans, Pellans and Dalrigians all sending regiments, at least the streets were calmer during the hours of daylight. Sometimes.

They left the plaza, taking one of the main routes towards the direction of the Middle Walls. Several of the buildings on the right hand side of the street had been demolished, and enormous piles of rubble and broken slabs of concrete rose above the height of their heads. Daniel kept his eyes open, scanning every heap of rocks, and every flat roof.

'Go back to Tara!' screamed an old woman by a street corner, her finger raised and pointing at the soldiers. 'You don't belong here; go home.'

The platoon ignored her. They had heard every insult the Evaders could think up, and Daniel had made it clear that no one on either side of fighting age should be arrested or pursued. Many were convinced that the rioters made the children and old folk of the Circuit taunt them in the deliberate knowledge that the troops would do nothing; or perhaps they were hoping that the Taran militia's restraint would crack, and then they would use the resulting casualties to rally more support.

A stone bounced off the shield of one of the soldiers, and they glanced around, looking for the source.

'Keep moving,' growled Monterey. 'Don't stop.'

The troopers kept on, as the sound of taunting laughter echoed from the nearby rooftops. Daniel could also hear the complaints murmured by the troopers; their frustration and anger all too plain to recognise. They reached another junction and diverted towards Candlemaker Row. Smoke was rising from the upper storeys of a large tenement block, but it looked derelict, so Daniel kept the platoon moving. The number of Evaders on the street increased the closer they got to the route the convoy had taken, and many scattered at the sight of the soldiers, clutching onto bags or sacks as they ran.

Daniel frowned. 'Clear the road, Sergeant.'

Monterey nodded, and took a whistle from round his neck. He blew and the whistle emitted a shrill blast of noise.

'Off the road!' he bellowed at the crowd. 'You have ten seconds.'

The crowd began to disperse, some shrieking as they ran in terror from the soldiers, while others slipped away quietly, taking their looted possessions with them. As the road cleared, a trail of debris was left behind. Crates had been smashed open, and barrels were lying upended, their contents leaking into the gutter. Up ahead, where the road intersected with Candlemaker Row, a wagon was sitting abandoned.

Daniel ordered the platoon forward, and they hurried up the

deserted road. Another four wagons came into view, and Daniel spotted the first bodies. Amid the ransacked wagons, two troopers were lying, their uniforms bloodstained.

'Secure the area!' Daniel shouted, and the two sergeants dispatched troopers to surround the wagons. Some of the crowds had returned, and were watching from a distance, their hands clutching stones. Daniel walked through the devastated convoy, counting another three bodies as he went. A trooper called over to report another slain wagon-driver, his body stripped and hacked to pieces by the side of the road.

'Sir?' said Monterey, his eyes dark. 'What are your orders?'

'Gather the dead, and put them all onto the back of a wagon. By my count we're missing four; three troopers and a wagon-driver. They may have been taken alive. Send two troopers back to the plaza to let the captain know there have been casualties, then we wait for reinforcements.'

The sergeant saluted. 'Yes, sir.'

Daniel walked over to the wagon where the troopers were beginning to gather the dead. Six bodies were picked up from the road and carried over. Some had been killed with a single wound, while others had clearly been tortured first. Daniel wanted to blame someone, but didn't know who. The people of the Circuit had killed them, but things didn't happen without a context. He could see the rage growing in his troopers' eyes as they regarded the dead. A final body was discovered lying half-submerged in the gutter. It was another trooper, her throat cut. Two of her colleagues waded into the sewage and dragged her body free.

'Someone needs to pay for this, sir,' said a young trooper, his eyes burning with anger.

'Quiet, trooper,' said Hayden; 'keep your eyes on the mob.' The sergeant turned to Daniel. 'That's seven fatalities altogether, sir; we've searched the rest of the convoy.'

'So we're missing three, if the captain's numbers were correct. They might have got away; fled back sunward towards Sander territory.'

'Or they might have been captured, sir.'

Daniel said nothing.

'Perhaps, sir,' said Monterey, approaching from the other side, 'we should take a few hostages from the crowd. It might keep the others from doing anything stupid, and we could always ask them a few questions while we've got 'em.'

The sergeants waited as Daniel considered their advice. He didn't know what to do, but had learned that Monterrey and Hayden rarely offered their opinions, and had decided that he should listen when they spoke.

'Two hostages should suffice,' he said. 'Send in a team to snatch them.'

'Yes, sir.'

Daniel watched as Monterey briefed four troopers. They dropped their packs to the ground, then the sergeant led them to the front of the convoy, where the crowd was closest. They acted as though they were going to move the lead wagon, then, at a shout from Monterey, they rushed at the crowd, their shields over-lapping as they charged. The mob began to scatter, but some were slower than the others, and Daniel saw two civilians hauled behind the half-circle of shields. The troopers retreated step by step as the crowd recovered its composure and began to re-form, and a few stones battered off their shields.

Daniel strode forwards as the snatch team returned to the convoy. The two civilians had their hands pulled behind their backs and their wrists tied. One was a middle-aged woman, the other a young boy, maybe around twelve years old.

The woman spat at Daniel when she saw his officer's insignia. 'Taran cowards! You'll never beat us, never. The Circuit will be your grave.'

Daniel wiped the spittle from his uniform. By the woman's side, the boy was standing defiant, but his hands were trembling.

'We have reason to believe,' Daniel said, 'that three Tarans have been taken alive by the mob. Where are they?'

'Look at you, the big officer,' sneered the woman. 'I bet you've never gone hungry a day in your life. You think that accent and that uniform impress us?'

'I'll ask again,' said Daniel. 'Do you know the whereabouts of the three missing Tarans? Did you see where they were taken?'

'I had a son your age; why don't you ask where he is?'

Hayden struck the woman across the face with his open hand.

'Do it again,' said the woman, her lip bleeding; 'it's all you've got, isn't it? And you have the cheek to call us savages.'

The sergeant raised his hand again, but Daniel shook his head. 'Secure them to a wagon. Make sure they're in sight of the mob.'

Hayden frowned. 'Yes, sir.'

The sergeant led the two hostages away and Daniel felt shame ripple through him. The other officers back at the soap factory talked as if they believed the purpose of the intervention was to prevent a civil war, but to Daniel it felt like he was already in the middle of one.

---

The sky went from pink to blue and then back to pink again as the day passed. Runners had been sent back and forth between Candlemaker Row and the large plaza, and reinforcements had been promised, along with ponies to replace those stolen from the convoy. The platoon had moved the wagons closer together to have a smaller area to defend, and the crowd shifted forwards on all sides to fill the gap.

At last, as the sun was dipping towards the horizon, a rumble of boots was heard along the road leading to the plaza.

'Thank Amalia,' muttered Hayden as they watched the first Taran soldiers come into view. The crowds on that street had scattered, and Daniel saw the long line of ponies walking beside the soldiers.

'Get the ponies hitched up to the wagons as soon as they arrive,' said Daniel. 'I want to be out of here in ten minutes.'

Monterey nodded. 'Yes, sir.'

Daniel stretched his limbs, stiff after so long on duty. At the head of the approaching column, he saw the captain march, leading what looked like half a company of soldiers.

'Good afternoon, Captain,' he said, saluting as the officer reached the convoy. The captain ignored him, his eyes scanning the scene. He walked over to the wagon where the dead had been gathered and pulled back the canvas sheet that had been covering them.

'Lieutenant,' he said without turning.

Daniel hurried over. 'Sir?'

'I have a new job for you.'

'Sir? I was just about to order my platoon to get the wagons back to the soap factory.'

'I've brought fresh soldiers who can take care of that. As the officer on patrol, it is your duty to follow up on any incident that occurs during your watch.' He handed Daniel a scrap of paper on which a rough street layout had been sketched. 'Some information came into my possession while investigating the attack on the convoy. Suspects were seen entering the premises marked on that map, and my source stated that they had at least one live captive with them.'

'This marked building is a large apartment block, and I have just the one platoon, sir.'

'I've brought soldiers for that too. Third Platoon, borrowed from the Eighth Foot. Take them and your own platoon, and make your way to the target building immediately, Lieutenant.'

'And what do I do when I get there?'

'If any of our people are alive, get them out safely. As for the Evaders, we don't have space in the prisons for any more, so use your imagination. Dismissed.'

Daniel turned to see two new sergeants by his side. 'You from the Eight Foot?'

'Yes, sir,' said one.

Daniel glanced at the map, while trying to smother a rising sense of frustration. 'Come with me.'

He led them to where Monterey and Hayden were organising the ponies.

'Leave that,' he said as they glanced at his approach; 'we've got a new job.'

---

Daniel divided his force into two as they approached the large tenement block marked on the map. It was a ramshackle, sprawling complex of grey concrete, multi-levelled, with several entrances. He didn't know either of the new sergeants, nor any of their troopers, but had no choice other than to assign them their positions and hope they would do exactly as he had ordered.

The locals saw them approach the building from different streets, and a cacophony arose as some fled, while others shuttered their windows and barred their doors.

'Seal the entrances!' Daniel cried as they reached an alleyway that ran down one side of the tenement. His troopers responded, spreading out to cover each of the doorways leading in. Daniel walked round to the front of the building, and gazed up at the towering block.

'Sir, your orders?' said Monterey by his side.

Daniel paused. People could live or die depending on the next words that left his mouth. He couldn't turn around and go back to the soap factory, not without at least attempting to rescue any Tarans that might be alive inside; but the only information he had was from a source he didn't know, and could easily be a mistake or a lie. He wanted to do the right thing, but had no idea what that was, or if it could even exist in such circumstances.

He lowered his eyes. 'Storm the building. Search the apartments for our missing people.'

The sergeant's eyes lit up. 'Yes, sir.' He turned to the assembled troopers. 'You heard the lieutenant; it's time to collect a little payback. Squads one and two, you're with me. Once inside...'

Daniel's attention drifted away from the sergeant's words. He felt sick. Was this what his expensive training and education had been for, so he could stamp on the weak and poor? The people who had killed the troopers and wagon-drivers of the convoy deserved to die, but the tenement in front of him looked like countless others, and he refused to believe that every single apartment within contained a nest of rebels.

Monterey blew his whistle, and the troopers charged into the building. With every second that passed, Daniel felt his spirit drain away. Screams and angry cries were coming out of the tenement, along with the sound of doors being kicked in. Anyone who tried to leave was forced back inside by the soldiers posted at every exit and before long crowds of them were straining to escape.

Smoke started to belch from an apartment three floors up, then a window directly above was opened, and a headless body was pushed outside. It landed on the cobbles next to Daniel and he stared at it. It was one of the missing Taran troopers, his neck sheared.

'Sons of dogs,' Hayden muttered.

More smoke was pouring from the upper floors and flames appeared at a high window.

'Call the squads back,' said Daniel. 'The building's burning.'

'Yes, sir.' Hayden blew three short blasts on his whistle.

More screaming rose into the air, and Daniel frowned as he tried to locate its source. Damn it, he thought, it was coming from the rear of the building, where he had posted the platoon from the Eighth Foot. He ran down the narrow alleyway that lay by the side of the building and emerged into a backstreet littered with bodies. Troopers in close lines were loosing their crossbows at Evaders trying to flee the tenement.

'Hold!' Daniel cried as he strode forward. 'I ordered no killing of civilians.'

'They were trying to escape, sir,' said a sergeant. 'They refused to listen to our warnings.'

Daniel glanced at the entrance. At least a dozen bodies were piled there, blocking the doorway.

'And anyway, sir,' the sergeant went on, 'if we're not letting them out, the fire'll get 'em anyway. If it was me, sir, I think I'd rather be shot than burnt alive.'

Daniel looked up. Flames were streaming from more windows,

and all of the upper floors were on fire. Thick, dark coils of smoke spewed into the air, and the screams were drowning out every other sound.

'Remove the soldiers from the doorway and let the civilians out.'

The sergeant frowned. 'Sir?'

'Do it.'

'Pull back!' cried the sergeant. 'Get clear from the doors and pull back.'

The troopers hurried away from the doors and a flood of civilians spilled out onto the street, running in a massed panic away from the burning tenement. The troopers held tight like a rock in a river as the swarm of Evaders moved around them. When they had passed, Daniel stared at the dozen bodies lying in the doorway and began walking back round to the front of the building.

What had he done?

The front of the building was in chaos. The troopers who had stormed the apartments were back outside, and were barricading the front entrance against the mass of people who had gathered there to escape the flames.

'What are you doing?' he cried.

'Following your orders, sir,' said Hayden. 'You told us no one was to leave.'

An explosion rocked the tenement, and flames burst from the windows on the lower floor, blasting the shutters to pieces. The troopers retreated, each gazing at the inferno engulfing the tenement. Daniel stared at it, his mouth open. No one still inside could be alive, he knew that as a certainty.

'Good job, lads and lasses,' said Hayden. 'Let's get out of here. Sir?'

Daniel tried to speak, but his mouth was dry. He nodded.

'Move out!' cried Hayden. He pointed to a trooper. 'Run round the back and tell those dozy beggars from the Eighth that it's time to go.' He pointed at another two. 'You pair, carry the body of the trooper back with us. It's evidence that we hit the right building.'

The troopers began to peel away from the tenement, forming up into a double column down the alleyway. Daniel walked to their rear, his head down.

Hayden caught his eye as he passed. 'That was well done, sir. Maybe I was wrong about you.'

―――――――

Daniel led the two platoons back to the soap factory. Runners had been sent ahead with the news, and the body of the fallen trooper from the convoy was taken away by stretcher bearers when they passed through the plaza. The locals eyed them with the same sullen expressions as they had when they had went out on patrol that morning, unaware that they were gazing at soldiers who had just carried out a massacre.

The barrier at the entrance to the factory's forecourt was lifted for them, and they returned to the relative security of the compound. Daniel left the platoons at the bottom of the stairs to get cleaned up, and ascended the steps to the commanding officer's office on the upper floor. He paused outside the door for a moment, then knocked.

'Enter.'

Daniel opened the door and walked in. The major-general was seated behind a table that was being used as a desk.

'Lieutenant Aurelian? I was half-expecting to see you this evening; I heard about what occurred, and your part in it.'

'I've come to explain, sir.'

'Explain what, Lieutenant? You have nothing to explain; in fact I intend to write a letter to headquarters in Torwood this evening, in which I will strongly recommend your elevation to senior lieutenant. Your actions today were exemplary; by all accounts you led two platoons in the elimination of a rebel stronghold, and got some measure of justice for the troopers that were so brutally murdered in the convoy.' He stood, walked round the table, and stuck his hand out.

Daniel shook it.

'Now come this way for a moment, if you please?' The major-general gestured to the door.

Daniel followed the commander along the passageway towards the officers' mess. He opened the door and strode in. The room fell into silence and around two dozen officers turned to look at their commander.

The major-general ushered Daniel forward. 'You've all heard what happened today,' he said to the watching room; 'and you all know what this young lieutenant achieved. With an iron will and firm leadership, he utterly destroyed a nest of rioters and murderous rebels. Ladies and gentlemen, I present to you Lieutenant Daniel Aurelian. Please show him your appreciation.'

The room erupted into cheers.

Daniel stood in stunned silence. A glass of something was thrust into his hand, and his back was slapped until he nearly toppled over. A regimental song started up, and within seconds the room was ringing to its sound as every officer present bar Daniel bellowed out the words.

He had finally been accepted, he realised. All it had taken was murder.

# CHAPTER 17

# THE BOY IN THE POOL

Ooste, Auldan, The City – 13th Koralis 3419

The barge bumped against the side of the wharf, and Aila stepped off.

'Good morning, ma'am.' said the Evader official waiting for her. 'Lord Naxor's carriage has just arrived.'

Aila smothered her reply. She was busy night and day dealing with the troubles in the Circuit, and had little time for her cousin's frivolities. They crossed a bridge over a wide canal and entered Icewarder territory. The local militia saluted her, and she noticed they had been heavily reinforced with Dalrigian troops.

She left the Evader official behind at the border and was joined by an Icewarder, who bowed low.

'My lady,' he said, 'may I take this opportunity to lay some of the district governor's concerns before you regarding the spread of violence into certain Icewarder regions?'

'Not today,' Aila said as she kept walking.

'But, my lady...'

She glared at him. 'Not today. Schedule a meeting like you're supposed to.'

'The local officials have tried, my lady, only to be continually told that you are not available.'

Aila spotted Naxor's carriage parked by the side of the large administrative building.

'The local governor has authorised me to issue a warning to you, my lady,' the man said, hurrying to keep up with her. 'She said that if you keep refusing to meet with her, she will be forced to take matters of security into her own hands.'

Aila paused. 'You, a mortal, are warning me, a demigod?'

The man's face flushed and he stared at the ground. 'Apologies, my lady, but the situation is fast becoming desperate. The governor says that if the violence continues to spread into Icewarder lands, then the militia will be forced to move into the Circuit to occupy key, strategic points.'

'Why not?' said Aila. 'The Tarans, Sanders, Pellans and Dalrigians are already there; why not the Icewarders too? Welcome to the party.'

She turned and strode away, leaving the official staring at her from the wharf.

'Cousin,' she said as she saw Naxor leaning against the carriage. 'This had better be important.'

He grinned at her, but his eyes betrayed his worry. 'Now, don't be angry with me, but I may have enticed you here under false pretences.'

'What? Is this some sort of joke? Do you realise how busy I am? People are dying; every hour the casualty list rises, and not just from the violence. Food shortages are as big a fear now, with the supply chains being cut and...'

'Save it, please. I'd hate for you to have to repeat yourself.'

'And why would I have to repeat myself?'

'Because you're getting in the carriage and I'm taking you to the Royal Palace in Ooste.'

She frowned. 'No, you're not.'

'I'm afraid so, cousin. You have been summoned.'

'By who? Your mother? Tough, tell her I refuse.'

'She thought you'd say that, so she made sure the summons was issued by the God-King himself.'

Aila felt the colour drain from her face.

Naxor shrugged. 'Sorry. You can refuse a summons from my mother, but from the God-King? Are you willing to incur his wrath?'

'You donkey turd; you set me up.'

'I am merely the emissary, cousin.'

'You lied to me.'

'Only to ensure that you turned up here this morning. Tell me honestly, would you have come all the way from Redmarket if you had known the truth?'

She glared at him.

'Please,' he said gesturing to the open carriage door.

'You're a devious asshole at times, Naxor,' she said. 'I'll go, but don't imagine for a moment that I'll be in a hurry to trust you again.'

He smiled as she climbed aboard the carriage. 'I'm sure you'll forgive me in a century or so.'

Naxor waited until she was seated, then jumped aboard and sat on the bench opposite Aila. A servant closed the door, and the carriage set off, the six ponies pulling it along the road in the direction of the Union Walls and Auldan.

They sat in silence for a few minutes as Aila glared out of the window. She didn't experience fear very often, but the thought of coming face to face with the God-King was terrifying. She hadn't laid eyes on him for over three hundred years, when he and the God-Queen had intervened to end the Civil War following the slaying of Prince Michael. Her last image of the two gods that ruled the City was of them taking two bodies back with them to Ooste; their dead son, and Princess Yendra. The God-King had shown mercy to Aila that day, and had sentenced her to two hundred years imprisonment rather than executing her, which was the fate he had decreed for Yendra.

'I hate you, Naxor,' she muttered.

'It'll be fine,' he said.

'Will it? I guess Ikara has blamed me for everything?'

'Yes, she has. My mother knows her daughter well, however, which is why she wishes to speak to you in person. I've seen my sister's reports; they are filled with inconsistencies and contradictions. Every success she credits to herself, and every failure is put squarely onto your shoulders.'

'I'm doomed.'

'As I said, my mother knows what Ikara is like.'

'Then why did she make her Governor of the Circuit?'

'You know the answer to that. With so many of our fellow demigods killed in the Civil War, she wasn't exactly spoilt for choice.'

'So the Circuit fell to Ikara by default? That tells me exactly where the Evaders fit in your mother's list of priorities.'

Naxor's eyes flashed with anger. 'I'm changing the subject.'

Aila glared at him, then turned to the window, where the wide streets of the Icewarders were racing past.

'I have some gossip for you,' he said. 'You interested?'

'Nope.'

'A pity, but I'll tell you anyway. As you know, news of what occurs within the Bulwark is often suppressed. Duke Marcus usually only lets out information that he feels will make him look good with the general population of citizens. You still not interested?'

Aila said nothing.

'I have contacts, however, as befits my role as emissary, and I hear things that others are completely unaware of.'

'Yes, yes, I know,' she sighed. 'Get on with it.'

He smiled. 'Well, the news is nearly a month old, but back in Izran, an attempt was made on the life of the new champion. He was returning from a sortie beyond the walls, and a madman ran at him, and plunged a six-inch blade into his side.'

Aila froze for a moment. Was he talking about Corthie? She needed to be careful. Naxor could read her mind any time he liked, and the last thing she wanted was for her cousin to find out that she had kissed the champion. She wasn't embarrassed by what had happened, and the knowledge would probably make Naxor laugh, but a part of her was hoping that the kiss might turn into something else; something more. She needed to stay calm, and nonchalant.

'You're being awfully quiet,' Naxor said. 'I thought my news would amuse you at least.'

'I assume you're talking about that muscle-bound oaf? I forget his name.'

'Corthie Holdfast? Yes, it was him.'

'And... is he alive?'

Naxor laughed. 'The way you said that makes me almost believe that you care, cousin. Yes, he lives; I don't think even Marcus could have suppressed the news if he'd been slain. Apparently he was up and about and fit for duty after only a few days. But I fear you're missing the point.'

'The point?' said Aila, trying to hide her relief.

'Yes. Clearly the duke was embarrassed by the lack of security that led to the assassination attempt. I mean imagine; the best champion in decades, maybe centuries, and he almost gets killed by a Blade?'

'Do they know why?'

'No. The champion's more... fervent followers tore the assassin to pieces before he could be questioned. The rumours are that my mother was somehow involved, but I don't need to tell you how ridiculous that suggestion is.'

'Your mother?'

'Malicious gossip, nothing more. Apparently my mother is jealous of his success.' He shook his head. 'Utter claptrap. Still, without transparency, these rumours tend to bubble away. My worry is that Duke Marcus will do nothing to suppress such nonsense. Being able to blame my mother would be quite convenient for him, I imagine.'

'Assuming it wasn't your mother,' Aila said, a slight smile on her lips, 'then who could it have been? Why would anyone want to kill the champion?'

'He has hundreds, maybe thousands of followers who think he is here to redeem us all. He has attracted a wide range of, shall we say, the more excitable elements of the citizenry. With that being the case, do we need to look further? The simplest answer is usually correct.'

'So, an insane individual? Some idiot working alone?'

'That would appear to be the case, yes.'

Aila looked back out of the window again as the wagon slowed by the Union Walls. For a moment she wished she were travelling in the other direction, towards the Bulwark. A part of her wanted nothing more than to see Corthie, to check with her own eyes that he was alright. What a fool she was. The champion had probably forgotten all about their drunken kiss, and she should forget him before her heart had a chance to care, and then break.

The carriage passed the walls and entered Auldan. She gazed out over the vast suburbs of Outer Pella.

'Is that smoke?'

Naxor glanced out of the window. 'It would appear so.'

'Has the trouble spread to Pella? Are the Reapers rioting as well?'

He shrugged. 'I'm sure my mother will tell you everything you need to know.'

---

The streets of Ooste were quiet as the carriage rumbled over the cobbles. They passed the Royal Academy, where Aila, along with every other demigod, had received her education. The bronze domes had turned green many years before, but the building retained a sense of elegance and grace. Beyond that, the carriage turned into the vast fore-court of the Royal Palace, home of the God-King. A servant opened the side door as the carriage drew to a stop by the entrance steps.

'After you, cousin,' Naxor said, gesturing to Aila.

She climbed down from the carriage, ignoring the servant's hand that was raised to assist her, and stepped onto the worn flagstones.

Naxor accompanied her into the palace, and led her through the shining hallways and marble splendour until they reached a small audience chamber. Guards opened the doors for them, and they strode through. Sitting in the throne of power was Princess Khora, and Aila noticed two of her own siblings were also in the chamber; her brother Lord Collo, and sister Lady Vana. Aila smothered a groan. It was bad enough that she was about to be humiliated by Khora, and the presence of her two sycophantic siblings only rubbed salt into the wound.

'Lady Aila, greetings,' said Khora. 'Please approach.'

Aila walked forwards. After three hundred years, that was how her aunt had chosen to welcome her?

'I was summoned by the God-King,' she said. 'Where is he?'

'His Most High Majesty is indisposed, I'm afraid.'

'So all this was just a trick to get me to come here?'

'As Guardian of the City, I hold the authority of the royal sceptre in lieu. My word should be taken as coming from the God-King himself.'

'Yeah, a trick, as I said. So, what do you want?'

Her sister glared at her. 'Show some respect, Aila. You are in the Royal Palace, not the backstreets of the Circuit.'

'Screw you, Vana.'

'Enough, both of you,' said Khora. 'Lady Aila, we need to discuss the contents of Lady Ikara's reports regarding the situation in the Circuit. Matters have deteriorated alarmingly over the last month and, with the troubles starting to infect Outer Pella as well, I fear the City is on the verge of a serious crisis.'

'I've read the reports. Are you going to remove me from my position?'

'Should you be removed?'

'If you believe what your idiot daughter wrote, then yes, I most certainly should.'

Khora said nothing for a moment and Aila could see that she had successfully managed to get under her aunt's skin.

'Politics is an art,' Khora said after a long silence. 'I understand the need to apportion blame but right now I'm more interested in bringing the violence and disorder to an end. What do you advise should be done to achieve this?'

'You know what the rioters are demanding?'

'My resignation, yes.'

'Well?'

'Is that your considered advice, Lady Aila; that the stability of the City will be secured once it has no functioning government? An interesting thesis. Fortunately for the City, it is not one I share.'

'They're not demanding no government, just that you are no longer at its head.'

'Then tell me, who do you imagine would step up to fill the void if I resigned? I am the last of the God-Children, if we discount Prince Montieth, but as the noble prince has not left Greylin Palace in Dalrig for over a thousand years, I hardly think he would suddenly develop a sense of duty now. Who else, then, Aila; please tell me.'

Aila paused for a moment. If Khora fell from power, then her children would fall too, along with the court of sycophants that included Vana and Collo. Who would be left? The running of the City would never be handed over to the mortals.

She smiled. 'Maybe the God-King and God-Queen should be encouraged to have more children.'

Khora shook her head, her eyes tight. 'Are you truly so blind, Aila? I've watched you for a long time, and have noticed many of your attributes and qualities. Being blind to the obvious I had not thought to be one of them. Think some more, then tell me; who would take over if I fell?'

Aila blinked, and her heart sank at the realisation.

'I think you're getting there,' Khora said; 'if the expression on your face is anything to go by.'

'Duke Marcus?'

Khora smiled. 'Indeed, Lady Aila. It took a while, but we got there in the end. Now, I am perfectly aware that you loathe me, and I don't want you to answer my next question out loud; just ponder it. Would you prefer him to me?'

Aila's gaze fell to the floor. Khora was right. As much as she detested her aunt, her cousin in the Bulwark was a different matter altogether.

'I seem to recall,' Khora said, 'that had my most glorious and divine brother, Prince Michael, survived the Civil War, he had plans regarding his son and you. Do you remember?'

Aila remained silent. Of course she remembered. Michael had arranged for her to marry Duke Marcus, as part of his plan to breed more demigods for the City. If Yendra hadn't cut him down... She shuddered.

'The duke is a very patient man,' Khora went on. 'A few centuries mean nothing to him, and I know for a fact that he still desires you.'

Aila turned to Naxor. 'Is this true? Tell me it's not, cousin.'

Naxor shrugged. 'My mother is stating the truth. My sources close to the duke have confirmed it.'

'Then why have you never told me?'

'What would have been the point? I was sparing you from three centuries of worry.'

Aila lifted a hand to her face; the thought of Duke Marcus anywhere near her making her nauseous.

'I would die before I let him touch me.'

'Quite,' said Khora, her voice lower. 'So, tell me again your advice for ending the riots.'

'There is something we could try.'

'Go on, Lady Aila; I'm listening.'

'We could try to implement Princess Yendra's reforms.'

'What, the reforms that plunged the City into Civil War the last time they were tried?'

'The Civil War didn't start because of the reforms, it started because Michael couldn't handle losing any of his power. Devolve decision-making to the mortals; let them set up their own assemblies and courts; and overhaul the unfair distribution of land ownership. It cannot be right that a tiny handful of Roser elites own most of the City. And, most importantly of all, repeal the laws that keep the people in servitude. You may deny it, in fact I know you will, but half of the City's population exists in a state of virtual slavery. The Circuit needs schools and hospitals, and so does Outer Pella, where the Reapers are almost as long-suffering as the Evaders. Should I continue?'

Her sister Vana glared at her. 'You reveal yourself as a rebel at last. I always knew you harboured sympathetic thoughts towards the revolutionaries that infest the Circuit, and now with your own words you have condemned yourself.'

'Shut up, Vana, unless you want me to come over there and punch you in the face.'

'You've never changed,' said her brother, Lord Collo; 'you're still a spiteful wretch. Perhaps we should have given you to Duke Marcus at the end of the war, after all, he seemed to do a wonderful job of taming Lord Kano.'

Rage flooded Aila, and before she knew what she was doing she found herself rushing towards Collo, her fists clenched and her teeth bared. Naxor gripped her arms and hauled her back as she kicked and writhed in his grasp.

'Not another word from either of you,' Khora said to Vana and Collo; 'in fact, it might be best if you leave us.'

Lady Vana widened her eyes, 'But...'

'I have spoken. Go.'

Vana and Collo shot furious glares at Aila, then walked from the audience chamber. Naxor released Aila's arms as soon as the door had closed behind them, and she staggered, almost falling to her knees. She wiped the tears from her face.

'Listen to me,' said Khora; 'of all the petty and cruel acts that Duke Marcus has performed over the centuries, I want you to know that what he did to your brother, Lord Kano, I rank among the worst. I apologise for the words of my advisors; they know not of what they speak.'

'I don't want your pity.'

'I know, but my feelings are genuine.'

Aila rubbed her face again, embarrassed that she had cried in front of her aunt. 'I assume you'll disregard my advice about Yendra's reforms?'

'For a start, we'll get nowhere by calling them that. Yendra is tainted as a traitor and murderer, and the God-Queen in Tara would instantly veto any laws associated with her name.'

'And the God-King; what does he think?'

Khora said nothing for a long while, and Aila noticed that she and her son were staring at each other. Aila frowned, understanding what it meant.

'I thought I was here for a meeting?' she said. 'Why are you and Naxor conducting a vision conversation in secret?'

Khora broke off her stare and turned to her. 'Because my son disagrees with what I am about to do, and I wished to give him a chance to lay out his reasoning.'

'It's a mistake, mother,' said Naxor.

'Perhaps, but I want to prove to Lady Aila that I trust her. We all know she hates and mistrusts me; would there be a better way of demonstrating that I think of her in a different way?'

Naxor shrugged. 'It's up to you.'

Khora stood. 'Indeed it is.' She stepped down from the throne and approached Aila. 'If you reveal to anyone what I'm about to show you, I will have you killed. Do you understand?'

Aila frowned.

'I said "do you understand?"; not even the God-Queen is aware of the secrets held within the Royal Palace, and certainly not Lord Collo or Lady Vana.'

'I understand. So, who else knows this... secret?'

'Myself, Lord Naxor, Prince Michael's daughter Lady Mona, and my youngest daughter Lady Doria. As you are aware, Doria, like Collo, possesses no god-powers except self-healing, and so I placed her in the Royal Palace a long time ago, to serve the God-King. It is to her that we shall go first. Please, this way.'

Aila glanced at Naxor as Khora walked towards a rear door in the chamber, but her cousin's eyes were dark, and he ignored her. They followed the princess deeper into the palace, through areas that Aila had never seen before; passing guards in shining steel armour. They came to a door and Khora opened it without knocking. As Aila stepped inside she saw her cousin Doria at a table, cutting flowers to go into a vase.

'Doria.'

The demigod looked up. 'Mother?' Her eyes flickered over to Aila in surprise.

'I have brought someone to see the God-King.'

'But...'

'It's pointless to protest,' said Naxor, frowning. 'Mother has made up her mind, it seems.'

'Hush, son; trust me.'

'I trust you; I trust that you're making a mistake.'

'Hey,' said Aila, 'you really don't want me to know, do you? Why? You know I never blab secrets to anyone.' She remembered telling Corthie about the other dragon as she said the words, but kept her face steady.

'It's not you personally, Aila. I just think that the fewer who know, the better.'

'Doria,' said Khora; 'take us to the God-King.'

Doria stood, glanced at Naxor for a second, then opened a set of doors leading into a quiet hallway of gold and polished marble.

'These are the Royal Chambers,' she said to Aila as they entered.

'Why is all the furniture covered in dust-sheets?'

'It wasn't always like this,' said Khora. 'Back when the God-Queen shared the chambers with the God-King, these rooms were bustling with life; now they are almost deserted.' They carried on, and entered a room that looked more like a cavern. Glistening stalactites hung from the rough ceiling, and water was trickling down several walls, forming into a pool set into the middle of the floor.

Naxor closed the doors behind them as Doria glanced around. 'Your Majesty?'

A young man appeared in the pool, his head rising from the water. Aila stared at him. The youth looked to be about sixteen; his eyes were wide and he had a grin on his lips. There was something familiar about his face, but Aila couldn't place it. He reached the pool's edge and climbed out of the water, and Aila saw that he was naked.

'Who...?'

'Lady Aila, this is His Divine Majesty, God-King Malik.'

'What?' Aila cried. 'Nonsense, I saw him, we saw him, at the end of the war. He looked nothing like this.'

The youth shrieked and ran towards the group by the doors. His eyes passed over Doria and Khora, then settled on Aila. He reached out and tried to touch her breasts.

'Hey!' Aila cried, stepping back.

Doria raised a finger. 'No, your Majesty. That's bad. I've told you before. No grabbing.' She turned to Aila. 'Sorry, cousin, he doesn't know what he's doing.'

The God-King shrieked again, then ran back to the pool and dived in.

Aila stared at him in the water. 'What's wrong with him? Why does he look so young?'

'His Majesty's mind has gone,' Khora said; 'poisoned by long over-use of salve.'

'Salve did this to him? Malik's breath… damn it, that sounds stupid now; I can't believe it. How?'

'After the God-Queen walked out on him,' said Khora, 'his Majesty fell into a deep depression. He over-indulged in alcohol, opium, women, and finally salve. He was bathing in its ointments for days at a time. His appearance stabilised for decades at about eighteen, but over time his behaviour began to become more erratic, and by the time we finally removed the salve from his reach it was too late.'

'And Queen Amalia doesn't know?'

'No. The God-Queen has refused to speak to King Malik for over three hundred years.'

'You should tell her; she should know what's happened to him.'

'I dare not.'

'What? Why?'

'Because the only reason that I am Guardian of the City, and not Duke Marcus, is because I have the backing of the God-King. Queen Amalia has always favoured the eldest son of her favourite child Prince Michael. Without the God-King's authority to bolster my regime, the

God-Queen would remove me from power and appoint Marcus to rule instead.'

Aila stared from her to the sight of Malik swimming in the pool. 'You mean all of this is a vast conspiracy to keep you in power?'

'Yes, and now you are part of that conspiracy, Aila.'

'What makes you think I won't tell everyone the truth as soon as I walk out of here?'

'Because you understand what the rule of Duke Marcus would entail, not only for you personally, but for the rest of the City. We come to the moment of truth, my awkward niece; you must choose. Work with me, or give yourself to the duke. There is nowhere to hide.'

Aila bowed her head. The authority of the City was built upon a gigantic lie. The God-King was mad.

'And if I said that I needed time to think about it, would you let me leave the palace alive?'

Naxor opened his mouth to say something but Khora raised her hand. 'Of course,' she said. 'Go back to the Circuit and continue to assist my daughter.'

'But what about her reports? I thought I was going to be punished?'

'I know Ikara's ways, and know that you are not to blame for what is happening in the Circuit. Dark forces are at work, distributing arms and gold to the gangs leading the riots. I'm depending on you to uncover those responsible so I can bring them to justice. In the meantime, if you decide you want to work more closely with me, I will be waiting.'

Aila frowned. 'I still don't trust you.'

'I know,' Khora said, her eyes shining, 'but I hope by this gesture today, that you realise that I trust you. Son, please escort Lady Aila back to the frontier of the Circuit.'

Aila took a last glance at the God-King. He was floating on the waters of the pool, a smile on his youthful lips, as if he didn't have a care in the world. She nodded to Naxor. Time to go home.

## CHAPTER 18
## A QUIET DRINK

Arrowhead Fort, The Bulwark, The City – 16th Koralis 3419

'Hey Buckler, ya dozy lizard; wake up!'

Corthie took a bite from the red apple in his hand as he stared at the dragon's perch from the roof of the Wolfpack Tower. He was sure he had seen the beast fly up onto his platform from the window of his room, but the angle from the roof to the eyrie made it difficult to see if he was there, especially if he was lying down.

'Buckler, you there?' he yelled. Nothing. He frowned, drew his arm back, and launched the apple at the perch. The little red missile arced through the air, and Corthie grinned as he watched it descend onto the platform. A surprised roar echoed out over the fortress, and dark red wings rose as Buckler's head craned up, his eyes gazing around.

'Over here!' Corthie cried.

The dragon flapped his wings and soared into the sky, then surged down at the roof of the tower. He stopped a yard over Corthie's head, his claws extended.

'Are you throwing stones at me, wolf-boy? I should reduce you to ashes for the insult.'

'It was an apple, so quit the dramatics.'

'It struck me on the head.'

'Oops. I used to throw things at my brother; he didn't like it much either.'

'You interrupted my afternoon nap to tell me about your brother? I demand an apology.'

'Alright, I'm sorry; sorry you're such an ugly lizard. Nature can be cruel.'

Buckler's eyes seethed with rage and he drew himself up to his full stature, his wings out. He opened his jaws and blasted a stream of fire up into the air. The dragon gazed down as Corthie folded his arms.

'You throw things at me, and now you bait me? Shall we see if I can be as cruel as nature, you measly insect?'

'You seem to be taking all of this a bit personally.'

Quill rushed onto the roof. 'Whatever's happening, stop it; now.' She glanced up at Buckler, her empty palms raised. 'Sorry about him, he's been a right pain in the ass all day; you know he doesn't mean any offence.'

Corthie chuckled. 'Why are you assuming it's my fault?'

She scowled at him. 'Isn't it?'

'It might be construed that way, I suppose.'

'I would be grateful, Sergeant Quill,' said Buckler from above, 'if you escort this foolish boy downstairs. If he annoys me one more time today, I shall not be held responsible for my actions.' He beat his great wings, and soared away into the pink sky.

'I wasn't finished,' yelled Corthie; 'I had a question for you.'

'I think it might have to wait for another time,' said Quill. She glared at him. 'Just what did you think you'd achieve by angering a dragon?'

Corthie walked to the stairs and began to descend. 'I'm bored.'

'Come on,' she said, following him, 'there are a hundred things you could do with your day off. Rest, read a book, take a long bath.'

'Have you bumped your head and forgotten who I am?'

'Alright, how about we bring some musicians and singers up to the rooms where Tanner and I live, and we could listen to some songs? We could get some dancers, and fancy food.'

'I'm not in the mood.'

They reached the bottom of the stairs and came out into his bedchamber. He strolled to the window and gazed out over the City. A pall of smoke was hovering over the Circuit beyond the Middle Walls in the distance, as it had for well over a month. To his right spread the vast area reserved for the Blades, laid out by a grand design around a series of circular plazas. To the left was the wall dividing the territory of the Blades from that of the Scythes. From the elevation of the Wolfpack Tower, he could make out endless fields stretching into the distance. Often, he would see the tiny figures of workers in the fields, but that was as close as he had come to meeting a Scythe.

'Or,' Quill said, 'we could just get drunk again.'

'Now you're talking.'

She sighed. 'Not downstairs in the common room, though; I can't stand the place since the commander locked down the fort.'

'Are you missing my worshippers?'

'Strange to say, but a little bit, I guess. They added to the sense of occasion. Arrowhead feels empty without the civilians.'

'I agree. Look, why don't we just forget about the day off? I could be kitted up and out there in an hour; let me slaughter a few dozen green-hides to work off my excess energy. We can have a few beers after that.'

'No way. The Wolfpack are adamant, and so am I. You must take one day off out of fifteen, so you can rest, and so that you don't get injured again.'

'I wasn't injured because of the greenhides.'

'It doesn't matter. Will you abide by the will of the Wolfpack?'

He sighed and sat on the edge of the bed. 'I guess so.'

She gave a half-hearted smile. 'Brandy?'

An idea popped into his head. 'Aye, but not here.'

'Then where?'

He glanced over at her. 'The Blind Poet.'

'Uh huh; no way.'

'I won't go to that shrine again.'

'It makes no difference,' she said. 'There are troops from Auldan and Medio swarming through the streets.'

He shrugged. 'It should be safe enough, then.'

'But if that Elsie's a rebel, then the authorities are probably after her, and the Blind Poet will be under surveillance.'

'That's a lot of "ifs" and "probablies". Come on, it'll be a laugh.'

'No it won't; and besides, Tanner will go mental.'

'Then let's not tell Tanner.'

'What, just slip away?

'There's never been a better time to do it; the fortress is deserted.' He got up and grabbed his coat. 'I'm going; come if you like.'

He went down the stairs, and smiled to himself as he heard Quill's boots on the steps behind him. He pulled his coat over his shoulders as he descended, passing the level where his two sergeants lived, then continued down to the ground floor. It was quiet, though a low noise was coming from the common room. Corthie strode out of the tower and across the empty forecourt, Quill hurrying to keep up. As they approached the gatehouse a burly sergeant stepped out.

'A fine afternoon,' the sergeant said as he watched them get closer.

'It is that,' said Corthie; 'so fine, in fact, that Quill and I are going out for a little walk.'

'Oh, I wouldn't be doing that, sir.'

Corthie halted a yard from him. 'And why not?'

'Perhaps because around four thousand of your more avid followers are camped outside the walls, and if you were to suddenly appear among them, then they might get a little excited, sir, and I don't think we want that now, do we?'

'You're right, Sergeant. Bollocks.'

The sergeant smiled. 'I can always organise a carriage for you, sir; then you could ride somewhere else for your little walk with Sergeant Quill.'

'You're a fine man, Sergeant. Thanks.'

'Not at all, sir. I'll just nip away and get that sorted for you.' He winked at Quill. 'You two have a lovely evening.'

The carriage bore them through the Bulwark and into Medio, the soldiers at the Middle Walls waving them past once they had seen that the famous champion was aboard.

Getting through the militia checkpoints in the Circuit was not as easy. Soldiers in Icewarder and Dalrigian uniforms stopped the carriage at several roadblocks positioned along the way to the centre of Evader territory, and when they reached Redmarket, Corthie and Quill left the wagon, ponies and driver with the palace stables and walked the rest of the way to the Blind Poet on foot. The building looked closed from the outside, but the door swung open after Corthie had knocked.

Nareen looked up from the deserted bar. 'The hero returns,' she beamed, as her husband slid home the bolts on the front door. 'Ale?'

'Aye, please,' said Corthie, his eyes scanning the alcoves. He muttered a curse to himself as he realised Elsie wasn't there.

'I didn't think you'd be coming in here again,' Nareen said, filling two tankards with ale, 'not with all the foreign soldiers swarming the streets. I hope they didn't give you any trouble.'

Quill frowned. 'Once he gets an idea into his head, there's no stopping him.'

'I'm surprised the soldiers didn't send you back,' Nareen said, placing the ales on the counter; 'I didn't think they'd want outsiders to see what they've been up to in the Circuit.'

'What do you mean?' said Corthie.

'Killings, beatings, you name it,' said Dorvid, coming over to the bar. 'The Tarans are the worst, as usual.'

'Tell them about the massacre in Candlemakers,' said Nareen.

Dorvid frowned. 'Just a few days ago, the Taran militia locked the doors of a tenement and set it on fire. They filled anyone trying to escape with crossbow bolts, and then watched the place burn. Eighty-three folk died in there; kids, women, old folk.'

'That's terrible,' said Quill. 'What's the governor doing about it?'

'Nothing, as usual. She sent her Adjutant to lodge an official complaint, but the Tarans told her they had evidence that the tenement was being used as a rebel stronghold.'

'And was it?'

'Of course not,' said Nareen. 'It was revenge, pure and simple, for a raid on a supply convoy. The Tarans just picked a nearby building to make an example of. They're treating it like a great success.'

'Aye,' said Dorvid, 'they even promoted the officer responsible.'

'Do you know the officer's name?' said Quill.

'Everyone in the Circuit knows his name,' said Nareen; 'it's Aurelian, some aristocratic beast from Tara. He's a dead man if the rebels get hold of him.'

Corthie frowned. 'So, would you say that the other tribes' militia are making things worse?'

'Aye. I mean, it was bad before, but the Circuit feels like it's at war now, occupied by a foreign enemy.'

'Give me a minute,' said Quill; 'I need to use the little girls' room.'

Corthie waited until the sergeant had disappeared through the door leading to the bathrooms, then leaned closer to Nareen. 'Has Elsie been in tonight?'

Nareen gave him a funny look. 'I've not seen her since you were last here. It's a shame; I've been dying to ask her what you two were up to.'

'Damn it. I thought she came here a lot.'

'She did, before the troubles started; before it became too dangerous to walk the streets.'

Corthie took a long swig of ale. 'Business bad, aye?'

'It's a miracle we're still open, son. The unpaid bills are stacking up, and without customers, we'll have to close soon.'

Corthie placed a bag of gold onto the counter. 'Our little secret.'

She opened the bag and glanced at the contents. 'I can't accept this; it's too much. I'll never be able to pay it back.'

'Just use it to stay open; I want my favourite tavern to still be around when these troubles are finally over. Oh, and don't tell Quill. Or Elsie.'

She slipped the bag under the counter as the sergeant returned from the bathroom.

'What's the plan, boss?' she said. 'Are we staying here and getting drunk or what?'

'Sorry to interrupt,' said Dorvid from the front door, 'but we might have a problem.'

Nareen frowned. 'What is it, dear?'

'Uh, there are a lot of folk standing outside; the whole street's full of them.'

'Soldiers?'

'Not yet, but with a crowd that size, they'll be along any minute.'

'What do they want?'

Dorvid glanced at Corthie. 'Him.'

'Me?' said Corthie.

Nareen shook her head. 'Were you seen on your way here, son?'

'Aye, maybe, but so?'

'What do you mean "so", son? You're the Champion of the Bulwark, did you not think the folk in the Circuit had heard of you? You're the most famous mortal in the damn City. I'm sorry, but I'm going to have to ask you to leave and come back another time. There's no telling what the soldiers will do when they get here.'

'Don't apologise, Nareen; it's my fault.' He downed the rest of his ale, then nodded to Quill. 'Let's get out of here.'

Corthie and Quill walked to the door, and Dorvid swung it open, the iron bar in his right hand. A roar of noise came in from outside, and Corthie saw that the street was packed with Evader civilians. They cheered as they saw him emerge from the tavern, and surrounded him and Quill. Folk were stretching their arms out to touch him, while others chanted his name to the beat of a drum that someone had brought along.

A woman in tears handed him a flower. 'You're our champion; the champion of all the oppressed mortals of the City.'

'Have you come to save us?' cried another.

'I just came for a drink,' he said, shaking his head as he pushed his way through the crowds.

A young man with earnest eyes grabbed his arm. 'You fight the eternal enemy, but don't forget the internal one; when will you fight them too?'

'I kill greenhides,' he said, shoving the man to the side, 'that's it.'

A harsh blast from a whistle pierced the air, and the crowd began to panic. Some scattered, running down any nearby alleyway, while a few reached for weapons.

'The Tarans are coming!' a voice cried.

A small group of youths remained in the streets after the others had fled. One had a crossbow, while the others had an assortment of makeshift weapons. Down the road in the other direction, the rumble of boots was approaching.

'Get out of here,' Corthie said to the group. 'I don't want your blood on my hands.'

One of the youths stared at him. 'I thought you were here to help us.'

'I was here to get an ale. Go home.'

The group glanced from him to the approaching soldiers, then scattered, fleeing from the militia. The soldiers arrived, filling the street. Protected by mail, shields and helmets, and wielding crossbows and long, steel-tipped clubs, they surrounded Corthie, who held his palms out to show they were empty.

'Evening,' he said to the officer.

'Corthie Holdfast?' the lieutenant said, her eyes glancing up at him.

'Aye.'

'We have orders to escort you out of the Circuit, sir.'

'Why?'

'Your presence is deemed to be an incitement to disorder, sir.'

'Are you Tarans?'

'Yes, sir,' she said, pointing to the badge of a black leopard on her arm. 'We're from the Third Loyal Regiment of Foot, sir, if you wish to file a complaint.'

'We have a carriage parked at Redmarket Palace,' said Quill. 'Can you take us there?'

'Yes, ma'am, if you promise to make your way out of the Circuit once we get there.'

Quill glanced at Corthie.

'Aye, alright,' he said.

The officer gestured to her troopers, and they moved into a flanking formation. Corthie glanced back down the street, seeing the crowd of youths standing fifty yards away, watching. What did they want from him? Wasn't killing greenhides every day enough? He turned as the troopers began to march off, their boots thumping over the rough cobbles.

---

Crowds followed at a distance as the troopers escorted Corthie and Quill back through the narrow, winding alleys to Redmarket Palace. The officer led them up to the checkpoint at the entrance to the palace forecourt, and handed them over to the custody of the Evader militia there. A palace official was also waiting, and he gestured to Corthie as soon as the Tarans had departed to resume their patrol.

'Pack Leader, welcome to Redmarket,' he said.

'How did you know I was here?'

The official raised an eyebrow. 'I think, sir, that the entire Circuit is aware that you are visiting. The governor, also, is aware, and has requested that you meet with her briefly.'

Quill frowned. 'The Tarans told us we had to leave the Circuit immediately.'

'And the quickest way to do that, ma'am, is to take a barge from the canal at the rear of the palace. The governor has arranged for her personal vessel to be available for your use tonight; it will take you right through into Icewarder territory close to the Middle Walls.'

'That's good of her,' said Corthie.

'But first, sir, if you would be so kind as to follow me into the palace; the governor is looking forward to meeting you.'

Corthie nodded, and the official led them across the forecourt, and up the wide steps into the palace. It was shabby compared to the Royal Palace in Ooste, and rough even by the standards of the Wolfpack Tower. They were shown to a small room laid out with comfortable chairs arranged by a fireplace. A woman was standing by a window. Corthie assumed it would be the governor, but one glance told him he was wrong.

'This is Lady Aila, Adjutant of the Circuit,' the official said.

Aila stepped forward. She was dressed in elegant robes with her hair up, and looked far more like a demigod than the last time he had seen her. Their eyes met for a moment, then she glanced away.

'You must be Corthie Holdfast,' she said, extending her hand.

Corthie took it, and raised it to his lips. 'A pleasure to meet you.'

'I, uh... yes, thank you. Of course. Ahh... would you like a drink?'

'I can do that for you, ma'am,' said the official, bowing.

'No need,' she said; 'you can leave us; I'm sure my noble cousin will be here shortly.'

The official bowed again, then left the room.

'A brandy would be nice,' said Corthie, unable to take his eyes off Aila as she walked to a cabinet.

'Just water for me, ma'am,' said Quill.

'No problem; you're guests here. As pleasant as it is to have a Champion of the Bulwark visit, I must ask, what are you doing in the Circuit?'

'The Pack Leader wanted to get a drink, ma'am,' Quill said. 'I told him that, under the circumstances, it might not be a good idea, but...'

'We went to the Blind Poet,' said Corthie; 'you heard of it?'

Aila turned and handed him the glass of brandy, their fingers brushing as he took it. 'I'm not familiar with every tavern in the Circuit, and with the troubles I don't get the chance to go out these days.'

Corthie smiled, and she glanced away.

'You've caused quite a commotion,' she said. 'I hear the streets are crowded with people trying to catch a glimpse of you.'

'Sorry about that. I didn't mean to give you a headache.'

Aila said nothing, and Corthie wished he could just push Quill out of the room for a moment so he could talk to the demigod properly, without all of the awkwardness of pretending not to know each other.

The door swung open.

'Welcome to my home,' said a woman as she walked into the room.

'This is my cousin,' said Aila; 'Lady Ikara, Governor of the Circuit.'

The governor stretched out her hand and Corthie shook it.

'Nice to meet you, ma'am,' he said.

She smiled. 'The pleasure is all mine. I thought the reports I was receiving were too far-fetched to be believed, but no, the famed Champion of the Bulwark is in the Circuit. I see my assistant has already got you a drink. Aila, be a dear and get me one too; there's a nice white from Port Sanders in there, I think.'

Corthie caught Aila rolling her eyes as she went back to the cabinet.

'So, tell me,' said Ikara, 'how is life in the Bulwark? I hear you've cleared the walls of the green devils that plague us.'

'I've separated a few from their heads.'

Ikara laughed. 'You're so funny. And how have you found the Circuit? I hope you'll not judge it too harshly; unfortunately there exists a bitter element among a small section of the Evader population, and trouble does occasionally flare up. It'll all be sorted soon, I'm sure, and perhaps then you can visit us again, in more peaceful times?'

'I'm sure I'll be back at some point. Maybe your... assistant could give me a tour of the place?'

'Nonsense, I would conduct the tour myself; your status demands it.'

Aila handed her cousin a glass of white wine.

'Sorry, ma'am,' said Quill, 'but your official mentioned a barge?'

'Of course, I won't keep you; I'm sure you're very busy. My assistant will escort you to the canal terminal in a moment. Before you go however, I would ask a favour.'

'Aye?' said Corthie.

'Yes,' she said, her smile vanishing. 'The next time you wish to visit the Circuit, I would be most grateful if you could send advance notice first. That way we could avoid the pitched battles that are already underway in the streets as we speak.'

She turned and walked from the room without waiting for a response.

'Something tells me that didn't go too well,' said Corthie.

'You think?' muttered Quill. 'Next time, boss, listen to me.'

'Don't worry about my cousin,' said Aila, 'you're completely beyond her jurisdiction.'

Quill eyed her. 'The barge, ma'am?'

'Sure, yeah. Follow me.'

Aila left the room and Corthie and Quill followed. He could feel a rising tide of frustration build inside him; he had come all the way to the Circuit to see Aila, and there she was, a yard in front of him, but he couldn't speak to her, or acknowledge what had happened between them. And now it looked as though they would be put on a barge and sent away before he had a chance to spend any time with her.

'Can I ask something, ma'am?' said Quill as they walked through the passageways of the palace.

'Yes?'

'It's about the building that the Taran militia burnt down with all of those folk inside.'

Aila narrowed her eyes. 'What's your question?'

'We heard, ma'am, that the Tarans said they had evidence the tenement was being used by rebels. Was that true?'

'So they claim. They say they recovered the body of a dead Taran inside; a soldier killed when rebels attacked a convoy.'

'And their officer, Aurelian, just stood there and watched the building burn to the ground?'

'That's what the rumours say, but it's unclear what happened exactly. I've interviewed survivors who claim a lieutenant ordered the rear doors of the building to be opened, so they could escape the flames.'

'Have you spoken to this Aurelian, ma'am?'

'I tried, but he's already been transferred back to Roser territory.'

'Thanks, ma'am. It's not every demigod who would answer the questions of a sergeant in the Blades.'

Aila smiled as they reached the rear door of the palace. 'I'm not every demigod.'

She opened the doors and they descended to a well-lit wharf. A few Evader militia were standing waiting for them under the oil lamps that hung from a long chain.

Aila gestured towards the barge. 'As my cousin said, this will take you close to the Middle Walls.'

Corthie turned to her. 'I'd like to come back to the Circuit.'

'I'm afraid that might not be possible for a while.'

He noticed Quill was a few yards away, and he lowered his voice. 'I'd like to see you again.'

'I'd like that too,' she whispered, 'but I can't see any way that this will work.'

'We can make it work.'

Quill glanced over. 'Boss, you ready to go?'

He turned his head. 'Aye, Quill; I'm just coming.'

A cry rang out behind him, and four hooded men appeared by the side of the wharf, carrying crossbows and running towards Corthie.

'Death to the Blade!' one of them cried, and the four men halted, raised their bows and loosed.

Aila sprang in front of Corthie, and three bolts hit her; two in the abdomen, and one in her right thigh. She cried out as she slid to the ground. The Evader guards charged at the four men, and they bolted back along the wharf. Quill stared at the body of Aila.

'Get after them!' Corthie cried.

Quill nodded, then sprinted up the side of the wharf, in pursuit of the hooded men and the Evader militia who were chasing them.

Corthie sank to his knees, and pulled Aila towards him. His mind was frozen in shock. Why had she done that? He stared at her, his eyes welling. It couldn't be happening; he was having a nightmare, he told himself, even though he knew it was a lie.

'Aila,' he gasped, holding her close, her blood covering his hands and the front of his coat.

She spluttered, staining her lips and chin red. 'Get them... out.'

'What? Aila, what? You're alive!'

'Get them... out of me.' Her hand came up and she brushed one of the bolts protruding from her abdomen. 'Out, or I can't heal.'

He blinked as realisation struck him. He took a grip of the first bolt, and ripped it out of her thigh. He grabbed the next bolt and pulled; then the final one. Aila cried out as he tore it from her abdomen, then she closed her eyes again.

'Aila? They're out, Aila; I got them.'

'I know,' she groaned. 'Just give me a minute, I'm healing.'

He held her close, and wiped his eyes so she wouldn't know he had been weeping. 'I thought you were gone.'

'It'll take more than a few bolts to kill me, Corthie,' she said, reaching up and turning his face towards her. 'I'm a demigod, remember?'

He gazed down into her eyes as relief and joy flooded him, along with the realisation of how close he had come to losing her. She smiled, pulled his face down, and their lips met.

## CHAPTER 19

# THE HARBINGER

Arrowhead Fort, The Bulwark, The City – 24<sup>th</sup> Koralis 3419

'There,' said Hilde; 'how does that feel?'

Maddie lifted her left arm, wincing at the small aches that remained, but marvelling at the sight of the limb without the splint and sling that had covered it for so long. She flexed her fingers.

'It feels good,' she said. 'Still weak, and it hurts a bit, but thank Malik the bandages are off at last.'

'And not too much longer for the leg; another ten days, maybe?'

Maddie lowered her arm, feeling it tire already.

'We'll build up to it,' Hilde went on; 'we'll start by getting you to exercise it more... are you listening?'

'What?'

The captain got to her feet. 'Never mind. Anyway, it's live-goat day, and I know how much you hate that, so rest your arm and I'll take care of it.'

Maddie frowned. 'I don't want to hear it bleating. Can you cover its mouth or something as you go past? I don't see why we have to give her live food; it's disgusting.'

'Come on, you know it's Blackrose's favourite day.'

'Yeah, she was telling me everything she was going to do to the goat yesterday, in great detail.'

'You know how much she exaggerates; she never actually tortures the goat. It's dead and eaten in about three seconds.'

Maddie made a face. 'Still.'

'Has your family never sacrificed a goat on New Year's Day?'

'I made them stop years ago. I'm not having live animals slaughtered in my home, and sacrifices are a load of superstitious nonsense anyway.'

Hilde smirked. 'You'd better hope the God-King's not listening to your wicked blasphemies.'

'As if. Do you expect me to believe that garbage? Do you really think the God-King's listening to what everyone says? It's a tale to frighten the children.'

'Quite possibly.' Hilde walked to the door. 'I'll be back in ten minutes or so; could you go to the kitchen and warm some soup for me?'

'Yeah, sure. Remember, no bleating.'

Hilde rolled her eyes and left the room.

Maddie raised her left arm again. It was stiff and sore, but the ache was bearable, and it felt like a pain of healing, rather than of injury or loss. She reached over and picked up her brush with her left hand, smiling as the fingers grasped it. She pulled the brush through her hair, feeling every muscle in her left arm tingle. She laughed, then glanced at her leg stretched out before her. Two splints were still in place, covered by thick bandages. Ten days, Hilde had said.

She heard a thump on the front door. Her first instinct was to ignore it, but she remembered that the captain was expecting a delivery of supplies for Blackrose, so she wedged the crutch under her left shoulder and pushed herself up.

The door was thumped again.

'I'm coming,' she yelled as she hobbled out of her room and down the hallway. She spied the soup pot on the stove as she passed the kitchen. 'Soup,' she muttered to herself. 'The captain wants soup.'

Another thump landed on the door.

'I said I'm coming; there's no need to break the door down.'

She reached the entrance, slid the bolts free, then turned the key in the lock. She swung the door open a few inches, and peered out into the red light of evening.

'Hello.'

She looked up.

'I recognise you,' he said. 'Maddie Jackdaw?'

'Eh, yes. Yes, that's my name; you remembered.'

Corthie smiled. 'So, can I come in?'

Fifty emotions flitted through Maddie's mind, none fully-formed enough to grasp. She was a bit scared, yes, but her curiosity was threatening to explode. What was he doing there? Had he come to see her? No, clearly that was ridiculous; then why? Oh. Of course.

She glanced around, but no one else was in sight. 'Tell me why you want to come in.'

He leaned down to her ear. 'Because I know about the other dragon.' He straightened, smiled and winked at her.

Maddie turned and looked back down the hallway, but Hilde was nowhere in sight. Time for an executive decision, she thought.

'Alright. Just you, though, yeah?'

He nodded. 'Just me.'

She leaned on the crutch and moved to the side, gesturing for Corthie to enter. He stepped over the threshold and Maddie closed and relocked the door.

'What happened to you?' he said, glancing at the crutch. 'Or was that a really stupid question?'

'It was her, I mean the dragon, but she didn't mean it. She was fighting Buckler at the time and I got in the way.'

'So it *was* her that wounded Buckler. The slippery lizard denied it as well. He told me that there was no other dragon when I asked him.'

Maddie started to hobble down the hallway and Corthie strode alongside her.

'Could you heat up some soup for me?'

'What? Aye, I suppose so.'

She led him into the kitchen.

'The soup's on the stove,' she said. 'If you could warm it up a little that would be great; oh, and remember to stir it.'

She watched him as he approached the stove. He picked up a spoon then took the lid off the pot.

'So,' she said, 'it wasn't Buckler who told you about the other dragon?'

'Nope,' he said, moving the pot onto the hot part of the stove.

'Then who was it?'

'I'm not telling.'

'I bet I can guess.'

'I bet you can't.'

'Was it someone else in Arrowhead?'

He smiled at her. 'Where is everyone? It can't be just you down here. I've been to Buckler's lair; he has about a dozen folk looking after him.'

'We're the poor relation. It's just me and Captain Hilde.'

He stirred the soup. 'And where is Captain Hilde?'

'Feeding a live goat to the "other" dragon. Did Duke Marcus tell you?'

'I'll answer that. No, and he doesn't know that I'm here, either.'

She opened her mouth.

'That goes for Lord Kano too, before you ask.'

'It's nice that you answer my questions before I ask them.'

'How about you answer some of mine?'

'I'll consider it,' she said. 'Well?'

'First, why is it a secret?'

'I think it's because she hates Duke Marcus and refuses to fly, so he's embarrassed I guess, and would rather not have to be reminded of it all the time. He hasn't executed her, or let her starve to death or anything, but the captain told me that was because Buckler said he would burn the duke to a crisp if he harmed her.'

'Here, this soup's ready.'

'The bowls are by your leg. One portion, please.'

She watched him lean over and pick up a bowl. 'What's your second question?'

'It's a request,' he said as he stood and served a large helping of soup into the bowl. 'I want to see the dragon. What's her name?'

'Blackrose.'

'Blackrose.' He nodded. 'Right, where do you want your soup?'

'Oh, it's not for me.'

'Maddie?' came a cry from the hallway. 'Where are you?'

'In the kitchen.'

The sound of footsteps came in from the hallway, then the captain walked into the room.

'Well, that was fun. I...' She tailed off as she saw the champion standing by the stove. She stared for a moment. 'What in Malik's name is Corthie Holdfast doing in my kitchen?'

'Warming your soup,' said Maddie.

'Ah,' he said, holding out the bowl for her, 'so this is for you? Are you Captain Hilde, aye?'

Hilde remained unmoving, so Corthie placed the bowl down onto a side table and wiped his hands.

'He knows,' said Maddie.

'Knows what?' said Hilde.

Maddie raised an eyebrow. 'About the, you know... other dragon.'

A slight change came over Hilde's face. 'There is no other dragon. I don't know what you're talking about. Pack Leader Holdfast, I'm afraid someone has been playing tricks on you, and without wishing to sound rude, I would like you to leave.'

He smiled. 'So her name isn't Blackrose?'

Hilde gave a scathing glance in Maddie's direction.

'What was I supposed to do?' she said.

'Deny it, of course.'

'Well, I was put on the spot, and he was standing at the door, and I didn't know what to do. I mean, you weren't here, so...'

'Don't blame this on me. I left you alone for ten minutes. Ten minutes, girl, and I come back to find... this in my kitchen.'

Maddie narrowed her eyes. 'Oh, sorry. I must have forgotten your lesson about what to do if the Champion of the Bulwark knocks on the front door.'

'Don't take that tone with me, girl, or you'll be…'

Corthie coughed. 'I want to see Blackrose.'

Hilde glared at him. 'Well, you can't.'

'So you admit that she exists?'

'I admit nothing. Until and unless you have a written command from Duke Marcus himself, I'm afraid I'm not at liberty to discuss this matter any further. I swore an oath, as did Maddie, although she seems to have forgotten all about it; and that, as they say, is that. I will show you to the door; this way, please.'

Corthie stayed where he was. 'I'm not going to speak to the duke about this; I want it to remain between the three of us in this room. The duke has no idea I'm here, and nor does Buckler for that matter.'

'It wasn't the duke who told you?'

'It wasn't,' said Maddie; 'I already asked him that. He wouldn't tell me his source.'

Hilde frowned at Corthie. 'Alright. If you tell me how you found out, then I'll consider letting you see Blackrose for one minute.'

'No. Let me see Blackrose, and speak to her, and then maybe I'll consider telling you my source.'

'I don't believe you.'

Maddie caught Hilde's eye. 'I'm sure Corthie would tell the truth if he got to, eh, speak to Blackrose.'

'Thanks for the vote of confidence, Maddie,' he said, 'but I'm not promising anything.'

'No,' said Hilde, 'perhaps my young associate is correct. Would you be willing to swear an oath to me first?'

'And what would the oath say?'

'That you would swear by everything you hold dear not to tell a single person about any of this; not a word about Maddie or me, or what we do, the location of this lair, of anything regarding the existence of Blackrose.'

Corthie laughed. 'Nope. I can't do that.'

Hilde's eyes darkened. 'And why not?'

'Because the future's not... because I can't be bound when I don't know what's going to happen.'

'Not good enough.'

'Then you have to decide,' he said; 'because I'm not leaving until I see Blackrose. Call the wardens and try to have me ejected from here, or let me speak to her.'

'If I asked Blackrose to incinerate you, she would do it,' said Hilde. 'Perhaps this is the answer. No one knows you're here, and your body would never be found. I could sweep it out with the rest of the ashes. Do you want to take that risk?'

Maddie stared at her. 'But he's the champion.'

'So?' Hilde said. 'The storms of Sweetmist will be arriving in less than ten days from now. The moats will refill with the rains, and the greenhides will retreat for a couple of months. If a champion were to go missing, this would be the best time for it.'

'Fair enough,' said Corthie. 'If that's your condition, I'm happy to take the risk. Make it quick, though, aye? I wouldn't want to be lying half-scalded for twenty minutes.'

'What?' said Maddie. 'This is insane, I can't agree to this.'

'Hush, Maddie,' said Hilde; 'I'm not asking for your agreement. This young man may be the flavour of the summer, but I've seen plenty of champions come and go over the years.'

'Not like him, you haven't.'

'His kill-rate is above average, I admit, but there are millions of greenhides out there. In the grand scheme of things, Corthie Holdfast's contribution will dwindle into insignificance, the fame of his exploits will fade, and before we know it, another champion will come along to thrill the hearts of the gullible.'

Corthie raised an eyebrow, and for a moment Maddie wondered if he was going to get angry. Instead, he smiled.

'You're completely right,' he said, 'except for one thing. My time here is short. I'll kill greenhides for the City, but not forever; perhaps not even for long.'

Hilde regarded him for a second. 'You have a deathwish?'

'No. My sister's coming to rescue me. I keep telling folk this, but no one listens. I just need to stay alive until then. Of course, if she were to get here, and find that you'd ordered a dragon to incinerate me, well, she probably wouldn't be too pleased; but I'll be dead, so hey. It'll be you that has to deal with the consequences.'

Maddie and Hilde glanced at each other.

'Your sister?' said Hilde.

'Aye. And if you think I'm powerful...'

'You're bluffing.'

'I'm sure Blackrose might have something to add to this,' said Maddie.

'Good idea,' said Corthie, 'though if she's like Buckler, I doubt it'll be anything sensible. As much as I love that red lizard, he's clueless about the history of dragons, or about anything other than fighting.'

'That's not his fault,' said Maddie. 'He was raised as a slave-merce-nary. Blackrose is always chiding him about his lack of dragony ways, whereas she used to be a queen.'

'Maddie, stop it,' Hilde sighed.

'A queen?' said Corthie, his eyes lighting up. 'Then she remembers her own world? By the way, I think the soup's gone cold.'

'I've lost my appetite anyway,' said Hilde. 'Amalia's ass, I hope I don't regret this. If Blackrose feels that I've betrayed her in any way it could destroy everything I've built here over the last decade. Her trust in me would vanish.' She glanced at Maddie and Corthie. 'None of us might be leaving the lair alive; do you both understand?'

'It'll be fine,' Corthie said. 'I'll take full responsibility. Tell her I bullied you into it.'

'Are you sure you don't have a deathwish?'

'All this worry can't be good for your health. You should try to relax more.'

Hilde strode to a cupboard and removed a flask of gin. 'I'm going to need one of these first.' She poured a glass, then downed it neat. 'Alright. Let's go and see Blackrose.'

The captain led Maddie and Corthie out of the kitchen and along the hallway.

'That door at the end leads to the lair,' said Maddie, keeping pace with her crutch.

Corthie smiled. 'The smell gives it away.'

They passed through the gate and entered the huge cavern that led to both lairs.

'That red door there,' said Maddie, pointing, 'that's where Buckler lives.'

'Right,' said Corthie. 'I've seen that from the other side. Buckler had the cheek to tell me it went nowhere.'

'And this black gate...'

'Hush, Maddie,' said Hilde. 'I think the champion can guess that for himself.' The captain opened the hatch in the gate. 'Blackrose? Me again. Listen, prepare yourself; we have a visitor.'

'Excellent,' murmured a voice; 'another live goat?'

'Eh, not exactly.' She turned to the others. 'Come on.'

They stepped through the doorway and entered the lair. Fresh blood was pooling by the dragon's forelimbs, along with a few scattered bones and scraps of goatskin. Blackrose was resting her head on her enormous limbs, her eyes glimmering as she watched them approach.

'This is Corthie Holdfast, Blackrose,' said Hilde. 'He's a champion; you know, one of the Wolfpack who goes out and fights the greenhides.'

'You've brought me an early dinner? How thoughtful. He looks as though he'd take a bit longer to eat than a goat. I hope he's clean.'

Corthie stared at her, his mouth falling open. 'Wow. You are just about the most gorgeous thing I've ever seen,' he said, walking closer to her claws. 'Buckler's a mere pup next to you. Maddie told me you were a queen, and I believe it, utterly. I've never laid eyes on anything more regal in my life.'

Blackrose smiled. 'A flatterer? It's been a while since I had one of those around. Go on, tell me more.'

Corthie halted a yard from her as Maddie and Hilde watched. 'Can I see your teeth?'

The dragon opened her jaws, and Corthie leaned in for a closer look.

'I can't watch,' gasped Maddie, clutching onto the captain's arm.

'The boy's mad,' muttered Hilde.

'Truly magnificent,' he said. 'It's your teeth that create fire, isn't it? My father could do it with his fingers. Can you show me?'

A spark of fire like lightning leapt across Blackrose's jaws and Corthie whooped and laughed.

Blackrose closed her jaws. 'Well, that was amusing. Should I eat you now?'

Corthie chuckled. 'When was the last time you ate a human? Do you not remember how bad they taste?'

'Good point, although I find it depends on what they themselves have been eating. Farmers are fine, but city-dwellers are generally revolting.' Her nostrils flared. 'From your scent I can tell that you would not be particularly tasty; you drink too much alcohol.'

'I have a scent? But I took a bath this afternoon, and I'm wearing clean clothes. I didn't think I was reeking.'

'A dragon can tell a hundred things about a human from their odour. For example I can discern a certain amount of hormones being released; enough for me to say with some certainty that you have met someone you like. It's not love, yet, but I can sense your growing interest in this woman. Am I correct?'

He smiled. 'Aye.'

'Who is it?' said Maddie.

'None of your business,' said Corthie. 'We're keeping it quiet.'

'But I'd really like to know. Can I guess?'

'You'll never guess, not in a million years.'

'But if I say her name, you'll confirm it? It's Sergeant Quill, isn't it? I've seen the way she follows you around and looks at you.'

'It's not Sergeant Quill.'

'No? Alright, give me a moment...'

'I have an idea,' said Blackrose. 'Shall we play a game?'

Maddie nodded. 'I like games.'

'You didn't like this one the last time we played.'

'Yeah, but I'm looking forward to Corthie playing.'

'What game?' he said.

The dragon fixed him with her eyes. 'Listen to me, little champion; in a moment you will feel some pain in your head. Do not worry about it, for sometimes the truth brings pain.'

He smiled. 'Ready when you are, dragon.'

'So cocky. Let's see if you remain so when forced to say nothing but the truth.' She narrowed her eyes, then opened them wide, her head rising. 'What is this! Impossible! What trick are you playing on me, insect?'

'I'm not playing any tricks. What's up? Finding it difficult to get into my head?'

Maddie stared as the dragon said nothing for a long moment. Blackrose moved her head round Corthie as he stood motionless, sniffing him and looking him up and down.

'You seem mortal enough, so how is this possible? I must know.'

'I don't understand,' said Maddie. 'Why isn't it working?'

Blackrose glared at her. 'That is precisely what I just asked him, girl. He is protected. A cloud surrounds him. No, not a cloud; a web of thick strands shields him, impenetrable. I'd guess that even the gods would struggle to break through.'

'They can't,' said Corthie; 'many have tried and failed. I'm immune to all powers.' He glanced back at Maddie and Hilde. 'It can be handy having a powerful sister.'

'Your sister did this?' said Blackrose. 'She must be a mighty god to have done so.'

'She's not, but I'll tell her you said that.'

'As well as the web of protection, I also sense a particularly virulent strain of battle-vision. The powers you possess are too dangerous for a mortal to hold. Why are you here? Who sent you? What is your purpose?'

'I was brought here against my will.'

'Yet you fight for Marcus. Are you his slave?'

'I'm nobody's slave. I fight because if I didn't I'd be dead, and I swore to myself that I'd stay alive, at least until I can escape this world and return to my own.'

'A cowardly compromise.'

'Aye, I know. If it was for Marcus alone, I'd tell him to go screw himself, but I like the folk that live in this City. I'm doing it for them.'

'You have a weak heart for feeling that way.'

Corthie shrugged. 'I'm a mortal man, with every weakness that comes with it.'

'I assume that if you had the means to return home, you would?'

'Aye. Lord Naxor brought me here, so I'm guessing he has the same sort of device that my sister used to have.'

The dragon came in closer, until her eyes were level with Corthie. 'Did you see it?'

'No. Naxor drugged me before we travelled here, but how else could he have done it?'

'So, there is a Quadrant hidden somewhere within the City? How interesting.' She turned to Hilde. 'You did very well in bringing this Corthie Holdfast before me; very well indeed.' She glanced back at Corthie. 'Do you plan on stealing it?'

'There's no need; my sister's coming for me.'

'But you said she "used to" have a Quadrant? Did she lose it?'

'It was stolen by the god who abducted me, but it'll be fine. My sister's very resourceful. When she comes, I'll ask her to help you get home as well.'

The dragon stared at Corthie for a long time. 'Thank you. You have no idea what your coming here today means to me. You are the first human to speak any sense about the other worlds that you and I both know exist, and the first to offer me the smallest glimmer of hope that I might one day see my home again.'

Corthie stepped back. 'I have to go to work now; I have a shift with the Wolfpack. It was an honour to meet you, Blackrose.' He lifted his hand and placed it on the side of the dragon's face. 'Farewell.'

He turned and walked over to where Maddie and Hilde were standing. 'Thanks for letting me see her; she's more amazing than anything I could have dreamt of.'

'You can't leave,' said Maddie, 'there are still a hundred things I want to ask you. What's a Quadrant?'

He laughed. 'Ask me next time.'

'You'll be back?'

'You can be sure of that.' He shook Hilde's hand. 'Have I earned your trust yet, Captain?'

'No,' she said. 'You didn't swear the oath.'

'Corthie Holdfast needs to swear no oath to you,' said Blackrose. 'He has my trust. He is here for a purpose, and the world of gods will tremble at his approach. Watch out for them, champion, I can sense that the rulers of this City will not take your presence among them lightly. Do not trust them. One or more will fear and hate you, and perhaps even try to kill you.'

He glanced at the dragon. 'There have been two attempts on my life so far, but I'm still here.' He turned to Hilde. 'I'll see myself out, Captain. Have a good evening.'

Corthie walked to the hatch in the gate, stooped down and passed through.

'Did you hear all that?' said Maddie. 'Other worlds? He's immune to the power of the gods! Malik's crotch, maybe he is the Redeemer.'

Hilde sighed.

'Alright, maybe not the Redeemer, but he's exceptional, you can't deny that.'

'He is an aberration,' said Blackrose. 'He goes against everything I thought I knew. Not even the gods can withstand my powers, yet he brushed them away like cobwebs. He is a freak of nature that should not exist; yet at the same time he is my last hope. What does it mean?'

'I don't want to know,' said Hilde. 'I don't like him, and I don't like the way he just walks in here and has you both eating out of his hand. He's trouble, and I hate to see him raise your hopes like that.'

Blackrose lowered her head to the captain. 'Hilde, you have served me well for ten years. You know my blackest moods, and my anger, and yet you stayed. We have argued so many times, you and I, and yet my spirits lighten every time you walk into my lair. You brought me Maddie, and now you bring me Corthie. I know you don't want things to change, but sometimes change is inevitable, my dear Captain; sometimes we just have to accept it.'

A solitary tear ran down Hilde's cheek. Before Maddie could say anything, Hilde turned and strode from the lair.

'I don't understand,' said Maddie; 'why is she upset?'

'Because she knows,' said Blackrose; 'she can sense it. Corthie Holdfast is the harbinger of events that will turn this City upside down.' She glanced down at Maddie, her dark red eyes lit with an inner fire. 'My ten years of being trapped in this prison will be coming to end, soon, one way or another.'

# CHAPTER 20

# INTRODUCTIONS

S unward Range, Roser Territory, Auldan, The City – 26th Koralis 3419

'Unless my colleague has any more questions for you, Lieutenant, I think we're done here.'

The other investigator checked her notes. 'I did want to ask a follow-up question regarding the orders to seal the doors of the tenement.' She smiled up at Daniel. 'Did you realise that this would mean those inside would be trapped, or was that your intention all along, Lieutenant?'

'You don't have to answer that question, Daniel,' said Nadhew, a lawyer and friend of his parents. He turned to the investigator. 'My client's answers are detailed within the written statement that has been submitted to the tribunal. I suggest you refer to that, madam.'

'Perhaps you are not aware that the statement has some... inconsistencies regarding the timing of certain orders.'

The older investigator coughed. 'As I was saying, I think we're done here. Thank you very much for your time, Lieutenant Aurelian. The findings of the tribunal will be sent to you as soon as they are available.'

Daniel nodded. 'Am I being posted back to the Circuit while I wait, sir?'

'No, Lieutenant. The commanders of the Taran militia feel that your presence there would not be conducive to creating a harmonious environment. The Evader mob knows your name, and the rebels have posted a bounty on your head. Remain here at your family villa, and get some rest; you deserve it.'

The two investigators stood, and Daniel and the lawyer got to their feet. They walked through the cool, marble-floored hallways to the veranda at the rear of the villa, where a carriage was waiting.

'I have a few words to say to an old friend,' said the older investigator. 'Please wait in the carriage; I'll just be a moment.'

The other investigator frowned, her eyes narrow. 'Yes, sir.'

As soon as she was out of earshot, the chief investigator turned to Nadhew. 'Sorry about that, old chap. She's new, and a little green behind the ears.'

'Not to worry,' said the lawyer; 'no harm done.'

'Between you and me, old chap, and strictly off the record, but young Daniel has nothing to fear from the findings of the tribunal. I've seen all the evidence and can categorically rule out a court-martial or other disciplinary measure. A few of the more soft-hearted civilians on the board may object, but nothing will come of it.' He glanced at Daniel. 'The Taran militia look after its own, son.'

'Thank you, sir.'

'What about his field promotion?' said Nadhew. 'Is it safe?'

'I will personally make sure that he retains his rank of senior lieutenant. If he keeps this up, he'll be a captain in no time.'

The lawyer and the chief investigator shook hands.

'A pleasure, as always,' said Nadhew.

'Until next time.'

The investigator turned, and strode off towards the wagon, his boots crunching on the sun-drenched gravel of noon.

'A good morning's work, Danny. Well done.'

'I hardly said a thing.'

'Exactly, my boy. You left it to the professionals, which is all I could have asked for.'

'The rebels have put a bounty on my head; did you hear him?'

Nadhew chuckled. 'Yes. To be loathed by Evader rebels is perhaps the highest badge of honour a Roser officer can earn; well, that's the way it will be perceived in Tara. It's marked you out as someone to watch, and I doubt you'll run into any more difficulties with your colleagues in the militia.'

'You heard about that?'

'You broke that boy's nose and jaw for insulting your family name, Danny. Did you think an old Taran gossip like me wouldn't come to hear of it?'

'I beat up a fellow lieutenant and I burned down a tenement in the Circuit; I'm a thug. How did this happen? Did you ever see me violent as a child?'

The old man shook his head. 'Never, but then your mother would always step forward to fight your battles for you. Lady Aurelian is a noble and great-hearted woman, feared and respected by all, and now you're getting a first glimpse of life without her protection.' He ruffled Daniel's hair. 'I would say that you've made a good start, my boy.' He turned. 'Ahh, here's my carriage.'

'Thanks for coming up here today.'

'I'm glad to be able to do a favour for you and your family, Danny. Now, spend a few peaceful days in the villa, and wait for the tribunal's letter. I'll arrange for a copy to fall into my hands at the same time, and shall be up here within a few hours of it arriving. Until then, take care and enjoy yourself.'

The lawyer strolled out to the carriage, waved to Daniel, then boarded. The driver urged the ponies on, and the carriage took off, its wheels rumbling over the gravel. Daniel stood in the shade of the veranda and watched as the wagon disappeared down the long, tree-lined driveway towards the road that led to Tara.

He turned and went back into the villa. He strode through to the central atrium, past the little channels that carried cooling water to dampen the heat of late summer. In a few days the rains and humid storms of Sweetmist would begin, and Daniel was almost looking forward to a break from the dry heat, although he knew that after five or six days of continuous downpours he would be tired of that too.

The villa was almost silent apart from the sound of the running water, and he savoured the peace. He still felt on edge from his month in the Circuit, and the old hands had told him it would take a while before he would be able to properly relax again. It was difficult for him to describe the relief he had felt at the news he would not be returning to Evader territory, but at the same time he felt guilty that so many other Rosers were still there in service of the City.

He passed a couple of Reaper servants cleaning the marble floor and went into the kitchen.

'Is sir hungry?' said a housekeeper, bowing.

'A long, cool drink would be better in this weather.'

'I'll have one prepared for you.' He snapped his fingers and a Reaper servant began to get his drink ready. 'Fresh ice came in from the harbour this morning, girl, make sure you put some in.'

'Yes, sir,' said the servant, her eyes lowered.

'And a small gin,' said Daniel.

'Yes, sir.'

'Shall I bring it to your room, sir?' said the housekeeper.

'No, I'll wait. Have one brought on the hour every hour after that, though.'

The housekeeper bowed. 'As you will, sir.'

Daniel gazed out the kitchen window at the view of the landscape. The rolling hillside was covered in terraced vineyards and olive groves, with alternating lines of spruce and cedar trees as windbreaks for the stormier seasons, lying perpendicular to the rays of the sun. Workers were out, pruning and tidying after the summer harvest had finished a few days previously. Daniel was glad that he had arrived after it was over, as the estate was filled with itinerant Reaper labourers for the harvest's duration.

'Here you are, sir,' said the housekeeper, presenting him with a filled glass on a tray.

Daniel took the glass. 'Thank you. I shall be in my room if I'm required for anything.'

'Very good, sir.'

He sipped the iced drink as he walked to his rooms. Once inside, he shut the door and closed some of the sunward-facing shutters to filter out the noon sun. He put down the drink and glanced around the small sitting room. How would he spend his days off? He caught sight of his well-stocked bookshelves and smiled.

---

Two hours later he heard voices in the villa. He put down his well-thumbed copy of *The Last Mortal Prince of Tara* and stretched his arms. The sound of voices got closer.

'Damn it,' he muttered. He had just got to the part where the God-King and God-Queen had exiled the Aurelian prince to a jail cell on the remote and wind-lashed Grey Isle in the Cold Sea, where he would spend the rest of his days.

There was a gentle tap on his door. 'Daniel, are you in there, darling?'

His mother. He thought about remaining silent, but his mother clearly knew he was staying in the villa. He was about to answer when the door opened.

'There you are,' she said, striding in, 'let me see my boy. Stand up, I want to look at you.'

He got to his feet and she gazed at him.

'Senior lieutenant at nineteen,' she said; 'promoted faster than anyone else in your graduation class; you should have seen the look on Lord Chamberlain's face when he heard the news. I'm proud of you, son; so, so proud.'

Daniel frowned. 'You know I was only promoted because the militia commanders didn't want to ascribe what happened at the tenement to a junior officer. Technically, I shouldn't have been given command of two platoons.'

Her mother waved her hand. 'Mere details, darling. The truth is that you were given the command, whether "technically" that was correct or not. It was what you did with that command that mattered.'

'And what did I do, mother?'

'You avenged the savage murder of innocent Roser wagon-drivers and troopers, Daniel. You showed those rebels that Taran officers will not stand by and watch our own people be cut down as if they were dogs.'

'There were civilians inside that tenement, children...'

'No,' she said, raising a finger; 'I'll not hear about that. War can be a rough business.'

'War, mother? We were supposed to be peace-keeping, not fighting a war.'

'You're right, of course. Personally, I feel we should withdraw at once, and let those Evader beasts fight it out among themselves.'

He sat back down and picked up his iced gin. 'For once I agree with you, mother.'

She took a seat opposite him. 'And the investigators' visit? How did it go? I trust Nadhew was up to his usual standards; he was such a dear, to represent you for free.'

'It was a complete whitewash.'

She raised an eyebrow.

'In other words, mother, I'm to be exonerated, and my promotion stands.'

'Excellent. The whole tribunal was a joke from the start. If it weren't for Lord Chamberlain making such a fuss, it would never have been convened in the first place. Still, I'm glad it's over; that's a weight off my mind.'

The housekeeper knocked at the open door. 'Your drink, my lady.'

His mother extended her hand and the housekeeper placed the glass into her fingers. He bowed, then left the room, closing the door behind him.

'It's difficult to believe it's only been a month and a half since I last saw you, darling; it feels like years. You look different, older. More mature. More dangerous, if I may say so. The dark glint in your eye has developed a slightly rogueish timbre; I like it. It makes you look like you have a ruthless streak, which, I suppose, you have proved. Not only in the Circuit, but I see evidence of it in Tara whenever I bump into that oaf Gaimer, and have to gaze upon his misshapen nose. He deserves what you did to him. He was always a brute, and now he looks like one too.'

She sipped her drink.

'How's Todd?'

'No idea. He was assigned to a comfortable position running errands for the commander of a fort in the Union Walls. Many of your graduation classmates were given easy positions; desk jobs in Tara, or within a garrison, like Todd. The militia's coffers must be bulging with all the bribes their parents paid to get them out of active duty on the front.'

Daniel attempted a smile. 'Did you forget to send our bribe?'

'It never even crossed my mind. I knew what the other parents were doing of course, but I saw it as an opportunity for you to win some acclaim and glory, and I was right. The other parents are riddled with regret, and all now wish they had done the same. You've no idea what this has all meant for me and your father; everyone is talking about you, even the lower classes in Tara have been singing your name.' She eyed him. 'Which brings me to another reason why I'm here.'

She gave him a smile.

'You're starting to worry me, mother; what have you done?'

'Oh, I didn't have to do anything, my dear; for once, they all came to me. It's extraordinary how one act in the Circuit can change the attitude of every aristocratic family in Tara with an unmarried daughter. Two months ago, they were shunning us, and enjoying the gold that Chamberlain had given them for that purpose, but now? I've been put in the frightful position of actually having to turn some away; can you imagine?' She leaned over and took his hand. 'Flowers have been arriving at our home daily, along with notes begging, sorry, requesting an introduction.'

Daniel shook his head. 'At least I'm here at the villa. I'll deal with this later, when I have time.'

'But, darling, don't you have a few days' leave while you wait for the tribunal's decision? You should use that time productively. By the time you return to active duty, we could have a whole new engagement organised. A winter wedding sounds wonderful. An heir to the Aurelians could be on his way within eighteen months.'

'You're getting a little ahead of yourself, mother,' Daniel laughed; 'and besides, Nadhew and the investigators told me to stay here at the villa, so unfortunately I won't be able to return with you to Tara.'

'Oh, I know that, dear. That's why I've brought the two most suitable candidates here with me today.'

Daniel spat out his drink. 'What? You did what?'

His mother reached over and rummaged in the small handbag she had brought. She withdrew some folded slips of paper. 'I've written some salient points regarding each of the two girls on these, to save you time.' She handed them to Daniel. 'Give them a thorough read, and then I'll take you to the first one.'

'But,' he spluttered, 'where are they?'

'I put one of them in the drawing room, and the other in the conservatory.'

'You left them alone?'

'Don't be silly. I asked each to bring a chaperone. Millicent brought her widowed aunt, and Emily brought her grandmother.'

'And you want me to meet them today? Now?'

'I want you get yourself cleaned up and suitably attired first, dear.'

'I can't believe this. I'm supposed to be resting.'

'And what could be more restful than spending some time with two lovely young ladies? Both seem to have gone to great lengths to prettify themselves in order to meet you; though I suppose they had little choice in the matter.'

'I'm not doing it, mother. I'm not leaving my room. I intend to get roaring drunk instead, and then perhaps I will roam the villa in my dressing gown, and play up to my new reputation as a boorish thug.'

'Are you quite finished, dear? I have one word to say to you: Clarine. You owe me.'

He stared at her. Was there no escape?

'If you even consider fouling this up, darling, I will be humiliated. I have just spent the last four hours sharing a carriage with them, regaling them with tales of your wit and bravery, and assuring them that you had matured somewhat since the failure of your previous engagement. Do you want me to seem a fool?'

Daniel stood, and walked to the shutters. Through the slats he could see the sky darkening from pink to red, the sun hovering just over the horizon of hills. Maybe one of the young women would be nice, he thought, trying to inject himself with some enthusiasm. A thought occurred to him.

'How old are they?'

'Read the slips of paper, dear, that's what they're for.'

He glanced at the first slip. Millicent Baccalaurian, second daughter of Lord and Lady Baccalaurian, aged seventeen. Enjoys pony-riding. Brown eyes, brown hair. Avoid discussing politics or history as it bores her.

He frowned at his mother. 'These notes, eh...'

'Yes?'

He shook his head. 'Nothing.' He read the second slip. Emily Omertia, only child of Lord and Lady Omertia, aged eighteen. Came first in her class for the end of year school certificate. Green eyes, blonde hair. Clever and pretty but, alas, she knows it.

'You'll do it, yes?' she said.

'How long will they be here for?'

'That depends. If, say, you were to approve of one, or both, then I've arranged that they can stay the night. Don't give me that look, Daniel; the chaperones will be sleeping in the same bedrooms as their charges; everything is respectable and above board. So long as you are discreet.'

'So if I talk to them each for five minutes, and don't like them, you'll send them away?'

'I require an actual effort from you today,' she said, standing; 'I want none of your nonsense. Even if it turns out that you despise them both, I want them to return to Tara saying nothing but good things about you. I'll leave you now, and shall inform the candidates that you are getting ready. Put on the drill uniform; it's not as formal as full-dress, and it makes you appear rather dashing.'

She smiled, then left the room.

Daniel stared out of the window, and almost wished he was back in the Circuit.

***

'Good evening,' he said, putting on his best smile; 'sorry it took so long to get ready.'

Millicent and her aunt rose from the couch where they had been sitting.

'Shall I serve some refreshments, sir?' said the housekeeper.

'Yes. I'll have a red wine, not too dry,' he said, 'and whatever the ladies desire.'

'Another round of what we had before,' said the aunt.

'Very good, ladies, sir,' the housekeeper bowed.

Daniel glanced at Millicent. 'Nice to meet you.'

She extended her hand and he kissed it.

'I hope you had a pleasant journey.'

'It was hot and sticky,' said the aunt. 'Ridiculous weather for travelling to the hills, but Millie's parents insisted. You seem to be flavour of the month, young Aurelian, and there has been a most undignified rush to your front door.'

'Aunt!' cried Millicent. 'You promised mother you wouldn't.'

The older woman sat back down on the couch. 'I have a tendency to speak the truth, however blunt, and that's how I see it. What's he done to deserve this attention; killed a few rebels? It takes a little more than that to make me go weak at the knees, girl.'

'I agree,' said Daniel. 'I was only doing my duty, and hardly expected anything like this upon my return.'

'Sit down, the pair of you,' said the aunt. 'I refuse to crane my neck any longer.'

Daniel and Millicent sat down opposite each other.

'Might I say how beautiful you are looking, Millicent?' he said.

The aunt snorted. 'You're either a liar or blind, lad. My niece is as plain as they come. The pretty one is waiting in the conservatory. So, let's hasten through the pleasantries, as we all know you're just being polite before you go on to the next girl.'

Millicent's face went a deep scarlet.

'That seemed a little uncalled for,' said Daniel, his embarrassment growing; 'and not true, either.'

'Come off it, boy,' said the aunt. 'It's not her you're trying to impress, remember; it's me.'

'But you seem to have already made up your mind.'

The aunt regarded him for a moment. 'You're correct, I have. I've seen what you did to that Gaimer boy; what guarantees can you give me that you won't raise your hands to Millie?'

He blinked. 'What?'

'You heard me. Millie's mother might be taken in, but my sister's always had a blind spot when it comes to brutish men. Therefore, I ask again; with your tendency towards solving your problems with your fists, how do I know that you won't turn them on my niece?'

'I... I would never hurt a woman.'

'Liar.'

'I'm sorry?'

'Weren't there women, and children, inside that building you burnt to the ground?'

Daniel froze as images of the flames shot through his mind.

'Your silence tells me everything I need to know. Before you go, do you have any other questions for my niece?'

He lowered his eyes. 'No.'

'Then goodbye, young Aurelian.'

Daniel stood. He glanced at Millicent, but she was keeping her eyes away from him. 'Thank you for meeting with me; it was a pleasure.'

He turned and walked towards the door just as the housekeeper was entering with a tray of drinks. He took his glass of wine and went back into the hallway, his mind spinning. He had done exactly as his mother had requested; smartened up, been polite, given compliments, and yet the chaperone had ripped him to shreds. She had found his weak spot and twisted the knife.

'Out already?' said his mother as she approached.

'Millicent's aunt didn't take to me.'

His mother nodded. 'I thought she might be a hard nut to crack. Should I arrange for a carriage to collect them or do you want to try again later?'

'A carriage, please.'

'Such a pity; the Baccalaurians were my first pick. Never mind. Are you going to the conservatory now?'

He nodded.

'Then either finish that drink or give it to me. It looks uncouth to walk in carrying a glass.'

Daniel downed the wine and passed his mother the empty vessel. Without waiting for her response he set off down the marble passageway. The warmth from the day was keeping the villa at a pleasant temperature, and he almost forgot what he was doing as he passed the water channels in the atrium, their spray glistening in the lamplight. He reached the conservatory, knocked, and entered.

Two women stood. One was elderly, and was leaning on a walking stick, while the other was young. His mother had been right; Emily was stunning, her blonde hair sitting curled on her bare shoulders. They both smiled as he approached.

'Good evening,' he said; 'how nice to meet you.'

'The pleasure is ours,' said the grandmother.

'Would you like a refreshment?'

'No, thank you; your servants have been keeping us well fed and watered while we waited.'

'What did you think of Millicent?' said Emily.

The grandmother gave her a quick glance. 'I'm supposed to ask the questions, dear.' She smiled at Daniel. 'After hearing your mother talk about your exploits, my granddaughter has been keen to meet you.'

'Please sit,' he said, selecting an armchair for himself; 'and I'm sure my mother was exaggerating.'

'Don't undersell yourself, Daniel. You acted, while around you others did nothing.'

'What was it like?' said Emily, her eyes sparkling.

'What was what like?'

'Being in the Circuit? Knowing that if you didn't fight, then you might be killed?'

He said nothing for a moment. 'I had one aim, I guess; to make sure all of my troopers returned back to camp every day alive.'

'Were you scared?'

'Emily,' said the grandmother, 'I know you're enthusiastic, but please, allow me to ask the questions.'

'Sorry, Grandma, but Daniel's done things that none of the other boys in Tara have done, and I have a hundred questions that I'd like to ask him.'

'They'll have to wait, dear. Remember that this is merely an intro-duction; you'll have plenty of time to get to know him if you get on well and like each other.'

Emily caught Daniel's eyes and smiled.

There was a low rumble from outside. Emily got to her feet and walked over to the window.

'A carriage has arrived,' she said, gazing out, 'and Millicent and her aunt are getting on board. Oh dear. I suppose that means she won't be staying the night.' She glanced at Daniel. 'What a pity.'

'Tell me, Daniel,' said the grandmother, 'what are your plans and ambitions?'

He smiled. He had practised this answer. 'I want to progress as an officer in the militia, then move into managing the family's estates and properties. I hope it'll be many years before I become Lord Aurelian, but one has to be prepared.'

'Are you going back to the Circuit?' said Emily.

'Not for the foreseeable future; the Evader rebels have put a bounty on my head.'

The young woman gasped. She walked back over to the couch and sat, her eyes fixed on Daniel.

'A bounty?' said the grandmother.

'Yes. I'm afraid I may have become a little notorious in the Circuit. However, I, we, are perfectly safe within Roser territory; the soldiers at the Union Walls will keep any Evaders from entering.'

'Good,' said Emily; 'I wouldn't want those savages anywhere near the civilised parts of the City.'

She looked like she was about to say more, but her grandmother interrupted. 'Do you have any questions for my granddaughter?'

'Yes,' he said. 'I heard you came top of your graduating class.'

Emily blushed. 'I did.'

'What subject interested you the most?'

'Political History and Law,' she said. 'I specialised in the Golden Age of Tara, and also the government and constitution of Prince Michael.'

The grandmother smiled. 'My granddaughter has whole bookshelves dedicated to the reign of Prince Michael; I've sat at dinners where it's all she could talk about.'

Emily glanced at Daniel. 'Have you read much about the prince?'

'Not too much.'

'You do read, though?'

'Yes. I have a small collection.'

'What are you reading just now?'

He cringed on the inside. '*The Last Mortal Prince of Tara.*'

She smiled.

'Well, I think that's enough for now, young sir,' said her grandmother. 'Would you be so kind as to let your mother know that I'd like to have a little chat with her; I feel this has been a very promising introduction.'

'As do I,' said Emily, her green eyes on Daniel.

Daniel stood and bowed. 'I hope to see you again, soon.'

Emily smiled. 'I'm sure you will.'

Daniel lay awake in bed, watching the dark purple light in the sky through an open shutter. A half-empty bottle of gin sat on his bedside table, drunk after his mother had told him to wait in his room so she could begin the serious negotiations with the Omertia family. He had heard her voice along with the grandmother's echoing through the walls, laughing and talking for hours as he had worked his way through the gin.

Could he marry Emily? She was clever but, like many in Tara, she might be a little too keen on Prince Michael, whom Daniel secretly loathed. He needed more time, to see if they would get on without a chaperone. He wished he could meet someone the ordinary way, like the peasants did, and fall in love without the pressure of both families watching. She was very pretty though, he couldn't deny it. He glanced at the entrance to his bedroom, then tried to banish the thoughts that were swirling through his mind. Of course she wouldn't come to his room. Her grandmother looked like the sort that would padlock her to the bed to ensure she didn't get up in the night.

He sighed, then heard it; a faint tap at the door. He rose, pulled on a pair of shorts, then went to the entrance and opened it. Emily was standing there in a silk nightdress, her hair down. She gazed up at him and smiled.

'Hi, Danny.'

'Your grandmother?'

'Don't worry about her; she's had one gin too many and is snoring her head off. Even a dragon wouldn't wake her.'

He reached out, took her hand, and pulled her into his room.

## CHAPTER 21

# THE TRAIL OF CRUMBS

Port Sanders, Medio, The City – 29<sup>th</sup> Koralis 3419

P ort Sanders, Medio, The City – 29<sup>th</sup> Koralis 3419

Citrus trees lined both sides of the road, and the morning was already hot under the late summer sun as Aila's carriage rumbled towards Port Sanders. She had two jobs to do; one official, one not. She gazed out of the windows as they passed the rows of orange and lemon trees. Another summer was coming to an end, and within days the first rains of Sweetmist would be turning the rich soil into mud. The preparations for the abrupt change in season were well underway throughout the City. The almost-empty underground cisterns would refill in readiness for the four dry months of winter that followed Sweetmist, and the cycle of the City would turn once more.

She wondered what Corthie would make of the coming storms. He had only known the City in the dry, hot summer months. Sweetmist would mean more days off for him, along with more chances for them to see each other. She shook her head, trying to dispel her desires. A demigod had no place falling in love with a mortal; she had to be strong. The next time they met, she would tell him that there was to be no more kissing or touching, and that she was not willing for her heart to go through the torture of watching him fade and die, while she remained forever young. It wasn't fair on him either. The best thing he could do was find a nice mortal girl, and forget about her.

She sighed. She had been through the same thoughts many times since she had taken the three crossbow bolts for him. Her instincts had kicked in the moment the four would-be assassins had aimed their bows at Corthie, but a dark place in her mind told her that she should have let him be hit. If he had died she would have mourned him, but if she kept seeing him the day of mourning would only be postponed, and the pain would be far harder to bear when it finally arrived. She didn't love him, but she knew that if they kissed again, she wouldn't be able to stop herself.

Other demigods had long ago reconciled themselves to this truth, why couldn't she? Many of her cousins and siblings had been with mortals over the centuries, having children with them, and then moving on once they had died. Several servants in the Royal Palace had God-Child or demigod ancestry, and the Chamberlains in Tara could trace their line to Lady Mona, the eldest daughter of Prince Michael. Aila had not only refrained from having children, but, apart from a few drunken liaisons, she had stopped herself from seeing mortals altogether.

But how was she supposed to forget him? She considered going into an opium haze for a few decades; emerging only once Corthie was gone and forgotten about, but that seemed a little extreme. Besides, her unofficial reason for going to Port Sanders was connected to the champion; she would need to get that out of the way first.

The carriage passed a crossroads flanked with lime trees and Aila knew they were approaching the outskirts of the harbour town. From the window she could see the red roofs of the outlying estates and farms, and it was hard to believe that somewhere so peaceful and beautiful lay only seven miles sunward of Redmarket. The concrete slums of the Circuit seemed like a different world compared to the rural tranquillity of Sander territory. She saw the outer suburbs of Port Sanders appear. The expansion of the town had been curtailed many centuries before, to preserve arable land, but with the general depopulation of the City since the Civil War, the pressure had eased. At its height, in the year before the catastrophic Civil War had begun, almost two million mortals had been packed into the three regions of the City, but three centuries later that total stood at seven hundred thousand fewer.

Many blamed Khora for the City's decline, whereas others thought it better to have fewer mouths to feed. Regardless, it was agreed by all that the City was past its prime.

The Governor of Port Sanders lived in a palace close to the harbour, and the carriage passed Lord Naxor's residence, where he stayed after bringing the champions to the City. Corthie would have slept there, she thought, then frowned and tried to think of something else.

The markets of the town were bustling, and the carriage had to slow down to pass through the crowds of farmers, merchants and shoppers. A flock of sheep barred the way for a few moments, the animals being taken from their pasture into shelter for the Sweetmist storms. The carriage turned left at the entrance to the harbour and she turned to glance at the sight of the Warm Sea stretching off into the misty horizon. Boats of all shapes and sizes bobbed in the harbour, the water reflecting the pink hues of the afternoon sun.

The carriage came to a halt outside the palace and Aila waited for the driver to reach the door. He swung it open and she stepped down to the gravel drive. A palace courtier was waiting for her, dressed in the yellow and black colours of the Sander tribe.

'Welcome back to Tonetti Palace, ma'am,' he said, bowing low.

'Is my cousin in?'

'Yes, ma'am, she is expecting you in her private study.'

'Thanks.'

She strode across the bridge over the narrow moat and entered the palace gatehouse, walking under a large banner of a honeybee. Sander guards saluted her as she passed, her face well-known. She crossed the inner yard and walked into the main palace building, ascending a tower to the governor's apartments. She went by more guards and knocked on the door of the study.

'Come in.'

Aila pushed on the door and walked into the room. It had a window overlooking the harbour and her eyes went to the view as they always did.

'Good afternoon, cousin,' said Lady Lydia, rising from behind a dark, oaken desk.

'Lydia. It's been a while.'

Her cousin smiled. 'I hear you've been rather busy.'

'You could say that; this summer's been a disaster.'

They sat and Lydia reached for a beaker of water and two glasses.

Aila watched her pour. 'Thank you.'

'For what?' said Lydia.

'The Sander militia is the only one occupying Evader territory that I've not had a major complaint about, and I know that you've had a lot to do with that.'

Lydia passed her a glass of water. 'I obey my mother. She told me to make sure my militia restrained themselves. It's her you should thank.'

'I met her, did you know?'

'Yes, she told me.'

Aila frowned. 'What did she say?'

'That you infuriate her. That you're stubborn, and that you tried to punch your brother, Lord Collo.'

'I should have done, the slimy little two-faced rat. I will punch him next time I see him, and that goes for Vana too.'

Lydia smirked. 'Dissension among the children of Prince Isra? I suppose some things never change.'

'And your family's any better? Try working with Ikara.'

'No, thanks.'

'Exactly. Your sister was a pain in the ass before the riots and occupation, but now she's a nightmare; and she blames me for everything.'

'I know; I read her reports.'

'And?'

Lydia glanced at her. 'I like being stuck away in Port Sanders. Others may think it's the backwater of the City, but that's precisely why I'm so fond of it. It allows me to keep out of the quarrels of the demigods. In the last year I've only spoken to you, my mother and Naxor. So, I think I'll keep my opinion of my younger sister to myself.'

Aila sat back in her chair.

'Oh, don't look at me like that,' said Lydia. 'That glower on your face is one of the reasons you don't get along with anyone. Perhaps Ikara would be easier to tolerate if you smiled a bit more.'

Aila put a big fake grin on her face. 'That better?'

'Now you're just being childish. Shall we get to business? I had a look at your request, but unfortunately the answer is no.'

'What? I thought I was here to discuss it? You know that the food supplies in the Circuit are almost gone; if you don't lower your prices, then people will starve this winter.'

'I don't set the prices; the merchants in the market do.'

'But you have the power to intervene.'

'I've decided to follow the advice of the merchant guild in this matter. They explained to me that lowering prices would put many of them out of business, and thousands of Sanders depend on them for their livelihoods. I felt there was little point in moving the suffering from your jurisdiction to mine.'

'But you have the reserves to cope, the Evaders don't.'

'Yes, but who would plant next year's harvest? Securing the future is more important than one season's pain.'

'So the Evaders will suffer, while the Icewarders and Sanders sit on enough reserves to feed everyone? No wonder the tribe feels everyone is against them; no wonder they rise up. I'm tempted to do the same myself.'

Lydia smiled. 'Straight to hyperbole? You sound like a mortal sometimes.'

'Some of the Evaders,' Aila said, her eyes narrowing, 'will take matters into their own hands if the food runs out. There are many weak points on the frontier between my land and yours that a starving mob could break through.'

'Are you threatening me?'

'No, I'm just stating a fact. If you don't want the fighting to spread into Sander territory, think again about lowering the prices of the supplies sold to the Circuit.'

'Or, I could mobilise another thousand troops and post them behind the frontier, ready to annihilate any such incursion. The Roser militia have gifted me a dozen of their new bolt-throwing machines and if what you say is true, I will use them to tear any mob to pieces. Tell them that, when you return to the Circuit. Shall I call your carriage now?'

'No.'

'But this discussion is over.'

'It is, but I intend to stay in the palace tonight.'

'Why?'

'Do you know how long it is since I spent a night away from the Circuit and your charming sister? I don't have any urgent meetings until tomorrow, so, may I please stay?'

Lydia sighed. 'Very well, although you'll have to amuse yourself; I'm busy this evening.'

'I wouldn't dream of intruding on whatever it is you do in the evenings, Lydia. I was planning on taking a walk, then enjoying some food in a harbourside tavern; perhaps I'll get a table by the pier and feed tidbits to the stray cats. After that, I'm going to get drunk, pick up a handsome sailor, and dance the night away.'

'Sounds truly dreadful; please don't waken the palace when you come in.'

Aila stood. 'Well, I can't say it's been a pleasure, but thanks for letting me stay.'

Lydia looked down at the paperwork on her desk. 'It's the least I can do.'

'Yeah, you're not wrong there.'

Aila glanced at the view of the harbour, then left the room. She knew the route to the guest quarters and made her way there, anger simmering within her. She hated having to ask Lydia for permission to stay, but it had been necessary; what boiled her blood more was her cousin's flat refusal to do anything to prevent hundreds or perhaps thousands of Evaders from starving. The tribal treasury was almost empty, and the granaries and depots had only four months' worth of food in them, nowhere near enough to last the winter.

A courtier caught up with her as she strode through the hallways of the palace.

'Ma'am,' he said. 'Lady Lydia has assigned me to assist you. Do you have any luggage, my lady?'

'It's in the carriage that brought me here. Could you bring it up?'

'Of course, ma'am. Will you be requiring anything else?'

'No, just carry my bags up and then leave me alone.'

'As you will, ma'am.' He bowed and hurried off in the other direction.

She needed peace and quiet for what she was going to do; but first she would eat, and drink.

---

Aila staggered back into her room, bumping off the doorframe and then hitting a table. She tottered for a moment, then shut the door and made for the bed. She collapsed onto it, her mind thick with brandy, and closed her eyes.

No, stop. She couldn't let herself fall asleep; she had work to do. She drew on her self-healing powers and sobered herself up. She groaned, and scrambled into a sitting position, rubbing her head. There was a lamp on the bedside table and she lit it, then rummaged in an open bag that was lying on top of the blankets. She dug underneath the spare dresses and pulled out the close-fitting black clothes that she had brought. In a pocket was the address she had already killed two people to obtain. She stared at the piece of paper as her eyesight cleared; her drunken night out already fading from her memory.

She left her dress on the floor and washed her face in a basin of cool water, savouring the relief from the heat that lingered throughout the night. She cleaned her teeth to remove any odour of alcohol on her breath, then dressed in her black outfit. The upper half had a layer of leather stitched between the fabric that would provide a limited amount of protection; it wasn't the most comfortable garment, but had been tailored to her precise measurements. Once dressed, she pulled on a pair of sandals then strapped a short sword to her waist and a knife to her lower leg. She stretched, loosening herself up, then glanced through a slit in her shutters. The inner yard of the palace was in silence. She could see a few guards standing by the gate that led to the moat, and more by the front of the tower where Lady Lydia had her residence.

She picked up a flagon of cold ale from her dresser, then threw a black cloak over her shoulders and stole to the door of her room.

*You see me as a palace courtier.*

Her chest tightened and she took a breath. Why was she nervous? She had done this a thousand times before. Yes, she thought, but never for Corthie Holdfast. It didn't matter that he had no idea that she was investigating on his behalf. There had been two assassination attempts already, and if she didn't act she could see no reason why there wouldn't be a third. She paused by the door, her hand an inch from the handle, and went over the arguments in her head again. If she stood aside and did nothing, and Corthie was murdered, then despite knowing it was futile, she would seek revenge on those who had done it. Surely it would be better to act first? It would be the last time she would get involved with his life; once she had destroyed the conspiracy trying to kill the champion, she would step back and forget him. Or so she told herself.

She opened the door and went out into the empty hallway. Enough people would have heard her drunken return to the palace to assume she would be in an unconscious stupor, and she could be back long before anyone noticed her absence. She hurried along the quiet passageways, and descended the spiral staircase to the lower floor. She crept to the opening that led to the inner yard and peered out, seeing the guards at their posts. The shifts had changed with the midnight bell, and the soldiers looked bored and hot in their heavy armour. She straightened her back and stepped out, striding across the yard with confidence.

The soldiers glanced at her approach.

'Evening, boys,' she said. She handed them the cold ale. 'I could see you suffering in this awful heat, and thought you could do with this.'

The two guards smiled. 'Thanks, you're a sweetheart. You came down here just for that?'

'No, I've a message for the night boat captains in the harbour. Her Ladyship wants fresh lobsters for breakfast.'

'And she's making you go out in the middle of the night?'

Aila shrugged. 'Demigods, eh?'

The soldiers laughed. 'You said it.'

She squeezed past them as they glugged down the ale. 'See you later, boys.'

She sauntered through the gatehouse and across the bridge over the moat. She kept her disguise until she reached the crossroads that led to the harbour, then ducked into the shadows.

*You see me as a soldier in the Sander militia.*

She re-emerged, then turned along a street that ran parallel to the harbour front. A few taverns were still open, their customers spilling out onto the side of the road as they drank the honeyed ale the town was famous for. She glanced at them like a soldier would, frowning at any misbehaviour while ignoring it at the same time, and continued on until she reached a quieter part of town. The old houses were stacked on either side of twisting lanes and she kept to the thick shadows until she reached the street written on her slip of paper.

Her eyes scanned the front doors. Each led to three or four apartments, and she read the names of the occupants as she walked by. She noted the position of the apartment she was looking for and kept going without breaking her stride. At the end of the street, she slipped into the shadows and worked her way to a back alley that ran along the rear of the apartments.

*You see me as Stormfire.*

She quickened her step, hastening along the alley until she reached the rear of the block she had noted before. The untidy backyard was heaped with household garbage, and she stepped through it with care until she reached the back door. It was locked, and she knelt, removing her picks from a small pouch on her belt. It had taken her many years of practice to become proficient as a picker of locks, but as a demigod, time was an advantage she could use. She felt the barrel of the lock turn, and pushed the door open. It made a soft creaking noise, but nothing that concerned her. She crept into the dark hallway, and ascended the stairs to the upper floor. There were doors leading to two separate apartments at the top of the final flight of steps, and she went to the one she was looking for, and listened. Silence. She knew there would be deadbolts on the other side of the door, so she glanced up. The hatch to the roof was within reach and she clambered up onto a window ledge and pushed it to the side, then pulled herself up into the attic. Her eyes took a moment to adjust to the darkness, then she crawled slowly through the low attic space, climbing over the thick roof beams. She found the building's water tank, and followed the pipes that led to the apartment she was after. There was a small hatch above the bathroom, and she placed her hand on it. It was locked. Damn it, she thought. She was going to have to make a noise, so she would need to be quick.

She half-stood in the cramped attic, then brought her foot down onto the hatch. The wood split, then swung free, the boards colliding with the wall of the bathroom. She dropped through the gap, landing on the floor and drawing her short sword at the same time. She kicked the bathroom door open and raced into the next room. A man was sitting up in bed, his hands scrambling for a crossbow on the table next to him. She pulled her knife from her leg-sheath and threw it. The blade struck the man's hand, fixing it to the surface of the table. She leapt over the bed as the man's mouth opened to scream and smacked the hilt of her sword down onto his temple. His eyes rolled up and he fell back onto the mattress, out cold.

Aila paused, listening. She waited a few moments to ensure no one else in the building was coming to check, then got to work.

It was nearly two hours before she could get the man to awaken. She had tied him to a chair, with one arm behind his back, and his ankles bound to the wooden legs. She had stuffed a pair of his woollen socks into his mouth, but had left his other hand secured to the table by the knife; it was a nice touch, she thought. She wiped the blood from his face and slapped him a few times, then splashed him with water until he groaned and opened his eyes.

He stared at her, panic and fear gripping his face.

'Do you recognise me?' she said. 'Nod if you do.'

He nodded.

'I'm going to remove the gag to let you speak. If you shout out I will torture you and leave you alive but broken, do you understand?'

He nodded again, and she yanked the socks from his mouth.

'Are you really her? Stormfire? I thought you were a myth.'

'Unfortunately for you, I'm quite real.'

'What do you want from me? I'm not mixed up in anything in the Circuit; I stay well clear of that cesspit.'

'I'm extending my remit.'

He was sweating and shaking as he stared at her. It was the scar, she thought, it always freaks them out.

'You paid four men to kill someone.'

His eyes widened. 'No, you're mistaken.'

'Don't lie to me. I've already spoken to, and killed, one of them. He gave up the name of his handler in the Circuit, and guess what? Yes, I killed him too. He was tough; it took a lot of... effort to get him to tell me where the money had come from. But, he did in the end, and so here I am.'

The man said nothing, the sweat trickling down his forehead.

'How did you know the champion was going to be in the Circuit?'

'Look, I'm only a middle-man, I was only passing on a job to a colleague. It was nothing personal against the champion; it's just business.'

'I know.'

'I have gold; take it, all of it. Tell me what I need to do to stay alive, and not... be broken.'

'You know what to do. Tell me who gave you the commission.'

He paused. 'And if I do?'

'Then I'll knock you out, untie you, and leave.'

'Do you promise?'

'Yes.'

'My life will be in danger; I'll have to run and hide somewhere.'

Aila shrugged. 'I'll leave you the gold; I'm not interested in money, I want the truth.'

'But you don't understand who you're dealing with here. The people who gave me the orders, they...'

'Yes?'

'They're demigods.'

'You saw them?'

'No. Not once. I dealt with one of their mortal lackeys, a man by the name of Tangrit.'

Aila almost cried out in rage, but managed to appear calm. 'Tangrit of Pella?'

'Yes. He works for...'

'I know who he works for.'

'Lord Naxor is a very dangerous man. If he discovers you've traced the money to him...'

'What did Tangrit say? Did he tell you who wanted the champion dead, or why?'

'He told me that Lord Naxor had received orders from his mother to make sure the champion was eliminated. We already knew he'd been in the Circuit, and I was told to prepare a team close to Redmarket in case he came back. As I said, it was only business.'

Aila frowned. Princess Khora had ordered the attempt? It didn't make any sense.

'Why?' she said. 'Why would Naxor's mother care about the champion?'

'Because he's a slave of the duke, and she's scared. She's heard that Marcus is thinking of moving against her, and if he does, and that champion is by his side, then nothing will stop him.'

She nodded. 'I think I might have to have a word with Tangrit.'

'You can't,' he said, 'unless you can speak to the dead. His body was found floating in a canal days ago. His eyes had been gouged out. You mean that wasn't you?'

'I never touched him.'

'Someone's covering their tracks, miss.' He glanced at her as she pondered his words. 'Have I said enough?'

She nodded, then got to her feet.

'Praise Malik,' he said. 'I promise I won't say anything about you being here.'

'I know you won't.'

She swung her hand, clubbing him with the hilt of her sword, then slashed his throat with a sideways swipe, stepping away to avoid the blood as his head slumped. She wiped the blade on the bed and sheathed her sword as she felt waves of rage course through her. She almost spat on the body, but controlled herself.

Her anger could be put to better use.

CHAPTER 22

# WRONG FOR EACH OTHER

Arrowhead Fort, The Bulwark, The City – 2$^{nd}$ Namen 3419

Lightning streaked across the dark red sky amid the torrential rains that battered down on the Great Walls. Huge, black clouds were rolling in from the direction of sunward, though no sun could be seen. Already the moat was starting to fill, after four months of almost no rain, and the parched earth outside the walls was transforming into thick mud. Many of the greenhides had begun their retreat; peeling off in groups towards the drier regions that lay sunward beyond the reach of the Sweetmist storms.

'Look at them run,' said Corthie from the shelter of a covered stretch of battlements. 'It's funny to think that they're scared of a bit of rain.'

'It's not the rain,' said Quill; 'it's the darkness. The City will be overcast for the next two months, so forget about seeing the sun for a while.'

'Bollocks,' he muttered. 'This is awful. Not only will I have nothing to do until winter, but it's going to be grey and miserable the whole time?'

'Namen's always the worst month; it's still overcast throughout Balian, but it's not as wet.'

'The weather here is crazy.'

'Don't you have seasons where you're from?'

'We do, they're just not quite as abrupt as here. I mean, yesterday it was still hot and dry, and now we have two months of this?'

'It's fine; we just move everything indoors. Sweetmist is a time of rest and recovery.'

'I need to find something to do. I can't hang around here idle, I'm already bored and it's only been a day.'

She shook her head at him. 'You're lucky; not many Blades are free to roam the City whenever they feel like it. You could visit Tara or Dalrig, or even Icehaven. The mountains there are supposed to be beautiful.'

'I'm not free to roam the City; I'm banned from the Circuit, remember?'

'Why would you want to go back there? The last time we went, you were shot at.' She eyed him as she said the words. 'And the adjutant saved you. Funny that.'

Corthie sighed. 'If you've got something to say, spit it out.'

'It's nothing; it's just that I think maybe she likes you. Why else would she have stepped in front of you?'

'She's a demigod; she healed in seconds.'

'Hmmm. I doubt she'd have done it for me.'

He shrugged. 'You're not the champion.'

'What, so my life is worth less than yours?'

'No, but maybe these demigods don't see things the way we do.'

'There's no "maybe" about it; every demigod in the City is an arrogant asshole who couldn't give a toss about mortals. They treat us all like servants, or slaves.'

'That adjutant answered your questions, didn't she? I remember you commenting on it at the time.'

'So you're defending one of them now?'

'She did save my life.'

Quill stared at him. 'You like her, don't you?'

'What? I'd only just met her.'

'I know, and that's what's bothering me.' She frowned. 'Something weird's going on, and I don't like it. I've also noticed you sneaking down the stairs some nights, past my room. Where have you been going?'

'I'm not going to the Circuit.'

'I know, you've not left Arrowhead; I checked with the sergeant on the gates. Look, I don't care if you're sleeping around, and I kind of appreciate you not bringing lots of girls up to the tower, but you don't need to keep it a secret from me.'

He stared out at the greenhides retreating through the rain, relieved with the conclusion she had reached. 'Alright. Sorry.'

She said nothing for a while, then walked from the battlements.

'Quill, wait...!' he shouted after her, but she kept going and disappeared down the stairs leading to the forecourt. He turned back to the greenhides, wishing he was down there with them. He had lied to Quill, his closest friend in the Bulwark, not just about Aila and the dragon, but about sleeping with other girls. He was trying to keep too many secrets, when blunt honesty was his usual approach to life.

Blackrose was right, he thought, humans existed on lies.

---

He had just dried himself when a knock came at the door of his bedchamber. He smiled. Quill?

'Come in.'

A young man in a wet raincoat opened the door but didn't enter. 'Sir? I have a message for you.'

Corthie pulled on a dry tunic and walked over. Under the man's raincoat, he could see the badge of a Blade messenger.

'Aye?'

'Sir, Lord Naxor has sent a carriage; he awaits you at the Fifth Gate in the Middle Walls, and asks if you would care to join him there.'

'Did he say why? Are we going on another tour of the City?'

'Lord Naxor didn't give a reason, sir.'

Corthie shrugged. 'I've nothing better to do, so aye; I'll be downstairs in five minutes.'

The messenger left and Corthie finished dressing. He glanced at the long, ugly raincoat he had been supplied with and left it hanging by the door. Hopefully Naxor was planning on taking him to a dry tavern somewhere, and maybe he would get a chance to slip in a subtle question about Aila. He smiled at the thought of her, then stopped himself. No. It had to end before it could become... something. His sister was coming for him, and he would leave as soon as she had arrived, while the City had been part of Aila's life for over seven centuries. He couldn't ask her to start something that he might not be able to see through. And if he fell in love with her, then parting would be even worse. He laughed at himself. 'If he fell in love with her'. If? He was already halfway there.

He tried to clear his mind as he laced up his boots, but the image of her lying in his arms after she had saved him in Redmarket was seared into his memory. He had turned down casual relationships because he had wanted to meet someone he liked; well, he had, and now he was doing his best to wreck it before it became serious.

He headed down the stairs to the level where Tanner and Quill lived.

'Hey, Tanner.'

The older warrior nodded. 'What did you say to Quill earlier? She came down here with a face that told me to stay well away, and she's not come out of her room since.'

'I was an idiot, Tanner. Tell her that when you see her.'

'Tell her yourself.'

'I would, but I'm going out. Lord Naxor has asked me to meet him at the Middle Walls.'

'Lucky you. Another night on the town, eh?'

'I hope so. See you later.'

He went back to the stairs and continued down to the lower floor. The carriage had pulled up outside the entrance to the Wolfpack Tower and Corthie got drenched in the five yards it took to climb aboard. He sat down, his hair and clothes dripping, then laughed. Next time he would take the raincoat. The carriage set off, leaving Arrowhead and joining the main road towards the Middle Walls. The rain battered down on the canvas covering, and the inside of the carriage was humid. Corthie wiped the windows with his hand but they steamed up again in minutes.

He gave up trying to see anything, leaned back into the carriage bench, and closed his eyes.

He awoke with a tap on the side door to see a soldier standing by the carriage with an umbrella.

'Morning, Pack Leader,' she said.

Corthie glanced at the dark clouds covering the sky. 'Is it?'

'Lord Naxor is waiting inside the gatehouse for you, sir.'

He climbed down and ducked under the umbrella as the soldier closed the door. They half-ran to the gatehouse and Corthie shook the rain from his hair as they entered. He gazed outside at the thundering downpour for a moment, then turned and followed the soldier into the interior of the large building. No one checked his identity any more, he noticed; they all knew his face.

He was led into a room and saw Aila sitting at a table.

His mouth fell open.

'Here he is, my lord,' said the soldier, bowing to her. 'Will that be all for now?'

'Yes. Leave us.'

The soldier backed out of the room and closed the door. Corthie gazed at Aila for a second, then strode across the floor towards her. He touched her face then leaned down to kiss her.

'No,' she said.

'Oh. Damn it. You're right.'

She raised an eyebrow. 'I am?'

'You said so yourself; you said you couldn't see how it could work.'

'I did? Why did I say that, again?'

Corthie sat on the table. 'I look at you, and I want you. When we're apart I tell myself that the next time I see you, I'm not going to try to kiss you, and it was the first damn thing I did.'

'Why would you tell yourself that?'

'Because despite how I feel, we're not right for each other.'

She narrowed her eyes. 'Why not?'

'Hang on, it was you who stopped me from kissing you. You said no for a reason I assume?'

'You idiot, it's because I look like Lord Naxor to everyone else; what do you think would happen if they came in and saw us kissing?'

'They'd think that Lord Naxor had excellent taste. Me? Not so much.'

She scowled at him.

'Not funny? Alright, sorry. Oh bollocks, I've screwed this up. Can I come back in and start again?'

'Just sit down. On a chair.'

He walked back round the table and sat opposite her. She was beautiful, he thought, why couldn't he have just kept his mouth shut?

'I, eh, need to tell you something,' she said.

'Aye?'

'Yeah. I did a little digging around into the attack at Redmarket, and it's led me somewhere unexpected. Not completely unexpected, but it was a surprise, if it's true.'

'Let me guess, it was a demigod?'

'Aim a little higher.'

'After the God-King and God-Queen, there's only Khora, isn't there?'

'Indeed.'

'Why would Khora want to kill me?'

'This is why I needed to see you in person, there's no one in the City I'd trust with a message. Except you, but that would be stupid, as the message was for you.' She paused, and rubbed her head. 'Amalia's ass, my words aren't working. Why do you think we're not right for each other?'

'Because my sister's coming, and when she does, she'll be taking me back with her.'

Aila squinted at him. 'How long ago was it that you were taken from your home?'

'About four and a half years.'

'Well, I hate to be the one who says this, but if she hasn't rescued you in four and a half years, what makes you think she'll be here any time soon?'

'You don't know her.'

'Obviously, but I'm picturing some armour-clad warrior goddess. Does she smite?'

He smiled. 'Occasionally, but not with a sword. I've never seen her hold a weapon in her life. Look, I know how it sounds. I said that I wanted you; I do. But how can I make any promises when I've no idea how long I'll be here?'

'Wow. This is not how I thought this conversation was going to go.' She fell into silence, her gaze on the surface of the table. 'Back to business. I'll get through this quickly, as I feel a sudden urge to get out of here as soon as I can.' She glanced back up at him. 'The source I spoke to said that Khora wants you dead because she sees you as a threat to her.'

Corthie laughed. 'In what way am I a threat to her?'

'The source said Khora had learned that Duke Marcus was going to try to remove her from power, and that you would help him do it. Do you know anything about this?'

'The duke said something to me once.'

She frowned. 'What?'

'He was talking about the problems in the Circuit, and how he thought that the tribal militia might not be enough to calm everything down.'

'And?'

'He said he might have to take a difficult decision.'

Aila's face drained of colour, and her hand gripped the top of the table.

'He wanted to know,' Corthie went on, 'if I would be loyal to him.'

'What did you say?'

'I told him I was a soldier. Look, if the demigods start fighting among themselves, I'm staying out of it. My job is to fight the green-hides, not help one group of demigods destroy the other.'

'But you can't stay out of it. If the duke does what I think he means, and sends Blades into the Circuit again, there will be carnage; and it won't stop there. He wants power, Corthie, he's always been jealous that Khora was given the job of ruling. As Michael's eldest son, he thinks it's his birthright.'

Corthie shrugged. 'I don't like him either, but at least he's not trying to kill me.'

'I hate Khora too, but she's not... not...'

'Not as bad?'

Aila lowered her head. 'Neither can be trusted, but we know what Khora's rule is like. Marcus would be infinitely worse.' She grimaced as if she hated to say the name. 'Please trust me.'

'You're saying I should side with the one who wants me dead?'

'Let me speak to her; let me ask her to her face.'

'And what will you do if she admits it?'

Aila looked into his eyes. 'Kill her.'

Corthie said nothing and they sat in silence. He glanced at her, and caught her glancing back.

'No one's come in,' he said. 'We could have kissed and no one would have seen us.'

'Don't, Corthie; you've already made your feelings clear.'

'My feelings? My feelings are telling me to pick you up in my arms and run out of here with you; leave this damned City and find somewhere we can be together.'

She reached across the table and pulled him towards her. Their lips touched and he put his hand behind her head, his fingers through her hair, his mind reeling. They could make it work, somehow.

She pushed him away, tears spilling down her cheeks. 'Right, we kissed; now go, please.'

'But...'

She sobbed. 'Go! I can't see you any more,' she said, standing and backing away from him.

'Forget what I said before.'

'No, you were right, though for the wrong reasons; we can't be together.'

He got to his feet. 'What are the right reasons?'

'You're mortal.'

His heart sank, and his spirits seemed to shrink. 'Aye, I am.'

'I can't do it.'

He tried to smile, but his mouth wouldn't respond.

'Go.'

Corthie turned, and left the room.

---

Corthie lay against Blackrose's long forelimb, his head leaning on her black scales. The dragon's head was resting on the ground close by, one eye open a slit.

There was a noise at the gate.

'I thought I heard you coming in,' said Maddie, leaning on her crutch. 'Two visits in three days, we are the lucky ones. What have you been up to then, with all this rain?'

'Quiet, girl,' said Blackrose; 'can't you see the champion's love sick?'

'I am not,' he said.

'There you go, being human again with your lies. I can smell it off you. Only a few days ago you weren't in love, and now you've already lost it. How long did the bit in between last?'

'A few seconds.'

'Oh no,' said Maddie, limping over towards them; 'that's awful. You do look a little forlorn sitting there; it's the first time I've seen you without a smile on your face. Did she break your heart?'

'No, I'm fine.'

Blackrose lifted her head a little. 'Your odour tells me something different. Corthie, I say again; stop lying to me; you know it is the one thing I detest most about your kind.'

'Alright, I feel terrible; is that better?'

Maddie crouched next to him. 'What did she do? Or was it you? You do have a big mouth sometimes; did you say something horrible to her?'

'Tell you what, go and get us a bottle of brandy and I might tell you.'

'Say please.'

'Please.'

Maddie got up, hefted the crutch under her left shoulder and hobbled off towards the gate.

'You have no intention of telling her anything,' said Blackrose.

'I said "might", so I wasn't lying. There was another reason I wanted her out of earshot for a minute, I want to tell you something regarding us getting out of here.'

The dragon came closer.

'When I arrived in the City,' he said, 'I was prepared to be patient. I fought the greenhides, and tried to make the best of it.'

'You know my opinion of that approach.'

'Aye, you called it cowardly, and I can see why. It's a choice I made, but at least I'm still alive to live with its consequences.'

'And have you had a change of mind? Has your approach altered?'

'Maybe the time for patience is over. Things in the City are getting worse, and it looks like the demigods are about to start fighting among themselves again. You've got Khora and Naxor on one side, and Marcus and Kano on the other, with everyone else picking between them. The problem is, they want me to pick a side too.'

'So what do you intend to do?'

'I want to stay out of the fighting, but I'm a Blade, and Duke Marcus is my commanding officer; while it seems it was Khora who was trying to kill me.'

'You have evidence of this?'

'No, but someone... close, who was close, told me, and I trust her.'

'Am I to infer that this is the same woman who has so recently broken your heart? Are you sure that this is not guiding your decisions? One must never rush these things, or make fateful choices when one's mind is clouded by loss.'

'Maybe. Maybe I was happy to stay here partly because I was hoping for... something more.'

'Why did she reject you?'

'How do you know that? My smell told you?'

'Yes. You may be immune to the powers of the gods, but my nostrils are working perfectly well.'

His face fell. 'She's a demigod; she finished it because I'm mortal.'

'Ahh, I see. You are a victim of their eternal tragedy.'

He narrowed his eyes.

'Imagine being one of them,' the dragon said, 'imagine falling in love, and then living to see the object of your love wither like a leaf in autumn, and then die, while you remain forever in the bloom of spring.'

Corthie blinked. Is that what had happened?

Blackrose tilted her head. 'From your expression I assume that this had not occurred to you. Did you think she was rejecting you because you were inferior? Corthie Holdfast, you are in no way inferior to any man. Now, your plan, before Maddie returns.'

'My plan?'

'Yes, I assume you have one.'

'Aye, I do. The only way to avoid getting involved in any new civil war is to leave the City.' He glanced at her. 'We need the Quadrant.'

'Go on.'

'There's one problem. If the plan works, and I manage to get my hands on it, I have no idea how to use it.'

The dragon smiled. 'Leave that to me.'

---

Corthie left Arrowhead for the second time that day, taking a carriage along the road sunward towards the mighty Fortress of the Lifegiver. The roads were sodden and the wheels got stuck in the mud more than once as the rain clattered down from the skies. He wished he had his mother by his side; her skills would be perfect for what he was planning – she had been an assassin before marrying his father and knew all about sneaking around in the shadows. Corthie was more like his father, a warrior rather than a spy, whose bloody-mindedness and refusal to compromise his principles had often got him into trouble. It was a noble approach, but it had also led to him being murdered by a god, while his mother had survived.

Thoughts of his family sent him into a downward spiral of bitter memories. Aila had looked at him with outright scepticism on her face as he had insisted his sister was coming for him. Others had done the same, and it hadn't concerned him in the slightest, but with Aila it hurt. Was he a fool to believe that Karalyn would suddenly appear, just in time, to carry him off to the safety of his home? Four and a half years he had waited. Every morning in Gadena's mercenary training camp on Lostwell, he had wondered if that would be the day she would come for him, but it had never happened, and now he was in the City of the Eternal Siege. How would Karalyn know where he was? How many worlds were there? He knew Lostwell was big, and he had only seen one tiny corner of it, maybe she would spend years and still be looking there.

If Aila was right, then he needed to act. If Karalyn was lost or delayed, or even dead, he needed to stop relying on her appearance to rescue him.

He closed his eyes, but the image of Aila in his arms appeared, so he opened them again. The damn dragon was right. A few days before he hadn't felt like this, he hadn't been in love, but after meeting Aila at the Middle Walls he felt bereft. It was his fault, and he knew it. He had taken a sledgehammer and wrecked everything to avoid feeling precisely what he felt at that moment. He had hurt her too, with some of the things he had said, he had seen it in her eyes. Had she only ended it with him to avoid the pain his mortal death would bring her?

The carriage passed through one of the massive gatehouses of Life-giver, and came to a halt in the forecourt close to the Duke's Tower. A soldier opened the side door, a raincoat keeping the torrential rain off her face.

'Pack Leader,' she saluted as he climbed down from the carriage.

'I want to see the duke.'

The soldier nodded. 'I'll take you inside, sir, where you can wait out of the rain.'

He nodded and followed her into the dry, entrance hall of the tower.

'Has no one issued you with a raincoat, soldier?' said a sneering voice.

Corthie turned, and saw Lord Kano approach. 'No, I've got one, sir. I just like getting wet.'

'Well, I'm not going to allow you upstairs to drip all over the duke's fine carpets. I assume that's why you're here.'

'It is, sir, aye.'

Kano nodded to the soldier that escorted him in, and she saluted and left.

'Come with me,' he said, turning towards a door.

Corthie went through into a warm chamber where garments were drying by a large metal water-heater. Steam misted the air, and water was dripping from the ceiling.

'Sit,' said Kano.

Corthie lowered himself into a chair, and Kano sat in another.

'What do you want?'

'To speak to the duke.'

'Yes, I gathered that. However, no one gets upstairs until they've been through me first. So, I ask again; what do you want?'

Corthie said nothing for a moment as he glanced at the young-looking demigod. How could this idiot be related to Aila? He saw a very slight resemblance in his eyes and he looked away.

'Is a civil war about to begin?'

Kano's eyes widened. 'What in Malik's name makes you say that?'

'Is the duke planning on moving the Blades into the rest of the City to restore order?'

'That's enough. These issues are far beyond your understanding. You are a Blade, and you take orders, nothing more.'

'So why did the duke tell me he wanted to bring me into his inner counsels?'

'If that is the case, which I seriously doubt, then Duke Marcus will come to you; you don't just appear at the front door of his tower uninvited. None of this is in any way your business.'

'No? Then why is Khora trying to kill me?'

Kano stared at him, his eyes tight.

The door to the room opened and a soldier leaned in. 'Apologies, my lord.'

'Yes, what is it?' Kano snapped.

'The duke, sir.'

'What about him?'

'He has asked that the champion be immediately brought upstairs, sir.'

Kano stared at the soldier with withering contempt. 'Is that it? Why are you still standing there like a fool? Get back to your post.'

The soldier bowed. 'Yes, sir; sorry, sir.'

Kano turned back to Corthie, the loathing he felt for the champion evident in his eyes.

Corthie got to his feet and smiled at him. 'You were saying?'

# CHAPTER 23

# THE ELUSIVE TRUTH

Arrowhead Fort, The Bulwark, The City – 18<sup>th</sup> Namen 3419

Maddie put the pencil down. It was useless. How was she supposed to concentrate when the rain was making such a racket? It sounded as though there were a thousand drummers standing outside in the forecourt of Arrowhead. She picked up the letter she had received from her mother and read it again. It was the first time her family had communicated with her since they had fought over a month before, and Maddie knew she needed to reply, but the damp, humid weather had drained all of her energy.

Her mother's tone had been almost formal in its politeness, but Maddie knew that was her way of trying to mend the bridges between them. So far, she had written three lines in response, all bland and inconsequential; grumbles about the rain, and hopes that the family were in good health. If only she could tell her mother the truth; that would make for a good letter, but the thought of having to fabricate some nonsense about repairing walls sapped her will. If she didn't lie, though, her letter would end up being pretty short. Maybe she should let Blackrose dictate it.

She heard a noise from the hallway and hoped it was Corthie. The champion hadn't visited since close to the beginning of the month, and she wanted him to see her walk without her crutch. She stood, unaided, and went to the door.

'Oh, it's you,' she said.

Hilde frowned, her long raincoat dripping onto the floor. She took it off and hung it onto a peg, then walked up the hallway.

'Have you finished writing that letter to your mother yet?'

'Not quite.'

'You've had four days, Maddie.'

'It's tricky; I can't tell them the truth, but lying seems wrong when I'm trying to make up with them.'

'You do what you have to; it's important to keep in contact with those who love you.'

Maddie smiled. 'See? You do have a heart.'

'I'm actually more concerned with making sure they don't turn up here again.'

'Maybe you should write the letter; you're good with words and stuff.'

'Maddie, you're one of the brightest girls I know; I'm sure that a simple letter is well within your capabilities.'

She decided it was time to change the subject. 'How did your trip outside go? Did you find what you were looking for?'

'No, but my suspicions remain firmly with the sergeant at the gate-house. He's one of the very few people in Arrowhead who knows the location of Blackrose's lair, and he probably could have been bribed by Corthie to give the secret away.'

'The sergeant would only have done that if Corthie had already known about her existence. It's not something that the sergeant would have randomly mentioned. "Oh, hello. I have a secret; do you want to give me some gold and I'll tell you?" Nah. The sergeant might have helped, but he's not the one who gave it away.'

'Hmm,' the captain said; 'you may be right.'

'You know,' said Maddie, 'one day you'll die.'

'What?'

'Or retire. What I'm trying to say is, I want to live up to your standards; I want to be the best looker-afterer of Blackrose, I mean the best carer...? Whatever, you know what I mean. I look at you, and think, yes, that's what I want to be like.'

'Is there a compliment somewhere in that twisted logic of yours?'

'You're my role model.'

'Malik's ass, please don't say that. I'm a friendless, grumpy misanthrope; why would you want to be like me? And do you really picture yourself putting up with Blackrose your entire life?'

'Of course I do, and let's face it, there's nowhere else they can send me now, not when I've learned so much.'

Hilde raised an eyebrow. 'Kano could cut your tongue out and send you to the Rats.'

'Is that...? What? He wouldn't, would he?'

'He's done far, far worse over the years, girl. Think of the cruellest thing you could to do someone; chances are that Lord Kano has already done it. He may look like a boy, but he has the mind of a monster.'

'I need to sit down.'

'Really? You're not usually this squeamish, except on live-goat day.'

'I'm not squeamish; my leg's sore.'

'Oh.'

Maddie limped over to a chair and sat.

'How is it?' said Hilde.

'A little bit stronger every day, but it's always stiff when I wake up each morning. Oops, that didn't come out right. Anyway... no, I'm distracted now, I can't even remember what I was saying.'

'Your leg.'

'Oh, yes; it's getting better, and now it only hurts if I stand up for too long.'

'You've healed well, but you're the right age for it. If that had happened to me I'd still be on crutches.'

'Come on, you're not that old. Are you?'

'Let's just say I was on the wrong side of thirty when I started looking after Blackrose.'

'Why is it the "wrong" side? Doesn't getting older bring some benefits?'

'Only a nineteen year old could say such a thing.'

'Do you regret not having children?'

'Not particularly. I've never felt myself to be excessively maternal.'

'Oh, I don't know about that; you're like a substitute mum to me.'

Hilde stared at her, and Maddie thought for a second that her eyes softened, then it passed.

'Get on with that letter,' she said, then strode from the room.

---

A roar from the lair woke Maddie, and she started.

'Wait,' she mumbled, 'I'm coming.'

She glanced around. She was sitting at her desk, the unfinished letter spread before her, a patch of drool blurring the few lines she had managed to add before falling asleep.

The roar came again. There was no pain in it, but it was insistent. Maddie got to her feet and rubbed her left leg, grimacing. She walked to the door of her room and peered out just as Hilde was emerging from a store-cupboard.

'Should I go?' said Maddie.

'Let's both go,' said Hilde. 'As far as I can tell, that roar means she wants the two of us.'

Maddie frowned. 'How do you know that?'

'A decade of practice.'

'That could be categorised as a benefit of getting older.'

Hilde halted as she drew level to Maddie's bedroom. 'You finished that letter?'

'Nearly. Maybe I should ask Blackrose for her advice.'

They walked to the lair's main gate, taking their time to account for Maddie's limp. The vast cavern was still, and they went through the hatch in the black gate. Blackrose had her head raised high, and she watched them enter.

317

'That took you longer than five minutes. What kept you?'

'Maddie's leg hasn't completely recovered.'

The dragon frowned. 'The frailty of you insects still astounds me. It is amazing that you have survived as a species.'

'What are you roaring about, then?' said Maddie. 'I was in the middle of writing a letter to my mother, but I'm not sure what to say. Do you think you could help me with it?'

'I could, but I most certainly won't, unless you wish me to force you to only write the truth; is that what you meant?'

'Eh, no.'

'Then I will not assist you in the writing of lies meant for the one who birthed you. Have you no respect for her, or for me?'

'Sorry I asked.'

'As you should be. Now, I have been thinking.'

Hilde and Maddie walked closer, and the dragon lowered her head a little.

'What about?' said Hilde.

'My life here. Ten years I've spent in this... cell, abiding by my principles. I resisted, because I refused to be a slave. Tell me, do you believe I have been right to do so?'

Hilde raised a hand to Maddie. 'Don't answer that; she's trying to trick us.'

'Come now, Captain; so suspicious? It was an honest question. You two know me better than any of the other humans in this world. When you look at young Buckler, and see him soar through the sky, do you think that my defiance has been futile?'

'No,' said Hilde, as Maddie said, 'Yes,' at the same time.

The dragon watched as Hilde glared at Maddie. 'Let's start with you, Captain. Explain yourself.'

'They're your principles; whether I agree with them or not is immaterial. Standing by what you believe in is never futile.'

'That doesn't make all that much sense to me. What if you believed that the sun never rose in the morning? Should you stay in bed all day with the shutters closed in case you are proved wrong?'

'But it's easy to prove if the sun exists or not; how is that the same as believing that if someone is forced to do something against their will, then that makes them a slave? You've often told me that you would never work for the humans for that reason. Would you now be content to live as a slave? Have you changed your mind?'

'No, I am merely canvassing the opinions of those I deem closest to me. Captain, isn't it written in the terms of your employment that part of your purpose is to try to persuade me to submit to the will of the City's rulers?'

'It is, yes.'

'Then why are you now doing your best to prevent that?'

Hilde shrugged. 'You won me over, I guess.'

'Good answer. Now, Maddie, tell me why you think my life is futile.'

'I didn't say your life was futile, what I meant was I don't see the point in resisting when your life could be so much better. Buckler can do almost whatever he pleases, he certainly has more freedom than most Blades, and I realise that it's the "almost" bit that gets you, but everyone lives under some kind of laws or rules that they need to obey. I can't just go around murdering someone, for example, so does that mean I'm not free? Life is a compromise, I guess is what I'm trying to say, although I can hardly believe I'm saying it. I'm a terrible example. I've been thrown out of regiments for not obeying orders, so maybe you shouldn't be listening to me.'

'I heartily concur with that last sentiment,' said Hilde.

'So, Maddie,' said Blackrose, ignoring the captain, 'you would say that swearing an oath to the Commander of the Bulwark would not mean degrading myself as a slave, but instead it could be seen as a normal, dignified course of action?'

'Well, look at Corthie.'

Hilde sighed. 'I wondered when his name would come up.'

'Does the champion act like a slave?' said Maddie. 'He remains his own man, despite fighting in the Wolfpack.'

'If I understand you correctly,' said the dragon, 'you would advise me to do the same as the champion?'

'Yes, I suppose.'

'And would that entail an oath to the Commander of the Bulwark?'

'I guess so.'

'Then summon him.'

Hilde's face paled. 'What? You can't be serious.'

'Do you think I am playing games with you, Captain?'

'I don't know what you're doing.'

'Summon Duke Marcus, as Maddie suggests. I wish to speak to him. That is all.'

The dragon lowered her head to the ground and closed her eyes.

Hilde turned to Maddie. 'With me. Now.'

Maddie bit her lip as she followed Hilde out of the lair, her limp making her lag behind as the captain strode away. Hilde went through the cavern and continued to her office, and Maddie's leg was hurting by the time she had caught up.

'Sit down.'

'I think I'll have to,' said Maddie as she fell into a chair. 'Oooh, that's sore.'

'I don't care about your leg right now. What in the name of Amalia's ass were you doing in there? Do you realise what you've done?'

'I don't understand; haven't we been trying to persuade her to give up her resistance all this time?'

'This is different. Before that idiot champion walked in here, she would never have said such things. He's got into her head, and filled it with the worst thing he could – hope. She'd already made her mind up before we walked in there, she just needed one of us to suggest it, so she could use that as her excuse. And you fell for it.' Hilde sank into her chair and put her head in her hands. 'This is a disaster.'

'But what's the worst that could happen? Assuming she doesn't just eat Duke Marcus... wait, do you think that's what she has in mind? That would be interesting.'

'That I could live with, but no, I think she's decided to pledge her allegiance as some kind of trick, or as part of an idiotic scheme concocted by Corthie. Why did you let him in, girl? Last time he was here, how long were they alone together?'

'Ten minutes, maybe? I'm not sure. I was still on a crutch back then, so I was taking a while to get around.'

'But long enough, though? Damn it.'

'It might be a plot or a plan, but I don't know if I care, if it means I get to see Blackrose fly. Imagine, if she takes the oath, then her chains would go, and she could fly again.'

Hilde said nothing.

'Don't you want to see her fly?'

'You've never seen her wings, have you?'

'How could I? The lair's not big enough for her to stretch them out.'

'Exactly. Do you know what happens to dragon wings after ten years of being in a cramped cell? I didn't either, of course, but I do now. Even if Blackrose is released today, she won't be flying again, not for a long while, if ever.'

Maddie stared at her. 'You're just saying that to put me off; you don't know.'

'I know what I've seen.'

'But dragons have self-healing powers.'

'They do, but remember that Dragons are mortal like us. She could certainly heal a broken bone faster than we would, but... oh, Maddie, her wings are in a bad state, her muscles almost withered away. It could take a very long time for them to recover.'

'But we have to start somewhere, don't we? Look how long my leg's taken to heal, but you didn't give up on me. Why would we give up on her? I won't.'

'It's not about giving up, it's about being realistic.'

'It sounds like you don't even want to try. I know it might be painful to watch, but if we take it one step at a time, just like you taught me, then it'll be worth it.'

Hilde looked away, and raised a dismissive hand. 'Fine. Go and summon the duke. If it has to be done, then I want it over with as quickly as possible.'

'Alright. Um, how do I do that?'

'Tell the sergeant at the gatehouse to send a messenger; tell him it comes from me. He'll understand.'

Maddie remained where she was for a moment. First the dragon had tricked her into suggesting that they summon the duke, and now Hilde was making her do it. Was this so she could take the blame if it all went wrong? So be it. People had blamed her for things all her life. But maybe, just maybe, it wouldn't all turn out wrong. Just maybe, Maddie would be right for once.

'Alright, I'll go.'

---

The sun had set by the time a carriage bearing Lifegiver markings pulled up in the forecourt of Arrowhead. Hilde had been watching the window all afternoon as she had made her way through a bottle of Hammer-branded gin.

Maddie watched the captain refill her mug. 'Did you drink this much before you started looking after Blackrose?'

Hilde glanced at her but said nothing.

'But what if Duke Marcus sees you drinking on duty?'

'I'm not on duty,' the captain muttered. 'You are.'

'Since when?'

'Since the moment you suggested this would be a good idea,' she said, her eyes drunk, and angry.

'Do you hate me?'

'Right now? Yes.'

'I don't regret it.'

'I know. If you did, then maybe I wouldn't hate you.'

A dark figure flanked by soldiers strode across the yard towards their front door.

'Here they come,' said Hilde. 'Go and greet them, and make sure you close my office door behind you. As far as they're concerned, I'm not in.'

Maddie stood. She glanced at the captain, then went out into the hallway as the front door was knocked.

'Coming,' she yelled as she closed Hilde's door.

She half-limped to the front door and slid the bolts free. A dozen soldiers seemed to be standing outside in the rain as she opened it. She looked for Duke Marcus, but Lord Kano stepped forward, a long raincoat covering him.

'Where's Captain Hilde?'

'She's not in just now, sir. I'm Maddie Jackdaw.'

'I don't care who you are,' he said as he barged his way past. He turned and pointed at the soldiers. 'You lot, go and camp yourselves in the Wolfpack common room; I'll send for you when I'm done here.'

The soldiers saluted and trooped off, then Maddie closed the door.

'Here,' said Kano, handing her his raincoat.

She took it, and hung it up on a peg by the door.

'When's Hilde coming back?'

'Tomorrow, I think.'

He glared at her. 'You think? And address me as "sir" when you speak to me, soldier; I am the Adjutant of the Bulwark.'

'Yes, I know that. Sir.'

'What is your rank, soldier? That uniform isn't standard; why has the captain allowed you to wear it?'

'I'm a private, sir. I guess we don't get many visitors with it being a secret and all.'

'You think and you guess. Do you actually know anything?'

'Does anyone, sir?'

'Is that supposed to be a joke?'

'No, sir, I was merely commenting on the elusiveness of true knowledge.'

'Is there something wrong with you?'

She pulled up her sleeve and showed him her list of previous units tattooed onto her skin.

'Ah, you're one of those. A reject. Fit for nothing. That explains why you're here; Hilde was an awkward bitch at the best of times.'

'The captain is a fine officer and a good person, sir.'

'In your opinion, which is utterly worthless. Are you the only Blade here?'

'Yes, sir.'

His eyes roved over her and she felt a knot forming in the pit of her stomach.

'So, we're all alone?' he said, taking her hand.

She tried to pull it away, but he tightened his grip.

'Do you know the authority I have, as Adjutant?' he said, pulling her closer. 'It means I can get away with doing whatever I want to whomever I desire; and right now, that's you.'

'We're not alone,' she said, as she squirmed in his grasp.

His eyes narrowed. 'Who else is here?'

She glanced at the door leading to Blackrose. 'There's a dragon right through that door; a dragon who has become quite protective of me over the last few months, sir. Just thought you should know.'

'That lizard cares about no one; you're bluffing.'

'Do you want to risk finding out if that's true?'

His eyes darted from Maddie to the door, then he shoved her away. She fell to the floor, her left leg aching as it hit the flagstones of the entrance hall.

'Get up, reject,' he said. 'Run ahead and tell the dragon that I am here. I will follow in a few minutes.'

He watched as she struggled to her feet. She pulled herself up, and straightened despite the pain. Asshole. Her fear lessened and her fury increased with every step she took away from him, and she could feel her eyes welling from the humiliation. She passed Hilde's office. Had she heard what had happened? Maddie hoped not, for if she had, and had ignored it, it was the end for her and Hilde.

She pictured Blackrose opening her jaws and incinerating him. She had heard that fire was one of the only ways to kill a demigod, but she was pretty sure that having his head bitten off would work as well.

She entered the cavern and hobbled towards the black gate. She paused, and tried to clear the anger from her mind. She needed to do what was best for Blackrose, and getting her to kill Kano might see them both executed. What would the duke do when he learned that his adjutant had been ripped limb from limb by a dragon that had refused to serve him for ten years? Blackrose was helpless as long as she had that chain shackled to her limb, as they could withdraw her food and starve her to death. Once she was free of it? Well, that would change things. Lord Kano would get what was coming to him, she just needed to be patient for the first time in her life. She would have to lie to Blackrose and pretend everything was fine; but she would explain it all later, when the chains were gone, and the dragon would understand; well, she hoped she would.

She hobbled through the hatch in the gate. Blackrose was in the same position as when they had left her, with her head resting on the ground.

'You have a visitor, but it's not Duke Marcus.'

'Don't tell me that he's sent that awful lackey of his. I told the duke years ago that I loathed that foul insect Kano; is he trying to provoke me?'

'I don't know.'

'Girl, listen to me. What I am about to do may seem to your eyes as unworthy of me, but I must; it is necessary.'

'Is it part of a plan you've cooked up with Corthie?'

The dragon gazed at her. 'You're a good girl. Very clever. Do not judge me for the things I must say to Kano over the next ten minutes. It is for a higher purpose.'

'Are you going to lie to him?'

'No, but I can shape words to make them seem true, and the gullible leave with a conviction that I have said things that I never actually uttered.'

'Sounds a bit like lying to me.'

'Which is why I am telling you this in advance. I loathe Kano, but it might not seem so from my words once he has arrived.'

'I hate him too, but for you, I will try to do the same.'

'Then we shall keep each other strong.'

'Can I ask something? Hilde said that your wings were... uh, not, eh...'

'My wings will take some time to heal, it is true.'

'But you will fly again?'

'How could you ever doubt it?'

'I don't, it's just from what Hilde said, she...'

'The captain is sad because she understands that things are about to change, and she is trying to resist it. Don't be angry with her; she needs your support now more than ever.'

Maddie nodded.

Footsteps echoed from the cavern and she turned to see Lord Kano enter the lair.

'Son of the noble and beloved Prince Isra,' said Blackrose, 'your reputation and authority precede you. Duke Marcus, I see, has sent his Adjutant in response to my request; will you be so good as to pass on what I have to say to him?'

'Dragon,' Kano said. He glanced over at the chain, as if to make sure it was securely attached to Blackrose, then noticed Maddie.

'What I have to say,' said Blackrose, 'concerns the future. Perhaps I have been here long enough; perhaps it is time to consider changing my mind.'

'Are you willing to swear allegiance to the Commander of the Bulwark, yes or no?'

'Would I have asked you here for any other reason? I would do almost anything to be free of this prison, and as I cannot remove these chains myself, it seems that swearing allegiance is the only option left to me.'

'Really? After all this time you've changed your mind?'

'The girl here has been most insistent. She has asked me to reconsider, and has told me of the many honours bestowed upon Buckler for his courageous service. Ten years is a long time to do nothing but sit and think; it is time for a change.'

Kano laughed and slapped his thigh. 'So, we'll have two dragons in the air in time for the winter fighting season? Ha. This will please the duke greatly, if you're not lying to me.'

'Do not insult me; dragons never lie.'

'And you'll fight?'

'I will. I do have some terms, regarding living conditions and so on.'

'I thought you might. Well, well. The duke thought this visit was going to be another waste of time; just wait until he hears.' He turned to Maddie. 'Leave us, Private; I do not wish you to be here while the dragon and I negotiate terms.'

Maddie nodded. Her eyes met those of Blackrose for a moment, then she turned and left the lair.

## CHAPTER 24
## EXCHANGE

Tara, Auldan, The City – 19th Namen 3419

'What a ridiculous time to be travelling,' Daniel's mother said as he boarded the carriage.

Four servants had lined the way from the regimental barracks with umbrellas, but the rain had still managed to get down the back of his dress uniform. He clambered onto the bench as the side door of the carriage was closed.

'The things I do for you,' said his mother from the bench opposite him. 'I once swore I'd never leave the house during Sweetmist, but your engagement has moved so far in such a short time that the inconvenience has become necessary.'

Daniel nodded. 'Where are we going?'

'To the Omertia townhouse; do you know it?'

He shook his head. 'Can we not meet them on neutral territory, like a restaurant?'

'They consider Emily's trip to the villa as being on our ground, so they expect this meeting to be held on theirs. This will be the fourth occasion I'll have met them; it's really you they want to see. They want to judge the young man who will take their only daughter off their hands.'

'Will Emily be there?'

His mother glanced at him. 'Why, do you hope she will?'

An image of Emily in his bed at the villa flashed through his mind. 'Yes.'

'Good. The fact that you actually seem to like her makes all this so much easier, but at the same time I feel a little sad. My boy is becoming a man, and soon I'll have to share his love with another woman.'

Daniel cringed. 'But I've been engaged before.'

'Yes, but Clarine was a girl, while Emily is quite clearly a young woman. A strong-willed young woman, whom I will need to evaluate carefully once you are married and she has moved into the mansion. I sense there may be some initial tensions, but I'm confident that I'll be able to tame her sooner or later.'

'You'll do no such thing, mother. She'll be my wife, and I'll not have you treat her like one of the servants.'

'Do you see what I mean? You're already taking her side over mine. I don't expect her to act like a servant, Daniel, I expect her to act like an Aurelian. How do you think your father's mother treated me when we got married? I had to leave my old family behind and not only join the Aurelians, but become one. And just as well I did, for had it been left to your father I fear the family line might well have ended with you, my dear boy.'

Daniel frowned. 'It still might.'

'Which is why you need to be on your best behaviour today; we cannot allow them any excuse to break it off. I admit, they do seem keen at the moment, but you know how quickly things can change. The Omertia family is a strange one, with a number of... eccentrics in their history, but they can boast a pure Roser heritage which can be traced back almost as far as the Aurelians. They are also rich, which helps.'

'Where does their money come from?'

His mother raised an eyebrow. 'For the sake of blessed Amalia, I pray that you do not ask questions like that when we're with them.'

'I'm not asking them, I'm asking you.'

'It's still a vulgar question.'

'Are you going to answer it?'

His mother frowned. 'They own substantial tracts of Medio, and the rental income they collect is substantial.'

'They own farms in Sander territory?'

'I said "rental income", son. They own much of the land the Circuit is built on. The recent troubles have hit them hard, as many of the filthy Evader peasants have been refusing to pay their rent, blaming the riots and suchlike, but the Omertias have deep pockets. They'll weather the storm.'

Daniel glanced out the window at the pelting rain. 'Will they? It seems to be getting worse, not better.'

'Yes. All the confident predictions that the troubles would end with the coming of Sweetmist seem to have been unfounded. A most unfortunate situation. Still, these things have happened before, and they always fizzle out eventually.'

'The Circuit has been paralysed for over three months, and Outer Pella is on the verge of boiling over; I wish I shared your confidence.' He caught her eye. 'That reminds me; I heard a rumour yesterday about a possible posting.'

'I thought you were settled into your new role at the militia headquarters; that's what I was told. Have they changed their minds? By Malik's eyes, please tell me you're not being sent back to the Circuit; it could completely ruin the wedding plans.'

'No,' he said; 'Pella.'

'Oh. Well, that's not so bad, at least it's still in Auldan. Doing what?'

'It was only a rumour, but I heard the regiment will be based close to Cuidrach Palace, to allow more Reaper militia to be deployed to Outer Pella to keep the peace.'

'Ah, the palace? This is sounding better all the time. A stint at Cuidrach will look good on your list of achievements, and the harbour front there is delightful. A junior lieutenant in the Circuit, and Pella as a senior lieutenant. Yes, I approve.'

Daniel laughed. 'I'm sure the commanders will be happy to hear that.'

'Let me know the details as soon as you find out, dear; I may need to adjust some of the wedding preparations.'

The carriage levelled off as they reached the bottom of the hillside. They turned left into a series of wide avenues, with townhouses set back from the road. They weren't as palatial as the mansions of Princeps Row, but their solidity and size denoted great wealth and status. They pulled up in front of a gate that had the Taran flag flying from a post, the black leopard looking wet and bedraggled in the rain.

'They are patriots, as you can see,' his mother said, 'so keep any wishy-washy opinions to yourself.'

A line of servants carrying large umbrellas formed between the carriage and the entrance to the townhouse, and the side door was opened. Daniel's mother took an offered hand and stepped down to the pavement, a hood keeping her hair from being disturbed in the crosswind. Daniel followed, and they hurried in a dignified manner to the front door.

'Greetings, Lady Aurelian,' bowed a man as they entered; 'and Lieutenant Aurelian.' He stuck out his hand. 'Nice to meet you at last.'

Daniel shook it. 'The honour is mine, Lord Omertia.'

A woman was standing next to the lord, her dress as formal as his. She glanced at him, extending her hand.

'This is my wife, Lady Omertia,' the lord said as Daniel bowed and kissed her hand.

'A pleasure to meet you, my lady.'

The woman kissed cheeks with Daniel's mother.

'You're looking well, Lady Aurelian.'

'And you, my dear. Thank you for inviting Daniel and me to your lovely home.'

'Well,' said the lord, 'we wanted to have a look at the boy before we give our little Emily to him.'

Daniel glanced down the hallway, but saw no sign of her. 'Is Emily at home today, my lord?'

'She is, however I have asked her to remain in her room. I will inform her of the outcome of this meeting once it has been completed.'

Lady Omertia smiled. 'She returned from the Aurelian villa quite struck with you, young man, so you needn't fear anything about my daughter's intentions.'

The lord shook his head. 'The girl will do as she's told, regardless of her intentions. But let's not stand out here in the hallway, we have had some refreshments prepared for you in the drawing room.'

He gestured to a doorway. Daniel and his mother handed their raincoats to a servant and followed the lord and lady into a large, high-ceilinged chamber, with tall windows that had been shuttered against the rain. Elegant lamps were bathing the room in a warm glow, and they sat on the comfortable couches that had been arranged around a low table.

'What's your drink, Daniel?' said the lord as he reached for an assortment of bottles and decanters on the table.

'At this time of day, I would say a red wine, thank you.'

'Good, good,' he said, picking up a bottle. 'Glad to hear you're not a gin-guzzler. As the Rosers make the best wines and brandies in the City, why anyone with any sense chooses to drink that vile stuff is frankly beyond me.'

'Some of the younger generation,' said Lady Aurelian, 'have been sadly influenced by fleeting fashion rather than good taste. Luckily for my sanity, Daniel appears to be an exception.'

'Well, that's me finished,' the lord said; 'I only had the one question.' He laughed. 'Only joking.'

Daniel smiled, despite the awkwardness, and his disappointment at Emily not being there. The lord poured white wine for the two ladies without asking what they wanted, then filled a glass with brandy for himself.

'So, Lieutenant,' he said, leaning back into the couch; 'tell me, how would you deal with the current crisis afflicting the Circuit?'

Lady Omertia shook her head. 'Really, darling? Politics?'

'It's important to know where he stands on such matters.'

'It's a trifle unbecoming, dear.'

'Nonsense. A man's politics is what defines him; you can always leave the room if it offends you.'

His wife lowered her eyes and said nothing.

'Well?' said the lord to Daniel. 'You can answer, boy.'

Daniel had been dreading this sort of question. He knew that if he gave his true opinions, then he and the lord would become embroiled in a potentially engagement-ending argument, and he would never see Emily again, let alone feel her body pressed against his. What was more important; his desire, or his integrity? He pictured the way Emily had looked as she had stood by his bedroom door, and made his choice.

'A firm hand is required,' he said, 'and a strong will. With rebellions such as this, there is no middle ground; either we concede to the demands of the mob, which would be a disaster for the City, or we remain steadfast, and crush them.'

A broad smile spread over the lord's face. 'You echo my thoughts precisely, Daniel. Good chap. There's been enough tip-toeing around; the entire governance of the Circuit should be placed into the hands of the occupying tribes, with Tara at their head, naturally. If all resistance was dealt with as ruthlessly as the way you handled things when you were there, then the situation would calm down soon enough. What about the root causes though, how would you deal with those?'

'Sorry, sir, I'm not sure I understand what you mean.'

'Perhaps I wasn't being clear. Why is it, do you think, that it's always the Evader tribe rising up?'

Daniel thought for a moment. The obvious reasons to him were the poverty and appalling conditions most of them lived in, but he knew that wasn't the answer the lord was waiting for.

'I'm not sure I know enough to be able to answer that, sir.'

'No? Well, at least you're man enough to admit it, rather than just make something up. Shall I tell you what I think? It's clear to me that the Evaders have never quite fitted in with the other tribes of the City, and that many of the problems we face can be put down to this basic, fundamental clash of cultures. The Evaders are too different to the rest of us, and, while they remain here, the City will never truly know peace and prosperity.'

'But, sir, what is the alternative?'

The lord smiled. 'Even I'm not ruthless enough to suggest that we kill them all!' He laughed. 'No, no. What I'm proposing is that we transport the entire tribe of the Evaders to the lands beyond the Great Straits on the other side of the Clashing Seas, where they would be free to build their own city. That way we all win; the Evaders get to run their own affairs, while we no longer have to put up with their backward customs and ways. Now, you're probably thinking that you'll be able to find a flaw in my plan, but rest assured that I have studied the possibilities extensively.'

'What would happen to the Circuit in this scheme, sir?'

'We would completely redevelop it; businesses, industry, new homes, and I propose that we move most of the Reapers from Auldan into Medio to fill some of the space. That way, Tara would directly benefit, as Outer Pella could be turned into farmland. See, I've thought of everything.'

Lady Omertia shifted very slightly in her chair. 'He's very proud of his plan.'

'He has quite the political mind,' said Daniel's mother.

'Indeed he has,' said Lady Omertia. 'If that's the politics out of the way, I'd like to move on to discuss the marital exchange.'

'An excellent idea,' said Daniel's mother. 'For our part, we were thinking of offering the Omertias an estate in Sander territory. It has six farmsteads, and covers forty acres of fertile land, where cotton is grown. It has been in the Aurelian family for over three hundred years, and is very pretty, as well as profitable.'

Lady Omertia smiled. 'Sounds charming. For our part, we wish to offer the Aurelians the ownership of ten acres of residential land within the Circuit.' She paused, but Daniel's mother didn't react in any way. 'Its average annual take in rental income is considerable. Of course, this year hasn't been quite as profitable, but I'm sure it will reap dividends once the troubles are over.'

'That seems perfectly acceptable to me,' said Daniel's mother, smiling. 'Shall I have my lawyer send over the fine detail for you to read?'

'Thank you, and I shall instruct ours to do the same.'

The lord coughed. 'I have a map of Sander territory somewhere. I don't suppose you would oblige me by pointing out where this estate of yours lies?'

'It would be my pleasure,' said Daniel's mother.

The lord stood, and ambled over to a large bookcase.

'I think I might use the bathroom,' said Daniel.

Lady Omertia smiled. 'Of course, it's down the hallway; the third door on the right.'

Daniel got to his feet and left the chamber. He kept the fixed smile on his lips as he passed a servant in the hallway, then went into the bathroom and locked the door. His face fell. The lord was a fool. A dangerous fool. He wanted to deport a quarter of a million peasants to a barren shore where the greenhides would rip them to pieces within days. He hadn't wanted to ask the question of what the lord thought would happen to the Evaders if they were sent across the straits, dreading what the response would have been.

He sat on the edge of the bath-tub and stared at the tiled floor.

A low, gentle tap came from the door. He stood, and opened it. Emily put a finger to his lips to quieten him, then pushed him into the bathroom and locked the door behind her. He placed his hands on her waist and pulled her close, then leaned down and kissed her neck. His hand moved down from her waist.

'Uh uh,' she said, pushing him away.

He stared at her, his desire burning.

'We're not in the villa now,' she said, smiling at him. 'I want to speak to you; we've never had a chance to talk alone. We'll have plenty of time for the intimate stuff when we're married, but first I want to make sure you're the right one for me.'

'Of course, I couldn't help myself; you're irresistible.'

'Good. I like that you want me, but I need more, Danny. What will you give me if we marry?'

'Um, I think our mothers are discussing the marital exchange just now.'

'I'm not talking about wealth or land, Danny, I'm talking about you and me. If I become your wife I will give you all of myself, my heart, my soul, my loyalty to the end. If you become my husband, will you give me the same?'

He took her hand. 'Yes.'

'I'll be the only woman for you?'

'Yes.'

'Loyalty is everything to me, Danny. I want to escape this house, and I need to be free of my father. He's controlling and treats me like an infant, and he treats my mother... I'd better not say. I need to know that you'll be different, that you won't sleep with other girls, and that you'll treat me with respect. I want to be your partner, Danny, not your quiet and obedient little wife.'

'You'll be Lady Aurelian one day,' he said, his body boiling over with desire, 'and I promise I'll be loyal. I'll be loyal, and I'll respect you, always.'

She gazed at him. 'I wish we were back in the villa.'

'So do I,' he said, reaching for her. He kissed her throat.

'But we're not,' she said, pushing him back. 'We're so close, Danny; let's not wreck it now. If my father even suspected I was downstairs he would call the whole thing off, and I'm not risking that.'

For five minutes with her, Daniel felt he would risk anything.

'Go,' she said; 'I'll wait here a little longer.' She pushed him towards the door. 'Go.'

He unlocked the door and slipped out, hearing the bolt slide home behind him. He felt like screaming, his thwarted desire pushing out every other thought. He knew she was right, but his body disagreed. He tried to control his breathing, then walked back along the hallway to the drawing room.

'Ah, there you are, Daniel,' his mother said, 'I thought perhaps you'd got lost.'

'Ehhh...'

She rose to her feet. 'You'll be happy to know that the marital exchanges have been agreed, and only await the paperwork from the lawyers being signed.'

'It was a pleasure to have you visit,' said Lady Omertia, also rising.

'You'll have to come over one evening,' said the lord, 'then I can show you both some more of my plan for the Evaders.'

'That's sounds... wonderful, thank you.'

They filed out into the hallway, and a servant handed them their raincoats. The lord shook Daniel's hand, and the two ladies kissed each other's cheeks.

'Until next time,' the lord said as the front door was opened.

Daniel and his mother crossed the driveway under a line of umbrellas as the wind and rain gusted around them. They climbed into their carriage and it set off.

His mother wiped the rain from her face and turned to Daniel. 'Do you realise how close you came to ruining everything?'

'What? I thought my answers were all right. I played along with his crazy ideas, didn't I?'

'I'm not talking about your answers, I'm talking about what took you so long in the bathroom. Do you think I'm stupid? That silly girl.'

Daniel stared at her, unsure of what to say.

'Well?'

'We were talking, that's all.'

'Really? And I suppose you were up all night "talking" in the villa too?'

'You knew about that?'

Her mother looked at him like he was mad. 'I have ears.'

Daniel grimaced. 'Please don't talk about it.'

'Look, I like to think I'm an indulgent parent, and I don't mind what you and Emily got up to in the villa; I actually thought it was quite cute, but in her parents' bathroom? Dear Amalia, spare me from stupid children.'

'Honestly, we were just talking in the bathroom. I wanted more, but...'

'Well, at least she has a tiny bit of sense, but her father would never have believed it was an innocent chat. Lord Omertia is a vile man, let's not beat around the bush, but once the marriage contract is signed, then Emily will become an Aurelian and she will move under my protection. Promise me that you'll do nothing stupid like this again until the contract has all of the required signatures; then, you can do as you please. Do you promise?'

Daniel frowned, and gazed out at the rain. 'I'll try.'

A messenger with an umbrella was waiting for him as the carriage reached the regimental barracks. He gestured to his mother to wait for a moment as he climbed down and took the slip of paper from the messenger.

'What does it say, dear?'

He frowned. 'My new deployment begins tomorrow. I'm to report to the Eleventh Royal Foot at dawn.' He glanced at his mother. 'Pella.'

'Good, then the rumours were true. I assume this means you have the evening off?'

'I do, yes.'

'Then I insist you spend it at home.'

Daniel turned to the messenger. 'Please let the commander know that I have received the order and will report as requested.'

The man saluted. 'Yes, sir.'

Daniel climbed back into the carriage and it pulled off again. 'I'll have to leave early,' he said. 'I need to collect a few things from my quarters before going to Pella.'

'I'll have a servant wake you.'

The ponies pulled the carriage up the hill towards Princeps Row. Somewhere behind the thick, black clouds the sun was setting, and Daniel missed seeing the sky. Water streamed down the slope of the road, filling the gutters and spilling over the cliff in little waterfalls.

'What a noise the rain makes,' said his mother. 'As I mentioned before, this is a ridiculous time of year to be travelling. I hope you're given a carriage tomorrow, I'd hate to think of you having to walk all the way to Pella in this. Have you ever met Lord Salvor?'

'No.'

'Well, he's the demigod you need to impress in Pella. He's one of Princess Khora's more, shall we say, competent children? Mind you, there's not much competition there. Ikara is a fool, and Lydia does nothing but sit on her hands in Port Sanders. Poor Doria is all but ignored, while Naxor swans around like he owns the City. The glory of the demigods has certainly faded.'

Daniel smiled. 'I thought you didn't discuss City politics?'

'This is not politics, it's gossip. I'm not demeaning their authority, just their personalities. Duke Marcus, now there's a man. It's a pity he's required in the Bulwark; he'd sort out the Circuit in a day.'

'Come on, now you're sounding like Lord Omertia.'

'Really? I'm hardly advocating the mass slaughter of the Evaders, am I? A little law and order might not go amiss, though.'

They pulled into their driveway, and the carriage came to a halt under a wide, rainproof awning. A servant opened the side door, and they hurried into the mansion to avoid the wind.

'Dinner's in an hour,' said his mother as they took off their rain-coats. 'Try not to drink too much gin before then.'

---

Daniel awoke with a finger pressed against his lips. He opened his eyes, and saw a hooded figure in his bedroom leaning over him.

He scrambled away, his hands gripping the covers as his heart raced. The figure pulled the hood back from her face.

'Emily? What in Malik's name...?'

'Shush,' she hissed.

He stared at her, and noticed her long, hooded cloak was dripping rainwater onto his floor. 'How did you get in? How did you know I was even here?'

'I'm pretty resourceful,' she whispered. 'My father kept drinking after you left; once he starts he doesn't usually stop until he's unconscious, and this evening was no different. My mother went to her room to pray, probably for a better husband, and I hope Amalia's listening to her.'

He said nothing, his eyes never leaving her face.

'Did you mean what you said, when we were alone before?'

He nodded. 'Every word.'

'Until your dying day?'

'Yes.'

'Then,' she said, unbuttoning the raincoat and letting it fall to the floor, 'I don't need to wait on a contract.' She pulled back the blanket and slipped into the bed beside him. 'I belong to you now, just as you belong to me.'

## CHAPTER 25

## THE FOG OF BALIAN

The Circuit, Medio, The City – 3rd Balian 3419

After thirty-two continuous days, the rain had stopped and a thick Balian fog had descended over the City. Aila didn't know which she hated more, but at least they were closer to the dry, crisp days of winter that were coming.

Fog would help a lot of assassins, she thought, as she followed the man through the twisting streets, but not her. Her disguise was herself; she didn't need anything that could make her lose track of her quarry, especially one that she had been hunting for so long. She had retired Stormfire for the moment; the appearance was too well known among the underworld, and she didn't want the notoriety to influence, or panic, her target. The man halted by the side of a canal, the mist drifting around him like a shroud. He tilted his head, as if listening, and Aila remained motionless in the shadows, her dark cloak covering every inch of her except her face, which she had told the world to see as belonging to an old peasant woman.

The man turned his head, scanning the street and the canal. A rumble of cries echoed through the fog, coming from a few streets away. Another disturbance, Aila thought, another deadly game between the rioters and the occupying forces. One or two soldiers from the other tribes were killed or seriously wounded every day by the insurgents, their bodies strung up from the balconies of abandoned housing blocks, or left mutilated in the gutters. The savagery of the rebels was matched by the ruthlessness of the Auldan militia. That Aurelian asshole had inspired his comrades by his actions in the summer, and there had been other tenement fires, where crowds of Taran or Dalrigian militia had stood by and watched as entire families had burned.

The man glanced in the direction of the noise, then turned and carried on walking. The bag over his shoulder looked heavy, and the man was tall and well-built, his shoulders wide and powerful. Her thoughts went to Corthie and she almost stumbled.

No, she chided herself. Not now. Concentrate. She had shed enough tears over him, and she would probably shed more; but not now. She slipped out of the shadows and followed the man. He led her into an area she wasn't familiar with. It had been knocked down and re-built within a decade or so, and she could remember the stinking tannery that had occupied the site before; now there was a maze of ramshackle streets, with houses piled up in ungainly stacks. More shoddy housing constructed by the Taran aristocrats who owned the land. Scum, she thought. Parasites who sat back and counted the gold fleeced from the residents by their teams of rent-collectors. Yendra's laws would have seen them lose their land, with it being redistributed to those who lived there. It had been the last straw for Prince Michael, who had taken the side of a few wealthy Taran nobles over the masses of suffering poor.

And what had Khora done to help? Nothing.

The man glanced around, then entered a housing block. Aila crept through the dark shadows, the fog clinging to the air as she hurried to the entrance. She listened at the door, then slowly pushed it open, half-expecting the man to be standing ready with a sword, but the hallway was empty. She entered, and closed the door behind her without a sound. The block had a dozen or so tiny apartments, and she went to the bottom of the stairs and glanced upwards.

There he was, ascending the steps above her. She timed her own steps to match his, and followed. He stopped on the third floor, and she heard a set of keys jingle for a second, and then a door opened and closed. She raced up the rest of the stairs, her soft-heeled sandals making no sound on the steps, and unclipped the little strap that held her sword securely in its sheath. She reached the landing and knelt by the door, listening for a few minutes. She could hear movement inside, but no voices.

She examined the lock. It seemed simple enough, but she knew there was probably at least one bolt also protecting the door. She took her picks from her belt pouch and got to work. It was slow going, but she knew silence was more important than speed. The mechanism clicked as she turned it, and she drew back from the door, waiting to see if the noise elicited a response from the man inside, her hand on her sword hilt.

Nothing.

It was time.

*You see me as Stormfire.*

She placed her fingers on the door handle and turned. The door opened an inch. No bolts?

He knew.

She edged to the side of the doorframe, drew her sword and swung the door open. A crossbow bolt flew past her, striking the concrete wall opposite and gouging out a two-inch hole. Aila burst through the entrance before he could loose again. She cursed as she saw him pick up a second loaded bow, then dived to the floor as the bolt whistled over her head. She pulled her knife from her boot and hurled it at him, but he brought the bow up to his face, and the blade embedded itself into the thick stock. She rolled to her feet and rushed him, her sword flashing in the dim light. He swung the crossbow, and the edge of her sword snagged among the cords of the pulling mechanism. He pushed, shoving the bow into Aila's face as he let go of it. Aila dropped her sword, and it fell to the floor with the bow in a tangled mess.

The man smiled at her as he pulled a knife. 'Stormfire. I wondered when you'd show up. Out of weapons? What a shame. Perhaps you're not as good as they say you are.'

*You see me as the worst nightmare of your childhood.*

The man's eyes widened and he let out a garbled cry. Aila grabbed the stock of the other bow and rammed it into his face. He fell, but slashed out with his arm at the same time, cutting through Aila's thin leather armour with the knife. She almost fell from the pain, but brought the stock down again, battering it against the side of the man's head. He collapsed to the ground, his eyes closed.

Aila fell to her knees, blood flowing from the wound in her abdomen. She powered her self-healing, first to rid herself of the pain, then to close the wound. She groaned as the pain faded, then checked her stomach, wiping away the blood to see that the injury had healed. She glanced at the man. He was good, and had been the first for over twenty years to get that close to Stormfire. But, more importantly, he was alive.

---

Aila didn't like torturing people. It made her feel like a demigod, but not in a good way. Inflicting agony upon a mortal when they were at your mercy seemed like something her brother would do.

She gazed at the man tied to the chair. She had secured the front door of the apartment, but no one in the block had come by to see what had caused the noise. The sounds of violence had become common in the Circuit, and folk ignored what was happening right under their noses, worried that they would be next. The contents of the sack that the man had been carrying were laid out on a table; piles of gold, and an assortment of weapons. She had also examined the unconscious man's upper left arm, and had seen the scarring that had removed the tattoos.

Another Blade in the Circuit.

She didn't relish what had to be done next, but it was necessary. She waited until the man began to stir.

*You see me as Lord Kano, Adjutant of the Bulwark.*

She slapped him across the face. He spluttered, his eyes opening. He glanced around, then halted, staring at her.

'My lord...' he gasped, his eyes wide.

'Stormfire is dead.'

The man let out a groan of relief. 'You killed her, my lord?'

'Yes. We knew she was tracking you, and followed her here. However, I now have a problem. You were alone with her in this apartment for longer than I'd hoped, and she may have had accomplices. I need to know what you told her.'

'Nothing, my lord, I swear it.'

'So you say. I wonder if perhaps you have outlived your usefulness. If your face is known, then the work you do may well be compromised.'

'There was no one else here with her, my lord, no one.'

She shook her head and scowled at him. 'Right now, I have thirty fighters positioned around this building; do you see or hear them? Of course you don't. How can you be sure she didn't have others with her? I also counted the gold. It's short.'

'What? No, my lord.'

'Did you think I wouldn't notice you taking your cut?'

'I would never, my lord, I swear. Stormfire must have taken it after I was knocked out. If I delivered less than was promised to the gangs, they'd kill me. They're already jumpy, and many are on the verge of calling off the riots; if I tried to short-change them, they'd stop the fighting tomorrow.'

'Have they threatened you?'

'Yes, my lord; they're losing too many of their young fighters to the Tarans, and they want more, my lord; more gold, more weapons. If I don't get that money to them by tonight, they might go on strike.'

'On strike?'

'Yes, my lord. They said they will lay down their arms and stay indoors unless the gold keeps flowing in. I've already had to increase the payments to account for the damn weather. I have done everything exactly as you commanded, my lord, but the Circuit is nearing exhaustion. To keep the troubles going, I need access to more gold.'

Aila paused, the knot in her stomach turning nauseous. Her brother had commanded this? The Bulwark was paying for the riots to continue? Much clicked into place in her mind, and she glanced at the man, knowing she had heard enough.

'Close your eyes, Blade.'

'But, my lord,' he cried, 'I have been loyal to you and the duke; faithful, always...'

'Close your eyes.'

He did so, his breath coming in gasps. She gripped the hilt of her short sword, and swung.

An hour later, Aila was in a carriage, travelling through the thick banks of fog towards the Union Walls and Auldan. She had returned to Redmarket after killing the Blade, and had tried to prepare herself as best she could for the confrontation she had been dreading. It had been over a month since she had been in Port Sanders learning about Khora's part in the assassination attempts made on Corthie's life, but after her meeting with the champion at the Middle Walls, she had avoided the entire subject.

She was still angry with him, still hurt. She had walked into the meeting with Corthie determined to end it with him, but when he had walked right up to her and tried to kiss her, everything had changed, and in that moment she had lost her heart to him. And then, a few seconds later, everything had changed again. She felt bereft, but how could she lose something she had never had?

She hated him for the things he had said to her, especially that nonsense about his sister. It was an excuse, nothing more, and how she had managed to restrain herself from punching him, she would never know. And then, he seemed to change his mind all over again, telling her that he wanted to run away with her so they could be together. Asshole. She had surrounded herself with work, buried herself in it, and sometimes hours would go by without the image of him entering her mind.

She loved him, she couldn't help it. She had never loved like this before, but it would pass, eventually; maybe. If she waited a few decades he would be gone forever; a few centuries, and her memories of him would fade, as had her recollections of all the mortals she had cared for. For the seven hundred and sixty-seven years of her life, this had been the case. Mortals bloomed and died, bloomed and died, while she and her family remained unchanging, but the way she felt about Corthie was different, and now she was on her way to speak to the God-Child who was trying to kill him.

The carriage went through the gates in the Union Walls and continued into Auldan. The fog outside remained thick and impenetrable, and they could have been anywhere. Khora had based herself out of Pella since the start of Sweetmist, and the thought of returning to her childhood home, and the place of her enforced house-arrest, weighed almost as heavily upon Aila as the prospect of confronting Khora. She had promised Corthie that, if the princess was guilty, she would kill her; would she?

Yes, she thought; she would do it for Corthie, and hang the consequences.

The carriage reached the shores of the Inner Bay, although no water could be seen through the fog. They took a road that ran by the beach and entered Pella through its old town walls. The day had not long passed noon, but the streets were quiet, and Aila could hear nothing but the clip of the ponies' shoes on the road and the rumble of the carriage wheels.

Then she saw it; Cuidrach Palace, the place of her birth, and her home for many years. Her father Prince Isra had ruled the Reapers from there for centuries until the Civil War, and she now loathed and loved the building with equal measure. The sprawling palace covered a large area of the town's harbour front, with wings and interior courtyards that had once resounded to the noise of her father's eleven children, and she remembered playing with Kano when he had been a boy. She had loved him dearly, but now he was an enemy.

The carriage halted before the main gates and Aila stepped down to the ground.

'A pleasure to welcome you home, my lady,' said a courtier.

'I haven't been here in over forty years.'

'Indeed, my lady; however, Lord Salvor has kept your rooms as they were.'

Aila smirked. 'Including the bars on the windows?'

'No, ma'am,' the courtier said, blushing a little; 'they have been removed.'

She walked up the steps and into the entrance hall of the palace, the courtier flanking her.

'Where is Princess Khora?'

'She is with Lords Salvor and Naxor, ma'am, in the governor's office. Are they expecting you?'

'Nope.'

'Perhaps, ma'am,' he said as he kept pace with her stride, 'I should go on ahead, if you'll allow me, so that I can introduce your arrival?'

'No, it's fine.'

'But...'

'I said it's fine.'

'I'm sorry, ma'am, but I may have to insist. Princess Khora does not like to be surprised.'

'As she and her two sons have vision powers, they probably know I'm on my way.'

They reached the door to the Governor's office. Two guards stood by, in the pale green uniform of Reaper militia. They glanced from Aila to the courtier.

'You know who I am,' she said; 'get out of my way.'

The courtier said nothing, and the guards stood aside. Aila pushed the doors open and strode into the large chamber. Khora was seated at a long table, with Naxor, Salvor, and a group of militia officers, some in Taran uniforms.

Khora's eyes went to the doors and she frowned.

'Good afternoon, aunt, cousins, mortals,' Aila said. 'How are you enjoying the Fog of Balian?'

Khora scowled at the mention of her slain son.

'Lady Aila,' said Naxor, rising; 'cousin, we weren't expecting the pleasure of your company. If you would care to wait for a few more moments; we were rather in the middle of things.'

'It can't wait.'

'Really?' said Naxor. 'What could be of such importance that you interrupt the business of the High Guardian of the City? My mother has summoned these officers here today due to matters of great urgency.'

'My words are not for them; dismiss the officers and make them wait.'

Khora took a breath, then nodded to her son. Naxor frowned.

'My apologies,' he said to the officers; 'as you can see, my cousin bears news for my mother that, quite clearly, cannot wait.'

The Reaper and Taran officers glared at Aila. She frowned. One of them seemed familiar from a drawing she had seen being posted around the Circuit. He was young, maybe twenty, and wore the uniform of a Taran lieutenant.

'You,' she said, as the officers were getting to their feet. 'What's your name?'

The Taran glanced at her, his face steady, but his eyes showing alarm.

'This is Lieutenant Aurelian of the Taran Eleventh Royal Foot, ma'am,' said a captain.

'Aurelian?' she said. 'You mean the criminal who burned a tenement of civilians to the ground? The one who was mysteriously transferred out of the Circuit as soon as I requested an interview with him. That Aurelian?'

The captain's eyes flickered, but he stood his ground. 'He is beyond your jurisdiction, my lady.'

She walked up to the young lieutenant. 'Why did you do it?'

The room stilled.

'I, uh... I...'

'He was doing his duty, ma'am,' said the captain, 'and I would appreciate it greatly if you would stop harassing one of my most promising young officers.' He glanced at Khora for support, but the princess's attention was elsewhere.

Aila smiled, her eyes never leaving Aurelian. 'Justice is very patient, and it never forgets.'

'That's enough,' said Naxor. 'You wanted them to leave, and now you're preventing them from doing so.'

Aila raised her hands. 'I'm done.' She turned and took a seat at the table opposite Khora as the officers filed out of the room.

Khora levelled her eyes at her. 'Speak.'

'Duke Marcus is paying gold to the gangs in the Circuit to keep the riots going.'

Lord Salvor's mouth opened, and he half-stood. 'What? Is this true? This is an outrage. What is he trying to achieve? Do you have evidence?'

'Sit, and calm yourself, son,' said Khora.

Aila smiled at her. 'You already knew, didn't you?'

Khora expression remained steady. 'Yes.'

Lord Salvor's face went red with anger, and he clenched his fists. He stared at his mother and brother. 'And did he know too?'

Lord Naxor nodded. 'It was I who informed our mother some time ago.'

Salvor banged his fist off the table.

'Go to your room if you cannot control yourself,' said Khora. 'I don't have to explain my actions to anyone, except the God-King himself. You are well aware that your brother is my closest advisor; this does not mean that I value you any less. My children all fulfil the roles I have given them, but there are things I would tell you that I would not utter to Ikara or Lydia for example.'

Salvor lowered his face.

Aila glanced at him. 'Maybe you should leave for the next part; I wouldn't want you to have to be sent to your room by your mummy for having a tantrum.'

'You disgust me,' he said, lifting his eyes to meet her. 'Having to watch you in an opium haze for years on end; debasing yourself like that; you should have been executed with the other traitors at the end of the war.'

'Lady Aila is right,' said Khora. 'Leave; now.'

Salvor stormed from the room, the door banging as he slammed it behind him.

'I would be obliged,' said Khora, turning to face Aila, 'if you would refrain from antagonising the very people who are on the same side as you, my niece. You like to think that you can remain apart from having to choose between me and Marcus, but if that were truly the case, you would not be here. Now, the Blades. Naxor brought me evidence some time ago that gold was being channelled from the Bulwark to the Circuit.'

'Why did you not tell me?'

'Because knowledge has to lead to action, and there is no action I can take. Do I announce to the City that Duke Marcus is behaving in this manner? Who would believe me, and what difference would it make? I cannot march an army into the Bulwark. Should I complain to the God-Queen? She would probably use that as an excuse to have me removed from power. What about the God-King; should I appeal to him?'

'So, you sit and wait for Marcus to make the first move?'

'Precisely.'

'There is one thing you could do, of course, that doesn't involve armies. What about assassinating those close to Marcus? His strongest allies?'

Khora raised an eyebrow. 'My. I don't know what to say. Are you encouraging me to murder your brother?'

'What? No, I didn't mean him.'

'Then who exactly? Marcus himself? This is dangerous talk, Aila.'

Aila glanced at the faces of Khora and Naxor. Who was trying to trap whom? She swallowed. 'What about his champion? He could be a powerful ally of the duke.'

'Funny you should say that,' said Khora.

Aila tensed, her hand inching towards the knife hidden in the folds of her cloak. 'Why?'

'Because Naxor here has suggested the same thing to me, more than once. I told him not to be ridiculous. Why would I want to harm the man who is keeping the walls free of greenhides?'

'Because he is a threat to you?'

'He's not a threat. If he ever becomes one, then I would consider it, but not before. If I went around assassinating everyone who might become a threat to me one day, there wouldn't be many people left in the City by now.'

Aila stared at Khora, but her aunt's face was unreadable. She turned to Naxor. 'Why did you kill your servant Tangrit?'

Naxor frowned. 'How did you know about that?'

'Why did Tangrit pay to have a team of assassins try to kill the champion?'

'Because he was a traitor,' said Naxor, 'which is why I killed him.'

'I see,' said Khora to her; 'you came here thinking it was I who was responsible for the attempts on the champion's life? Tell me, what would you have done had it been I?'

Aila frowned, knowing they were going to read the thoughts from her head no matter what she said next. 'I was going to kill you.'

Khora and Naxor glanced at each other, then stared at Aila. She felt a burning sensation behind her eyes for a moment as they trawled through her thoughts and memories, feeling as powerless as she ever had. It was done, though, and at least she had discovered another part of the truth.

'Oh, Aila,' said Khora; 'oh dear.'

'You impersonated me at the Middle Walls?' said Naxor. 'I'm impressed. And kissing the champion, three times?' He laughed. 'You wicked girl.'

'Son, please,' said Khora, 'can you not see how much she is hurting?'

'I don't want your pity,' said Aila.

'Stay here tonight,' said Khora; 'sleep in your old rooms. I must resume my meeting with the officers of the militia, to finalise our plans for opposing an invasion by the Blades into Medio and Auldan. I do not wish you to be at that meeting, especially after seeing how you talked to that Taran officer. I'm not your mummy, but I would very much like you to go to your room. Tomorrow, we can discuss Stormfire, and how we can work together to save the things we love.'

Aila got to her feet.

'I'll send you up some brandy,' said Naxor, winking; 'you look like you need it.'

---

Aila sat on the huge bed, gazing around at her old possessions. Her room looked like a museum, an image of her life from before that had been frozen in time; only tidier. For hundreds of years she had been confined within those walls, the windows barred, and the doors locked. She knew that, on this visit, she could walk out any time she liked, so why did she feel so trapped?

Khora and Naxor had read her every thought, every fear, every desire. She lay back onto the bed as she imagined Naxor laughing at the way she felt about Corthie, and tears welled in her eyes. Khora was different. She wanted to trust her, but could never forget how the princess had betrayed Yendra at the end of the war.

A knock came at the door.

'Yeah?'

The door opened and a servant walked in with a trolley. 'Dinner, ma'am.'

Aila remained where she was until the door closed again, then she got up and wandered over to the trolley. Covered dishes and plates filled the surface, along with a bottle of brandy and a note. She unfolded the slip of paper.

*Aila,*

*Sorry for laughing; it's been so long since my own heart was broken that I had forgotten how it feels. Drink the brandy, rest, and tomorrow we'll work out how to beat Marcus.*

*As long as there is breath within me, I will never let the duke hurt you.*

*My love, Naxor.*

Aila felt the tears roll down her face, and she succumbed to them. She would do as her cousin asked and then, in the morning, she would do the unthinkable; she would make her peace with Khora.

## CHAPTER 26
## CHANGE OF PLAN

Arrowhead Fort, The Bulwark, The City – 3$^{rd}$ Balian 3419

'There is something seriously wrong with this City's weather,' said Corthie as he gazed out of the tall windows of his bedchamber. 'Where's the rain gone? Is it morning?'

'It's nearly sunset,' said Quill; 'You didn't stop drinking until dawn and you've been sleeping since.'

'Really? Oh.'

'And this,' she said waving her arm at the view, 'is the first day of the Fog of Balian. It's come a couple of days late this year, but it hardly ever starts precisely on the first of the month.'

Corthie shook his head. The Bulwark was invisible, shielded by a thick blanket of fog. The top of the Wolfpack Tower was poking out like an island in the middle of an ocean of mist. The sky remained dark and brooding, and there was no sign of the sun through the endless clouds.

'So what did this Balian guy do to deserve having a fog named after him?'

'Nothing. He replaced Princess Yendra in the calendar after she was executed and he was slain in the Civil War.'

'He wasn't a rebel, then?'

'No, he was Princess Khora's son.'

'Did Yendra kill him, aye?'

'No.' Quill smiled. 'The killing was actually carried out by two people, one of whom you've met.'

'Aye?'

'Yeah. Lady Aila, the adjutant who saved your life.'

Corthie tried to keep his face expressionless. 'She killed him?'

'She had a warrior who was helping her. Lady Aila used some kind of trick, and the warrior chopped Balian's head off.'

He wasn't sure why, but somehow the news made him feel deflated. 'A warrior?'

'Yeah, she was pretty amazing by all accounts.'

'The warrior was a she?'

'Yeah, that's what I said.'

His heart lifted again and he realised that, for a moment, he had been jealous of a man from three hundred years before who hadn't even existed. Why couldn't he get Aila out of his mind? It had been a month since their fight at the Middle Walls, and yet every day he thought of her, wondering if she was still angry with him, or if their last kiss had meant as much to her as it had to him. He had to forget her; he had made a promise to Blackrose, and if his plan worked, then the dragon and he would be leaving the City forever. All he had to do was make it through another month without seeing Aila, then it would be done, and he could regret his choices later.

He could do it, he told himself, he just needed to stay in the Bulwark and behave himself. Obey orders and get cosy with the duke, just enough to allay the demigod's suspicions without appearing like a sycophant. A month of discipline and patience, and then he would be free.

The fog might help with his plan, he thought.

'So, how long does this mist last?'

'Until the end of Balian,' said Quill. 'Give or take a few days in either direction.'

Corthie nodded.

'The change will be just as sudden,' she said. 'One day it's fog as normal, and the next morning it's all sunny and dry. Cold, though, but clear and bright. The first greenhides usually get here about three or four days after that, and you'll be busy again, praise Malik.'

'Sorry I've been such a pain in the ass this last month.'

She glanced at him. 'You drink too much.'

'It's to keep me out of trouble. If I just stay here, in the fort, and go drinking in the common room, then at least I won't be up to no good, like going to the Circuit, for example.'

'What, so you can visit the adjutant?'

'No, so we can go to the Blind Poet, if it's still standing.'

'Your eyes looked away when you said that. You should practise lying more.'

There was a knock on the door. 'It's me.'

'Come in.'

Tanner opened the door and strode in. 'Is this you up at last? Seen the fog, have you?'

'Lasts a month, apparently.'

'Yeah, one more month of idleness. Suits me fine. Any day we don't have to go beyond the walls is a good day as far as I'm concerned.'

'Winter's not as bad as summer,' said Quill, 'and with Corthie and Buckler in action, we should do alright.'

'Not as many greenhides?'

'Not as many, and they're slower. They really hate the snow.'

'I thought it was dry and sunny in winter?' said Corthie.

'It is, most of the time, but there are blizzards now and again. Wait until you see them slipping on the ice,' she laughed; 'their claws are useless.'

Tanner chuckled. 'That'll be a sight.' He turned to Corthie. 'Listen, lad. The reason I'm up here is that the duke is after you. He wants you to head along to Lifegiver.'

'Again?' said Quill, eyeing Corthie. 'You're very popular with the duke these days.'

Corthie smiled. 'Just cultivating my career prospects. All I actually do when I go there is sit and nod while he talks. And, Lord Kano is always really annoyed that I'm there; it's worth it just for that.'

'What's he like?'

'Which one?'

'The duke?'

Corthie considered his words, as stating his true feelings might jeopardise his plan. He hated lying to his two friends, but he had promised Blackrose, and he wouldn't let her down.

'He's a clever guy,' he said, 'and he knows it. He understands every detail of the Great Wall, every fort, every turret, every catapult...'

'Yeah, fine,' said Quill, 'but what's he like as a person?'

Corthie shrugged. 'He's a demigod.'

'What about Kano?' said Tanner.

Corthie smiled, feeling on slightly safer ground. 'He's an asshole.'

'Makes sense,' said Quill, 'after all, he's a demigod too.'

Tanner chuckled as Corthie walked to the bed. He sat down and reached for his boots.

'I should be back in a few hours, if I don't get lost in the fog. Shall I meet you in the common room?'

'Give us a shout when you get back, and we'll come down,' said Tanner.

Quill groaned. 'Not another night on the brandy?'

Corthie shrugged from the edge of the bed. 'It's either that or the Circuit.'

'Fine, brandy it is.'

Little yellow lamps lined the main route by the Great Walls, guiding the carriages and soldiers that travelled through the thick fog. Corthie's attention soon wandered in the carriage; with nothing to see, he leaned back and closed his eyes.

Aila popped into his mind. He pictured her lying in his arms, covered in blood, and remembered how he had felt, then saw her in the room where they had argued in the Middle Walls. He went back further, to the time they had shared by the roses in the Shrine of the Three Sisters, and he felt his body ache with longing.

He shook his head, telling himself to stop. Thinking of Aila only caused him pain. The words of Blackrose had haunted him since the moment they had left the dragon's mouth, that Aila had broken it off because she couldn't bear the thought of him growing old and dying. If that was the real reason, then he should go to her and tell her it didn't matter; tell her that what mattered was spending as much time together as they could; but maybe that would just make it worse, maybe he should stay away for her sake. He didn't want to be the cause of her pain.

One more month. No, less than a month, because he had decided to bring his plan forward by a few days to make sure it coincided with the last days of the fog. The dense mist would make things easier, and he needed all the assistance he could get. He hadn't shared his entire plan with Blackrose, because much of it remained only half-formed in his mind. Lord Naxor was a hard man to track down, and the Quadrant in his possession was a secret to all but a tiny handful of demigods in the City. Aila would know what to do, but the thought of asking her to help him leave the City forever was not something he was going to consider. Aila. He clenched his fists in silent frustration as the carriage rumbled towards the Fortress of the Lifegiver.

If he was leaving in under a month, why did he feel so bad? This was his first broken heart, he realised, the first time he had understood what the phrase meant. He felt ill, his stomach twisted in knots and his chest tight. He remembered being with his sister when she had broken up with Lennox, a man Corthie had idolised. He had never understood his sister's reasons for ending it, but he would never forget the period she had spent grieving afterwards. Every time he had walked past her room, he had halted, listening to her tears through the door. Karalyn had always been his closest sibling, and he had wanted to reach out to her, but her pain had seemed too strong a barrier for him to breach.

This was different, he thought. He wasn't crying in his room, he was lying to every person he met, hiding himself and waiting for his moment to escape. His heart would heal, in the end.

He was almost relieved when the carriage pulled into the Fortress of the Lifegiver; anything to distract him from thinking about Aila was welcome, even Duke Marcus's company. He stepped down from the carriage outside the Duke's Tower and went inside, the guards nodding to him. He no longer had to sit through a preliminary meeting with Lord Kano to gain access to the duke, as the commander had made it clear to his adjutant that the champion was welcome. He ascended the stairs to the duke's study and knocked on the door.

A servant opened it, saw who was waiting, and stepped aside.

'The champion is here, my lord.'

'Ahh,' said the duke, glancing up from his desk, 'good. Come in, lad, take a seat; I'll just be a moment.'

He went back to his paperwork as the servant left the room. Corthie sat in his usual chair, and glanced at the full bookshelves. There were volumes on strategy, history and political theory.

'Feel free to borrow any of those,' said the duke, noticing where Corthie was looking.

'I've not noticed many books in the City,' he said, standing to take a closer look at the bookshelves; 'why is that, sir?'

'The cost of paper is prohibitive,' the duke said, his eyes on his work. 'Every tree that is felled in the City is accounted for, and most are set aside for urgent repairs, or go to the fishing fleet. There's not a lot left over for books.'

Corthie noticed a large volume entitled *The Governance of Prince Michael* and he slipped it from the shelf. It had a painting of the prince on the cover, looking mighty and regal, and holding a sword almost as tall as the God-Child himself.

'Is that sword painted to the right scale?' he said.

'Yes. It's mine now. The God-King gave me my father's sword at the end of the Civil War. It has a name; the "Just".' He put his pen down and glanced at Corthie. 'I have never used it in battle, but, I fear, the day I shall have to wield it is drawing near. This is why I called you here today.' He gestured to the seat and Corthie placed the book back onto the shelf and sat.

The duke glanced at him for a long moment in silence.

'The situation in the City,' said Marcus, 'is no longer tenable. It pains me to admit it, oh how it pains me, and I wish it were my father who were in my shoes, for he would know what to do.'

Corthie nodded.

'With every day that passes,' the duke went on, 'I feel my range of options diminish. If I stand aside and do nothing, then Auldan and Medio will rip themselves to shreds. It is with deep regret that I say this, but Princess Khora's government has proved unequal to the challenges it has faced. For three hundred years the City has slid inexorably into decline and ruin, and I have watched with growing sadness and concern, but done nothing, as the constitution of the City decrees.'

He glanced at Corthie, but the champion said nothing.

'Therefore,' the duke said, 'I have had to make an unprecedented decision. I have approached the God-Queen of Tara, and have gained her approval for the actions I am about to take.'

'The God-Queen?' said Corthie. 'I thought she was above politics.'

'She is. However, Queen Amalia and the God-King remain, ultimately, the supreme authority in the City, from whom all sovereignty derives. Her Majesty's word is law, and she has granted me permission to make some adjustments to the way the City is governed. At last, some hope for this tired, angry land and its long-suffering people. I am anticipating resistance, of course. Some will misunderstand my motives, while others will work actively to thwart my plans. Princess Khora, for example, will not relinquish her authority willingly; she will fight to cling onto her last vestiges of power, even if it means the destruction of the City.' He paused for a moment, his eyes on Corthie. 'I cannot, will not, allow that to happen.'

The duke stood, and turned to his window. Like Corthie's bedchamber in Arrowhead, the Duke's Tower was high enough to rise above the thick blanket of fog covering the land. The champion watched him for a minute, conscious that he was waiting for him to make some sort of response.

'How can I assist, my lord?'

'What was that?' the duke said, pretending not to have heard. 'Sorry, my mind was distracted by the woes of the City and the burden of leadership.'

'I asked how I could best assist you, sir.'

The duke turned. 'I have one command for you, Champion of the Bulwark.'

'Name it, sir, and it will be done.'

'No,' the duke said, shaking his head; 'perhaps you are not ready for such a task.'

'Have I ever disobeyed an order before, sir?'

'Never. If you had, do you think you would be sitting here with me?' He turned back to the window. 'Timing is everything in this. Tonight, at midnight, I shall embark upon a ship, along with two thousand selected Blades, and sail to Tara. By the time I arrive, I require you to have completed the task I am about to set you.'

'What do you need me to do, my lord?'

'I require you to travel to Pella, enter Cuidrach Palace, and bring Princess Khora's reign over this City to an end, soldier. Kill her, and every demigod that you find in the palace.'

Corthie felt his heart sink. 'You want me to murder the princess, sir?'

The duke turned, his eyes flashing. 'No, not murder. Execute. Princess Khora has been judged, and has been found guilty; guilty of negligence, corruption; and let's not forget her numerous attempts upon your life. If she had her way, you would be dead, soldier. Of course, I know that in an ideal world, we would arrest her and put her on trial, but the situation is so dire, so urgent, that I cannot afford such luxuries. If Princess Khora is permitted to escape justice, she will resist the changes that the City needs, or worse, she will flee to the God-King, seek his aid, and plunge the City into a devastating civil war. I am relying on you to prevent these outcomes, soldier; I am placing great trust in you.'

'I shall do as you command, sir, as always. May I ask, which other demigods are known to be in the palace?'

'Lord Salvor, naturally, as Cuidrach is his home. I also believe Lord Naxor is present. Be very careful with that one. He is utterly lacking in any morals or compassion, and is a willing accomplice of his mother's misrule.'

'May I ask one more question, sir?'

'Proceed.'

'Why me, sir?'

'Several reasons. You are permitted to travel throughout Medio and Auldan, and your absence from the Bulwark would be unlikely to alarm my aunt. Secondly, and Lord Kano would not like to hear this, but you are the best warrior I have. There is no one else among the Blades I believe to be capable of entering a guarded palace and eliminating a powerful God-Child and two of her demigod sons. I would need to send an entire division to do the job, and there would be a large number of civilian casualties, which is something I am trying desperately to avoid. If those three are the only fatalities of the night, I will be well pleased. Do you understand?'

'Aye, sir.'

'Good. Your prospects are rising all the time, champion. If you succeed in this task, you will be rewarded with a place at my side in the new regime that will take over the running of the City. You and Lord Kano will be my trusted lieutenants, and you will answer directly to me, not to him.'

'Thank you, sir.'

The duke smiled. 'I thought you'd appreciate that. I know how you and Kano don't particularly see eye-to-eye, but I like that there is an element of competitiveness between the two of you.' He nodded. 'Very well, I think we are done here. I'm leaving all of the details to you. I don't want to know how you intend to carry out your task, just ensure that it has been completed by the second hour following midnight. I shall set a flare from my ship as I enter Warm Bay, and when you see the red glow in the sky above Tara, you will know that I have almost arrived. Remain in Cuidrach, and I will come to you.'

'Aye, sir; understood.'

'Dismissed, and may the spirit of the Blessed Amalia guide your hand this night.'

Corthie stood, saluted, then left the chamber.

His mind was turning cartwheels by the time he reached the bottom of the stairs. His entire plan had been ripped to pieces, and he had no idea what he was going to do.

He left the tower and jumped into the carriage.

'Back to Arrowhead,' he called to the driver.

The dragon; he needed to warn the dragon.

***

'Sorry, Captain, but I need to speak to her alone.'

Hilde glared at him as she stood blocking the door that led to the lair. 'Why?'

'Because there's something I need to tell her.'

'Tell me, and I'll pass it on.'

Corthie frowned. 'Have I done something to offend you?'

'My personal feelings are not important. You have no right to be here; I was foolish to have allowed you in before. Please leave.'

The door to Maddie's room opened and she poked her head out. 'What's going on? Why are you fighting?'

'We're not fighting,' said Hilde.

'It sounded like you were. Hi, Corthie; you here to see Blackrose?'

'Aye, but, eh, we might have a problem.'

'What?'

'The captain doesn't want to let me into the lair.'

'Oh,' she said, walking out from the doorway. 'Why not?'

Hilde frowned. 'He shouldn't be here.'

'Yeah, well, isn't it a bit late for that? He's been here a few times, and you didn't stop him on any of those occasions.'

'I should have.'

'Captain,' he said, 'I respect you, but if I don't get in there to speak to Blackrose, there could be serious consequences.'

'Are you threatening me, champion? If you intend to physically remove me from this doorway, then do it; I'm not scared of you.'

'I'm not a bully, Captain, and if I can't persuade you, then I'm not going to force you.'

'I'm glad to hear it; now leave.'

'Alright. I hope Blackrose doesn't incinerate you when she finds out.'

He turned, and strode back down the hallway toward the exit.

'Wait!' cried Maddie, hurrying after him.

He paused by the front door and waited for her to catch up. 'Aye?'

'Buckler,' she whispered. 'You can get inside through his lair.'

'Buckler's out exercising his wings; who knows when he'll be back.'

'Maybe that's better,' she whispered, and opened her hand to reveal a key on her palm. 'That'll get you through the door in the red gate. Do you promise to bring it back?'

'Aye,' he said, smiling at her as he took the key. 'Thanks, Maddie.'

She gave him a nervous smile in return. 'Just don't tell the captain.'

He nodded, then went through the door and emerged back into the thick fog. He walked across the forecourt then through the rather more grand entrance to Buckler's lair. The guards on duty let him pass, and he descended into the huge underground caverns that made up the home of the young dragon. His footsteps echoed off the stone floor as he reached the red gate. He glanced to either side, but no one was around. He took the key and found the hatch cut into the enormous gate. He unlocked it, and pushed it open. Captain Hilde was still standing by the doorway opposite, and he could hear her arguing with Maddie. To his right was the black gate, and he stepped through into the cavern. The door creaked behind him, and Hilde turned.

'You!' she cried.

He sprinted for the black gate as she ran to cut him off. He powered his battle vision and jumped through the hatch, then swung it shut and bolted it as Hilde arrived on the other side. She pounded her fists against the hatch.

'Five minutes,' he shouted through the door; 'that's all I need. Five minutes.'

He turned, and saw Blackrose watching him.

'I wondered when the dear captain would attempt to prevent you from seeing me; it seems I have my answer.'

'Aye,' said Corthie as he walked towards her. 'This will probably be the last time I come here until, you know...'

'Until you have the Quadrant?'

'Exactly, only that might end up being a lot sooner than we'd planned.'

'I don't understand. I require a month for my wings to properly heal, and the process has only just begun. How soon were you thinking?'

He glanced at her. 'Tonight.'

'Out of the question.'

'But your chains have already been removed. In theory you could leave right now, if you wanted to.'

'No, I could leave right now, if I could fly. I cannot. My wings are in poor shape and they will need time to heal. Tonight, Maddie is due to help me again; we swing the black gate open so I can stretch my wings out. The girl has soft hands, and is very good at rubbing in the ointments I need.'

'That's nice, but tonight I've been ordered to assassinate the ruler of the City. I can't refuse, but at the same time, there's no way I'm going to do it. That leaves me one option; steal the Quadrant tonight, and get back here with it. I have one thing in my favour, Lord Naxor is in the same place as Khora, and if he has it with him... well, it could just about be done, I think.'

'You think? You're not filling me with confidence, champion.'

'How do you think I feel? I'm just back from seeing the duke; he's planning on launching a coup overnight. When he learns that I've not killed Khora, he's going to come after me.'

'Unless...'

'Unless what?'

'Unless you actually kill her. Is she not the one who was trying to have you assassinated? Kill her, and Naxor, then take the Quadrant. There's no need to do everything tonight. And besides, it remains impossible for me to fly at present, so we have no choice other than to wait.'

'No. I'm not doing it that way. You don't need to be able to fly to activate the Quadrant and get us out of here; the flying part was always a luxury.'

'A luxury? What nonsense. Flight will be a necessity from the moment we arrive on Lostwell. How long do you think a flightless dragon will survive in that place?'

'I'll protect you, I swear. I'll never leave your side until you're able to fly.'

'No. I need time to heal, and that time would be better spent here, in safety, rather than risk the poisoned wastes of Lostwell.'

'Look, if I come running in here later tonight, with the Quadrant in one hand, and four thousand Blades chasing me, we aren't going to have any choice.'

The dragon glared at him. 'Then make sure that doesn't happen. You promised me you would do whatever it takes to get us out of the City. Are you going back on your word?'

'No, of course not.'

'Then the answer is clear. Kill Khora and Naxor, hide the Quadrant, and wait for my wings to heal. I appreciate that you may have to toady for the duke a while longer, and for that you have my sympathies, but please do not destroy our hopes for the sake of someone who has tried to kill you.'

The pounding on the hatch in the gate resumed. 'That's five minutes,' cried Hilde. 'I want you out now, or I'm summoning the wardens.'

Corthie glanced towards the gate.

'Go, champion,' said Blackrose, 'and do what must be done.'

He strode to the gate without a word, and unbolted it.

Hilde pushed it open, and put her hand out. 'The key.'

Corthie placed it into her hand, then squeezed past her and made for the other door, where Maddie was watching.

'Sorry.'

She shrugged. 'I'm glad you got in to see her. I hope it works out alright, whatever it is.'

'Thanks. Take care.'

He walked down the hallway.

'Hey,' she called after him. 'Why did you say that? You are coming back, aren't you?'

He didn't reply. He left the building and strode to the gatehouse, where the sergeant was leaning by the gates.

'I need a carriage.'

'Coming right up, sir,' the sergeant said. 'No Quill this time?'

'No, just me.'

'And where is sir off to this fine, foggy evening?'

Corthie caught his eye. 'Pella.'

# CHAPTER 27
# THE DRAGON PORT

Arrowhead Fort, The Bulwark, The City – 3<sup>rd</sup> Balian 3419

'You're done here,' Hilde cried; 'I want you out, tonight.'

'What?' said Maddie, her eyes wide. 'You can't...'

'Don't tell me what I can and can't do, girl, I'm your superior officer, and I am relieving you of your duties in this lair. Pack your things, and go.'

'No, I won't.'

'I am a captain, and you are a private. Are you disobeying a direct command? I can have you locked in the cells, girl, and don't think I won't. You betrayed me; you gave the key to Corthie behind my back when you knew I didn't want him in here. How can I ever trust you again?'

'I was doing what I thought was right.'

'And by doing so, you proved that you are of no more use to me.'

'But what am I supposed to do? I have nowhere to go, except the Rats.'

'Where you'll have Corthie to protect you; and Blackrose, if she ever actually flies again.'

'You know she will. That's what the problem is, isn't it? You don't want Blackrose to fly again, you want her to stay here so you can keep her all to yourself. She's not your pet dragon, Captain, she's a champion of the Bulwark, or will be soon, and you can't stand that you might lose her. Well, tough, she's not yours, and never has been.' She strode into her room and sat down, her arms folded. 'You'll have to call the wardens and get them to drag me out of here, because I'm not moving.'

'You don't know what your talking about, girl. That champion's filled her head with nonsense, and I'm starting to think you're part of it. What are they planning? Tell me.'

'I don't know. They haven't let me in on their little secret.'

Hilde walked over, and crouched by the chair. 'And that drives you crazy, right? You're dying to find out what they're up to, aren't you? Listen, if you go in there and speak to Blackrose, and find out their plan, then I might reconsider dismissing you from your post.'

'No way; I'm not your spy. Besides, Blackrose would see through me in a second.'

'Fine, I don't need you anyway; I already have a rough idea of what they're up to.'

'You do?'

'She wants to go home, wherever that is, and she thinks Corthie can help her.'

'They're trying to escape? I thought they were waiting for his super-amazing sister to turn up.'

Hilde shook her head. 'What else could it be?'

'Then we should help them.'

'Are you out of your mind? Do you hear what you're saying? What you're suggesting is treasonous, and would see us both hanged. We each swore an oath.'

'Screw the oath; we should do what's right for Blackrose.'

'Bravo, Maddie,' came a booming voice from the hallway.

Hilde and Maddie both turned, but there was no one standing outside the room. Hilde got up and walked over. She glanced towards the entrance of the lair.

'How long have you been listening?'

'Long enough,' said Blackrose.

Maddie got to her feet and joined Hilde in the hall. Part of the dragon's face was visible through the open doorway.

'Now that I am unchained,' Blackrose said, 'I can come to you, instead of you having to come to me. It's more civilised than roaring, I find. I heard you arguing, and so I swung the black gate open and here I am.'

Hilde frowned. 'It's not polite to listen to other people's conversations.'

'Whoever said I was polite? Now, let me make one thing clear, Captain; you will not be dismissing Maddie Jackdaw from her post, is that understood?'

'It's not up to you.'

'Very well, let me be even clearer. If you dismiss her, I shall kill you.'

Hilde's face paled, and she stared at the dragon through the doorway. 'But, after all this time? After everything we've been through, you'd choose her over me?'

'She has faith in me, while you seem to have lost yours. In truth, I want you both, but if I had to choose, then yes, I would choose her. Do not force my hand.'

'This girl is nothing,' Hilde said; 'I made her.'

'And then you abandoned her to Lord Kano, while you hid in your room and got drunk. Perhaps you should do the same thing now, and in the morning we'll pretend that none of this happened.'

Hilde's shoulders sagged, and she turned away.

Maddie winced as she watched the captain disappear into her office. 'Oh, poor Hilde. You wouldn't really kill her, would you?'

'Do dragons lie? Now, fetch my ointment, and bring a ladder this time.'

---

The anxious anticipation of seeing Blackrose's wings had been worse than the reality. With the dragon standing in her lair, she was able to stretch out one wing at a time into the neighbouring cavern. For several nights in a row, Maddie had been rubbing gallons of thick, waxy ointment into the dried folds of her wings. It had a healthy, medicinal scent, and Maddie found it quite relaxing.

'I only treated this section last night,' she said from atop the ladder, 'and it's healing already. Your wings are beautiful.'

'Indeed they are, but at the moment they are also very painful. I haven't stretched like this in a long time.'

'A decade?'

'Longer. I was imprisoned for years before I was brought to this world.'

'How were you captured?'

'With a very large net.'

'That's not what I meant. You're always a little evasive when I ask you questions about where you came from. I know it's "another world", but what does that even mean? And does Corthie come from the same place?'

'I'm evasive because such knowledge will do you no good.'

'How does somebody get from one world to another?'

'Rub a little slower.'

'What realm were you a queen of?'

'Not that slow.'

'Will you ever tell me anything?'

'Perhaps; I haven't decided.'

'Oh, so there's hope, then. That's all I need, a little glimmer of hope to keep me going. Hang on, I need to move the ladder.' She hopped to the ground, then wobbled as her left leg throbbed. 'Ow. Too soon for hopping.' She wiped her hands on her tunic and pushed the ladder a yard to the right. She stood back for a moment, surveying the wing. The healed parts looked like waxed black leather, sleek and strong, but there were still several dry areas. She rubbed her chin, smearing it in ointment. 'Damn it,' she muttered.

'What's wrong?'

'Nothing, just got ointment on my chin.'

'Well, back up the ladder, girl; I want as much done tonight as possible.'

'Why, thinking of going somewhere?'

The dragon hesitated for a split second. 'What a ridiculous notion.'

'I notice you didn't deny it. What's going on? Was Hilde right; are you and Corthie planning an escape?'

Blackrose said nothing.

'If you don't answer, I'm going to take that as a "yes". You can tell me; I could help.'

'You would help me flee the City?'

'You heard what I said to Hilde; of course I would. It's wrong to keep you in this dungeon, and I'm glad that you'll soon be out flying again; but I'd be even happier if you were free.'

'Do you wish to be rid of me?'

'Seeing you go would be... it would be hard, I know that. I'd be sad for a while, I know that too, but I'd also know that you were living the life you should be, and that would make me feel a bit better.'

'And what life should I be living?'

Maddie smiled. 'A dragon queen life. Doing whatever dragon queens do.'

Blackrose fell into silence, so Maddie climbed back up the ladder and began to rub in more ointment.

'A touch slower.'

Maddie scowled at the back of the dragon's head, then did as she had been asked.

---

For hours, Maddie worked her way along the wing, until her arms were aching.

'Time for a break,' she said as she stepped down from the ladder.

'Are your puny arms exhausted?'

'They are, as a matter of fact. I need a drink.'

'You're too young to be drinking.'

'I'm nineteen; I'm old enough. You worried about me?'

'I'm worried about you pickling the tiny brain inside your skull.'

'Aww, that's nice; thank you.' She picked up a cloth and began to wipe the ointment from her hands. 'Have you decided if you're going to tell me anything yet?'

'No. How does the wing look?'

'Shiny, but that's all the ointment. Great, actually. What you need to do now is exercise it.'

'And how exactly am I to do that in here?'

'Stretch it back and forward a hundred times; then shift around and do the other wing.'

The dragon drew her wing in slowly, groaning as she did so, her eyes clenched shut. She pulled her wing in close to her body, then began to stretch it out again.

'That's it,' said Maddie; 'that's what I had to do with my arm and leg, over and over, after, you know, you broke half the bones in my body.'

'Leave me,' the dragon said; 'this is humiliating. I will do as you suggest, but I will do it alone.'

'Alright. See you later.'

Maddie turned and went back through the door into the hallway. She walked into her bedroom and stripped off the ointment-plastered clothes, dumping them into the laundry basket. She needed a bath, but it was too late in the evening and there would be no hot water. At least the ointment made her smell clean, she thought, as she pulled on a fresh uniform. She wandered down towards the kitchen, but stopped outside the door to Hilde's office. She put an ear to the wooden surface and listened. A gentle sound of snoring was coming from inside, so Maddie pushed the door open, and looked in. The captain was at her desk, her head resting on its surface. There was a couple of inches of brandy left in the bottle that was sitting by her elbow, and Maddie crept in and picked it up.

Hilde stirred. She lifted her head and squinted at Maddie. 'You? I trusted you.'

'You still can.'

'To do what? Stab me in the back again? I gave you somewhere to stay when no one else would take you; I gave you a purpose. Well, you can have her. First thing in the morning I'm requesting a transfer.'

Maddie smiled. She had heard Hilde threaten that before, always after a few brandies.

'This time I mean it, and then it'll be you that has to put up with Blackrose's crap; I'm sick of it.'

Maddie sat, the bottle of brandy sitting on her knee. 'What would happen if you actually went ahead and did it? Would they put another captain here to replace you?'

'How should I know? I'm the only officer that's ever been assigned to her. Maybe if you're lucky, they'll put Kano in charge.'

Maddie stood and went to the door. 'In the morning, I'll help you write your letter of resignation, if you like.'

She stepped out into the hallway before she could either shout or cry. She clutched the bottle to her chest, anger coursing through her. Hilde had claimed to have heard nothing on the night Lord Kano had visited the lair, but Maddie had retained a tiny bit of doubt in her mind. It was the brandy; she hated when Hilde was drunk. She walked into the kitchen and put the bottle down. She had been intending to finish it off, but the thought was making her feel sick. She needed some fresh air.

She walked to the entrance hall and pulled a coat from a peg. The Fog of Balian had started that day, and she hadn't even seen it. It had been one of her favourite days in her childhood, the day when the awful rains had finally stopped, and the mysterious fog had descended, shrouding the Bulwark. She pocketed the spare set of keys in case Hilde got up and locked the door, then stepped outside.

It was like being inside a cloud, she thought. The forecourt was invisible, hidden behind the thick blanket of mist. Dozens of tiny yellow lamps marked out the openings to the barracks and the Wolfpack Tower, and she began walking, breathing in the cool night air.

'A beautiful night, miss, isn't it?' said a voice.

She turned, and saw a figure emerge from the fog. It was the sergeant from the gatehouse.

'Yes,' she said; 'I love it.'

'I see you had the champion visiting you today.'

'How did you know that?'

'I see pretty much everything that goes on here, miss. So, how's the Old Lady doing these days? I heard a whisper that she's reconsidered, and we might see her flying alongside Buckler this coming winter. Do you have any gossip for me?'

'She's in the process of exercising her wings; it's been a while, I guess, but she's coming on fine. Is the champion drinking in the Wolf-pack common room? I thought I might go and speak to him.'

'No, miss, he left in a carriage a little while back, after he came out of the Old Lady's lair.'

'Oh.'

'He's in there most nights though, I'm sure you'll catch him tomorrow. Boy, that lad can drink.'

'He's got battle-vision; he has an unfair advantage over the rest of us.'

'That he does. Do you remember when we mocked the idea? How wrong we were, eh? Just shows you, there's more to all this than we think.'

She nodded. 'I think I'll go and see if Buckler's in.'

'Right you are, miss. Watch your step in this fog.'

Maddie turned and guessed the way towards the entrance to the young dragon's lair. She had never been in before, and wasn't sure what she would say to him, but an idea was forming in her mind. She saw the large gate to the lair loom ahead of her through the mist, and she walked up to the guards.

'Hello,' she said. 'I'm Maddie Jackdaw, and I want to speak to Buckler. Could you please let him know that I'm here?'

One of the guards glanced at her. 'No.'

'But I want to speak to him, didn't you hear me?'

'Your name means nothing to me, girl.'

'Buckler knows me. Go on, don't be assholes. I said "please".'

The guard sighed, then turned and walked inside. Maddie smiled at the other one while they waited, but he didn't even look at her. Idiots. They would know her soon enough, she thought.

'Fine,' said the first guard as he emerged from the gate.

The other guard blinked. 'Buckler said "yes"?'

'He did,' the first guard said; 'he told me that she's always welcome in his lair.'

Maddie grinned. 'That means I can go in?'

The guard rolled his eyes. 'Yes.'

She glanced at them. 'Well, well, so he does know me; and now you know me too.'

She walked past them, and entered a long hallway. A few Blades were working by a storeroom, rolling barrels of food supplies, and she squeezed past. A huge cavern opened up, and more Blades were around. She frowned at them, wondering what it was that they all did, when Blackrose had only her and Hilde.

Another large cavern led away through an open gate, and she saw a flash of red scales.

'Hey, Buckler,' she yelled. The young dragon twisted his neck and gazed down at her.

'Maddie Jackdaw,' he said. 'Have you come to ask if you can work for me, instead of... her?'

'Umm, not exactly. Can I speak to you without all of these other humans about?'

The dragon said nothing for a moment, then turned to the group of Blades. 'Out, all of you; I wish to speak to this one alone.'

The Blades saluted the dragon and left the cavern.

'Thanks,' she said as the last one filed out. 'How many of them know about Blackrose?'

'A small number of the humans who work for me are brought into the secret, but they must swear an oath never to reveal it. I heard a rumour, though, that might mean many more will learn of her existence. Is that why you are here? Have you come to tell me what's happening with her? I would appreciate some news, instead of gossip.'

'I thought Lord Kano would have told you.'

'The demigod tells me nothing, but I know he visited Blackrose recently. That's what started the rumours.'

'It's true,' she said. 'Blackrose has agreed to cooperate. For about ten days or so I've been rubbing ointment into her wings. It's going well, but she's feeling down. Her wings are sore.'

'That is to be expected after such a long interval without flying. My heart is moved by her suffering, but I'm more surprised than anything else. You, no doubt, remember the last time I tried to persuade her?'

'My leg still hurts.'

'So, who is responsible for her change of mind?'

'Have you heard any other rumours?'

Buckler lowered his head to the level of Maddie's face. 'Corthie?'

Maddie nodded.

'I guessed as much, after he came here one day and asked me directly about her existence. I was caught off guard, and I'm afraid to say that I lied to him. I denied it. It was a mistake, I now feel, but there we are. I will apologise to him when I next see him. What did he say to her?'

'He told her how amazing she was, stuff like that, and then they spoke alone.'

'And then she swore an oath to Lord Kano?'

'I wasn't there for it, but yes, I believe so.'

The dragon said nothing.

'I thought you'd be happier.'

'I would be, were I convinced she will go through with it. To have her fly alongside me this coming winter would be wonderful; the sky is big enough for both of us. However, I fear that she might change her mind again. She's spent the last ten years telling me she would rather die than be a "slave", as she puts it, so forgive me if I'm finding it all a little difficult to accept.'

Maddie smiled. 'I have an idea that might help.'

'Blackrose,' Maddie called out as she stepped through the hatch in the gate.

The dragon glanced around.

'Over here.'

Blackrose narrowed her eyes. 'Why are you emerging from Buckler's lair? What have you been doing, girl? Do you find the child's company preferable to my own?'

'We're moving onto the next stage of your recovery,' she said, 'and, logistically, that required me to go into Buckler's lair.'

'Why?'

Maddie frowned and looked around. 'Do you see any way for you to get out of this lair? Anywhere? How were you imagining you would get outside again? Do you not remember how you got in here in the first place?'

'I was drugged. I awoke here.'

'Oh. Well, the only way out is through Buckler's lair.'

'I see. Am I to assume therefore that the young buck is now aware that I have agreed to assist the City?'

'Well, yes; I had to tell him.'

'Most unfortunate. He will now believe me to be a hypocrite.'

'He's pleased for you.'

'Of course he is. Pleased that he has won the argument; pleased that he has been proved right. I cannot bear his mocking eyes upon me.'

'Well, he's waiting for you, but he won't mock you. Buckler's alright, you know. The one thing he's missing is a bit of wisdom and guidance from an older, more mature dragon, one who can show him a trick or two.'

'If he mocks me, run, for I do not wish to accidentally break all of your bones again.'

'Then you'll do it?'

'Wait. Is it a clear night? Are there stars? Is there a moon?'

'No to all of those, sorry. Thick dark clouds overhead, and a blanket of fog on the ground.'

Blackrose nodded. 'That is better. Fewer humans will be able to observe me. Open the red gate.'

Maddie laughed and ran to the gate. She poked her head through the hatch. 'She's ready.'

The enormous gate began to swing open, and Blackrose stepped back as it slid past her. She glanced up, and her eyes met those of Buckler, who had been standing on the other side.

'Blackrose,' he said, tilting his head and lowering it a fraction; 'greetings. My heart is sad, as Maddie has told me of the agonies you have experienced in the healing of your wings; but it is also happy, to think that you will soon be ruling the skies of the City.'

'Ruling?' Blackrose said. 'Are you mocking me?'

'No, I am acknowledging your power, and your authority. I am still in my first century of life, and you are nearing your prime. I bow to you. Will you teach me?'

Maddie's heart swelled to hear him say the words. He had promised he would, but she had doubted it until they had left his mouth. Blackrose did not respond for a moment, as she regarded the younger dragon.

'I make no promises,' she said; 'not yet. Let's see if I'm worthy first.'

'You need prove nothing to me, Blackrose.'

'Thank you, but I have a lot to prove to myself.'

Buckler backed up along the cavern, and Blackrose entered his lair, her wings tucked in, while Maddie strode alongside. All of the other humans had been told to leave, and the enormous spaces were deserted. Buckler turned, and led them up a long, wide ramp that led from his entrance hall, and Maddie began to smell the fresh air. Blackrose sensed it too, her nostrils flaring in the light breeze. They ascended further, until Maddie could make out a wide, rectangular area of sky. Blackrose halted.

Buckler noticed, and turned. 'This is the Dragon Port. This is how I fly in and out of my lair. Come and see the fog; it's quite something.'

Blackrose hesitated.

'What's wrong?' said Maddie.

'My heart is breaking,' the dragon said; 'hope is overwhelming me. If I see the sky and feel the wind, there will be no turning back.'

'Then don't turn back.'

'I'm sorry that Hilde isn't here to see this.'

'Yeah, me too.'

'But I have you now, Maddie Jackdaw.'

'And me,' said Buckler. 'The girl and I both love you.'

Blackrose said nothing, but resumed her stride, and they walked up to the lip of the Dragon Port. It had been cut out of a high section of the inner walls of the fortress, and commanded a view of the entire landscape facing out from the City. The plains where the greenhides assembled each summer and winter were covered in an impenetrable layer of fog that rolled all the way to the outer walls, swallowing up the moat completely. A night breeze was lingering in the air, and Maddie watched as the two dragons sat side by side, each absorbed by the sky and land.

Without warning, Blackrose swung her neck round and picked Maddie up in her jaws.

She screamed in fright, and for a moment thought the dragon was going to drop her off the side of the walls, but Blackrose instead placed her onto her back.

'Hold on tight,' she said.

'What are you doing? Your wings aren't ready; please!'

Blackrose laughed, then launched herself from the lip of the Dragon Port, her wings extending to their full length. Maddie screamed again as they tumbled down towards the fog, her hands grasping onto the folds on the dragon's shoulders. At the last second, Blackrose beat her wings and they soared up, her tail trailing through the fog.

'Mela,' said the dragon.

'What?' cried Maddie, the cold air freezing her.

'I promised my rider my name, and now you have it.'

'Mela? It's beautiful.'

'But?'

'I don't know.'

'You were expecting more? There is more. Mela is my first name, the one given to me by my mother on the day I was born, but I have many. I'll give you another each time you ride upon me.'

The dragon wheeled round, and Maddie saw the Great Walls of the City as she had never seen them before, from the point of view of the greenhides. The fortress of Arrowhead jutted out like the prow of a ship; to her right was Stormshield, while the towers of Lifegiver were visible to her left. Despite the cold, it was the greatest thing she had ever seen in her life, and she felt a happiness that made her start to cry. Blackrose circled one more time, then came in to land back inside the lip of the Dragon Port.

'Bravo, my lady,' said Buckler, tilting his head.

'It was a mere minute or two,' she said, 'and my wings are already exhausted. But, after more than ten years, I finally feel alive again.'

Buckler laughed, then launched himself off the lip of the port, and soared away towards the clouds. Blackrose reached up with her jaws, and plucked Maddie from her back.

'You're trembling,' she said once she had placed Maddie back onto the ground. 'Were you that scared?'

'No, I'm freezing. That was the best thing I've ever done, but next time I'm taking a blanket.'

'You wouldn't need a blanket on my world. It's warm and sunny all the time.'

Maddie smiled. 'Did you just tell me something about your world?'

'Yes, and in answer to your earlier question; getting from one world to another requires a device called a Quadrant.'

'What? Why are you telling me this?'

'Because I have decided.'

'Decided what?'

'You are my rider, Maddie Jackdaw, and when I escape this place, you shall be coming with me.'

# CHAPTER 28
# PRINCE OF TARA

Pella, Auldan, The City – 3$^{rd}$ Balian 3419

'Remember, Lieutenant,' said the major, 'everything you heard in there is confidential and must not be repeated, to anyone.'

'Yes, sir, and thank you for letting me sit in on the meeting.'

'I've had my eye on you, Daniel, ever since your return from the Circuit. If you do well, I shall see about having you appointed to my staff permanently.'

'Thank you, sir.'

The major nodded and Daniel saluted. The carriage waiting to take him back to the barracks was parked outside the side entrance to Cuidrach Palace, and Daniel walked in that direction. In truth, he had hardly heard a word the major had just said to him, as his thoughts were occupied by the news that Princess Khora and Lord Naxor had delivered.

Daniel didn't believe it. Surely the God-King and God-Queen would not stand by and allow the Blades to invade the rest of the City? Preposterous. Only once in a millennium had they marched through the Middle Walls, and then only to crush the last vestiges of rebellion in the Circuit at the end of the Civil War. Daniel had been ordered to say nothing at the meeting; he was a mere lieutenant after all, but he had bitten his tongue several times. The very idea of Blades patrolling the streets of Auldan was a ludicrous prospect.

A small group of Taran militia saluted him as he passed. Most of the guards in the palace were Rosers, and their arrival had allowed companies of Reaper militia to be redeployed to the troubled parts of the sprawling peasant suburb of Outer Pella. The ancient town centre of Pella was quiet enough, and the streets by the harbour front were deserted as he stepped outside into the fog.

Lady Aila had called it the Fog of Balian, right to Princess Khora's face. The crass comment had shocked the Tarans, but, in hindsight, Daniel was glad she had said it, because when the demigod had insulted him only a few moments later, all of the officers present were already viewing her with contempt.

He nodded to the driver and climbed into the carriage. It had been a lucky escape. Lady Aila's words had struck deep, and he had been rendered speechless, his mind as foggy as the weather as he had tried to formulate a response. She had asked him why he had done it; a simple enough question, but it had been the first time anyone had asked him to his face. He wondered what he would have said had the captain not interceded. 'I didn't mean it,' or 'It wasn't my fault,' or some other pathetic excuse.

In a way, he admired Lady Aila. Everyone else acted like he was some kind of a hero for what he had done, but he knew the truth. He had overseen the murder of defenceless civilians; women and children; peasants who had done nothing wrong except to be born as Evaders. If it had been the other way round, and Circuit militia had burned down a tenement full of Rosers, those responsible would be hunted down and executed as criminals, instead of being promoted, praised, and allowed into secret meetings with the High Guardian of the City.

His mother would call him wishy-washy if she heard him voice such thoughts aloud, and he had kept his feelings to himself, preferring the safe life of a hypocrite to the troubles honesty would bring.

The meeting had gone on for a few hours after being reconvened following the appearance of Lady Aila, and Daniel was looking forward to resting in his quarters in the barracks. They were luxurious compared to the place he and his platoon had stayed in the Circuit, and he felt his recurring sense of guilt return at the thought of his clean sheets and towels, and the hot water that ran from the taps in the large bathroom. Why did he deserve such things, when the majority of the Taran rank and file were suffering in the grey slums of the Circuit?

It was a short ride to the barracks, and before long the carriage pulled over. The view his mother had talked about was completely obscured by the thick fog lying over the Inner Bay, and he could barely see the boats in the harbour, let alone Ooste or Tara. The Roser soldiers at the gates saluted as he entered the main barracks building. The green and red standard of the Reapers had been taken down from the flagpole, replaced by the black leopard of Tara. In Outer Pella this would have been seen as a grave insult, but the affluent residents of the old town had made no comment.

He reported to the desk sergeant, then climbed a flight of stairs to his quarters. He had a bedroom with a balcony, a bathroom almost as large, and a small study for entertaining. He had yet to use it, as he had spent most evenings in the quarters of the more senior officers, playing cards and listening to them drone on drunkenly about politics. He had managed to evade an invitation for that evening however, and all he wanted to do was to sink into a hot bath with a bottle of wine and a book.

Once inside his quarters, he removed his uniform jacket and hung it up. Reaper servants would collect his laundry each morning, and return it clean and ironed later in the day, and a fresh pile of clothes was sitting on the end of his bed. He poured himself a glass of wine and walked out onto his balcony. Maybe if his posting lasted into winter, then he would be able to enjoy the view; but at that moment the thick fog suited his mood. He was hiding so much of himself from others that he felt no one truly saw him as he was. Maybe except for Lady Aila.

The demigod had threatened him. It sounded impressive, and no doubt Emily would be thrilled to hear it, but he wasn't worried. Lady Aila was one of those demigods who seemed to have nothing divine about them except their ability to stay alive; no vision or battle-vision, and certainly no death powers. That wouldn't be what he would tell Emily, though; for her he would make it sound a bit more dramatic as she seemed to relish danger.

Emily. It had been fourteen days since he had seen her, and without her presence, a few doubts had crept into his mind. She didn't know him, and he didn't know her; they had shared two nights together, but not a meal, or a walk, or even a proper conversation. Emily wanted to be free of her father, that was certain, but what else did he know about her? He had her letters, which arrived at the barracks in Pella every other day, but they had clearly been overseen by her parents, and the language was formal and stilted; full of generalisations about the weather. She seemed attracted to the notoriety he had earned in the Circuit; what would she do when she discovered his true feelings about what had happened?

It was done, though; the engagement contract had been signed, and the marital exchange of land was sitting at the lawyers awaiting the marriage itself, after which, the Aurelians would become the owners of a tract of slum housing in the Circuit. If it were up to him, he would give it to the peasants who lived there, but he knew his mother would never agree. He wondered what Emily would make of the idea.

Someone thumped on his door. 'Lieutenant Aurelian?'

Daniel walked in from the balcony, and heard more sounds, as if every door on that level was being knocked. He opened the door, and saw a colonel and a pair of sergeants standing outside in the passageway.

'Sir?'

'Urgent orders from Tara, Lieutenant,' said the colonel. 'The entire regiment is being recalled immediately. You have ten minutes to pack your things and report to the gatehouse.'

'Recalled, sir?'

'Are you deaf? Yes, back to Tara. We have to be out of Reaper territory before midnight.'

'Why would Princess Khora...?'

'The orders come directly from the God-Queen,' the colonel said as he turned away, 'not from the High Guardian.'

Daniel watched the officer move on to the next door along, then went back inside.

Tara? What was going on? He pulled his trunk from under the bed and threw his clothes in. If the Tarans withdrew, there would be hardly any soldiers left to protect Cuidrach Palace. At the meeting with Princess Khora, she had talked about how vital the Roser contribution was to keeping the peace in Pella, so why would an order arrive that countermanded that? A riot in the local vicinity was unlikely, but if the rebels in the outer suburbs heard the news the palace would be vulnerable. The Reapers must be returning, he thought. As the City authorities would never leave Pella undefended, that could be the only answer.

He frowned, realising that he would have to wait for the famous view of the two bays from his balcony. He filled his trunk, then dragged it out into the passageway, where Reaper servants were waiting to pick it up for him. He led them down the stairs and watched as his trunk was placed onto the back of a wagon in an inner courtyard. The open space was filled with Tarans. Troopers were lined up, and some were already marching out of the gates, their packs strapped to their shoulders. Daniel scanned the yard, seeking out the major.

'Sir,' he said, saluting when he found him amid a group of officers.

'Lieutenant,' he nodded. He glanced around at the assembled officers, many of whom looked a little dishevelled from the bar. 'It seems our time here has been cut short,' he said to them. 'The briefing will have to wait until we return to the regimental barracks in Tara, as our orders are clear. Those who have troopers under their command, ensure that you and they are clear of Reaper territory by midnight at the very latest. For those of you on my staff, I have hired carriages to take you back to Tara immediately. You'll find them lined up on the harbour promenade. Four officers to each carriage.'

'When shall we report, sir?' said a captain.

'Let's say noon tomorrow; that should give you enough time to sort yourselves out after tonight's little journey. We'll hold the briefing in the officers' mess; keep it informal.'

A junior lieutenant spoke up. 'Sir, do we know why...?'

'No, and there's no time for questions, even if I did. Dismissed.'

Daniel strode through the arched entrance to the courtyard and emerged into the fog of the waterfront. He joined the queue of officers standing by the five carriages waiting to collect them, then boarded one along with two captains and a fellow senior lieutenant.

Tara was only three miles from Pella by boat, but the journey was three times as long from palace to palace by road. The captains swapped theories along the way, but the consensus was that the Reaper militia must have unexpectedly returned early from duty in the suburbs to relieve the Tarans. Daniel glanced out of the window for most of the journey, wondering instead what he was going to do with the rest of his night. With the briefing called for noon, and the carriage due to arrive in Tara around midnight, he could pop into the taverns by the harbour for a few drinks before climbing the hill to the barracks. Or he could try to break into Emily's house, the way she had broken into his?

He shuddered. No chance. Her father would have his head if he caught him with his daughter. The redeployment of the regiment might be permanent for all he knew, and he would have plenty of time in Tara to see her; in fact, his mother might even bring the date of the wedding forward, and they could be together without having to sneak about.

The carriages rumbled along the road that ran by the waters of Warm Bay, and Daniel gazed at the bank of fog until they reached the little lamps that ringed the centre of Tara. The carriages halted by Prince's Square, and the officers disembarked. A bell from a clock tower rang out; midnight.

Daniel walked up to the others. 'Drink?'

---

'I have another theory,' said the captain who had joined them in the tavern.

A lieutenant groaned. 'Another, sir?'

'Why, thanks; I'll have a large brandy. Anyway, what if we've been brought back here because we're being sent to the Circuit? We all know things there are still bubbling away, and the casualties are starting to mount up. Aurelian, you've been there, well, obviously; do you fancy another crack at the Evaders?'

'Any time,' said Daniel, swigging from his brandy glass. 'Bring it on.'

'That's the spirit,' laughed the captain.

One of the other lieutenants shook her head at Daniel. 'You can't be serious. My cousin was there, he said it was the worst time of his life. He still has nightmares.'

'It wasn't so bad; I miss it, sometimes.'

'That's why the major has his eye on you,' said the captain. 'After what you went through, well, that would have broken some junior lieutenants, but you came out the other side smiling, as if it had been nothing particularly special. You've got a tough hide on you, and that attitude will take you far.'

Daniel got to his feet. 'I'll be back in a moment.' He made his way through the almost-deserted tavern towards the toilets. He went into a cubicle and closed the door. What had he been saying back there? It was like his brain had no control over his mouth. The thought of going back to the Circuit made him feel physically sick, and he could feel the waves of nausea begin to rise from the pit of his stomach.

He calmed himself. It wasn't going to happen. He had a bounty on his head, and the Adjutant of the Circuit had clearly threatened him in front of the major and the other officers; they wouldn't send him back, would they? He took a breath, his eyes going to the narrow window slit. He frowned. Through the fog, a red glow was hanging in the sky. It looked like something was burning, only the light was coming from out over the waters of the bay.

He washed his hands and returned to the tavern. The captain had gone, and only the lieutenants were still sitting round the table.

One glanced at him as he sat. 'We were thinking of heading up the hill to the barracks; you coming?'

'Yeah.'

They all stood and went outside into the cool air. The fog lay thickly over the harbour, but Daniel could see small groups of people gathering; soldiers, and courtiers from Maeladh Palace, the black leopard of Tara emblazoned on their uniforms.

A lieutenant pointed. 'Look at that.' The others turned, and they all stared at the red glow over the bay. 'Someone's set off a flare.'

'Maybe a boat's in distress,' said another.

Daniel frowned. 'Then why are all those folk from the palace here? It's like they're expecting someone.'

One gasped. 'Maybe we'll get to see the God-Queen; maybe it's her that's arriving.'

'Why would she be out on a boat in this weather?'

More groups were gathering by the harbour, and soldiers had set up a long cordon that stretched down to the quayside. Daniel and the others went forward, and stopped by the edge of the cordon.

A shout rang out from the direction of the town. 'Make way for the God-Queen!'

They turned. A glow of torches was coming from an avenue by Prince's Square, and civilians were emerging from taverns and their homes to see what was happening.

'I was right!' said the lieutenant. 'The actual God-Queen is coming! Malik's breath.'

'But she's not arriving by boat,' Daniel said, 'and she surely can't be leaving. So, who's she here to meet?'

More people were spilling out into the streets, crowding round the area where the torch light was approaching. Daniel craned his head to look, but there were too many palace guards and courtiers blocking the way.

'There she is!' came a cry from the crowd.

Emerging from the fog like a vision strode the God-Queen; tall, regal, beautiful. A slender crown was on her head, and she was wearing dark blue robes studded and embroidered with golden threads. By her side, a few paces back, walked Lord Chamberlain, her most trusted mortal advisor, also dressed in robes of state. Tarans were falling to their knees at the sight of Queen Amalia, but she kept her expression serene as scenes of near-hysteria gripped the public. Palace guards pushed back the crowds, wielding long batons and clubs, and striking anyone who tried to get too close to the living God walking among them.

The procession reached the quayside, and the guards formed up in thick lines around the area.

'I can't see anything,' said Daniel. 'Come on, let's get a better view.'

He and the other lieutenants began to circle round the crowd, looking for a way in to see the God-Queen. The noise by the harbour front was reaching a crescendo, with screams and shouted prayers punctuated by weeping. Amid the crowds were many aristocrats as well as folk from the lower classes, and one of the lieutenants pulled Daniel's arm.

'Danny, look,' she said. 'Lord and Lady Omertia. Is that Emily? Malik's ass, you've done well for yourself.'

'Thanks,' he cried amid the noise. 'I'll see you lot later.' He pushed his way into the crowd towards them. The lord and lady had brought half a dozen Reaper servants to keep the crowds back from them, but they were tightly pressed together in the confusion. Emily was standing by her mother, trying to see what was happening, but she was being pushed and shoved from all sides.

Daniel barged his way past a group of peasants and neared them.

'My Lord,' he said, trying to bow amid the mob.

Emily's father glared round, then his features softened a little as he saw it was Daniel. 'Over here, lad; I could do with some assistance.'

Daniel pushed more of the peasants away, clearing a little space around the noble lady and her daughter.

'Thank you, Daniel,' said Lady Omertia, her eyes shot with anxiety at the proximity of the crowds. 'Do you know why the blessed God-

Queen has emerged from the palace? Is her Majesty leaving us? Has she reconciled with the holy God-King?'

'I don't know, ma'am,' Daniel said, keeping himself between the Omertias and the swarming groups of peasants.

The crowd surged, and Emily was swept up alongside him. He reached for her hand and squeezed it.

'Why are you here, Danny? I thought you were in Pella?'

'Got recalled a few hours ago.'

'Why?'

He shrugged. 'No idea, but it must be connected to whatever's happening now.'

'Emily!' cried her mother's voice.

Daniel turned. Lord and Lady Omertia were being pushed back by the crowds, the distance between them and their daughter increasing.

The lord caught his eye. 'You look after her, Daniel,' he shouted; 'you look after my little girl.'

'Yes, sir,' Daniel called back, then turned to smile at Emily, his hand still gripping hers. 'Come on, let's get closer to the front.'

He used his shoulders to shove his way through the tight mass of peasants and nobles towards the quayside, his arm never leaving Emily. His uniform and strength got them close to the cordon, and he pulled Emily near as the crowds swayed and surged. The line of palace guards surrounding the God-Queen was three deep, but at least they could see her. She was standing alone, her eyes gazing out into the fog, where the red glow had faded. The prow of a ship appeared through the thick murk, and Daniel frowned, not recognising its shape or identity.

He gasped. It was a warship.

'Blades,' he muttered, his heart racing.

'What?' said Emily. She lowered her voice. 'Did you say "Blades"?'

The sail of the ship came out of the fog, and the crowd stilled, their voices trailing off as everyone stared at the crossed swords on the huge standard fluttering from the mast.

'Blades!' someone screamed.

Daniel thought the crowd was about to panic, but the God-Queen turned and raised her hand.

'People of Tara, do not be afraid,' she said, her clear voice carrying over the harbour front.

The crowd silenced, her calm presence lending them courage. The ship reached the side of the pier, and a dozen huge soldiers disembarked, each in plate armour, their faces shielded by steel visors. They walked up the pier as others tied the boat up, and bowed low before the God-Queen. Another ship emerged from the fog to the right, then another, until half a dozen warships of the Blades had docked. Armoured soldiers were filing down the gangways, each as tall and broad as the first had been. All bowed to the God-Queen, then formed into ranks, flanking the ship that had landed first.

'There are hundreds of them,' whispered Emily. 'Are they in charge now?'

Horns and trumpets blasted out before Daniel could respond, and the Blade soldiers turned and bowed towards the lead ship as a man began to walk across the gangway. He had a silver band on his brow, and was taller than any of his soldiers. He had a full set of plate armour covering him, and the largest sword Daniel had ever seen was strapped to his back. He strode down the gangplank, then halted with one step to go.

The God-Queen raised her hands. 'By my will, I repeal the restrictions upon the Blades from entering Auldan and Medio. It is done, and I welcome Duke Marcus to Tara.'

The crowd stood in stunned silence as the duke took the last step and set foot upon Roser soil. He strode up the pier, and got down onto one knee before the God-Queen, his head bowed.

'Eldest son of my eldest son,' she said, her voice ringing clear, 'it is time you were given responsibilities that match your talents. For three centuries you have fulfilled your duty as Commander of the Bulwark, keeping the City safe from the eternal enemy, and for this, we give you the thanks you are due. It has come to my attention that discontent and disharmony are threatening the security and tranquillity of this beloved

City, and so, therefore, I hereby pronounce the following.' She reached out a hand, and Lord Chamberlain passed her a long, slender sword. 'You are duke no longer,' she said, holding the tip of the sword an inch over her grandson's head. 'Arise, Prince Marcus of Tara, the new High Guardian of the City.'

The crowd gasped, and cheers broke out from some sections, while others stared in bewilderment.

Marcus got to his feet, seeming like a giant compared to the mere mortals around him. He reached behind his back and drew the massive sword, then held it aloft in one hand, the blade almost as long as he was.

'With the permission of the divine and blessed Queen Amalia, I accept the great honours bestowed on me. With my father's sword, I pledge to bring peace and a new golden age to this City of ours. Even now, as I address you here in Tara, the failed regime of my predecessor is being brought to an end, and when the dawn of tomorrow comes, it will herald a new beginning for us all. I humbly thank the God-Queen for the great favour and trust she has shown in me. I will pray to her Majesty daily for assistance, and with her divine help, I have no doubt that this City shall flourish once again.'

He sheathed the sword, then he and his grandmother embraced. The crowd cheered at this, but many still looked nervous and unsure.

'We have a prince again,' said Emily.

'I'm sure your father will be very pleased.'

'No doubt, but I know the truth.'

He glanced at her. 'The truth?'

She leaned over and whispered in his ear. 'It should be you, Daniel Aurelian.'

The Blades began to move, with two flanks pushing back the palace guards and the crowds to clear a path towards Maeladh Palace. The new prince took the God-Queen's hand, and they walked side by side, processing between the thick lines of soldiers. More Blades were disembarking from the ships, and many began to follow the royal party, while others remained to secure the harbour district. The torches surrounding the God-Queen and her grandson faded into the fog as they drew away into the distance.

'Disperse!' cried a Blade officer, his sword drawn. 'This crowd must disperse!'

A group of Blade sergeants and armoured soldiers began piling into the crowd, shoving them back.

'All Taran militia must return to their barracks immediately without exception,' yelled a sergeant as he eyed a few uniforms in the crowd, 'and all civilians must return to their homes. Failure to comply will result in punitive measures being taken. Disperse!'

The crowd began to break up as groups of Blades forcibly moved them on.

'Are you stationed in Tara now?' said Emily as Blades approached them.

'Yes.'

'We should marry as soon as possible. I missed you, and I don't want to be separated from you for long.'

He held her close and they kissed. 'I'll send a message to my mother in the morning.'

'You two,' cried a Blade as he strode forwards. 'Off the streets. Soldier boy, get back to your barracks, and girl, run on home before I break your heads.'

Emily's mother rushed up and pulled at her daughter's arm. Daniel gripped her hand, then felt her fingers leave his palm.

'Goodbye Danny,' Emily said as her parents bundled her away.

He watched her go, then turned to the approaching Blades, his hands raised. 'I'm going.'

'Too right you are, boy,' said a sergeant. 'We own this City now.'

# CHAPTER 29

# INSIDER KNOWLEDGE

P ella, Auldan, The City – 4<sup>th</sup> Balian 3419
      Despite the brandy, Aila had trouble sleeping. Her mind went over every word that Khora and Naxor had said to her, trying to decide how much of it was true. Perhaps all of it was. Perhaps she was being paranoid, but her history with the princess and her children had been filled with lies and deceit. With them reading her head, she no longer had any secrets; they knew everything, whereas she had no idea if anything they had told her was true.

She considered getting up, putting on a false appearance, sneaking out of the palace and returning to the Circuit. Or maybe she should keep going, pass right through the Middle Walls into the Bulwark, and look for Corthie. She would need a disguise, as Lady Aila of Pella was barred from entering the Bulwark, just as the Blades were barred from entering the rest of the City. The rules had protected her from the attention of Duke Marcus for three hundred years; if he overturned them, she would have nowhere to hide.

Her blankets felt suffocating and she threw them off. She would die before she allowed Marcus anywhere near her. She snorted. It was easy to say; not so easy for a demigod to carry out. Where could she run if he came after her? Nowhere, especially if her treacherous sister

Vana was around to track her down. No, working with Khora was the only option, no matter how much it violated her principles. Only together could they beat the duke if he ordered the Blades in. She almost wished Naxor had sent up a lump of opium to her room instead of the brandy, then she could have blotted everything out and surrendered to oblivion. She sat up and lit a small lamp. The half-empty bottle was sitting on the bedside table and she poured herself a small measure.

If Corthie were by her side, then she would feel like she could take on anyone. He never seemed to despair, or give up; the only time she had seen him at a loss was when she had told him they were breaking up because he was mortal. It hadn't been her most tactful moment, but she had needed to say it.

She took a sip, then her eyes were drawn to the shutters. A faint red glow was visible between the slats. She smiled. Maybe Tara was burning. She imagined the wealthy Rosers running around shrieking as their massive villas and mansions caught fire; what a dreadful shame that would be. She got up and opened her balcony doors. The fog lay thick and heavy over the bay, and she squinted at the red glow. It seemed to be coming from somewhere at sea, rather than from Tara or Ooste. A boat was in trouble, maybe, but no one down at the harbour front in Pella was hastening to their aid. She frowned, and looked down off the balcony; no one seemed to be about at all. The quayside was deserted, as were the guard posts in front of the palace. Where had the damn Tarans gone? She listened, but the only noise was coming from that faint splash of water against the harbour walls below. She turned, and went back into her room. She swapped her nightshirt for a loose dress and strapped a belt round her waist. She knew Naxor would be sleeping, so left her quarters and padded through the hallways of the palace in her bare feet.

She came to a door and knocked on it. 'Hey, Naxor?'

Nothing.

She turned the handle and the door opened. 'Are you in?' When there was no reply, she strode into the large room, her eyes scanning the table and furniture. She went to the bedroom and knocked again. Silence. She wondered if the demigod kept a diary.

'Ma'am?' came a voice from behind her. 'Can I help you?'

She turned. 'I was looking for my cousin; have you seen him?'

The servant inclined his head. 'Lord Naxor went out this evening, ma'am; he departed not long after the last meeting finished. He told us to expect him back later tonight.'

'Has he gone out to a tavern?'

'I believe so. His last words were, "I'm going to get blind drunk; don't wait up," ma'am.'

She smiled, then remembered the missing Tarans. 'Where have the soldiers gone?'

'They have been recalled, ma'am.'

'What? Why?'

'I don't know, ma'am. Her Highness the Princess is currently discussing the matter with Lord Salvor.'

'Oh, right. Well, that's good; they've got it in hand, then.'

The servant nodded, and waited by the door.

'Fine, I'll go,' muttered Aila. 'I wasn't going to steal anything, just have a poke around.'

'Quite, ma'am. I will be sure not to mention this to Lord Naxor upon his return.'

'Good.' She walked past him and back into the hallway, then he followed her out and closed the door. 'Actually,' she said, 'I'm a little hungry. Are the kitchens open?'

'For you, ma'am, always.'

'Don't try to suck up to me now, not after throwing me out of Naxor's quarters.'

He looked a little nervous at the remark, so she winked so he would know she was joking. That seemed to make it worse, so she attempted a smile and turned away. She descended a flight of stairs and turned to the right, where she knew a kitchen with a bread oven was located. Perhaps there would be some hot pies or fresh cakes available, she thought, her stomach rumbling. She walked past the palace's small library, and noticed the door was open. She heard an intake of breath, and halted, listening. Oil lamps were burning in the passageway, but she could see no one. She turned to the library and peered through the open door into the dark chamber.

'Hello? Is there someone in there?'

A hand went to her mouth as another pulled her into the room. She struggled, and lashed out with her foot, kicking the man's shin. The door swung closed and the room was cast into darkness.

'Don't make a noise,' whispered a voice in her ear as the hands released her.

She stumbled back a step, her mouth opening. 'Corthie?'

'Quiet,' he hissed.

'What are you doing here? Sneaking about the palace like a thief or a... an... No.' She backed away.

'I'm not here to kill anyone.'

She heard a low noise as he lit a lamp. Her eyes squinted in the change of light, then Corthie came into focus, standing before her. He was dressed in his ordinary uniform, the same one she had seen him in when he had visited the Blind Poet, with no armour, and not even a sword on his belt.

'Hello,' he said, his eyes fixed on her.

'Hello.'

'My shin's a bit sore.'

'Well, that's what you get for grabbing me.'

'I didn't want you to shout. Sorry.'

They stood in silence for a moment.

'Well,' she said. 'This is a little awkward.'

'Awkward? It's a complete disaster.'

'Oh, thanks. It's nice to know you think seeing me again is a disaster.'

'It is, because I knew I would only be able to go through with my plan if I never saw you again. Now I have, I don't ever want to leave you. I know you finished it, and I'm not going to be an asshole about it, so I promise I'll say this only once, and if you tell me to shove it, then... then

I'll accept it.' He took a step forward, and she looked up into his eyes. 'I love you,' he said. 'I want to be with you, no matter the barriers in our way.'

'Oh Corthie, stop.' She rubbed her face. 'I can't...' She took a seat by a reading table. 'I love you too.'

He laughed. 'You do?'

She smiled, despite the pain she felt in her heart. 'I do, but it doesn't change anything.'

He approached, and crouched by her. 'It changes everything. Look, as much as I want to talk about this, you have to leave the palace.'

She blinked. 'What?'

'Was there a red glow in the sky, in the direction of the bay?'

'Yes.'

'Then Blades are sailing here. We don't have long.'

Her skin felt cold, as if an icy wind had blown through the library. She stared at him, a hundred questions bubbling to the surface. 'Start at the beginning.'

'The duke is launching a coup, tonight. He's sailed for Tara, and is sending soldiers here too.'

'Then why are you here? If you're not an assassin, then what are you?'

'I'm trying to be a thief, but so far I've not proved to be a very good one.'

She glared at him. 'And it never occurred to you to warn Khora about what was happening? The Blades are invading, and you're trying to steal something?'

'She tried to kill me, you told me so yourself. Why would I warn her?'

Aila groaned. 'Malik's ass. Uh, I might have been mistaken about that. It was the duke who was paying to keep the riots in the Circuit going; it might well have been him trying to kill you and make it look as if Khora was behind it.'

'Oh. Bollocks.'

She stood. 'We'll have to tell her.'

'You should, but I can't,' he said, getting to his feet. 'I made a promise, and I'm going to keep it.'

'What promise; to whom?'

'To a very large dragon. I told her I'd help her get out of here, and I will.'

'What do you mean by "out of here"? Leave the City?'

'Aye.'

'And go where?'

'Take her home, back to her world.'

'And... and you were going to leave me?'

'You broke it off. I thought I'd never see you again. That's what I meant about it being a disaster, because now I can't do it; I can't leave you, but I can still fulfil my promise. If I find the Quadrant, then I can take it to the dragon and she can use it to go home, and I'll stay here, with you. That's what I'm saying; if you want me, I'll be here. If you don't...'

'You would stay for me?'

'Aye,' he said, his eyes gazing down at her. Aila gazed back, her mind torn. She wanted Corthie, and knew how easy it would be to sink into his arms and kiss him, but soldiers would soon be storming Cuidrach Palace, and she needed to warn Khora.

'Come on,' she said, pulling her gaze away and walking to the door.

'Where are we going?'

'To see Khora, then I'll help you with your promise to the dragon.'

'And then?'

'One thing at a time, Corthie; my brain can't handle any more than that at the moment.'

They stepped out into the hallway and she led him to the centre of the palace towards Lord Salvor's personal suite of rooms. A servant watched them pass, his eyes widening at the sight of the Champion of the Bulwark. A solitary Reaper guard was on duty at the entrance to Salvor's rooms, and she saluted as Aila and Corthie passed.

'But, mother,' she heard Salvor shout through a closed door; 'I have no troops available to redeploy, they're all miles away in the suburbs. I've recalled the closest ones, but I can't get them here any quicker.'

Aila glanced at Corthie. 'Could you stay out here for a moment? I think I might need to build up to you being in the palace.'

He smiled. 'Aye, sure. Call me when you want me to come in.'

She knocked on the door and entered. Salvor and Khora were standing by a table, and they turned as Aila approached.

'Niece,' said Khora, 'grave news. The Taran militia have withdrawn from Pella. At this present moment, the palace is undefended.'

'I have even worse news, but I also have other information that might help.'

Khora faced Aila. 'Go on.'

'You were right. The duke's going to try to take over, tonight.'

'Tonight?' cried Salvor.

'I have spies on the Middle Walls,' said Khora, 'and they have reported no movement from the Bulwark.'

'They're coming by ship.'

Khora looked like all breath had left her for a moment. 'When will they arrive?'

'Soon. The duke's going to Tara.'

'Then the God-Queen must have granted her permission.' Khora lowered her head. 'That's why the Tarans have been withdrawn, to make the things easier for the Blades.'

'We may not have any militia,' said Aila, 'but we do have someone else on our side.' She glanced at the door. 'Come in.'

Corthie strode through the entrance and walked up to stand by Aila. He nodded to Khora.

'He came here to warn us,' Aila said. 'It was Corthie who gave me the news about the ships.'

'The duke told me himself,' he said.

'And you came, all this way?' said Khora, frowning. 'Against orders?'

'Not exactly. The duke sent me here to kill you, but, as you can see, I don't intend to do any such thing.'

'And what do you intend to do when the Blades arrive? Are you pledging your service to me?'

'He will,' said Aila, 'he just needs your help with something else.'

'Let me deal with the "he will" part first.' Khora glanced at her son. 'Summon every remaining servant and member of the Reaper militia and tell them to gather here, then break open the armoury; we'll need weapons and armour for our champion; oh, and wake up Naxor.'

'That won't be necessary,' said Aila; 'He's out getting drunk.'

'As a mother it makes me glad that he is safe, but as the High Guardian of the City...' her expression darkened; 'I told him to stay in tonight.' She glared at Salvor again. 'Why are you standing here? Go.'

Salvor nodded and hurried off, then Khora turned back to Aila and Corthie. 'On to the next item on my never-ending list. What assistance does the champion require from me?'

Aila glanced at Corthie.

'I was letting you do the talking,' he said.

'But what was the name of that thing you wanted?'

Corthie smiled. 'Khora would never give it to me willingly, and I don't even know if it's worth asking. If we do, then she'll know that I know about its existence.'

Khora raised an eyebrow. 'If you don't ask, then you'll never know what I'd say.'

'I can guess,' he said; 'but don't worry; I'll fight for you tonight. It sickens me to think I'll be up against Blades; I have a tattoo on my arm that says I'm one, but I have to do what I think is right.'

'Corthie,' said Aila, 'you were correct about letting me do the talking; you've just given away any leverage you had. No, this isn't good enough. If Corthie's going to risk his life, go against his commander's orders and fight to save you, my dear auntie, then I want you to promise that you'll give him what he asks for.'

Khora frowned. 'Without knowing what it is? I think not.'

'Wait!' Aila cried. 'It's coming back to me... Quarter... Quatran... oh, damn it, something like that.'

'The Quadrant?' said Khora, her eyes like ice.

'Yes, that's it. The Quadrant. I've no idea what it is, but could you please give it to Corthie?'

A silence fell over the chamber as Khora stood frozen, her eyes unreadable. Sounds filtered through from outside the room, of guards arriving and preparing themselves.

Khora finally took a breath. 'He wants to go home?'

'I want someone to go home,' he said, 'but I'll stay, if Aila wants me to.'

The princess laughed. 'Oh, she wants you to, believe me. Listen, I cannot hand over what is not mine to give, and besides, I do not have it.'

Aila felt her face turn a shade of red, and she cursed her aunt's vision powers. She glanced at Corthie, and met his eyes; he was gazing back at her, oblivious to Khora's words.

'Oh, please,' said the princess, 'stop these glances. Did you hear me? I don't have it.'

Corthie turned to face her. 'Naxor has it, doesn't he?'

'I deliberately refrain from knowing anything about its location, so it cannot be read out of my head by any God-Child or demigod in the City; it's safer that way. But, and this is important, I'm not saying no. There may be a way to let you borrow it, under supervision.'

'You mean Naxor takes this someone home?'

'Precisely, then he can return here. With it.'

'Alright, I'll agree to that. As long as I can go too, to make sure he does it right.'

'You don't trust my son?'

'No.'

'Can this wait?' said Aila. 'We need to leave the palace before the Blades arrive.'

Khora walked to the door, and opened it to the small crowd of staff and the handful of Reaper militia.

'Thank you for gathering,' she said to them; 'I'll keep this brief. We are under attack. All non-military personnel, I am ordering you to flee into the fog, immediately. Militia, you will assist them.'

Several of the servants and staff cried out.

'Guards,' said Khora, 'escort them all out, there is no time to waste.'

'What about us?' said Aila, as the staff were pushed out of the hallway by the militia. 'Where do we go?'

Khora glanced at her. 'I called for a ship to be prepared as soon as I noticed the Tarans had gone.'

'A ship? Are we going to Port Sanders?'

'That was the plan. You could then enter the Circuit to rally resistance to the duke, I could do the same from Sander territory, and in that way we could cut him off from the Bulwark. However, I anticipated any Blade invasion coming from overland, rather than by sea, and the harbour no longer looks like a safe option.'

'Why don't we take a carriage?' said Corthie.

'Unfortunately, the Tarans requisitioned every carriage and wagon to transport their militia back to Roser territory.'

'Then we'll walk,' said Aila. 'Remember, I was born and brought up here; there are secret ways through this palace that no one else would know, not even Salvor.'

'Speaking of my son; where is he?' said Khora, her eyes tight. 'I'm not sure we can wait much longer for him.'

One of the militia burst back in through the door. 'Blades are landing at the harbour, ma'am, thousands of them!'

'Did the staff get away?'

'Most of them, ma'am; some have been arrested.'

Khora gazed at the young soldier. 'When they come, do not resist. Lay down your arms and surrender to the Blades. There is no need for any bloodshed. Now, go.' She turned to Aila. 'Time to use your local knowledge, my niece. Lead on.'

'And Salvor?'

'He has his orders.'

'I'll need a weapon if he's not returning,' said Corthie glancing around the hallway. He went back into the large chamber and walked to the hearth, where Aila saw him pick up a heavy, iron poker.

'This will do for now,' he said, returning to the hallway.

Aila nodded. 'Follow me.' She led Corthie and Khora down a

passageway, and entered a servant's area through a door. She paused for a moment, scanning the walls. 'This used to be, long ago, my brother Irno's quarters. As my father's eldest child, he always got the biggest rooms, but he used to let me play here when I was a girl.' She spotted the stone in the wall she had been looking for. 'Ah, here we are.'

She crouched down and tried to shift the stone, but it was stuck solid. She glanced at Corthie. 'I might need a little of your brute strength.'

Corthie knelt by her. 'Who are you calling a brute?'

She smiled at him. 'You. Now, see if you can shift that stone, brute.'

He grabbed it, his large hands grasping it easily, then wrenched it from the wall in a cloud of dust, leaving a hole in the wall. 'Like that?'

'Yeah,' she laughed. 'That'll do.'

She put her hand into the gap in the wall and found the lever. She pulled it, and there was creaking noise as a hatch a few yards along opened an inch. Corthie pushed the stone back into place, then they went to the hatch. The hinges had long rusted, but the passageway beyond looked undisturbed. She pushed the hatch open.

'I'll go first,' she said, 'then Khora, and Corthie defends the rear, yeah?'

'Wait a moment,' said Khora, 'I think I hear my son's voice.'

They crept back to the doorway, and peered through the crack. Lord Salvor was visible in the hall, but he was surrounded by Blades, and had his hands raised. A Blade officer ordered him to his knees, and the demigod complied.

'I surrender,' he said. 'I am unarmed.'

'Where's your mother?' growled the officer.

'The High Guardian of the City has already fled the palace,' said Salvor. 'As Governor of Pella, I alone remained. May I speak to your commanding officer?'

'Oh, I'm sure he'll want to speak to you.' He gestured to the other Blades. 'Take him away, and search the palace. If Khora's here, I want her found, dead or alive.'

Salvor was hauled up by two burly soldiers and escorted out.

'Coward,' whispered Aila.

Khora shot her a look of anger. 'He is doing exactly as I instructed him. Tell me, what good would his death bring?'

Corthie glanced at the hatch. 'Time to go.'

They hurried back to the secret passageway and entered, squeezing through the low hatch and emerging into the musty corridor. Corthie closed the hatch behind them, and they were plunged into darkness. A moment later, boots echoed along the hallway, and the three fugitives remained silent, listening to the sound through the hatch. When the noise passed, Aila reached out with her hand and found Khora.

'We should have brought a lamp,' whispered the princess. 'I can see nothing.'

'I can see fine,' said Corthie. 'I'll lead.'

Aila felt him move past her. He took her hand and placed it onto his belt.

'Alright,' he said, keeping his voice low. 'I'll move slowly; keep a hold onto me.'

He began moving, and Aila followed, hearing Khora's breath just to her left in the utter darkness. She shuffled her feet forward, her hand clinging onto Corthie's belt. After a few minutes, he halted.

'Left or right?' he whispered.

'Left.'

They trudged on in the pitch darkness, and Aila began to lose track of time as she concentrated on not stumbling.

'There's a doorway ahead,' whispered Corthie; 'low, like the hatch we entered.'

'That's it,' said Aila as they slowed to a halt; 'it leads out to a small gate by the old clock tower that was walled up centuries ago, but there's a gap we can climb through, and then we'll have a short run to get to the streets. I have contacts in Outer Pella.'

'Good girl,' said Khora.

'Girl? I'm seven hundred and sixty-seven years old.'

'You'll always be my niece.'

'You're how old?' said Corthie, chuckling. 'Wow.'

'When we get out of here I'm going to slap you.'

She felt his hand touch her waist. 'I can think of a few better things to do.'

'Save it,' said Khora; 'and when we reach Outer Pella, for my sake, please get your own room.'

Aila's heart lurched at the thought, and she put her hand on Corthie's. Screw the heartbreak, she thought; she wanted him, and all her worries about his mortality paled next to that simple fact.

Corthie withdrew his hand, and she heard him crouch by the hatch. He remained silent for a moment, then gently eased it open, letting light flood the corridor. He squeezed through the gap.

'It's deserted,' he whispered back through the hatch. 'Come on.'

Khora and Aila followed him and emerged into an old gatehouse, long abandoned. Aila went up to a window and peered through the slats in the rotten shutters. Outside in the fog stretched an ornamental garden, and the rear walls of the palace compound were visible. The old gate was down there, and then beyond, freedom. She went to the door and tried to move it, but beams had been placed across it, and the rusty nails were still in place. She glanced at Corthie and he nodded. He stepped up to the door, and gripped a beam in both hands. Making almost no sound, he pulled it from the door, easing the nails out of the frame. Once all three had been removed, he swung the door open and they peered outside. The gardens lay empty before them.

'Stick to the flowerbeds,' Aila said, 'not the gravel path.'

They crept out of the gatehouse into the swirling fog and stole to the thick beds of earth that lay by the path. The soil was damp and they made no noise as they went. They passed lines of high hedges, checking the way was clear each time, until Aila saw the old gate in the walls. It had been bricked up, but she knew there was a gap a little further along, where she had played centuries before, that no one else who hadn't been brought up in the palace would know was there.

'This way,' she whispered. They left the flowerbeds and entered a small enclosure with walls on three sides. She walked over to the bricked-up gate, then began searching for the gap behind the bushes and shrubs.

'So predictable, sister,' came a voice from behind her. She turned on her heels.

Kano was standing by the hedges in full battle armour, ranks of Blade soldiers arrayed before him. 'Did you think I wouldn't remember how you used to get out of the palace, sister, all those years ago?' He turned to Corthie. 'And so predictable, Champion of the Bulwark. I knew the duke's trust in you was misplaced; I knew you would betray us.' He gestured to the soldiers. 'Kill him.'

# CHAPTER 30

# BROKEN PROMISE

Pella, Auldan, The City – 4<sup>th</sup> Balian 3419

Pella, Auldan, The City – 4<sup>th</sup> Balian 3419
A dozen Blades lowered their crossbows and took aim at Corthie. He launched himself forward, hurtling at breakneck speed towards them, the heavy poker in his hand. A bolt flew past his face, and another grazed his shoulder; he rolled and struck a soldier across his kneecap with the iron bar, shattering his leg. Then he was in amongst them, too close for them to loose their crossbows, the poker lashing out, breaking arms and battering off the soldiers' helmets.

Kano took a step back, his mouth opening as the champion laid low anyone within range. Corthie grabbed a soldier by the back of his neck, and held him up as a shield, while all around Blades writhed on the ground, clutching their broken limbs and howling in agony. The remaining Blades were starting to pull back, pointing their bows into the scrum of bodies, but unable to take a shot. Corthie laughed as he saw the fear in Kano's eyes. He threw the human shield at the demigod, then prepared to close in.

'Corthie, run,' cried Aila.

He let his battle-vision process what was happening in an instant. Aila and Khora were edging away to the left, where a tall clock tower stood. By the corner of the tower, where it met the outer palace wall, there was a gap in the ancient stonework. In the other direction, dozens more Blades were approaching, attracted by the cries of pain from the injuries he had inflicted. He lunged at Kano, then, as the demigod flinched, he turned away, and sprinted towards the side of the tower. A yard from Aila, he felt a searing pain rip through his right thigh, and his leg gave way. He crashed to the ground, a bolt embedded in the back of his limb. More soldiers aimed, and he pulled himself into a crouch. The gap in the wall was too far; he would never make it, so he threw himself at the wooden door of the clock tower. It flew open and he landed on the stone floor in agony, the bolt wound excruciating. Aila and Khora ran in after him as the air filled with a hail of crossbow bolts. Aila slammed the door shut and secured it with a thick bar, then she rushed to his side.

'Corthie,' she cried, her eyes wide at the blood.

'Is there another way out of here?' said Khora, staring at the door they had come through.

Aila shook her head.

'Then why did you lead us in? We're trapped.'

'I wasn't thinking, I saw Corthie get hurt and... I didn't think.'

Corthie rolled onto his side, gripped the shaft of the bolt, and ripped it from his thigh. He closed his eyes for a moment, trying to use his battle-vision to mask the pain, then felt Aila's hands touch his leg. She tore a strip of fabric from her dress and wrapped it round the wound, pulling it tight.

He opened his eyes. 'Thanks.' He grabbed the poker and hauled himself up, putting his weight onto his left side.

'You are surrounded,' came Kano's voice from outside.

'Aila,' said Corthie as he leaned against the wall, blood dripping down his leg; 'I'm going to need you to tell me something.'

'What?'

'He's your brother; can I kill him?'

She stared at him for a moment, her eyes wide. 'I... but, he...'

'Yes,' said Khora, 'by all means; if you can.'

'He's my brother,' cried Aila.

'And I'm sorry for that,' she said, 'but he is well past any possible redemption.'

'Surrender!' called out the demigod's voice from outside the clock tower. 'You have five minutes, or we'll burn you out.'

'Kano!' Aila shouted through the door. 'Why are you doing this to us?'

'I'm not after you, sister,' he said. 'Duke Marcus wants you unharmed.'

'What, so you can hand me over to him? You'd give your sister to that vile beast?'

Kano was silent for a moment, and Corthie turned to Khora. 'What does she mean?'

'I swear to you, sister,' Kano said, 'that if you walk out of there, alone, I will let you go.'

'He's lying,' said Khora.

'Five minutes,' said Kano, 'that's all you have.'

Boots sounded on the gravel outside, then faded away.

'What did you mean about Marcus?' said Corthie, as Aila turned from the door.

'The duke has desired Aila for a very long time,' said Khora. 'It was Prince Michael's intention, before he died, to pair the two together.'

He glanced at Aila. 'Why didn't you tell me?'

'What difference would it have made? Until tonight, the duke was confined to the Bulwark, and the chances of him getting his hands on me were nil.'

'But, you're cousins.'

Aila shrugged. 'Yeah, I know. Prince Michael had a lot of crazy ideas; he wanted the demigods to come together to breed a new generation. After Yendra slew him, those ideas died away.'

'They died away because I killed them,' said Khora. 'Do you think for a moment that I would have countenanced such foolishness?'

'You tell me,' said Aila, 'you were close to Michael, you must have known what he was like, and yet you betrayed Yendra to help him.'

'Aila, you must stop this. I did not betray my sister Yendra.'

'But you did murder your sister Niomi.'

Khora's face fell. 'I killed Princess Niomi, yes, it's true. If I hadn't, she would have killed me. But Yendra was different. I know why you think I betrayed her, but you're wrong.'

'This all happened hundreds of years ago,' said Corthie, keeping his right leg still as the pain coursed through him. 'Maybe it's time to forgive and forget.'

'I'm prepared to forgive,' said Aila; 'that's why I'm here. But I don't think I'll ever be able to forget; I'll always want answers.'

'Answers I can give you, my niece, but right now we need to think our way out of this. The duke wants me dead, that much is clear, and the God-Queen is on his side.'

'Then what about the God-King?' said Corthie.

'Unfortunately, his Majesty is in the Royal Palace in Ooste.'

'Aye, but you have vision powers, don't you? My mother, sister and brother have them too, and any of them could easily vision a few miles to Ooste. You're a God-Child, surely your powers aren't any less than my idiot brother's?'

Khora and Aila glanced at each other.

'Oh dear,' said Corthie, shaking his head. 'That look told me a lot. Is there something wrong with your powers?'

Khora said nothing.

'Alright, then there's something wrong in Ooste, aye? There's something wrong with the God-King? Has he already taken the Quadrant and fled the City? I don't think anything would surprise me any more. So, we're on our own?'

'We are, yes.'

'On our own, in a building with one exit that's about to be set on fire. Hmm.'

Khora frowned. 'Are you thinking of a plan?'

'A plan?' Corthie laughed. 'There's no plan going to get us out of this. Right, here's the best I can come up with. We wait until the flames take hold, then I'll burst outside and charge the Blades. That way you two might have a chance to escape. Not much of a chance, but it's better than sitting here and burning to death.'

'No way,' said Aila. 'You're already wounded.'

'Exactly. I can't run; I would just slow you down.' He shook his head. 'Blackrose is not going to be happy about this.'

'Screw Blackrose,' cried Aila, 'I'm not happy about it. I don't want a dead hero, Corthie.'

'Alright, you think of a plan.'

The gravel crunched outside. 'Time's up. Aila, I ask you again, as my sister, listen to me. You don't have to die today. I have a hundred Blades out here with me; not one of you would last a step before we cut you down. And the champion, he's injured isn't he? I saw it; a nasty blow to the thigh. He fought well, I admit it, but he won't be able to protect you or Princess Khora any longer. He's finished, Aila, and like a wounded dog, all that remains is to put him out of his misery.'

'Then come in here and try it,' Corthie yelled; 'there's somewhere I want to ram this poker.'

'I'm going to spit on your body, champion,' Kano said, 'then feed it to my dogs. Your friend Tanner, I will put in the Rats, while I think Quill would do well in my personal harem.'

'You shame no one but yourself,' said Corthie. 'I hope the Blades outside heard every word you just said. What a great and noble man you are. Fancy a fight? I could take you, wound or no wound.'

There was nothing but silence from outside, then a low, 'So be it,' came from Kano and he walked away.

Aila lowered her head, then glanced at Corthie. 'Kill him if you have to.'

He glanced at her. She still loved her brother, despite everything, and he knew that killing him would leave a scar across the heart of their relationship that she would never be able to forget. He took a breath. With every moment that passed, it looked less likely that he was going to survive. Kano had been ordered to kill him, and without the ability to run, or even walk properly, he was never going to be able to flee. All that remained was ensuring Aila was alive, and that his promise to Blackrose was fulfilled.

'Khora,' he said. 'If I die here, and you get away, I need to know something.'

'Don't say that,' said Aila.

Khora glanced at her, then turned to Corthie. 'What?'

'I need to know that you'll try to get Blackrose home.'

'Blackrose? Is she another champion on the wall?'

'She's the other dragon, the one that's been kept a secret.'

'Oh. I didn't ever learn her name. Yes, I will try, you have my word.'

Corthie began to smell smoke drifting through from outside. 'Then get ready.'

'What for?' said Aila.

'My wonderful plan,' he said, trying to smile. 'As you two haven't come up with anything better, I'm going to do it. As soon as I'm out of the door, run for it, and don't look back.'

Aila approached him. 'No,' she said, her eyes beseeching him. 'There has to be another way.'

'Do you smell the smoke? It'll be getting warm in here soon; we're out of time.'

She ran into his arms and he put his right hand round her, as his left was supporting his weight against the wall. He grimaced as he felt the wound in his thigh ache, but pulled her close, her head buried into his chest.

'Listen,' he said; 'when my sister comes, tell her I missed her, tell her I thought about her every day. Tell her what I miss most is when I used to hide around the house, wait for her to pass, and then jump out and wrestle her to the ground.' He laughed. 'She always hated that.'

Aila pulled her head back and gazed up at him, tears coming down her cheeks. 'You can't die.'

'I'm mortal, Aila. I can die.'

She leaned up and they kissed, and he forgot everything else for a brief moment, losing himself in the touch of her lips. He had few regrets, he thought, but leaving Aila would be his greatest.

Khora approached as Corthie looked up.

'Thank you,' she said.

He nodded, then picked up the poker and staggered towards the door. He threw down the beam that was barring it, and peered through the thin crack. Firewood from the garden was piled up outside the tower, and several patches had been lit, while Blades were standing back in a thick line, shields up, crossbows levelled. Kano stood behind them, his height towering over the mortal soldiers.

Behind him, he heard Aila and Khora by his back, ready. He turned and glanced down at them, so he could see Aila's face.

'Everything's going to be fine,' he said, then he burst through the door in an explosion of speed. He charged at the soldiers, roaring, and had crossed half the distance before the first crossbow bolts struck him. Right shoulder, left side, stomach. He clattered to the ground, skidding through the gravel, and trailing a smear of blood behind him. He gasped for breath, twisting his head to see if Khora and Aila had made it to the gap in the wall, but Aila was standing frozen by the tower door, staring at him, as Khora tried to drag her away. Soldiers rushed them, jumping over Corthie or running round him, and Aila went down, pinned by two Blades, as Khora was surrounded. Lord Kano stepped forward. He glanced down at Corthie lying on the dirt, and spat on him.

'I'm not dead yet, you asshole,' he gasped.

'You will be soon enough, boy,' Kano said. He looked around. 'Secure my sister,' he said; 'bind her hands.' He drew his sword and walked towards Khora.

'I surrender to you, Lord Kano,' she said, standing proud. 'Let me speak to Duke Marcus.'

Kano raised an iron-clad fist and punched her in the face. Khora collapsed to the ground. Kano watched her groan in agony for a moment as she self-healed, then leaned over and took a fistful of her hair. He dragged her across the gravel and into the tower. The door slammed behind him, and Corthie heard Khora scream.

Aila was struggling in the grip of the two Blades, trying to reach where Corthie was lying, but the grip of the soldiers remained firm.

After a few moments, the screaming from the tower cut off in the middle of a cry, and Kano emerged from the tower, the front of his armour covered in blood.

'You're not my brother!' shouted Aila.

Kano approached her and slapped her across the face. Corthie tried to move. He lifted his arm an inch, and gasped. His sight was starting to swim, and the pain was almost unbearable.

A cry echoed from somewhere else in the garden, then another, from a different direction. Several Blades turned, and Kano glanced round. A third cry rang out, along with the sound of steel striking steel.

'Whoever that is,' cried Kano, 'find them!'

The Blades began fanning out, moving between the high hedges into the thick dark fog, until only a handful were left by the tower. Kano walked over to Corthie.

'Now it's your turn,' he said.

Behind him, Naxor appeared from nowhere, a sword in one hand, and a copper-coloured metallic device in the other. Corthie's eyes widened. The Quadrant. Naxor powered his battle-vision, and his sword flashed out, cutting down the two guards holding Aila.

'You?' cried Kano, his eyes wide.

Naxor glanced over to the tower, and saw the blood trickling through the open door. Kano raised his sword and charged at him. Naxor stood his ground, then grabbed hold of Aila.

'No,' she cried, 'Corthie!'

They both vanished, and Kano ran through the empty space where they had just been standing. He turned, his mouth hanging open as he stared around the enclosure.

Sir,' cried a Blade officer, 'there's no one out in the gardens. We've searched everywhere.'

Kano said nothing as he continued to stare at the spot where his sister had last been.

'Sir?' said the officer.

Kano blinked. 'It's done. Send a messenger to Duke Marcus that the High Guardian's rule is over. Princess Khora was murdered in cold blood by Corthie Holdfast, and the criminal was apprehended and executed by myself, Lord Kano. Do you have all that?'

The Blade officer hesitated for a second, then saluted. 'Yes, sir.'

'Who killed the princess?'

'Corthie Holdfast, sir.'

'Dismissed.'

The officer turned and hurried away. Kano walked over to Corthie, then knelt down by him.

'You lost,' he said, 'as I knew you would.'

Corthie tried to respond, but he was too weak, and could feel his life ebbing away as the blood flowed from his wounds. Of all the places to die, he thought. At least Aila had got away. He closed his eyes.

Kano stood, and walked away.

---

Darkness, movement. Pain. He tried to open his eyes.

'Don't move an inch,' hissed a voice, 'and make no sound.'

The bumping continued, and he realised he was lying on the floor of a wagon that was being driven at speed over cobbled streets.

He groaned, then a hand came down over his mouth.

'Shut up,' the voice whispered, 'or we're both dead.'

The carriage slowed to a halt, and Corthie heard voices; the gruff accents of Blade soldiers. The talking continued for a moment, and the wagon took off again.

'Praise Malik,' whispered the voice.

Corthie managed to turn his head, but his vision was blurry. He saw the rough shape of a man. 'Who are you?'

'You don't recognise the man who has just saved your life?'

'My eyes... not working...'

'I'm Salvor.' The voice came closer. 'Now listen to me, mortal, very carefully. I saw what they did to my mother. They're trying to spread the story that it was you, but I know. One day I shall have revenge upon Kano, and you are a part of that; which is why you must live, champion.

Those fools left you for dead, and ordered me to dispose of your corpse.' He laughed, but it was strained, and had a tinge of near-hysteria about it. 'Imagine my surprise to find that you were still alive.'

Corthie spluttered, the agony rolling over him in waves.

A hand grabbed his shoulder. 'Do not die, mortal, I forbid it. I'm sending you away, far away, and it's not going to be pleasant, let me tell you, but it's the only place out of reach of my cousin Vana. She can sense powers, and would be able to tell if you were alive and in the City, just as she will be used to track down my brother Naxor. The coward that I am, I will kneel and beg and swear whatever they want me to swear, but I will be waiting, waiting for news of your return.'

He came even closer, and Corthie could feel the demigod's breath on his face.

'And when you return; you will kill them all.'

## The Mortal Blade - The Royal Family

| The Gods | Title | Powers |
|---|---|---|
| Malik | God-King of the City - Ooste | Vision |
| Amalia | God-Queen of the City - Tara | Death |

| The Children of the Gods | Title | Powers |
|---|---|---|
| Michael (deceased) | ex-Prince of Tara, 1600-3096 | Death, Battle |
| Montieth | Prince of Dalrig, b. 1932 | Death |
| Isra (deceased) | ex-Prince of Pella, 2001-3078 | Battle |
| Khora | Princess of Pella, b.2014 | Vision |
| Niomi (deceased) | ex-Princess of Icehaven, 2014-3089 | Healer |
| Yendra (deceased) | ex-Princess of the Circuit, 2133-3096 | Vision |

| Children of Prince Michael | Title | Powers |
|---|---|---|
| Marcus | Duke, Bulwark, b. 1944 | Battle |
| Mona | Chancellor, Ooste, b. 2014 | Vision |
| Dania (deceased) | Lady of Tara, 2099-3096 | Battle |
| Yordi (deceased) | Lady of Tara, 2153-3096 | Death |

| Children of Prince Montieth | Title | Powers |
|---|---|---|
| Amber | Lady of Dalrig, b. 2035 | Death |
| Jade | Lady of Dalrig, b. 2511 | Death |

| Children of Prince Isra | Title | Powers |
|---|---|---|
| Irno (deceased) | Eldest son of Isra, 2017-3078 | Battle |
| Berno (deceased) | 'The Mortal', 2018-2097 | None |
| Garno (deceased) | Warrior, 2241-3078 | Battle |
| Lerno (deceased) | Warrior, 2247-3078 | Battle |

| Vana | Adjutant of Pella, b. 2319 | Location |
| Marno (deceased) | Warrior, 2321-3063 | Battle |
| Collo | Khora's Secretary, b. 2328 | None |
| Bonna (deceased) | Warrior, 2598-3078 | Shape-Shifter |
| Aila | Adjutant of the Circuit, b. 2652 | Shape-Shifter |
| Kano | Adj. of the Bulwark, b. 2788 | Battle |
| Teno (deceased) | Warrior, 2870-3078 | Battle |

**Children of
Princess Khora**

| Salvor | Governor of Pella, b. 2201 | Vision |
| Balian (deceased) | Warrior, 2299-3096 | Battle |
| Lydia | Gov. of Port Sanders, b. 2304 | Healer |
| Naxor | Royal Emissary, b. 2401 | Vision |
| Ikara | Governor of the Circuit, b. 2499 | Battle |
| Doria | Royal Courtier, b. 2600 | None |

**Children of
Princess Niomi**

| Rand (deceased) | Warrior, 2123-3089 | Battle |
| Yvona | Governor of Icehaven, b. 2175 | Healer |
| Samara (deceased) | Lady of Icehaven, 2239-3089 | Battle |
| Daran (deceased) | Lord of Icehaven, 2261-3063 | Battle |

**Children of
Princess Yendra**

| Kahlia (deceased) | Warrior, 2599-3096 | Vision |
| Neara (deceased) | Warrior, 2601-3089 | Battle |
| Yearna (deceased) | Lady of the Circuit, 2604-3096 | Healer |

# THE NINE TRIBES OF THE CITY

There are nine distinct tribes inhabiting the City. Three were in the area from the beginning, and the other six were created in two waves of expansion.

**The Original Three Tribes – Auldan (pop. 300 000)** Auldan is the oldest part of the City. United by the Union Walls (completed in 1040), it combined the three original tribes and their towns, along with the shared town of **Ooste**, which houses the Royal Palace, where **King Malik** lives.

1. **The Rosers** – (their town is **Tara**, est. Yr. 1.) The first tribe to reach the peninsula where the City is located. Began farming there in the sunward regions, until attacks from the Reapers forced them into building the first walled town. **Prince Michael** ruled until his death in 3096. **Queen Amalia** governs the Rosers from Maeladh Palace in Tara.

2. **The Gloamers** – (their town is **Dalrig**, est. Yr. 40.) Arrived shortly after the Rosers, farming the iceward side of the peninsula. Like them, they fought with the Reapers, and built a walled town to stop their attacks. **Prince Montieth** rules from Greylin Palace in Dalrig.

3. **The Reapers** – (their town is **Pella**, est. Yr. 70.) Hunter/Gatherer tribe that arrived after the more sedentary Rosers and Gloamers. Settled in the plains between the other two tribes. More numerous than either the Rosers or the Gloamers, but are looked down on as more rustic. **Prince Isra** ruled until his death in 3078. **Princess Khora** now rules in his stead, but delegates to her son, **Lord Salvor**, who governs from Cuidrach Palace in Pella.

**The Next Three Tribes – Medio (pop. 400 000)** Originally called 'New Town', this part of the City was its first major expansion; and was settled from the completion of the Middle Walls (finished in 1697 and originally known as the Royal Walls). The name 'Medio' derives from the old Evader word for 'Middle'.

1. **The Icewarders** – (their town is **Icehaven**, est. 1657.) Settlers from Dalrig originally founded a new colony at Icehaven to assist in the building of the Middle Walls, as the location was too cold and dark for the greenhides. After the wall's completion, many settlers stayed, and a new tribe was founded. Separated from Icehaven by mountains, a large number of Icewarders also inhabit the central lowlands bordering the Circuit. **Princess Niomi** ruled until her death in 3089. Her daughter, **Lady Yvona**, now governs from Alkirk Palace in Icehaven.

2. **The Sanders** – (their town is **Port Sanders**, est. 1702.) When the Middle Walls were completed, a surplus population of Rosers and Reapers moved into the new area, and the tribe of the Sanders was founded, based around the port town on the Warm Sea. Related closely to the Rosers in terms of allegiance and culture. **Princess Khora** rules, but delegates to her daughter, **Lady Lydia**, who governs from the Tonetti Palace in Port Sanders.

3. **The Evaders** – (their town is the **Circuit**, est. 2133.) The only tribe ethnically unrelated to the others, the Evaders started out as refugees fleeing the greenhides, and they began arriving at the City c.1500. They were taken in, and then used to help build the Middle Walls. The largest tribe by population among the first six, though the other tribes of Auldan and Medio look down on them as illiterate savages. **Princess Yendra** ruled until her death in 3096. **Lady Ikara** rules from Redmarket Palace in the town's centre.

**The Final Three Tribes – The Bulwark (pop. 600 000)** The Bulwark is the defensive buffer that protects the entire City from greenhide attack.

Work commenced on the enormous Great Walls after the decisive Battle of the Children of the Gods in 2247, when the greenhides were annihilated and pushed back hundreds of miles. They were completed c.2300, and the new area of the City was settled.

1. **The Blades** – (est. 2300.) The military tribe of the City. The role of the Blades is to defend the Great Walls from the unceasing attacks by the Greenhides. Their service is hereditary, and the role of soldier passes from parent to child. Officials from the Blades also police and govern the other two tribes of the Bulwark. Their headquarters is the **Fortress of the Lifegiver**, the largest bastion on the Great Walls, where **Duke Marcus** is the commander.

2. **The Hammers** – (est. 2300.) The industrial proletariat of the Bulwark, the Hammers are effectively slaves, though that word is not used. They are forbidden to leave their tribal area, which produces much of the finished goods for the rest of the City.

3. **The Scythes** – (est. 2300.) The agricultural workers of the Bulwark, who produce all that the region requires. Slaves in all but name.

# NOTE ON THE CALENDAR

In this world there are two moons, a larger and a smaller (fragments of the same moon). The larger orbits in a way similar to Earth's moon, and the year is divided into seasons and months.

Due to the tidally-locked orbit around the sun, there are no solstices or equinoxes, but summer and winter exist due to the orbit being highly elliptical. There are two summers and two winters in the course of each solar revolution, so one 'year' (365 days) equates to half the time it takes for the planet to go round the sun (730 days). No Leap Days required.

New Year starts at with the arrival of the Spring (Freshmist) storms, on Thanalion Day

New Year's Day – **Thanalion Day** (approx. 1st March)
　-- **Freshmist** (snow storms, freezing fog, ice blizzards, high winds from iceward)
　　- Malikon (March)
　　- Amalan (April)
　-- **Summer** (hot, dry)
　　- Mikalis (May)
　　- Montalis (June)
　　- Izran (July)
　　- Koralis (August)
　-- **Sweetmist** (humid, stormy, high winds from sunward, very wet)
　　- Namen (September)
　　- Balian (October)
　-- **Winter** (cold, dry)
　　- Marcalis (November)
　　- Monan (December)

- Darian (January)
- Yordian (February)

Note – the old month of Yendran was renamed in honour of Princess Khora's slain son Lord Balian, following the execution of the traitor Princess Yendra.

## AUTHOR'S NOTES

AUGUST 2020

Thank you for reading *The Mortal Blade*! The idea of writing stories about a city besieged for thousands of years was one that had been floating around my head for a very long time, and I'm glad I had the opportunity to finish it.

It was written in strange circumstances, during the COVID-19 lockdown – an unsettling time, but one where I was suddenly presented with more time to write than ever before. It gave me a glimpse of what life could be like if I moved to becoming a full time author – a step I have recently taken.

This book also marked my first foray into a world away from the Star Continent of my earlier books – though I have no doubt that I'll be heading back there at some point in the future!

## RECEIVE A FREE MAGELANDS ETERNAL SIEGE BOOK

Building a relationship with my readers is very important to me.

Join my newsletter for information on new books and deals and you will also receive a Magelands Eternal Siege prequel novella that is currently EXCLUSIVE to my Reader's Group for FREE.

www.ChristopherMitchellBooks.com/join

# ABOUT THE AUTHOR

Christopher Mitchell is the author of the Magelands epic fantasy series.

*For more information:*
www.christophermitchellbooks.com
info@christophermitchellbooks.com

Made in United States
Cleveland, OH
01 November 2024

10399213R00259